Assassin's Manuscript

D1593871

William J. Carl

LeConte Publishing LLC
Maryville, Tennessee

"Ending lives and saving them are two ways to feel God-like. Making peace is the third."

William J. Carl

In memory of Alex Haley who told me

I should write a novel—

Thanks Alex

Acknowledgments

My favorite dedication for a book was written by a scholar who said, "I dedicate this book to myself without whom it could not have been written." Clever, but not always entirely true. I believe that no book can come to life without the help of others. That is certainly the case with this one. There are too many people to thank, so the list here will be short. I begin with Alex Haley to whom I dedicate this book. Read the Author's Note at the end for an explanation of why he told me to write it. I also want to thank my brother-in-law, Lamar Alexander, and his wife, Honey, for allowing me to write large portions of this novel at their East Tennessee home in the mountains.

Charles Cornwell, former Professor of English at Davidson College, a wise and seasoned editor, and a former student of mine at Union Seminary in Virginia, has been a mentor and writing coach for decades. He's shared the journey with me through all twelve revisions of this book. Fellow authors, Mike Farris, Ray Flynt, Cathy Adams, Scott Brunger, L.A. Starks, Elizabeth Lawless, and Katharine Rhodes Henderson deserve credit for helping me improve the manuscript. Raymond Rose is an editor with a sharp eye for detail and an ear for how things sound on a written page. Thanks to Marty Callaway, Lee Walthall, John Tally, Lindsey March, Gordon Lindsey, and Jean Cole for proofreading, and the late Ian Boyd for help with the scenes in London and all things British.

My actor son in New York, David Carl, his big brother, Jeremy, and their mother, Jane, have lived with this book since the mid-1990s, and are still alive to talk about it! Jeremy and David, both writers themselves helped their dad's sentences sing. Hiking buddies, Margaret Stevenson,

Henry and Jim Callaway, Bob Merriman, and Rick Hughes, made sure my Smoky Mountain scenes were authentic. Buck Revell, former Associate Deputy Secretary at the FBI (in charge of Counter-Terrorism and Counter-Intelligence Activities) and a consultant for Tom Clancy and Frederick Forsyth on their novels, was my consultant on terrorism. A gallery warder at the British Museum told me how well the security system works there.

I can't even begin to name all the people I met while doing research in London, New York, Washington, DC, Moscow, Rome, Jerusalem, St. Catherine's Monastery at the foot of Mt. Sinai in Egypt (where Tischendorf discovered the Codex Sinaiticus), the Smoky Mountains, and Maryville, Tennessee. I'm thankful to the Patriarch of the Greek Orthodox Church, based in Istanbul, who got me entry into the library at St. Catherine's, and for the monks there who told me stories that gave me insights I could never have discovered on my own. Former Ambassador, Sichan Siv, got me onto the White House tennis court so I could write that scene in the novel, and my older son, Jeremy, who also worked at the White House, got me into the Oval Office.

The interviews I did with several real hit men were chilling, revealing, and helped me get inside the mind, heart, and soul of my main character, Adam Hunter. One assassin was a Russian mafia chief who became a minister in the Ural Mountains. Another was an Israeli who told me he had Arafat in his sights twice, but the order never came to take the shot. I learned about one assassin from his son (a Philosophy professor at a small college) who said his father revealed on his deathbed what he'd done on all those trips overseas. He said, "I was shocked. I had no idea about his true identity. He was a regular, Little League Dad in the neighborhood who never appeared to be a violent person."

Table of Contents

PART ONE: PREMISE

Revenge is Sweet

Cairo

The Bedouin, a dark-skinned, pockmark-faced Arab stared out the window at the American tourists who filled the streets below him. He hated the way they flaunted their money and sauntered through the market as if they owned the place. "Infidels," he muttered under his breath. He blamed them for problems that kept the Middle East stirred up like a boiling cauldron.

He rubbed the scar just above his left cheekbone and turned away from the window. Something caught his eye—a picture of his woman on a side table. Next to it lay a yellowed newspaper clipping that described the New York bombing where she'd been killed years earlier, but it seemed like yesterday to him.

He knew eventually he would find her killer, but there was no rush. He would take his time. That was the Bedouin way. Americans would never understand. Bedouins always planned long term. It had been that way for a thousand years. Patience, camouflage, and surprise were the best arrows in the terrorist's quiver.

He turned his gaze to the wall in front of him filled with pictures of the Twin Towers of the World Trade Center and the Pentagon thinking of how successful 9/11 had been.

The phone rang.

"*Salaam Aleikum*," he said.

"*Aleikum Salaam*," replied Conrad Docherty.

"Tell me who's going to steal the Codex for me."

"I think I have the right man for the job. Why do you want this old manuscript?"

"I promised it in return for another manuscript a monk at St. Catherine's Monastery in Sinai is creating for me."

"What's involved?" said Conrad.

The Bedouin wondered why the American kept peppering him with questions.

"He has to find the right vellum skin palimpsest over which he will write what I tell him. He has to make what will appear to the naked eye as ancient ink. The lithography alone is painstaking. He has to distress it to make it look centuries old."

"He's willing to go to this much trouble for an old Bible?"

"Not just any old Bible. The oldest one in the world, stolen from St. Catherine's Monastery in the nineteenth century by a German scholar named Tischendorf. The monks here talk about it as if it happened yesterday. They want it back because they are its rightful owners."

"I just want my money."

"You Americans are all alike. You'll get what's coming to you. Tell me about the man who will help you."

"He's a gallery warder at the British Museum. His name is Nigel Rupert."

Nigel's Temptation

Nigel Rupert was a man of habit. His route to the British Museum had been the same every day for thirty years. From his south London home on Hamilton Road, he walked across Merton High Street every morning at exactly the same time to catch the Northern Line at the dingy South Wimbledon Underground Station where he always got a seat since it was the first stop after Morden. At exactly the same time every day, he got off the train at the Tottenham Court Road stop, emerged under the great awning of the Dominion Theatre at St. Giles Circus, and turned onto Great Russell Street for the five-minute walk to the Museum. Nothing ever changed in his routine.

There was nothing really complicated about Nigel Rupert's life either. Never more than average to below average work in school, a stint in the Royal Army Service Corps after basic training in Farnsworth, with a spot of service in the British zone in Germany, where all he did was security duty. He was proud to be a gallery warder at the British Museum, so proud that he made sure everybody he met knew it. It made him feel important to talk about it. People got tired of hearing his stories about the Rosetta Stone, the Greek statues, and all the dusty, old books, especially at The Grove Tavern, the pub near his South Wimbledon stop where he got lathered up every night on the way home from work.

A few weeks earlier, he'd met a man from the States

named Conrad Docherty who actually enjoyed listening to Nigel talk about his job. His bar buddies were ecstatic to have someone else give them a break.

Nigel and the Yank, as they called Docherty, would sit in the same booth every day and talk about the British Museum while they downed a few pints of Tetley's bitter. The American gave Nigel money to do odd jobs for him. Simple deliveries after hours. It was a way for Nigel to make a few extra pounds and it made him feel even more important. Soon they became fast friends.

One evening, after a few laughs and a few drafts, Conrad asked Nigel about one particular palimpsest called the *Codex Sinaiticus*.

"Yes, we used to have that one," Nigel said proudly. "It was displayed right next to *Codex Alexandrinus* in Cabinet 42Q in Room 30, the one at the south end of the King's Library."

"What do you know about it?" said Conrad.

"What would you like to know?"

"Everything," replied Conrad.

Nigel grinned broadly and ordered another round of ciders. For the first time in his life, someone wanted to listen to him. Off he went with the whole story about the German scholar named Constantin von Tischendorf, a real nineteenth century Indiana Jones, who'd discovered the fourth century Bible at St. Catherine's Monastery in Egypt in the mid-1800s then stole it from the monks and delivered it to the Czar of Russia. When the Bolsheviks killed the Czar, they sold the Codex to the British Museum in 1933.

Conrad never blinked. He acted as if he had never heard it before.

No one else in the pub could hear them since the whole place was glued to a football match on the telly. They were too busy yelling, shaking fists, and cursing at the screen.

"But," said Nigel, "we don't have it anymore,

4

permanently anyway. They moved it and other manuscripts to the British Library on St. Pancras. It was an outrage. Some of those documents had been at the British Museum since the 1820's. Now they are all gone."

"People are able to see them in their new location, aren't they?"

"Right," said the Englishman, "but in a more sterile, hi-tech environment—nothing like the old-world look of the British Museum."

"So, it was good-bye to them forever." said Conrad.

Nigel nodded. The sad thought wrinkled his face. "But it's back now for a short period?"

Nigel's eyes brightened. "Yes! I'm so glad to have *Sinaiticus* back in its original location for a few months, just like old times!"

"That is good news. Hey, let's go for a walk," said Conrad after a few moments of silence. "I'd like to talk to you in private. You don't live far from here, do you?"

Nigel was surprised at the request, but felt like he could trust Conrad enough to take a little walk with him. But why couldn't he just tell him what was on his mind here in the pub?

"My place is just around the corner," Nigel said.

"I want to make you a proposition, but not here. It's a little dangerous and involves a lot of money."

Nigel's heartbeat quickened. What the hell, he thought. Might as well see what he has in mind. All he'd be doing that evening was watching another old Cold War espionage movie anyway. He was a big fan of John le Carré. They took off down Merton High Street for a little walk.

After they'd gone a block, Conrad said, "I'd like for you to make a switch."

"What?" Nigel was feeling dizzy now but not from the cider.

"I want the *Codex Sinaiticus*."

"You want me to steal it?"

5

"No. Just put this facsimile in its place." Conrad removed an old hardbound document from a large satchel. He opened the old book and laid it on the bonnet of a car.

Under the dim lamplight, Nigel could see it was written in the same Greek uncials as the original. He'd heard about facsimiles, but had never seen one. Its similarity was remarkable.

"Where'd you get this?"

"Copies exist in various libraries around the world. I purchased this one for a handsome price from a university that had two of them then hired one of the retirees from the British Library's Conservation staff to distress it to make it look like the original."

Nigel sucked air. He had gotten used to the extra money his new friend had given him for little odd jobs, but to switch documents at the British Museum? He collapsed onto the boot of the Vauxhall parked at the curb behind him, feeling faint.

"Do you remember how much the museum paid for it in 1933?"

"Of course, £100,000."

"Well, I'm going to pay you five times that much when you do this job. In fact, you get half of it right now if you agree. No questions asked."

Conrad waved a fat envelope under Nigel's nose.

Nigel felt like someone had just socked him in the stomach. His palms turned moist.

"It's just a switch. The Museum would never know. Neither would the public. No crime. And you keep your same old job until retirement, but you're a helluva lot richer."

"Why don't you have someone steal it?"

"With you in charge of security? Think how hard it is to steal anything from the British Museum. And it has to be done before it's moved back because the security at the new British Library is even tighter. You're the man for the job. Besides, now that I've told you, you would be even more on the alert. If I had someone else steal it, I would have to kill you," he said with a little laugh.

Nigel swallowed hard. He could tell the American wasn't joking.

"How would I make the switch without getting caught?"

"You work out the details."

Nigel's heart raced. He'd never done anything this exciting or terrifying in his whole life.

"Perhaps this will help you think more clearly." Conrad handed him a plump parcel.

He quickly thumbed its contents—£250,000. He had never held so much money.

"I'll call you later when you have had time to work out your plan."

"Yes . . . later."

When he looked up, Conrad had disappeared into the darkness.

More Than Meets the Eye

Maryville, Tennessee

Adam Hunter, the tall, lanky pastor of Hope Church on the outskirts of Maryville, stood in line at the bank not far from his church. The clock on the wall read 3:55 p.m., nearly closing time. No one talked much. In East Tennessee people minded their own business, especially in the bank.

Suddenly, two armed men wearing black ski masks burst into the lobby. "Everyone on the floor, now!" People who had queued up to cash checks turned, startled, but no one moved.

One of the thieves raised a shotgun, finger tensed on the trigger, repeated the command. "On the floor!"

He squeezed—a deafening explosion echoed as bits of ceiling plaster fell like mountain snow all over them. "I said down!"

Old men and women toppled onto the marble floor. Adam dropped to one knee, surveying the area as an elderly security guard appeared, fumbling for his gun.

"Drop it, old man," the other thief said, thrusting his weapon in the guard's chubby face. When he hesitated, the assailant whacked him across the right cheek with his pistol, knocking him to the floor.

"Everyone down now. Hands behind your heads!"

"Somebody, do something!" a woman screamed.

A young man lurched forward, targeting the nearest thief who turned and fired with no more thought than swatting a fly. The shot grazed the young man's arm, a streak

8

of blood red across his sleeve. He dropped to the floor, curled into a fetal position.

"Anyone else want to play hero?" the gunman asked. He seemed to be the leader. "Don't touch that button," he said to the teller behind the counter.

The woman backed away.

Adam lifted his head slightly, sizing up the scene. He didn't want to do anything that would out him as a martial arts expert, exposing a life he wanted to leave behind. He knew he'd better keep his cool.

"Keep down or I'll blow it off!"

Adam dropped his head.

Throwing a bag at the teller, the leader said, "Fill it up, Lady. Be quick about it!"

At that moment, local attorney, Renie Ellis, walked through the front door. She was a member of Adam's church and the real reason he'd come to Maryville.

The one nearest her grabbed her from behind, his arm around her throat.

Adam flinched at her yelp, but stayed on the ground as she fought to free herself.

"Hurry up with that money! Hold still!" he said to Renie. "Hey, Eddie, maybe we should take this one with us."

Renie stomped his foot then elbowed him in the stomach and wriggled free.

The man doubled over, grabbing his gut.

Adam stood up and began walking his direction slowly.

"I told you to stay down!"

Adam continued to walk toward him. "You don't really want to do this. Leave now and I will let you and your friend go," Adam said.

All eyes were on Adam, especially Renie's.

"I'm gonna shoot you, man!" said the thief with a pistol in Adam's face.

"You do not want me to do what I'm about to do to

9

you," Adam said calmly.

"You're a fool, buddy."

Before the thief could fire, Adam jerked the pistol from his hand, reversed it, pitched it under a kiosk, then whirled the man around and onto the ground in seemingly one whirlwind motion.

The thief was out cold.

The other masked man charged Adam.

Stepping aside, Adam tripped him and catapulted him head first into a pillar. He lay on the floor unconscious.

It all seemed like slow motion to Adam, yet he could see it happened in an instant to those in the bank. He was more Kung Fu than heavy-weight boxer. More skirmish by deception and deflection than brute force, effortless. Something he'd learned long ago.

Everyone was stunned at how fast it all happened.

Adam began helping people up as Renie joined him.

He heard people around him whispering, "Did you see what the Reverend just did?"

Renie was bolder. "Where'd you learn all that, Adam?"

"Seminary," he said. "An extra-curricular course for handling rough parishioners...." Then with a smile, he added, "Just kidding. I worked as a security guard part-time in the Bronx when I was a student at Union, and took some self-defense."

"Looks like you learned it pretty well."

"Well, you did too," Adam said, pulling the young man who'd been shot in the arm to his feet.

"Oh, that? It's nothing. Just a little feminist, karate course I picked up when I was in school in Boston."

Police cars pulled up with sirens whining.

Officers swarmed the lobby, handcuffing the two startled thieves and asking questions about what had happened.

Everyone pointed at Adam.

When the officers tried to get some answers, all Adam said was, "People shouldn't steal things."

Sleight of Hand

London

Nigel Rupert surprised himself at how calmly he developed the plan to take the *Codex Sinaiticus* and put the facsimile in its place. It would have been easier a couple of months earlier, but just a week before there had been a terrorist bomb threat. The British Museum had been under red alert which meant all bags, even those of the gallery warders, had to be checked. Normally, security was so lax that guards, tourists and readers came and went as they pleased without being searched. But now, everyone had to be frisked. The alert increased the challenge for Nigel. Instead of going through the front door of the Museum to the information booth for check-in, he had to pass by old Arthur Bledsoe in the warders' quarters. Arthur had worked at the Museum nearly as long as Nigel had.

"Morning, Arthur!"

"Morning, Nigel. What's in the bag?"

"Oh, just a present for a friend," said Nigel. "Going to a birthday party after work."

"So, what's the present? Looks like a big book."

"Good guess."

"You know I'm going to have to make you unwrap it and show it to me, Nigel."

He'd never been very good at lying, but for once he felt calm and said, "Arthur, if you can't trust me, who can you trust?"

Arthur got off his stool and stepped toward Nigel.

"Come on, Nigel. You know the rules. Don't play games with me. Open the bloody package or I'll have to call security."

"I am security!" said Nigel.

Arthur blocked the entrance. "Nigel, open that package or you don't go in."

"Okay. You've caught me." He paused for a moment. "I didn't want to tell you, but this present is for you."

"For me?" Arthur said, back on his heels.

"That's right, for you. I didn't want to tell you. Thought I could slip by with this story about it being a birthday present for a friend. But you really did your job and caught me."

"Oh, I get it, this is a test."

"Right again, Arthur. You're sharp today. No way to slip anything by old Arthur."

Arthur beamed. Relieved. "So," he said in little more than a whisper, "it's a present for me?"

"Yes. But not much of a surprise now, I'm afraid. That is, unless . . ."

"Unless what?" barked Arthur.

"Unless you act surprised at the party after work."

"A party for me? Oh, I can act surprised."

"But you won't be able to fake it very well if you open your present now."

"Then I won't open it now. I'll wait until after work and open it," he said with a broad smile, exhibiting a brown row of crooked teeth.

Nigel walked right past him with his fully wrapped package and said, "There's no way anyone could ever get anything by old Arthur."

"And don't you ever forget it," Arthur said, beaming.

In the guards' quarters Nigel removed the package, placed it at the bottom of the locker, and began his rounds. He moved from room to room throughout the British

Museum, his normal route. He waved to other warders, even stopping to speak with them as was his practice. At 11:00 am, he went into Room 29, the British Library Bookshop, and purchased *The History of Alexander the Great,* a book the same height and width of the *Codex Sinaiticus.* Although it was thinner, he knew he could pad the package and make it appear the same size. Returning to his locker he unwrapped the large package he'd placed there and slid the facsimile of the *Codex* into a large brown bag often used by inventory staff to carry documents in and out of Rooms 30 and 30a. With sellotape, he covered the book he'd just bought with the same kind of wrapping paper he'd used for the *Codex* so that the package looked exactly like the one he'd shown Arthur.

Tiny beads of sweat surfaced on his forehead. He wiped his brow, gathered the brown bag, and started toward Room 30 where the real *Codex Sinaiticus* sat next to the *Codex Alexandrinus* in a sturdy wooden case. With his best official face, he sauntered through the long King's Library, Room 32. At the entrance to Room 30, he surveyed the entire space with its tired walnut paneling.

He checked his watch and began walking by a circuitous route toward Cabinet 42Q. Along the way he passed Chaucer's *Canterbury Tales,* Elizabeth Barrett Browning's *Sonnets to the Portuguese*, Joyce's *Finnegan's Wake*, Handel's *Messiah*, a display of Beatles' memorabilia and the *Magna Carta*. He nodded to tourists from around the world, but never lingered long with anyone since warders were not supposed to. No one slowed him on his way to his destination. He kept checking his watch because everything had to be timed perfectly.

The Supervisor entered from the Library Bookshop to his right and looked directly at Nigel then headed his direction with a purse-lipped look on his face. Fifteen feet and closing.

Suddenly a large-bosomed, elderly woman stepped

right in front of the Supervisor and blocked his path. She asked him a simple question about Dickens' *Nicholas Nickleby* then one about Eliot's *Middlemarch*. In the seconds it took for the Supervisor to brush her off, Nigel set the *Codex* facsimile on the floor next to the case that housed Schumann's *Sonata in F* then turned and walked in the direction of Room 30a. It happened so quickly, Nigel was sure no one had seen him do it, least of all the Supervisor.

"Nigel Rupert!" said the Supervisor with an air of authority in his voice, having dispatched the woman. "May I have a word with you?"

Nigel turned on his heels, his heart racing. "Why, of course."

"Over here," said the Supervisor, motioning to the corner.

Nigel noticed no one had removed the brown bag, which leaned against the side of the cabinet in plain sight. He and the Supervisor walked right past it.

"We've had a tip," the Supervisor said, "that someone might try to pull off a theft. Everyone needs to be on high alert."

"But the moment someone bumps one of these cabinets the whole museum shuts down."

"I know that. But pros have their ways. They're a lot smarter than you and some of the other gallery warders we have around this place. Just keep your eyes open."

"Right." Nigel wanted to give him *two fingers* as he walked away, but others were looking. Besides, the buxom intruder had a bead on the Supervisor again, and Nigel decided that was punishment enough.

As soon as the Supervisor moved to another room, Nigel zigzagged his way to the spot where he'd left the facsimile. It was still there! He checked his watch once more. It was almost time. The Supervisor's interruption had nearly blown the whole thing.

He nodded to a man who slipped into Room 30a

where, at exactly 11:45 am, there was a large disturbance. People screamed and began calling for help.

Everyone, including the two inventory staff workers who'd just opened cabinet 42Q, looked up to see what the ruckus was.

Nigel knew they'd signaled the man in the security surveillance room to turn off the alarm while they counted documents, which meant he had a window of only a few seconds.

Gallery Warders, including the Supervisor, poured into Room 30a. Room 30 emptied as visitors from around the world crammed through the door to get a good look.

Nigel quickly unlocked the case that held *Codex Sinaiticus* and removed it carefully from the two thin membranes of binding. Sweat blurred his vision. He pulled a handkerchief from his pocket and mopped his shiny forehead and face.

As far as he could tell, everyone seemed focused on the commotion next door. He handled the Fourth century manuscript like a fragile eggshell as he set it on top of the glass case then slid the facsimile into its place.

He opened it to the exact page to which the original had been spread. Fortunately for him, no camera panned the room. Quickly he closed the case then placed the ancient *Codex* inside the brown bag and set it on the floor at the side of the cabinet since another warder had just walked in from the Library Bookshop.

At that very moment the Supervisor burst through the door.

"Nigel, what are you doing? Someone's having a seizure in there! Radio the front desk now so they can call for an ambulance. I'm going into the King's Library to make sure nothing is being stolen. Get the warders back to their stations."

Nigel nodded and put a radio to his mouth, pretending to make the call to the front desk for the

16

ambulance. A quick glance at his watch told him the ambulance with Conrad and his men would be there any minute.

"Move on out of here, please," Nigel said to the tourists in Room 30. "Go quietly to the lobby. There is no reason to panic."

Nigel pushed his way into Room 30a and saw the man writhing on the floor, foam bubbling at his mouth.

The warders did their best to move sightseers along as they jostled each other on their way out the door.

Nigel thought about the manuscript he'd left on the floor next to the cabinet. He had to get back there as soon as possible. The commotion provided some camouflage, but he knew it wouldn't last for long.

"You've got this under control?" he said to one of his subordinates.

"Yes. We'll stay with him until the paramedics arrive."

Nigel made a beeline for Cabinet 42Q. To his shock the brown bag with the manuscript was gone! His light blue uniform shirt was drenched with sweat under the navy-blue sweater with royal crown shoulder epaulettes. His face was flush. The room suddenly looked like a slow-motion kaleidoscope.

"Sir," said a young woman.

"I'm sorry, Madam," Nigel said, looking furtively around the room, "I have an emergency." He started to walk away but she called to him again.

"Sir? Sir?" She was insistent.

"What is it, Madam?!"

"Does this belong to the Museum? My son picked it up."

A flood of relief washed over Nigel as he stared at the bag, the woman and her curious seven-year-old son who asked, "Is it important, Mister?"

"Oh no," Nigel said, practically wrenching it from

17

the woman's hands. "Just another old book. Look. We have lots of them up on the shelves." He waved his hand across the room. "Thanks for returning it. Now, please move to the lobby. Paramedics will be here soon."

More tourists spilled in from the King's Library to see what had happened. Some coming from the Library Bookshop collided with those being pushed through the door.

Finally, the paramedics arrived with a stretcher on wheels. One of them was Conrad Docherty. Nigel moved right in behind them with the brown bag and slipped it to Conrad, who with one quick motion slid it into a special side compartment in the stretcher and covered it with a sheet. By the time they'd reached the man who writhed on the floor next to the *Lindisfarne Gospels*, neither Nigel nor Conrad had the bag or the manuscript.

Nigel moved back to Room 30, clearing a path by running interference all the way to the lobby.

One of the warders at the front door said, "Nigel, we should search them to make sure they didn't take anything."

Under the glaring eyes of the Supervisor, Nigel managed, "This man could die if they don't go now. How could they have taken anything? They just got here. Besides, I've been with them the whole time. Let them go before it's too late!"

Suddenly the man on the stretcher began convulsing violently.

"It will be your responsibility if this man dies!" Nigel said.

"Get him out of here then." The warder waved them on.

At that moment, the paramedics, the man faking the seizure and the *Codex Sinaiticus* went right out the front door of the British Museum. Nigel smiled nervously. Everything had worked perfectly. They'd settle up at The Crown later that night.

18

At closing time, as Nigel approached Arthur, he was stopped by the Supervisor. "What's this I hear about your bringing a present in that wasn't checked thoroughly?"

"You told him about your surprise?" said Nigel to Arthur.

Arthur's face fell in embarrassment. "I had to. He asked me if there had been anything unusual today."

"And there was," said the Supervisor. "Come now. Open up."

Nigel said confidently, "It's your present Arthur. You open it."

Arthur tore the wrapping off, uncovering *The History of Alexander the Great.*

"Thanks, Nigel. What a great gift! And such an expensive one at that."

When Nigel said, "Only the best for my friend," the Supervisor scowled and stomped off in a huff.

Psychic Pain

Maryville

Adam sat comfortably, his feet on an ottoman in the back room of his cabin nestled near the foothills of the Smoky Mountains in East Tennessee. They were like home to him since he'd grown up in Townsend, the "peaceful side" of the Smokies. After high school he'd gone to Vanderbilt where he was recruited by the CIA, and disappeared for years. Hardly anyone in the area was left who remembered him.

From his house, he could see Thunderhead, Rocky Top and Spence Field rising up in Walland Gap between the foothills that were spread out before him to the right and the left.

He peered at the old book again then shut it. Something he'd read stirred it up again—the explosion in New York. His wife, Emma, and the young man sprawled on the street in front of him. He closed his eyes, hoping the image would disappear, but it remained seared in his mind. His attempt to kill a terrorist and destroy his biological weapon had killed them instead.

He cradled his coffee mug and walked to the window. Steam rose from his cup like the diaphanous vapors that drifted in layers over the old hills. The mountains blazed so that fall that Moses would have turned aside at every bush and tree. He glanced at the seminary diploma on the wall and thought about the young, black theology student who had nursed him back to health, then got him started on the road

20

to healing through those dreaded stages of grief. It would take a lifetime to get over Emma's death. God may forgive him someday, he thought, but he would never be able to forgive himself.

His phone chirped. Adam answered.

"Hey Adam, it's Renie. You free for a visit if I come by your office this afternoon?"

"Sure. I'm at home now, but will be back around 2:00. I'll just be working on a sermon and will welcome the break. See you later."

Irene Ellis, "Renie" as nearly everyone in Maryville called her, had the rough-hewn beauty of a mountain woman. Her body was trim and firm, evidence of years spent pounding the trails, especially her favorite, the steep one that wound past Alum Cave Bluff on its way to Mt. LeConte. Like that trail, her own life had taken some hard twists and turns. Fresh from Harvard Law, she'd turned down lucrative offers from prestigious New York firms to come home and take over her Daddy's small practice in Maryville right after he died.

She'd waited a long time to get married. Eric was the only one she'd ever known who was smart enough to keep up with her, then suddenly his life was over on a street in Manhattan a few weeks before their wedding day.

She and Adam hadn't shared more than a few paragraphs since he'd moved to the small college town near Knoxville the year before. Having grown up nearby, Adam knew how folks in the foothills of the Smokies tended to keep their own counsel, but she seemed more withdrawn than most. They'd caught each other's eye once or twice but nothing had ever come of it. Neither one was ready for any sort of serious relationship. There was still too much hurt for both of them. Besides, he couldn't imagine her ever thinking about him that way after what had happened in New York— if she ever found out.

The turning point in his life years before would not

go away no matter how hard he tried to erase it from his memory. As if it were only yesterday, he remembered how, disguised as a homeless man, tethered to a brown-bagged bottle, he had hunched on the pavement in front of an old apartment building on West 114th between Broadway and Riverside in Manhattan not far from a giant boulder the people in the neighborhood called "Rat Rock." Across the street, a black minivan he'd wired with a bomb waited for its mark, its driver sleeping soundly.

The target had been involved in planning the 9/11 attacks. His contact had assured him the mark's van held a biological weapon that would be released somewhere in New York. Adam's job was to eliminate both. As ex-CIA, he was doing this last hit free-lance. Emma was there because she'd seen a note he'd written with the address.

He remembers squinting, shading his eyes from the smoggy afternoon sun that slanted between dull, gray buildings. The quiet street seemed as empty as his life had been. This final hit was going to be the end of an old life for him, the beginning of a new one. After this, he would make a clean break.

Or so he thought.

*   *   *

Adam settled into a chair back at the church and rubbed his eyes. The day had been long, and he hadn't gotten much done. The bank robbery was still on his mind. He'd tried to write a sermon, but couldn't get past the first sentence.

The knock at the door startled him.

"You here?" Renie said, peeking in.

Adam stood up. "I didn't hear you come in. Evelyn's off this afternoon."

Renie entered slowly. "Is it okay to visit now?"

"Sure," he said, waving her to the old couch. He took the seat opposite her.

She stared at the pictorial book of Jerusalem on the coffee table. The Dome of the Rock was on the front cover.

"Ever been there?"

"Long time ago," said Adam.

"I've always wanted to see it."

"Maybe you will someday."

Renie looked down and rubbed the arm of the sofa.

"What is it?"

"Thanks for this afternoon," she said. "You saved my life."

"Looked to me like you had things pretty well under control when you stomped his foot. Good move."

"Sheer anger and adrenaline." The start of a smile curled the side of her mouth. "But, your moves—that had to be more than a little Tae Kwon Do course in seminary?"

"Picked it up, here and there . . . but you didn't come by to talk about that, did you?"

"No."

He waited.

"What happened this afternoon . . . it reminded me of what happened to Eric."

"Thought you didn't want to talk about him."

"I never do, but I think about him all the time," she said. She crossed her leg and bounced it anxiously.

So do I, thought Adam. "He must have been very special. Tell me about him."

"He was the light of my life. Smart, funny, loved my food even though I'm a terrible cook. He wasn't perfect. Not by a long shot. Sometimes he didn't listen even though he pretended. Or maybe he just didn't hear me. He had this annoying way of telling me I was always right. Just once I wanted him to argue with me about something." She paused reminiscing. "Oh, and his foot rubs were heavenly. Put me right to sleep every time."

She looked out the window at nothing in particular then broke the silence with "God, I miss him. I wasn't there when he was killed, but I've seen the explosion in my mind a thousand times."

The blast flashed through Adam's psyche, stirring old pain. He saw Emma and Eric sprawled across the sidewalk. He saw himself stumbling toward her and bundling her broken body in his arms.

"I never got to say good-bye."

Her words snapped Adam back. He rubbed his side to ease the pain.

"It's like whoever killed Eric killed me, too. Who'd have thought an explosion in New York would shatter my life here? A two-for-one bomb."

Adam said nothing.

An awkward silence settled in. Grief is like that, he thought. It has a way of striking you strangely mute. Words seem to hide in deep places of pain.

"Is there something else about Eric you want to tell me?"

Up to then he'd had her eyes, but with that question they'd found the floor as if she'd suddenly decided to count his shoelaces. "No. I don't want to talk about it anymore," she said.

Neither did he. A fleeting glimpse of the man approaching the black minivan in New York flashed in front of him.

"You don't talk much for a preacher."

"Words are precious," he replied. "They shouldn't be wasted."

Renie raised one eyebrow, smiled and shook her head. "We all have our secrets, don't we?" Before he could answer she said, "You've lost someone dear. Your wife?"

Startled, he replied, "Oh, yes. Emma was her name."

"I can tell she meant a lot to you."

"She was my all in all. She finished my sentences for me. Made me a better person. Don't know if I'll ever love anyone again like that."

"Same here. How do you get over it when someone that important to you dies?"

"I'm not sure you ever do."

"How did she die?"

Adam stared at her, knowing he couldn't tell her. "It was an accident."

"I'm sorry."

"You seeing anyone?" he asked. "Sometimes that helps."

"No one measures up. I've just thrown myself into my work."

"You haven't dated since he died?"

"Dead people don't date."

Adam looked away, wondering what to say next. "It must be hard letting him go."

She nodded, tears surfacing.

"Sooner or later, you have to."

"Perhaps, if . . ." she stopped.

"If what?"

"If I could meet the one who killed him. See him face to face. Ask him why he did it. Maybe then I could let Eric go."

Adam looked away then back at her. "Maybe you will someday." The words were out before he could stop them.

Hoping to change the subject, he said, "Hey, you want to have a coffee sometime?"

"Actually, I'd like that."

Pleased, he said, "Okay. Vienna Coffee on College Street?"

"Sure, that's a staple for me. Gets me ready for clients or meetings with judges. You pick the day and time and let me know."

"Deal," he replied.

Renie rose and extended her hand. "Thanks for listening, Adam. You're a good man."

Adam stood and took her hand in his.

When she had left, he returned to his desk and opened the middle drawer. Staring back at him was a picture of Emma.

Everyone has a dark side, he thought. It's the human condition. He knew his was darker than most. He didn't need biblical scholars to teach him that. Not even three years of seminary could scrub him clean. Theologians called it Original Sin. Some called it Total Depravity. That's the way he felt—depraved, "totally." There were days in his earlier, more violent life when he was so close to death, he was sure he was going to taste it. But he always dodged it. After all, he was trained to help others breathe their last breath while narrowly avoiding it himself. But, when the most precious thing he had left to live for had died, and at his own hands, he wondered why he was still around. If there is a God, something he was still sorting out even after studying with the best and the brightest at Union New York, Adam imagined keeping him alive was evidence of Heaven's cruel sense of humor. Death would be better than the guilt that plagued him daily.

But, if he could help Renie whose fiancé died the same day Emma did, maybe the guilt wouldn't taste so bad. If death came, he was ready for it. Other than helping Renie, he had very little to live for. He'd read books on death in divinity school, but they didn't help. They were too theological and philosophical, not practical enough for him. He imagined death would make its final house-call when he least expected it.

The phone rang.

"Adam, it's Conrad," a voice said when he answered. "Conrad Docherty. Remember me?"

Adam's stomach tightened. He wished he didn't. He massaged his belly trying to rub the pain away. "What do you want?"

"I need your help with something."

"I'm out of all that now."

"Nobody ever retires from what we do."

"I did." Adam felt the old numbness settle in. "I've got a whole new life now."

"Yeah, I heard—a church. Those people know who and what you really are?"

Adam exhaled deeply then said, "All I want is out."

"You owe me, man."

Conrad had him there. You do owe those who save your life.

"Any wet work?"

"We don't do that anymore. Remember? At least not officially. Besides, the transition from wet work to God work can't be that hard. After all, there's a lot of killing in the Bible if memory serves me from my Sunday School days. Even Jesus was killed."

"You went to Sunday School?!"

"Sure, can't you tell?"

"No comment."

"There's a lot you don't know about me," Conrad said.

"Obviously."

"I'll be sending you a page from an old manuscript that I want you to deliver."

Adam remained silent.

"Well, you in?" Conrad asked.

"No."

Adam hung up.

Conrad's Ruse

London

At the Crown, a pub on New Oxford Street a few minutes' walk from the British Museum, Nigel and Arthur met Conrad and a few other gallery warders for Arthur's "surprise party."

"Hey Arthur, we're glad you gave us an excuse to enjoy some Samuel Smith lagers!" Nigel said.

"That's right," said the others. "Happy Birthday, Arthur!"

Arthur smiled and waved then took a big gulp of his pint.

He even bought a round for everyone in the pub, which made him instantly popular.

Arthur got pretty tanked that evening. At around half-past midnight, when most of his colleagues had already left, he said, "I have to go to the Gents then I'd better head home."

"Me too," slurred Nigel and Conrad, chortling the way old sots do at their unison response.

"Right," replied Arthur as he twaddled to the little door in the center.

The barman leaned over to those who were left and said in a heavy cockney, "Poor Arfer, 'e's only 'alf thar!"

They exploded in robust laughter.

Nigel and Conrad followed Arthur to the loo, swapping stories and singing songs as they waited for Arthur to finish at the urinal.

While washing his hands, Arthur looked over his shoulder. "Nigel, there's one thing that doesn't fit." He sobered a bit, steadying himself on the sink. "What's that?" Nigel glanced at Conrad.

"This morning you had a present for me, a book."

"You guessed that, Arthur, from the shape and the size," laughed Nigel, slapping him on the back.

"Yes, I did. But the book you gave me is *The History of Alexander the Great*. About the only place you could have bought that particular book was in the British Library Bookshop. And if you bought it there, then what was the book you had in the package on the way in?"

Before Nigel could answer, Conrad pointed his silenced 380 caliber Walther PPK at a spot just behind Arthur's right ear and pulled the trigger.

Bloody pieces of scalp and skull splattered the wall.

Arthur slumped onto the hard floor, a jumbled tangle of arms and legs. Blood seeped onto the bathroom floor from the tiny hole in his head.

Nigel threw up in the sink.

Conrad hauled Arthur in by the toilet and dumped him on the tile.

"My God, what have you done?" said Nigel.

"He was asking too many questions." Conrad handed him another fat envelope that bulged with British pounds. "Here's the rest of your money. Let's go."

"I can't leave old Arthur here like this!" Nigel staggered back into the wall, sobbing. His knees buckled; he slid to the bathroom floor, his trousers sponging some of the brown-red smear of Arthur's blood that streaked across the tile to the toilet.

Conrad grabbed him by the arm and pulled him up. "It couldn't have been helped, Nigel. Come on. We have to go."

"What have I done?" Perspiration beaded up on Nigel's brow.

"Get hold of yourself, man. You're too plastered to travel on the tube by yourself with all this money. Come on. I'll drive you home."

As they emerged from the Gents, no one paid them any attention.

*   *   *

The two teenagers gamboled in Cannizaro Park on Wimbledon Common nearly every night. A great spot for lovers, if not a little dangerous. Since it had been a popular dumping ground for murderers and assassins for decades, more dead bodies had appeared in Wimbledon Common than anywhere else in the Greater London area. But neither the boy nor the girl had ever seen one. So, they kept meeting there, necking and kissing under the bushes, under the trees, wherever they could find some privacy.

A couple of nights after Nigel and Conrad had left the pub together with Nigel still visibly shaken, the two teenagers walked holding hands through the park in the dark.

Suddenly the girl stopped and stared at something in the brush, something she could barely see in the moonlight. It was a man's hand. As their eyes focused, what they saw a few paces away sickened them.

Lying under the azaleas and rhododendron were remains of a man who had been beaten to a pulp. His head was deformed, obviously bashed in by blunt objects. They'd seen it in movies but never in person.

Rigor mortis had come and gone. The man's belly was distended. Discolored, protruding eyes bulged and stared directly at them. The man's raisin-tinted tongue pointed straight ahead. A gray-black-purplish pigment had stained his face.

They saw a tattered British Museum guard's uniform on one what was left of him.

Suddenly the wind shifted. The fetid stench of

decomposed death hit the inner lining of their nostrils causing both to empty their stomachs. A yo-yo of spit swung from their lips as they stumbled in a lop-sided, off-balance gait on the pathway that led back to the old Cannizaro mansion.

"We can never tell anyone about this!" she said. "Especially, not Mum and Dad."

"But we have to," he said, wiping rancid bits of lunch from his lips. He wished he could wash the foul taste from his mouth and the sight of the man out of his mind.

"Maybe" she said, "if we don't tell anyone, it will be like it never happened."

*　　*　　*

Cairo

The Bedouin sat in his flat watching a replay of the World Trade Center Towers collapsing. First one, then the second. He kept replaying it, freeze-framing it at his favorite spots. Even the ongoing noise of riots in the streets did not deter him.

His subordinates remained quiet. They knew not to speak unless spoken to.

The Bedouin switched to the crash into the Pentagon, and smiled. He couldn't decide which he liked better. Now back to Manhattan, one more time.

"Did you ever see anything more beautiful?"

"Nothing in all my life, Great One," said one of them.

"If only we could have hit the Capitol and the White House, too. That would have surely wounded the American psyche."

"Brave men died trying," said one of his lieutenants.

The Bedouin nodded. "And to think, the Americans thought it was bin Laden. Fools!" he said, smiling. "They wanted a target and Osama was the most visible one. Then they went after Saddam, and finally got both. How quickly they bought my ruse. Americans always need a concrete enemy to attack. Then it was ISIS, but it's really the one who lurks in the shadows that eludes them."

The Bedouin's cell phone vibrated, so he put it on speakerphone and heard Conrad's voice.

"I have the *Codex*."

"Excellent."

"The Russians have agreed to the plan to help me sell it."

"Why do they want it?"

"It was theirs after Tischendorf stole it," Conrad said. "But the real reason is money, and the secrets I promised them. They want to mess with the next presidential election and I'm going to help them. Their cyber-technology is even better this time."

"Americans and Russians working together. Who would ever have imagined it? The press was always suspicious but could never prove it."

"Doesn't matter now. The money will be ours soon. Some old Greek woman is willing to pay an exorbitant amount for it."

"Hard to believe for an old Bible. The original Koran, yes. But a Bible? What about Hunter?"

"I'll have him roped in soon."

"I would never have guessed him to be hiding behind a cleric's garb."

"Yep, an odd cover for a murderer."

"Everything is coming together. This one will make September 11 look like a picnic."

"I'll be long gone by the time it happens."

"I will too."

From Russia Without Love

Moscow

Vladimir Petrovich Kulikov was a massive hulk of a man. He was tall, handsome in an earthy sort of way, with a large head, huge hands and an ego to match. A General in the Russian Army for only a dozen years, his bravery in battle against the Mujahadeen in Afghanistan and his leadership in Chechnya when he was young had catapulted him into the spotlight in the Russian military. A soldier at heart, he cut a wide swath wherever he went. The men on the front line would march through fire at his command.

Everyone revered and dreaded Kulikov. That is, everyone except Aleksandra Vasilyevna Beserdechnaya—Sasha, to him and those who knew her well. She rolled over and stared at him as he slept beside her. Sasha remembered when she'd first seen him as she reached for a cigarette on the bedside table. She tapped a Kosmos from its pack, lit it with the flick of a match then sucked on it hard and deep. A billowy cloud rose from her mouth like the sweet vapor of incense in a Russian Orthodox Church.

She smiled as she recalled the event at the Hermitage. At first it had been all business and politics. But the more they saw of each other, the more they liked what they saw. Their lives and their sex were always Stalinesque—violent and passionate.

Sasha stood and threw on her robe. She walked to the kitchen and poured herself a cup of strong, black coffee. She was No. 2 at what was left of the KGB, now the FSB–Federal'naia Sluzhba Bezopasnosti, the Federal Counterintelligence Service or Federal Security Service, more powerful than the GRU or the SVU, other spinoffs of the KGB. A celebrated alum of the elite Alpha Unit, Sasha scanned the report from England about the theft of the original *Codex Sinaiticus* from the British Museum in London, then rested what was left of her cigarette on the tray.

The General moaned.

She called to him. "Volod'?"

He muttered something incomprehensible in response.

"Would you like some tea?"

"Love some," he mumbled. "You know I like it hot."

Sasha moved toward the bed, scalding cup in hand. She stood over him for a moment then said, "I could burn you up if I dumped it on you."

"You've already burnt me to a crisp," he laughed. "There is nothing left of me but ashes."

"Just remember that," she said as she set the cup down and loosened her robe. She dropped it to the floor and pushed her tall, statuesque body against his for one more kiss.

Together, Vladimir and Aleksandra made a formidable alliance. They had both learned how the game was to be played in the new Russia and, with the Russian Mafia's help, had amassed more power than anybody had ever imagined. They both liked the freedom of the new capitalism. Especially the fact it hadn't worked very well, which made everyone—the starving military, big industry, and small business—dependent on them and their protection. Money and Mafia made Russia tick; Vladimir and Sasha needed both to accomplish their plans.

They also needed the ongoing war to come to an end. It hadn't started well, and it was wrecking the Russian economy. The people didn't like the idea that it was sidelining and isolating Russia on the global stage. Vlad and Sasha needed money to achieve their goals. But first, they needed the Russian Orthodox Church and a strategy that would gather them all in.

"Boris has a good plan," said Sasha, "that involves a former CIA operative named Conrad Docherty who's an old friend."

"Can we trust him?"

"Who can we trust these days, Volod? Boris Viacheslavovich Gromilov, former chief of the Brighton Beach's Little Odessa in Brooklyn, has a very hot manuscript called the *Codex Sinaiticus*. The plan he's concocted with the American over this *Codex* in London is superb. We will have another go at manipulating American elections."

"I just hope you know what you're getting us into. Boris can be very dangerous."

"Trust me darling." She ran a fingernail down the side of his face, "I can, too."

Running From Something

Maryville

Adam, who'd spent a lifetime running, decided he needed to clear his head, and a good jog through the woods was the ticket. Fortunately, he knew a nice cycling/jogging trail right there in town. Pulling into the Blount County Library parking lot, his typical starting point for tackling the trail, he readied himself for the run. The crisp air and fall colors were calling his name.

Once he'd slipped on his new Hokas, he stretched for a minute then set his watch for an Outdoor Run and took off around the left side of the Library. When he crossed the bridge, he headed down to the right going North on the Maryville/Alcoa Greenway. One more little bridge and he was into the woods, snaking his way toward Springbrook. Neil Diamond serenaded him through his earbuds with "Solitary Man," "Holly Holy" and other classics.

Halfway through "Sweet Caroline," a gray jogging suit with hair flying under an orange UT Vols baseball cap flashed by him in a blur. "Pick up the pace, Preacher!"

It was Renie!

"I didn't know you ran!" he yelled as she flew on down the trail in front of him.

"There's a lot you don't know about me. See you at Springbrook!" Off she went, leaving him behind.

Despite his best effort, he couldn't catch her, so he decided to circle the lake at the end, a shorter distance to the porta potty and the parking lot. When he rounded the lake's corner, she was already there, stretching and cooling down.

"You took the shortcut and I still beat you!" Renie said.

"Guilty as charged." He forced a smile between labored breaths. "You have younger legs," he said as he stretched his.

"Excuses, excuses."

"Wanna walk up to the Wellness Center," Adam said, "catch our breath and get a drink? I belong there and they'll let you come in, I'm sure."

"Of course, they will, I belong there, too! But I'm neither tired nor thirsty. We just did a little 5K. Let's do one more."

"Okay. Why don't we run back and get that coffee we keep talking about?" He wanted another chance to beat her. "Where'd you park?"

"The Library. You?"

"Same."

"Race you back," she said, "but I'll give you a head start." She was already stretching again.

"You think I need it?" He felt like teasing her, but realized trying to feel comfortable around her was making him feel uncomfortable. He just wanted to be close so he could help her, not fall in love with her. She replied with an affirmative smile.

"Okay, well make it a good one!" Adam said.

"Loser buys coffee at Vienna."

"That will be you!" He took off sprinting.

In spite of a big lead, she passed him halfway back, gliding like a gazelle through the woods.

When he rounded the library, he could see she'd already changed her shoes and thrown a little jacket on to ward off the chill in the air.

"Glad you made it, slow poke. I was about to send out a search party for you."

"Okay, you won today, I want a rematch sometime. But for now, I owe you a coffee. Meet you at Vienna."

"I'm ready for it! See you there." She hopped in her Subaru and took off.

She was ordering hers when he entered and walked up behind her.

"You gonna beat me at everything?" he said.

"Probably. What do you want?"

"I thought drinks were on me today."

"Are you kidding! I know what you make. And I'm a rich lawyer. You can pick up the tab next time. I'm having my basic black. What's your pleasure, Adam?"

"I'll take a Crème Frappe with nonfat milk, and a chocolate hazelnut crepe."

"Geez, this is costing me. I should have let you buy!"

Two women who were members of Adam's church walked in the door and saw him with Renie, both still sweating from their runs.

"Adam, how good to see you here! Hello Renie. You two been jogging?" said Mrs. Delozier.

"Actually, we ran into each other on the trail," Renie said with a touch of red in her face, which drew a nodding grin from both women. "Well, it's true. It was a good day for exercise and there was Adam, and…oh never mind, enjoy your coffee, ladies!"

Renie turned to the barista and said, "Just bring ours to our table." She threw a twenty on the counter. "Keep the change." Then she shepherded Adam by the arm to a table in the corner.

"See you Sunday!" Adam said over his shoulder as Renie hurried him along.

"Well, that was fun," she said.

"Yeah, it was. Not everything is in ministry. God only knows what they're thinking now!"

She looked at him with a furrowed brow.

"What?" he said.

"Been thinking about death."

"Wow, are you this good at non sequiturs in the courtroom?"

"Not really. I was just wondering... after we talked the other day...have you ever been close to death?"

"Why do you ask?"

"I don't know. Just curious. Well...have you?"

"Yes."

"What happened?"

"I'd rather not talk about it. It was a long time ago."

"Okay."

He could tell she knew she'd hit a nerve, but she seemed stuck on this theme.

"Have you noticed how people you really love die before they should no matter how old or young—isn't that the way it always happens?"

Adam muttered a tepid but pained agreement.

As the barista placed their steaming cups in front of them accompanied by Adam's enticing crepe, Renie continued her train of thought. "My parents are gone, and as an only child it's just me now with Eric gone."

"I'm sorry." He tried his best not to telegraph the pain he was feeling.

"Our wedding was to be a couple of weeks after he died. Your predecessor was all lined up to do it as one of his last. Instead, Eric's was one of his last funerals."

Adam didn't know what to say, so he said nothing. She needed to talk as if grief had its own way of articulating itself in fits and spurts, whatever comes to mind at the moment.

Renie glanced at her watch. "Crap, I have a deposition in an hour. Need to shower and put my face on. Thanks for the run and the coffee. Maybe I'll let you win next time...or maybe not!"

She stood quickly then leaned forward and brushed her face against his cheek in a half sort of hug, surprising both of them.

"Okay," he said standing close, but not touching her. "Till next time then."

"Yeah, next time." She smiled and dashed out the door, waving at the two church ladies who still looked surprised.

Adam sat there for a bit finishing his coffee and nibbling at what was left of his crepe.

He wondered what road he was going down now and where it might take him. He wasn't sure he was ready for it, whatever it was. In church work, he mused there are good days and there are bad days. This had been a good one. But not all of them are like that, he thought.

Old Parchments

The Sinai Peninsula in Egypt
St. Catherine's Monastery

In a musty, fire-lit cell of the old monastery, shadows danced on the wall as Father Nicodemus, a white-haired Greek Orthodox monk robed in black, put the final touches on a manuscript with a quill pen. He held the vellum goatskin up to the light and adjusted his wire-rimmed spectacles as he examined his work carefully.

Behind him stood the Bedouin in the meager attire of a steward with a red and white keffiyeh on his head. Two men, dressed in black, remained in the corner.

Father Nicodemus turned to the Bedouin. "It's finished."

The Bedouin took the two-page manuscript from him and studied it as Father Nicodemus waited. "Is everything here?"

"Everything. Now for your end of the bargain," said the monk. "The *Codex Sinaiticus*. I want it back."

"It's coming." The Bedouin nodded to the men in black as he moved to the fireplace to peruse the manuscript more closely.

One of them slipped behind Father Nicodemus and snapped his neck like a twig.

The old monk's body dropped to the floor with a thud.

The Bedouin handed the other man one page of the manuscript, but kept the second one. "Go."

The two men dressed in black ducked through the ancient door.

The Bedouin punched a preset number on his cell phone. He glanced at the body on the floor then turned back to the fire as he spoke into the phone. "It's done."

* * *

Washington, DC

The President and the First Gentleman had just finished a late dinner in the private dining room upstairs. Roast rack of lamb, buried in bourbon molasses, wild rice, julienne vegetables, and a chocolate decadence torte topped with raspberry sauce.

They had relished a quiet evening together with no interruptions, the first one in weeks.

The red light on the phone near the President's chair began to blink like sparks from a heap of burning coals. The silent metronome throbbed, a pulsing splash of red on their faces. They knew it flickered only in an emergency.

The President's face tightened. She picked it up then listened for a moment. "Yes, I see. I'll talk to him. Let me pick it up in the study."

She stabbed at the hold button, but missed at first. Her hand shook a little as she returned the receiver to its cradle.

She mustered a glimmer of a smile. "Be back in a minute." She conjured a wink, but her husband had already turned away. He was used to it. Interruptions were normal in the White House. Besides, their marriage had been on the rocks for years. It was common knowledge.

Maybe the Irish/Hispanic match wasn't as perfect as they had originally thought.

Sean Kelly knew he was merely a trophy spouse who'd swept Victoria Sanchez off her feet at Notre Dame, but soon realized her family's money, her tough mind and ability to sell people on her personality would soon leave him in a cloud of dust. He may have been the life of the parties, but she surpassed him in every other way. He'd only stayed with her because he enjoyed the ride to the top, and campaigns provided plenty of side distractions, not to mention all the free booze he ever wanted. Why would he leave now? He was hanging out in the most powerful house in the world with servants at his beck and call and, best of all, no responsibilities except to grin and wave from time to time.

As she hurried off, he cupped a glass of Armagnac and walked to the window. Like a horizontal Christmas tree, the nation's capital glistened in a constantly moving blur of red and white.

The President turned on the speakerphone and collapsed into her favorite chair in her private study. Personal political memorabilia from a raucous campaign littered both the old, mahogany desk and the high-ceilinged walls of her dimly lit, oak-paneled study. No one had ever expected her to win, least of all her. But here she was in the White House, the first Hispanic, the first female and the third Catholic; now she was the most powerful woman in the world with everyone wondering how long she would last. She knew the next presidential election would be a challenge.

Victoria Sanchez was both tough-as-nails and charming—the perfect package for a female leader—channeling Margaret Thatcher and Hillary Clinton one moment and Laura Bush and Michele Obama the next.

"Tell me again," she said.

The voice on the other end of the line repeated the whole thing with the husky timbre of a heavy breather.

"An old monk was murdered. The manuscript is on its way."

President Sanchez squirmed in her chair. She tried to

43

think, but could not. More a woman of action, she'd decided early on that the White House doesn't lend itself to serious thought anyway; handlers and spin-doctors were a waste of time in her mind. She trusted her own judgment and, never having an unspoken thought, she tweeted most of them to the world regularly. It seemed to be the newest way to communicate directly with the public.

"Keep me informed, but only me. You understand?"

"Yes, Madame President. I understand perfectly."

She hung up and looked out the window for a moment then headed back to her dinner that had turned cold by now—just like her marriage, she thought.

Hidden Dreams

Maryville

Adam stared at the sermon on his computer. It was the same old stuff. He highlighted the whole thing and hit the delete button. He'd speak from the heart again this week. He'd been doing a lot of that lately.

He needed inspiration and some fresh air. He punched the intercom button. "Evelyn, I'm going for a drive."

No answer. She must have stepped out for coffee.

He left by the back door, his quick exit when he wanted to avoid troublesome members. He got in his car and headed out of town with no particular place to go.

Cruising along the winding Sevierville Road, he negotiated the treacherous thirteen curves and pulled into the long driveway of Coleman Ashburn's wooded estate outside of town. Feathery thin clouds drifted in strands and threads across the Smokies that loomed in the distance before him.

Coleman, a confirmed bachelor, was Professor Emeritus of Classical Greek at Maryville College. Long retired but not much admired, he was a bit too eccentric for most people's tastes. He'd been known to give whole lectures with one foot in a wastebasket or spend an entire semester on a single sentence in Plato's Republic.

Townspeople thought him sort of an odd duck. A few admitted the old professor had, on occasion, shown signs of brilliance. But he'd never published anything because he always got into huge arguments with his editors. Unfinished manuscripts of books he'd started over the years filled his garage. He loved repeating the phrase, "Nothing stinks like a stack of unpublished writing," but couldn't remember who'd said it first. His housekeeper had threatened more than once to set a match to the whole lot. "Go ahead" he'd say. Thus far, his writings had escaped the torch.

After retirement, he'd started a rare bookstore in the small house behind his home with the Smokies in the background. The only one like it in the area. Its wood-paneled, Persian-rugged, tapestried look added to its old-world charm and, by word-of-mouth, brought tourists in from Knoxville, Gatlinburg, and Pigeon Forge. Some even came from Chattanooga and Kingsport.

Adam, a bibliophile himself, loved hanging out there on his days off. He'd spent hours by the old fireplace examining Rousseau's *Confessions*, Pascal's *Pensées* or trying to piece together a few Greek sentences in Aristotle's *Rhetoric*. Old man Ashburn's collections specialized in leather-bound European literature and Greek philosophy. The older and the mustier, the better. He called the place RARE FINDS.

Adam parked out front, then walked around to the antiquarian bookshop in the back while watching a thick mantle of mist blanket the range of blue mountains before him. The "Back Later" sign was on the door. Must have taken his dog, Socrates, for a walk.

Adam figured he'd catch him later.

*   *   *

Moscow

The Bolshoi Theater on Sverdlova Ploashchad was packed to capacity. Gold leaf glittered in the shadows. Despite the poor economy, war, hunger, and crime, Mussorgsky's *Boris Godunov* helped Russians who could afford to attend the opera forget their troubles. Vladimir and Sasha preferred the Director's box, which was second row, stage left. Only the Russian President could use the Czar's Box any time he wanted. Entranced by the power of Mussorgksy's music, Vladimir and Sasha felt as if they were part of the stage.

As the actor playing the Tsar entered the Cathedral of the Archangel, the chorus sang, "Long life to Tsar Boris! As we praise the sun in the sky, so we praise Tsar Boris of Russia, Glory! Glory! And long life!"

"*Spasibo Spasibo!* Thank you very much!" said Boris Gromilov with a bow, startling Sasha and Vladimir as he entered their box.

"Borya!" hissed Sasha. "Are you daft?"

"You like my opera house? I own it now. But in time we will all own something even more precious."

"What are you talking about?" whispered Sasha.

"The old Codex will soon be in our hands," said the Mafia chief, sipping champagne and munching crackered caviar he'd smuggled into the box.

On stage the curtain raised on a night scene in a cell in the Chudov monastery. Father Pimen was writing by the light of an oil lamp. Grigory was asleep nearby. Father Pimen sang about one final story, about the industrious monks, who in the future would shake the dust of the centuries from old manuscripts and transcribe truthful stories.

"Very appropriate," said Boris as monks called from offstage, awakening the singer who played Grigory.

"What the devil are you talking about?" said Sasha.

"Old monks and old manuscripts, and the secrets hidden in both. What else?"

Off and Running

Maryville

Adam had just settled into the chair in his study, a stack of mail on his desk. A subdued sunlight peeked through tall oaks and leaded windows as he thought about his flock in the small Tennessee town. He felt a bit of a fraud on Sundays because of his pockmarked past, but no one knew. Maybe all clergy were frauds some days, he thought, pretending to promote what they only half-believed when they were really honest with themselves. Most of them were closet agnostics; he certainly was.

He'd made a clean break from his old life. Eventually, he figured he'd switch to full-time academia or help old man Ashburn run his rare bookshop so the congregation could get a real pastor. But the little church and the part-time teaching job had provided the perfect place for him to hide out and try to forget about all the killing he had done.

It had been hard enough leaving it all behind since the CIA never liked letting go of one of its own, especially one who knew so much. It had been even harder convincing them that he wouldn't share any secrets, that his life as he had known it was over. They wouldn't see him around doing Company business any more he'd told them in his exit interview. It was a clean slate. No turning back.

At least that's what he'd thought until the phone rang that afternoon.

He answered it himself. "Hope Church."

"Bet you thought you'd never hear from me again."
Conrad said.

Adam recognized the voice immediately. "There's always hope." Adam weighed his words carefully, never sure who might be listening in.

"We have a job for you. A manuscript from Egypt. We want you to take it to one of our contacts in the Vatican, a priest you know from an earlier life."

"What is it?"

"The find of the century, discovered in an old monastery in the Sinai. But, it's better you don't know in case you get caught."

"I never get caught," Adam said, rallying to the challenge.

"That's why we want you."

Adam hesitated, backing away. "You people promised—no more jobs."

"What happens when your congregation finds out who you really are?"

"I'll get over it," Adam said, then hung up.

Adam glanced at his desk and began fingering a small stack of letters.

A large manila envelope caught his eye, marked *Confidential* with no return address. He opened it carefully. There were no names, no signatures. Only a simple typed note: "Thought you might balk at the idea. Here's the manuscript page. Better give your old professor friend a call to make sure he's all right."

Adam unrolled the ancient vellum goatskin. Old manuscripts had been more than a passing hobby with him in his code-breaking days at Langley. This page reminded him of *Codex Sinaiticus,* the one German scholar Baron Constantin von Tischendorf had discovered in 1859 at St. Catherine's Monastery at the foot of Mt. Sinai in Egypt. Scripted in the same Greek uncials, it had been preserved with remarkable care. He wondered about its authenticity.

He recognized some of the letters but couldn't make out the words.

The phone rang.

When Adam picked it up, he heard Coleman Ashburn screaming in his ear, something about a fire!

*　　*　　*

As his car squealed onto the gravel driveway of the Ashburn estate, Adam saw smoke billowing from the back. Neighbors had gathered to help, some to gawk. Firefighters had just arrived. Behind the house, the professor pounded a smoldering stack of tattered volumes with an old blanket and yelled incomprehensible expletives in ancient Greek.

The rare bookshop was a shell of itself. Adam could tell it had been gutted by an inferno. The backyard looked like an old-fashioned book burning.

Coleman's dog lay lifeless on the ground, a bullet through the head.

Adam ran to Coleman. "What happened?" Adam asked, now at his side.

The old man's face glowed with soot and sweat, his eyes aflame with anger. Hands blackened from failed attempts to rescue a seared tome or two. Dozens of his prize possessions lay charred before him. They flickered then spit sparks.

He kicked one of them and watched cinders float up in the sky.

"Who would have...?" the professor muttered under his breath. "Why...?"

"What can I do, Professor?"

"Nothing." The old man hurled a blanket at the ground in disgust. He hoisted the dead weight of his dark lab and staggered toward the house.

"Let me help you carry Socrates," said Adam.

The old man never replied.

50

Others tried to console him, but he spoke to no one. Adam's insides blazed. The hazy outline of the Smokies melted into the azure blue of the night sky. He stumbled in a daze back to his car and sat there weighing his options.

He jumped at the sound of his cell phone chirping.

"Will you take the job now?"

Adam sat stunned, watching his world unravel before him. He stared out the windshield at nothing in particular.

"I'll take your silence as compliance."

The phone went dead.

Back at the church, Adam flicked on a couple of fluorescents in the entryway and shaded his eyes. He made his way into the dark sanctuary. Shafts of light from the narthex splintered across old wooden pews.

He walked down the aisle surrounded by shadowy stained-glass saints, ghostly members of the heavenly host. A darkened biblical figure loomed high above him in the chancel. He stood for a moment in silence, wondering if he would ever see any of it again, then slid into one of the pews, palming his face in his hands.

They'd caught up with him. Langley's tentacles would never let him go!

He leaned forward, elbows on his knees, trying to pray, but nothing would come. He sat there a long time, until a thought crossed his mind. He remembered an old friend in Georgetown, the one man he knew he could trust.

He opened his cell phone and punched in the numbers for American.

"Knoxville to Reagan National."

PART TWO: PREDICATE

An Old Friend

Langley, Virginia

Andrew Farley, head of the CIA, stared out the window of his seventh-floor office. His meeting with the heads of all his directorates had not gone well that morning. They'd argued with him entirely too much, as they had done the week before. There were moments when he wondered why the President had appointed him. Some days he felt prepared for it all, but most days not.

He picked up the secure phone to call his contact on the outside. The line was still busy as it had been for an hour. The clock on his desk read 4:00 p.m. He turned to his computer to check email while he waited.

Career CIA to the bone, Drew Farley had toughed his way up from the bottom. A Cajun at heart, he'd partied his way through LSU with mediocre grades and a lifeline of booze at the Tiger Lounge. But when he went to work at Langley, his Mensa-level IQ exposed him as a serious underachiever. Farley was a large man in every way with a round, owlish face, a huge heart, and an expansive, disarming laugh. An avid fisherman, he knew how to angle with the best of them for redfish and speckled trout in the Gulf at Grand Isle. Divorced three times, he was now married to his job.

Lately his job had been a real nag.

The secure phone rang. He punched the speaker button hard.

"Mr. Farley?"

"I've been trying to reach you all afternoon. Who the hell have you been talkin' to?"

"The man who's setting everything up."

"Well, why don't you get call waiting or something?!"

"A little testy this afternoon. Meetings not go well today?" The man spoke in a patronizing tone.

"What are you, my shrink?"

"You could use one. Are we still meeting tomorrow night?"

"Only if you've got what I asked for."

"I've got it."

"Same time, same place."

*   *   *

Washington, DC

Adam pulled into the last spot left on a tree-lined side street in Georgetown. The two-story row house where his old friend lived was nearly dark, but he could see the light on in the kitchen. Having driven around a little before he parked, he was positive no one had followed him.

"That you, Adam?" said the elderly man at the door. He squinted at Adam's shadowed face.

"May I come in?"

"Of course!" A grizzled-looking man, he wore baggy khakis and a forest green sweater.

The two men embraced like old friends. "You're the same old, washed-up spook," said Adam.

"You look pretty bad yourself. Want some pasta?"

"Only if you didn't cook it."

The old man smiled. "You're a sight for sore eyes. Make yourself at home."

As his mentor ambled off to the kitchen, Adam wandered the house he had known so well. He remembered the first time he'd come to visit the former head of the CIA, Stump Stevens. The odor of stale cigar smoke lingered in the air. It turned the filtered light from the kitchen into a pale shade of brown. The place had the same dumpy furniture and the same ugly drapes. Stump detested decorators and was never much for show. Fusty didn't begin to describe the sepia-toned and moldy ambience of the place.

The hallway to the kitchen was filled with pictures of Stump, the first African-American CIA director, shaking hands with former Presidents and dozens of dignitaries. The kind of photographs that always looked staged, ones that Stump hated the most. Next to the photo-ops were snapshots of the old man's two wives, both of whom he'd outlived, his children, and his prize German Shepherd, Montana, that he mourned more than either of his women.

With an Ivy League education and early experience in the espionage business, Richard K. "Stump" Stevens had risen quickly in the ranks but, unlike other fast burners, had not burned out. Two Presidents had recognized his brilliance and rewarded him with the Directorate, under which Adam had felt the Company had been the best place to work in the government. It hadn't been the same since Stump had left.

Adam waited for dessert to unload his story.

Since patience was one of Stump's virtues, he kept the conversation going with small talk until his prize student finally opened up. It didn't take Adam long to spell out the facts, sketchy as they were. When he'd finished, Stump didn't say a word. Instead, he pushed his chair back from the table, lit a long, Cuban cigar and stared off at a point somewhere northeast of Adam's right shoulder.

When he spoke, all he said was, "Do you have the page with you?"

Adam unrolled it on the table.

Stump eyed it carefully. "Can't make anything out of it. You?"

"Only a few words here and there. Nothing

consequential."

"You were the best code-buster I ever knew, but you may need help on this one. Conrad wants you to deliver it to a plant in the Vatican, one of ours?" continued Stump.

Adam nodded.

"Doesn't pass the smell test," Stump said. "Certainly not the Company. Who else knows about this?"

"I have no idea. Think the Chief is in on it?"

"Farley? I doubt it. It's not his style. But it sounds like somebody pretty high up."

"Can't you use your pull inside to help me?"

"Are you kidding? I can't pull crap over there. But I do know the Chief well enough to confront him on this. Tell me about the hit in New York."

Adam hesitated.

"Everything went wrong."

"Why'd you use a bomb?"

"He had anthrax in the van. An explosion would kill the spores."

"You saved a lot of lives," said Stump.

"I killed the wrong ones," said Adam looking away. "They assured me he'd be in the van."

"Who is he?"

"Not sure. Only that he's a terrorist with many disguises."

A noise at the back door caused Stump to put his finger to his lips. He waved Adam toward the kitchen, turning out lights as he went. For a moment they stood silently in the dark.

Stump found his 40 Caliber Glock 23 in the drawer next to the silver and Adam produced a Sig Sauer.

"Expecting someone?" whispered Adam as they tiptoed, guns raised.

Stump shook his head.

By the time they reached the door, they saw the digital timer of a bomb that was attached to the back door.

Adam raced to the hallway as the back of the kitchen exploded. He tried to re-enter the kitchen but flames licked his body and smoke filled his eyes.

"Stump! Stump!" He coughed as he covered his mouth and backed away in horror.

He turned and ran to the front of the house then out to his car. He knew it would be better to flee the scene than to get implicated.

He careened around the corner, checking his side view mirrors while plowing through the blur of lights that filled his windshield.

Then suddenly his cell phone rang. It was Conrad. "You took a detour."

"Bastard!"

"What are you talking about?"

Adam hung up and turned the corner, then crossed the Key Bridge and headed for Dulles. There was no turning back now.

*   *   *

Langley

Drew Farley pushed the button and listened once more to the conversation between Stump Stevens, and a former operative named Adam Hunter. At the end of the recording, he picked up the phone.

"We need to talk sooner than I thought," he said. "Yes, tonight...No, it can't wait!"

Smooth as Silk

The eastern coast of Sicily thrilled Vicenzu Mazzini that morning as early light warmed the rooftops of the little town of Taormina, tucked among the hills. The snow-capped volcano, Mt. Etna, loomed large in the distance while sunlight danced on the Strait of Messina, a clear cerulean blue. The old man loved his private view of it all more than anything, even more than the local officials who bowed and scraped to kiss his ring. Don Mazzini had everything with one exception—papal absolution for all his sins. He knew the Pope would never give it to him.

Vicenzu's other great sorrow was the absence of a worthy heir. He couldn't imagine leaving his kingdom to his son, Luigi, since the boy lacked both discipline and backbone. Though the Don had hated his own father for beating him when he failed and always pushing him to the brink, he did the same to Luigi. It was the way of the family. No one dared call it abuse.

A servant appeared with a mobile phone on a silver tray.

Vicenzu creased his brow.

"A call from the Vatican, Don Mazzini," the steward said with a quaver in his voice. "Cardinal Carbonari."

The Don snatched the phone from the tray.

"Lorenzo, *mi amico. Buon giorno!* How are you today?"

"Something awful has happened! It's a page from a

58

manuscript from St. Catherine's Monastery that I'm worried about!" the Cardinal said.

"What's that? Calm yourself, Lorenzo, or you'll have a heart attack. It can't be that bad."

"It is that bad! They say it looks like an old codex."

"What codex? What are you talking about?"

"My sources tell me that someone will be trying to bring it to Vatican City."

The Don said nothing. He knew, since Lorenzo was Secretary of State, the second most powerful position in the Vatican, only a whisper away from the Pope, that his Vigilance officers regularly monitored all telephones in the papal state, carrying out whatever covert activities he commanded. He knew Lorenzo was susceptible to periodic tantrums. He dipped a hunk of bread in a thick pool of olive oil and stuffed it in his mouth.

The panicked priest did his best to explain the implications.

"I just faxed you a brief description and a photo of the man my sources say might be coming to Rome with the vellum page from Egypt," said the Cardinal. "He must be dealt with!"

A servant appeared with the fax and placed it in front of the Don.

The Don stared at the picture for a moment then said, "Renzo, you worry too much. Don't fret. I will take care of everything. *Ciao.*"

*   *   *

Marcello Zanetti, a delicate-featured man with large, dark eyes and jet-black hair pulled into a ponytail in the back, strode toward the godfather's chair. He winked at one of the Don's daughters. His gait was fluid, graceful, his manner genteel. Everything he wore seemed tailor-made, as unruffled as his personality.

"Come close, my boy," the Don said, his cupped hand raised slightly. Although they were alone, Marcello leaned over and placed his ear to the old man's mouth. The Don whispered something briefly, then handed Marcello the fax with Adam Hunter's picture.

"Your target. Do not to return unless you are successful. *Capisce?*"

Marcello nodded. He knelt, kissed the old man's ring, and made his way down the back steps of the villa.

Vicenzu Mazzini returned to his breakfast and his view of the Ionian Sea. The others knew to keep their distance when the old man talked to Marcello Zanetti, the deadliest of his hit men. A soft-spoken professor of ancient literature who had tried the academic life but found it a direct route to semi-poverty, Marcello had entered the killing business for one reason and one reason only—the money.

Ancient Ruins

Rome

A dam had carried on a lover's quarrel with Rome all his life. Although his Italian was a little rusty, he had no trouble making his way to the Borghese Gardens overlooking the Piazza del Poppolo where he was to meet his contact.

Rome seemed to Adam like one large inhabited work of art. In the distance Saint Peter's rose majestically above the Tiber. Next to San Pietro, he could see the top of *Tosca's* Castel d'Angelo. Large stone lions guarded the Egyptian obelisk in the piazza below him where artists and lovers gathered and gypsy children targeted unsuspecting tourists.

A quick glance at his watch told him his contact was late. He tried to remember how long he'd known Giovanni, a Jesuit who'd mastered the priestly curriculum at the Catholic seminary in D.C. before signing on at Langley. They'd met first at the Farm, CIA's grueling training center at Camp Peary, Virginia and later at the Pentagon's School of the Americas at Ft. Benning in Georgia, otherwise known as the "school of the assassins." Though he hadn't seen Giovanni for years, he knew one thing about him—he was always on time.

Then he saw him. A monk in muslin alb, emerging from the trees.

The hooded man walked toward him with a look of panic on his face.

He began yelling in Italian, but was silenced by a

sniper's bullet that caught him at the base of the skull.

He was dead before he hit the ground.

Adam sprang into action.

Tourists screamed and scattered, running for cover.

A bullet nicked his hand as Adam ran as fast as he could, zig-zagging his way down the hill to the piazza.

He hopped the hood of a red Fiat then dodged a large BMW flying toward him.

The Beemer nailed the Fiat, turning traffic into a pileup.

Cars banged into cars.

Italians and Germans emerged from their cars screaming and shaking their fists at each other as Adam fled down the hill.

By the time he'd reached the door of the Santa Maria del Poppolo, winded but unharmed, he'd slowed to a walk. He wondered how he remembered exactly what to do. It had been over a decade since he'd done anything like this.

Inside the old church, Adam stared at the Carravagios displayed before him while he watched for non-tourists out of the corner of his eye.

Glancing at the floor, he saw drips of blood from his hand. He wrapped the wound with a handkerchief then hid his hand in a pocket.

He scraped the red blotches, smearing a thin, scarlet streak on the marble floor. Directly above him, he saw more blood spilled on Caravaggio's colorful canvas, the *Martyrdom of St. Peter.*

He spotted his predator. Definitely not a tourist, Adam thought. Years of observation had taught him how to read people by watching their faces, their eyes, their manner.

There was something about the way this one examined the paintings that was different.

When the man glanced away for an instant, Adam made his move behind one of the Carravagios. Hiding was something he knew how to do well. He'd been doing it all his life in the oddest places with disguises of all kinds, but now in the church.

When the man passed the painting, Adam approached the priest peddling post cards in the sacristy and crossed his palm with 50 euros—his ticket out the side door. He clutched the briefcase with the manuscript close to his body as he made his way through festive crowds where musicians serenaded sidewalk diners. The back streets of Rome were Adam's old friends.

*　　*　　*

His little *albergo* was a plain bed and breakfast, a typical *pensione* run by an old man, who looked like he had spent his life in a permanent nap in the little dump.

"*Buon giorno*," whispered Adam.

"*Giorno,*" grunted the man in a husky whisper with a slight nod of his forehead, eyes down.

Hoping no one had followed him, Adam looked both ways down the hallway then entered his room. He closed the shutters, which muffled the din from the nearby piazza. Turning on the light next to his bed, he opened the parchment and spread it out before him. He saw the same Greek uncials he'd seen in pictures of Tischendorf's famous fourth century codex.

ЄΝΑΡΧΗΗΝΟΛΟΓΟC

Careful not to tear the delicate vellum, he began to translate the best he could. Hours passed. Dark came, but he kept working deep into the night. The candle's wick sizzled and crackled as its light flickered across the page. Without a lexicon, he could only pick out a few of the words but enough to begin to get the gist.

As morning light spilled into the room at dawn, he tried to rub the sleep from his eyes. By noon the next day, he finished all he could and collapsed on the old chair in the corner. Something seemed to be missing, something to complete the story. Perhaps another page that would finish the odd tale. But where was it?

He hated it when things were left hanging, unfinished...like his life.

It was then that he heard the sound at the door.

*   *   *

Maryville

"But where does his aunt live in Charlotte?" Renie asked Evelyn Hastings.

"I'm not sure," replied Evelyn. "He left in a hurry without telling me."

"Oh, I get it. You're covering for him. I understand. My administrative assistant does the same for me."

At first Evelyn Hastings thought to ignore the comment, then said, "I really don't know where he is in Charlotte, Renie."

"Well, that's too bad, because I'll be taking a deposition there tomorrow and I had hoped to see him."

Evelyn wondered why Renie had volunteered such information but she tried not to read too much into it.

Fresh out of Vassar, Evelyn Hastings had worked in Washington, DC, but got fed up with the young-eyed ones who came to save the world, then fell from grace like all the rest. She'd given up finding a decent man anywhere inside the Beltway. So, she did the only thing left for her to do. She came home. At least the guys in Tennessee had their feet on the ground and didn't have their heads up their...

"Evelyn? You still there?"

The counselor's voice snapped Evelyn back to reality.

"Yes."

"Well, if he calls, tell him I'll be in Charlotte tomorrow. Maybe we could do lunch."

"Okay. I will."

Evelyn Hastings said good-bye, but Renie had already hung up.

Puppet On a String

A dam froze, more out of precaution than fear, his body poised for action. He was surprised at how dry his throat seemed. He swallowed hard and held his breath.

Another noise.

Under the door appeared a thin brown envelope followed by the sound of receding footsteps.

He opened the door slowly.

Nothing.

He cradled the large envelope like a piece of delicate porcelain, then sniffed the glue in the envelope. Semtex? No.

He opened the envelope and deciphered the note written in code:

Wait an Hour. Go out the side door of the pensione to the outdoor cafe in the southeast corner of Campo di Fiori. Wait there for my call.

*   *   *

Campo di Fiori teemed with activity when Adam entered it that day. Townspeople and tourists loitered about the piazza. Portrait artists offered to recreate him on canvas for only a few euros. T-shirt salesmen hawked their wares. He could have worn Mona Lisa or a Botticelli on his chest for a very small price. Booksellers guarded large rectangular tables laden with old and new volumes to peruse. Old men argued art. Young lovers sauntered arm in arm. Professors debated

philosophical ideas before anyone who would listen.
Women pulled up laundry hung between old wooden
shutters stripped of paint. Faded ochre and burnt orange
walls surrounded the piazza as motor-peds sped through with
minds of their own.

Adam decided to call Tennessee to check in,
calculating it would still be morning there.

"Hope Church, may I help you?" It was nice hearing
Evelyn's voice in Maryville.

"Evelyn, it's Adam."

"Adam! How's your aunt?"

"Oh...she's doing better. Thanks for asking. How's
Coleman?"

"Still picking up the pieces from the fire. The police
have no clues."

"Tell him I may need his help with an old Greek
text."

"I'll let him know. Oh, by the way, Renie called."

"Renie?" He heard the lilt in his own voice and tried
unsuccessfully to smother it.

"Is she okay?"

"She's fine. Just wanted to talk to you. Are you
alright?"

"Who me? I'm fine. Gotta go now. Talk to you later."
He hung up before she could say goodbye.

Sunlight glanced off ancient Roman buildings. Since
jet lag had settled over him like a large, sluggish cloud,
Adam massaged his eyes, wishing he could join the
homeless men for a nap.

He felt his phone buzz the watch on his wrist. It was
Conrad.

"Good to see you're still with us."

Adam ignored the comment.

"How are your archaeological skills these days?"

"I'm no Indiana Jones, if that's what you mean."

"What about Constantin von Tischendorf? Ever

heard of him?"

"I didn't think you read that much."

"You're going to re-trace his steps," Conrad said.

"Oh, God."

"Yeah, well, he may be there too. You're heading to Sinai."

"Why me?" Adam asked, dodging a motor-ped that zipped by him.

"Think of it as a calling," Conrad said. "It's in your blood—these old manuscripts. Like Petrarch and Boccaccio in Florence. See the man at the third table from the end being serenaded by that sidewalk singer?"

Adam glanced at the top floor of the building in front of him wondering where Conrad was.

"Focus on the man at the table. He has your tickets and instructions in a different briefcase you can use. Don't go back to your hotel. They're looking for you there."

"You're going to pay for this."

"Is that any way for a man of God to talk?"

"It's the way they've talked in this town for centuries."

"Ciao, mi amico."

"Go to hell!"

"I'll see you there."

The phone went dead.

Adam slipped into the chair opposite his contact as if they were going to have a drink together, but no words passed between them. After a minute, the man rose and left the table.

Adam saw the briefcase under his chair. Leaning over to pick it up, he glanced in the window in front of him and caught the reflection of the sidewalk singer, who pulled a Beretta 92 from behind his guitar and pointed it at the man who had just left.

A single strike to the head dropped his contact in a heap.

Adam hurdled the café's perimeter rope, sending one man's Genoa salami cascading in all directions.

People screamed as they collapsed in accordion-like fashion, creating a clear view between Adam and the assassin.

Adam hit the ground, rolling to the side. Then, quick on his feet, he ran around the corner of the building in front of him.

A barrage of bullets glanced off the side of the building just missing him.

He ducked into the nearest bar then slowed down. He looked for the sign for the toilette and headed that direction. Once he'd changed into some soiled clothes he'd brought along, he pulled a dark brown cap down over his forehead, smudged his face, morphing himself into a homeless beggar.

The crowded bar provided the camouflage he needed.

The assassin charged through the door, scanning the room.

The room quieted to see who the target was.

Adam turned and extended his hands.

"Alms for the poor," Adam said in Italian.

"Outta my way, old man!" barked the assassin as he shoved Adam aside and left in a huff.

Adam stepped out the front of the bar and walked down the street. When he could see his attacker was gone, he switched the manuscript page Conrad had sent him to the new briefcase Conrad's contact had left and glanced at the tickets he retrieved from inside it. Turkish Airlines. Milan to Sinai via Istanbul and Cairo.

What Does She Know?

The Washington Monument soared high above the bushes that camouflaged the White House tennis court. President Sanchez hated being interrupted in the middle of a match. She'd played on the varsity team at Notre Dame, but chose politics over the pro circuit.

At the end of a point, an aide stepped on the court and whispered something to her. She grabbed a towel and turned to her guests. "Duty calls. Just hit a little or have a drink," she said to three of her biggest financial supporters, then disappeared into the bushes and made her way through the Rose Garden.

Back in the Oval Office she put her racquet on the gigantic desk given by Queen Victoria to President Hayes and made from the oak timbers of the British ship HMS Resolute. She surveyed the White House Lawn. It was a hazy day. A soft natural glow crisscrossed the most powerful room in America with angular, fragmented beams and long shafts of light.

She tapped the speakerphone. "Talk to me."

"There's a new wrinkle."

"I'm listening."

"It's the other player who's got the manuscript," said the man on the phone. "He's one of ours who left a few years ago."

"You're kidding…why did he leave?"

"No one knows. Probably got tired of government

70

wet ops, so he went on his own for a while. Made a few hits freelance, then one day he quit completely. He sort of freaked out, got religion or something. Some of our people wanted to put him out of his misery because he knew so much. But he swore himself to silence, so we let him go."

"Did he deliver the page?"

"No. They terminated his contact—another one of ours."

"Pity. What about the manuscript?" the President asked.

"He still has it."

"Why didn't they kill him, too?"

"He slipped through their hands."

The President's eyebrows lifted. "He's that good?"

"He was the best, which is a good thing—he's out there on his own."

"What if he turns on us?" said the President.

"If we have to step in, we will. But intervening prematurely could jeopardize everything. He's expendable."

The President shifted her weight from one foot to the other. She watched a plane glide lazily in the direction of the Washington Monument.

"Where is he now?"

"Not sure. He seems to have gone dark. But my gut tells me he'll head to Egypt."

"Why there?"

"It's where his manuscript came from."

"If he turns into a loose cannon, this whole thing could blow up in our faces. You may have to take him out to provide plausible deniability. You'd better know every move he makes."

"I will, Madame President, once I locate him." said the man on the phone.

The leader of the free world hung up and returned to the tennis court to finish her game. As she made her way through the Rose Garden, she wondered how the real game

71

she'd set in motion would turn out. It was not one she could afford to lose. But failure was the farthest thing from her mind.

Saints and Sinners

Vatican City

Cardinal Lorenzo Carbonari's gaunt face and skeletal frame masked an unbridled ambition. The cleric entered the Pope's private chapel quietly so as not to disturb the Holy Father during his personal devotions, which always followed morning mass.

He watched the old man sitting in what seemed to be a permanent state of genuflection. Lorenzo knew he could never be that pious. His models were more Machiavellian, much more worldly. Like the Medicis and the Borgias, he told the truth, but told it slant.

Papal piety was a good thing as far as it went and often impressed the faithful, Lorenzo had said to sycophants, but it would never feed the starving millions; it would never find a cure for cancer. He was much more practical.

Lorenzo raced through his own self-imposed compulsory prayers the way the laity often tipped their hats to God at the mass.

Finally, the Pope rose and turned. His face lit up briefly at the sight of his old friend.

The Cardinal nodded in respectful obeisance. He could tell his superior was exhausted from his recent hectic schedule.

"Lorenzo, my friend. Would you join me for a cup of tea?"

"As you wish, Holy Father," he said, turning his eyes to the ground in veneration, a studied pretense he'd mastered over the years.

They moved to the Pope's private study and slipped into large Florentine chairs around a small table. An attendant appeared with a tray of cups, saucers and a small pot. As they sipped chamomile tea, Roman sunlight streamed through the windows as if to coax the shadows from the pontiff's face.

"Why was Giovanni killed?" the Pope asked his Secretary of State.

"No one knows. It's as mysterious as the murder of those Swiss Guards a few years ago."

"Tragic," said the Pope with not a trace of suspicion, completely unaware of the subterranean awkwardness that lurked between them.

"Yes, it is. He was an excellent worker and loyal," said Lorenzo. Although he'd known for some time exactly who Giovanni was, he still wondered who'd killed him. The CIA plant hadn't been the target he and the Don had discussed. But he surmised his order had somehow set Giovanni's murder in motion.

"I'd like for you to assist me in his memorial service and burial day after tomorrow."

"As you wish, Holy Father." He thought of the public exposure he would enjoy. It bothered him that this pontiff had dispensed with the royal "we," only one of the many things about the Pope that irritated him.

"Perhaps you could offer the eulogy."

"Me?" said the Cardinal as his teacup rattled against its saucer.

"*Si*. Consider it a personal favor to me."

Lorenzo nodded, noting the irony.

"May God rest his soul," said the Pope.

"Yes, Your Holiness."

"What is this about a manuscript from Sinai and the murder of one of St. Catherine's monks?"

"I am only just now hearing reports of it," Lorenzo

said. Lying came easily with so much practice.

"It would be fascinating to read what is written in it," said the Pope.

The Cardinal bristled at the pontiff's naïveté. "Why would you want to? What if you found something that might be damaging to the Church?"

"The Church is always in need of reform. Besides, I've been looking for a sign. Perhaps this is it."

Lorenzo did not argue. The pontiff had his own ideas and Lorenzo knew it was useless to express his real opinions. For a time, they sat quietly.

Since the Pope's priestly background had been mostly monastic, an avid reader of Thomas Merton's written works, he would on occasion stop to meditate. He'd become speechless, transfixed in a state that bordered on a trance. Lorenzo thought it smacked of Zen. It reminded him of the time the Dalai Lama came to the Holy See. Neither he nor the Pope said anything for the longest time. They simply sat and stared at each other. They smiled and nodded like kindred spirits entwined in interfaith contemplation, driving everybody else crazy.

Il Papa would launch into one of his private talks with God at the oddest moments. If others were present, they'd just have to wait until he finished as he sat in complete stillness. Sometimes with his eyes open, sometimes closed. These "spells," as Vatican inhabitants often called them, could last anywhere from five to ten minutes. Foreign dignitaries who visited were warned. Heads of state nearly came unglued. But Lorenzo always calmed them.

There were times when he thought the whole thing was a charade, a false and arrogant piety. But deep down he knew the old man's faith was real. It unnerved him. He didn't agree with the Pope's theology or his direction for the Church. He believed the pontiff would soon lead the whole thing down the drain if allowed to continue, especially if he ever got his hands on that codex.

The Cardinal took the opportunity to scan his daily mail. He'd learned early on to bring something along to read in case the old man slipped into one of his holy catalepsies. There were times when he wondered if he were to get up and leave and then come back if the Pope would even notice. But he was afraid to try for obvious reasons.

Suddenly, the Pope snapped out of his catatonic communion with the Almighty.

"Lorenzo, how long have we been friends?"

"A very long time, Holy Father."

"I don't know what I'd do without you."

"I am ever your servant."

The noise of the faithful on the Piazza San Pietro began to grow outside. It had gathered momentum throughout their visit, starting as a low hum but building to the clamor of a civilized riot. The people readied themselves for the Pope's general public audience when he would lead them in the Liturgy of the Word.

The Holy Father looked worn and tired.

"The crowds await you. They love and respect you. They yearn for you."

"Do they really? Or is it not anyone who stands at this window?"

Lorenzo winced. He wanted more than anything to stand at the most powerful perch in the world. He always thought himself a *papabile*, a man of papal timber. After all, he'd prepared all his life for this position. How long he wondered would he have to wait?

"No," he lied, "it is you they love, not anyone else."

"I thought it was Christ. I'm just a stand-in," muttered the Pope with a glimmer of a grin.

A hint of color brushed Lorenzo's face as he corrected his obvious theological error. "Yes, of course." Recovering quickly, he said, "But they also love the stand-in."

The old man nodded then smiled. He leaned forward

and placed his hands on the Cardinal's. The gold pectoral cross dangled from his neck. "You're a good man, Lorenzo."

Lorenzo tilted his head, dipped his knee and grazed the Fisherman's ring with his lips.

The Pope rose with the help of his priest secretary, moved to the window and waved.

The roar from the square shook the Cardinal to the core. It was more than he could stand.

*   *   *

When the Cardinal returned to his own palatial office in the Secretariat of State on the Third Loggia of the Bramante and Raphael building across the Court of St. *Damasus,* he was on the phone to the Don.

"He's going to ruin everything. He's nothing but an old fool."

"Patience, Lorenzo," replied Mazzini. "His day will come."

Strange Bedfellows

In the country outside Moscow

Aleksandra Vasilyevna Beserdechnaya and Boris Viacheslavovich Gromilov met the Patriarch and the Metropolitan of the Russian Orthodox Church at the Mafia chief's dacha, a 30,000 square foot palace about 20 minutes outside Moscow. The wooded castle overlooked the Moskva River. Limousines and chauffeurs waited on the circular drive, surrounded by a row of massive fir trees. Body guards sentried themselves in front of the mansion. The day was steel-gray cold, so Sasha, Boris, and the two clerics stayed inside.

"Your home is lovely, your property beautiful, Boris Viacheslavovich. But you did not invite us here to admire the view," offered the Patriarch.

"Very perceptive," replied the Mafia chief with an expansive grin.

Sasha flashed a quick smile at the two aging clerics and turned toward the river. She stared out a large picture window at the forest that sloped down to the Moskva-reka as it moved majestically by the estate. With her back to them, her voice was calm and firm. "We have something for you, something very special. But it comes with a price."

The Patriarch and the Metropolitan looked at each other expectantly then at Sasha.

"But first, let us sit down and have a drink," said Boris. His servants appeared with glasses of Stolichnaya vodka, china and a samovar of tea.

All four sat down and shared afternoon refreshment. The Metropolitan broke the silence. "Tell us, Madame Beserdechnaya, about this precious gift. And what we could possibly offer in return."

"Do you remember the manuscript a German scholar named Tischendorf brought to the Czar in the 1800's?" said the woman.

The Patriarch thought for a moment then replied, "*Codex Sinaiticus?*"

"You know your business well."

The aged cleric smiled. "I wish all the questions were that easy. It's only the most famous manuscript in the world."

The Metropolitan leaned forward. "The Bolsheviks sold it to the British Museum for 100,000 pounds in 1933. It's long gone. End of story."

"Now the story continues," said Sasha.

The Patriarch's eyebrows arched.

"We have it in our possession," intervened Boris, "and are prepared to return it to the Russian Orthodox Church. It is a matter of national pride that it has come home to its rightful owner. And we think you should have it, that is if..."

"If what?" the prelates replied in unison.

"If you agree not to oppose our continued ventures into nuclear buildup."

"How can we oppose something we know nothing about?" replied the Patriarch.

"Yes, but you do know about it," countered Sasha. "We have it on good authority. We cannot worry about the church publicly contesting something that is in the best interest of Mother Russia. Of course, we have to tell the rest of the world that we are not doing more nuclear buildup. But we cannot afford to stop preparing ourselves."

"But, how can you continue nuclear buildup when there is no money?" said the Metropolitan. "The people are poor; our military troops are dying as we speak. The recent war has turned the world against us and nearly ruined our economy."

"There are funds available," boomed Vladimir Kulikov with a deep resonance as he paraded into the huge room. He thrust his lower jaw out and lifted his chin in a regal manner. "You just have to know how to find them."

"General," replied both religious men, standing to attention. "*Kak dela,* Vladimir Petrovich?"

"Fine, thank you and how are you?" He bowed to them with a flourish.

"We are well," replied the Patriarch as they all took their seats again.

"Do not worry yourselves about the money," continued Kulikov.

Boris and Sasha nodded in agreement.

The Patriarch and the Metropolitan exchanged nervous glances wishing they had never agreed to such a meeting. They'd learned long ago that alliances with the government were always fraught with danger and potentially illicit compromise. But they also knew of monks who had been murdered for not going along.

"Could we have a moment to confer?" said the Patriarch to the other three.

"But, of course," said Boris. "Take your time. Come, Volod', have a drink!"

One of the servants handed him a tumbler of vodka.

The Patriarch and the Metropolitan wandered toward the window and stood their ground with their backs to the others. The sun peeked through the clouds and began to warm the snow.

"What do you think?" said the Metropolitan, studying his superior's face for a sign.

"I don't know," said the old man, gazing into the woods. Sunshine sparkled as a crystalline sheet of ice crusted up on the thawing snow.

"We should never have come."

"But you thought they were going to give us money for restoration of churches and monasteries."

"I know," said the Patriarch staring out the back window. "I had no idea what they wanted." He paused for a moment of brief meditation lost in another world.

"Think of the possibilities if it's the real thing," said the Metropolitan. "The *Codex* back in our hands. We should never have let it go in the first place. Stupid Bolsheviks."

"They needed the money," mused the Patriarch as if he had been around when it happened. "Some think it should be returned to St. Catherine's in Egypt, and frankly I'm one of those."

"But they gave it up," said the Metropolitan.

"Tischendorf stole it. He promised to return it but never did."

"Yes, but we are the true church."

"I know that," said the Patriarch, "but I've been reading some Catholic theologians like Hans Kung, and wondered lately if we need to rethink that…whether God wants us to be more open to our Christian brothers and sisters."

"What?!" said the Metropolitan. "The Vatican will never believe you if you do."

"I don't know about that. The present Pope is the most ecumenical one in history."

The Metropolitan said, "Do you suppose the Codex is the real thing?"

"Why would they lie?" replied the Patriarch. "They have nothing to gain."

"But we can't agree to keep silent about a nuclear build-up. It wouldn't be right."

"We don't have a choice now."

The Patriarch turned and gazed deeply into his subordinate's eyes. "God help us. The things we do for the church," he said shaking his head sadly. Then an idea brightened his face. "I think we should ask for one thing more in return for our silence," said the Patriarch.

"What?"

"Follow my lead and you will see."

The Metropolitan nodded.

The two clerics returned to their chairs.

"Well, Your Holinesses, what is your decision?" pressed Sasha.

"We would like to see it first."

"Not very trusting," said the General.

"Not very gullible," retorted the Patriarch, obviously miffed.

Boris stared at the prelate for a moment, surprised at his sudden surliness. He raised his left index finger and nodded to one of his assistants near the door. Into the vast parlor emerged a tall, severe-looking man who carried what appeared to be a very large book wrapped in brown paper.

"Gentlemen," Sasha said, "Meet Mikhail Igorevich Pritvorny, Special Agent, FSB."

"Your All Holiness, Your Eminence," Pritvorny said with a bow. "*Zdravstvuyte.*"

"Hello to you too, Mikhail Igorevich."

"I believe I have something you would like to see." Mikhail removed the brown paper covering carefully and held it before them. "The original *Codex Sinaiticus.*"

For a moment the Patriarch and the Metropolitan stared in awe as if someone had just unwrapped the Holy Grail. Finally, the Metropolitan took it, and cradled it like a newborn as an attendant moved decanters, cups, saucers and glasses to make room on the table. The two old clerics leaned over to get a better look.

When they saw the old Greek uncials, they realized it was the real thing.

As tears surfaced in the old men's eyes, Sasha and Boris glanced at each other. They knew the deal would be made.

The two prelates carefully turned several of the paper-thin parchment pages to make sure. They could hardly believe it. Finally, the Patriarch looked up. He stroked his thick beard. "How did you get it? Or should we ask?" He picked it up again to examine it more closely.

Sasha smiled. "Let's just say that God moves in mysterious ways. So, do we have a deal?"

After what seemed an eternity, the Patriarch finally spoke. "I don't think we can agree to your terms."

Sasha, Boris and the General exchanged glances then Sasha blistered the two clerics with a chilly stare. "Think long and hard before you say that again."

The Patriarch's face blanched turning whiter than his gleaming vestments. He knew her reputation for living up to her last name in Russian—"the ruthless one." He could tell she wasn't kidding. His hand quivered with a slight palsy as he laid the old Bible on the table.

After some thought he spoke. "One thing more."

"*Shto*?" replied Sasha.

The Metropolitan peered at the Patriarch, wondering what he would say.

"We know that the law that established four traditional religions—Orthodox Christianity, Judaism, Islam and Buddhism—and banned all others has been changed to include other forms of Christianity like Protestant faiths. Even though we believe that Russian Orthodoxy is the true church, we want the government to be more open to the Vatican for the first time in history."

Dumfounded, the Metropolitan stared at the Patriarch. It was a brash request at best, much too ecumenical for Russian Orthodox worshipers and silly to people who thought all religions were alike and one was certainly enough.

Kulikov and Boris eyed each other and nodded. "Why not?" Sasha said. "The President may not like it. It might take a little time to sell, but we will do our best."

"Then," said the Patriarch, "we have an agreement."

"Excellent!" said Boris to the others. "Let us drink to celebrate."

"No, thank you. I think the Metropolitan and I have had quite enough. We must be going. Are we to take the *Codex* with us now?"

"That would not be wise," Kulikov said. "You never know what sort of treachery you might run into along these roads. We will have it brought to the monastery at Sergiev Posad by the end of the week."

"It would be wonderful if we could make a big demonstration of its return to Russia, but we don't want the Brits to know we have it now, do we?" Boris said.

"We will keep it in a safe place," said the Metropolitan. "At least we will know it has finally returned home."

"Well, one of its homes anyway," the Patriarch said, causing the Metropolitan to give him a sideways glance.

*   *   *

When the two ecclesiastics had left the dacha, Sasha waved Pritvorny away and called to a young man who had been waiting in an adjoining room. "Sergei, you can join us now."

A 30-year-old, bespectacled man with bright eyes and a slight build entered slowly. "Boris and Volod, meet Sergei Smirnov, the top graduate of our Cyber-hacking program at the GRU. Also, like our two previous guests, a very pious man—probably the only IT person I know who actually goes to church." The two men nodded and smiled at the young nerd without getting up. He returned the nod but did not smile.

"Did you hear all that?" Sasha asked.

"Yes," Sergei said. "What an honor to have both the Patriarch and the Metropolitan here. The Church is blessed to have them as leaders."

"I'm glad you think so. Now tell us, have you made contact with Conrad Docherty to begin the process of interfering in the next US presidential election?"

"Yes, he has opened the doors for me as we agreed."

"Good. He will be paid handsomely when we sell the Codex."

"What do you think about the deal with the Patriarch and the Metropolitan? I know how devout and religious you are."

"It sounds reasonable. I'm also glad to hear of your plan to sell it to someone who will make sure it returns to St. Catherine's in Egypt, which is its rightful home. But what about what you promised the Patriarch and the Metropolitan?"

"We've secured another excellent facsimile we will give to them."

"Won't they know it's a fake?"

"Probably, but who cares? They've made a promise and will have to keep it."

"Does the Museum know the real *Codex* is missing?" Kulikov asked.

"They will soon," Sergei said. "The facsimile the guard put in its place is a good one, but not that good. A trained eye will be able to tell it's a fraud."

"Won't they initiate a world-wide search when they discover it's missing?"

"Not publicly. They'll keep it watertight from the press at first. Too much pride in their security system. They wouldn't want to admit it failed. Eventually, someone will leak that it's gone."

Boris smiled. "The perfect crime."

"Yes," Sasha said, "and now to sell it to someone who will reward us handsomely for this old Bible."

Righting a Wrong

Toronto

Anastasia Paleologos took in the skyline of Toronto from her fifty-sixth story corner office window atop the Commerce Court West building of the Canadian Imperial Bank of Commerce. She'd made it worth their while for them to lease the top floors to her.

She turned and gazed across Lake Ontario.

It was a bright, clear, Indian summer day in November. Through her telescope she could see the freighters in the distance as they entered the first lock of Welland Canal near the town of St. Catharines. Welland helped ships bypass the Niagara River en route from Lake Ontario to Lake Erie. Her scope targeted the Brock Monument at Queenston Escarpment. She backed away from it and glanced down to her left at her 48-foot C &C sailing yacht docked at the Royal Canadian Yacht Club.

The widow of shipping magnate Dimitrios Paleologos, Anastasia was one of the wealthiest women in the world. When he died, she surprised everyone by taking over all his businesses and expanding them with risky leveraged buyouts. No one actually knew how much she was worth. She didn't even know herself. She owned spacious homes in Athens, Toronto, Melbourne, Monte Carlo and the modest house where she'd grown up in a neighborhood called Astoria in Queens, New York.

She plowed ahead as if she were going to live forever. Her only ailments in her early 80s were a touch of osteo-arthritis and a lymphoma that had invaded her body and gone into remission under a massive assault of radiation and chemotherapy. When all her hair had fallen out and those around her had already planned her funeral, she declared, "Enough of this nonsense, I have too much left to do!" She fooled all the doctors by getting well. She said she was cured and that she would outlive them all. Except for the arthritic hip, she felt fine.

"Yes, Mrs. Paleologos?" said her male administrative assistant who had just entered her office suite, responding to her summons.

"I want to see Ian as soon as he arrives."

"I believe he just walked into the building. I will get him up here immediately."

Ian McPherson, former British SAS, had been in charge of security for the Paleologos Enterprises, Inc. for twelve years. Anastasia had learned early on that he was the best and could be trusted. His grandfather had moved from Scotland when Ian's father was a child, so his roots were in the highlands, but his experience was strictly urban, his upbringing English, and he had only a touch of brogue.

The tall, barrel-chested Brit felt out of place in a suit. But he always wore one well. Especially the fashionable Brionis his boss sent him to buy on her account at Holt Renfrew on Bloor Street. Ian's rugged face was a juggernaut. His soft hands could turn to iron. But on the surface, he was a true British gentleman. He was always "on call" for her. He rode the elevator directly to her floor and was at her door in less than two minutes.

He entered without knocking, the only one on the payroll with unfettered access to the matriarch of the company.

"Mrs. P.," he said with a slight nod of the head.

"Welcome home, Ian." She waved a letter in his face. "This just came from my old friend, Father Nicodemus, the monk at St. Catherine's. Listen to it."

Anastasia slipped a pair of gold, half-moon spectacles onto the bridge of her nose and began reading aloud.

Dear Anastasia,

I have been asked to create a manuscript to look very old, a two-page manuscript that will be delivered to the Vatican to be translated there. There are two meanings to the manuscript—the surface meaning and a deeper meaning I have hidden in code. The man who had me create the manuscript only knows the surface meaning. The answer that will help crack the code is in the original Codex Sinaiticus that will be stolen from the British Museum. Lest this letter fall into the wrong hands, I cannot tell you what is hidden in code, but if you can secure the original Codex Sinaiticus and give it to the man delivering the manuscript which I created to the Vatican, perhaps he can crack the code. Bishop Nikopoulos in Jerusalem can help him. Once you have accomplished this mission, please return the Codex to St. Catherine's, which, as you know, is its rightful home. If you receive this letter, I am probably dead. I asked Father Euthymios to send it to you if anything happened to me.

Your old friend,
Father Nicodemus

Anastasia removed her reading glasses and gazed at McPherson, a tear running down her cheek. "I can't believe Father Nick is dead."

"He was a good man."

"Have you heard anything about the old codex?"

Ian hesitated.

"What?" prodded the old woman.

"This game will get pretty rough."

"Tell me."

"I understand that the Codex has been stolen."

"Who has it?"

"The Russians."

Anastasia stared at him. Her roots were in Russia.

"And they are willing to sell it," Ian continued, "but the price is high."

"How high?"

"One billion, American."

"I want it."

Ian fell silent.

"A billion is actually a bargain. You have no idea how long I've waited for a chance like this," Anastasia said. "I can't let it slip through my fingers. Make all the arrangements."

Enigmatic Options

Maryville

The cursor on Evelyn Hastings' computer blinked at her. Cursed. That's the way she felt sometimes—trapped in a life that didn't seem to be going anywhere. Adam was the most exciting thing that had happened to her in years. But he hadn't given her a moment's encouragement. Theirs had been a platonic, professional friendship—nothing more. She wondered if she would ever find a decent man, or if it made any difference any more. After all, she'd decided there were worse things than living alone.

But to hear Renie Ellis carry on about Adam made Evelyn's heart skip a beat. Renie was younger, smarter, certainly more interesting.

Evelyn took the compact out of her purse and studied the tiny wrinkles around her eyes. She knew she'd let her weight go, but rationalized it made her look younger. She glanced at her watch. She had a lunch date with an old friend. She saved what she'd typed, and shut down the computer. Flicking off the lights, she locked the door behind her.

She got in her car and turned the key.

At first it didn't start. There was a click, a whine.

Finally, it started.

She knew a tune-up was long over-due.

* * *

Washington, DC

The search for Stump Steven's remains and the mystery surrounding his presumed death delayed his funeral for a couple of weeks. Following a majestic memorial service at National Cathedral, complete with the kind of pomp Stump would have detested, the motorcade lined up for the trek to Arlington Cemetery. Paparazzi jockeyed for position as limo drivers started their engines on a drizzly gray day. A mushroom field of umbrellas popped up over a trench coat convention. The police-escorted cavalcade snaked its way through the streets, turning rush hour traffic into a tangled snarl.

Since there was no body, there was no graveside service. Just a few words muttered by a Navy Chaplain, the booming gun salute through the rain and fog, a moment of silence and a quiet procession back through town.

While most of the limousines peeled off to their destinations, the ones carrying Drew Farley and the President went directly to the White House. The meeting in the Oval Office had been called that morning.

The President's Aide de Camp, Beau Miller, showed Farley in when the President was ready. From the Cabinet Room, Farley passed through Esther Adrian's office suite then through the door between the windows and the fireplace. The President stood beside her desk talking to her Chief of Staff, Pete Ashton, who'd been her campaign manager and was her right arm. Ashton, an African-American graduate of Howard University, had caught her attention early in her career. She thanked Ashton and excused him.

He and Farley exchanged nods as he left.

Farley knew better than to sit in the President's old chair, a blue leather wingback she'd had for years. Instead, he plumped down on one of the two-seaters, glad to take a load off. The President's brow creased as she stared at the DCI. "I met yesterday with the National Security Advisor, the Director of the FBI and the Attorney General. They have no idea who could have done this. Your people got anything yet?"

"Nothing, Madame President."

"Stump nurse-maided you when you were still in spook diapers, Drew. I wasn't just bullshitting the country in the eulogy this afternoon. He was a great man."

"Everyone agrees on that, and we have top priority on this case. But we have to be careful not to step on the FBI's toes."

"I can't believe it," snapped the President. "Best intelligence forces in the world and we can't solve a simple murder case."

The CIA Chief sat stone-faced.

"Come on, what do you really think?"

"Straight up, Madame President?"

The President's nervous nod said, I think so.

"My gut tells me it's an inside job."

"How high?"

"I don't know."

The President's face tightened.

"You do have your enemies," said Farley.

"Name a President that doesn't."

The room got very quiet.

The President broke the silence as she stood, which caused Farley to rise as well.

"Thank you for coming. If you get anything…anything at all, I want to hear it from you before I read it in the papers or catch it on CNN, MSNBC or Fox News. Understand?"

Farley nodded, shook the President's hand then left.

Minutes passed before the President punched a button on the speakerphone. "You get all that?"

"I got it," said the man on the other end of the line.

"Where is Hunter now?"

"Egypt."

PART THREE: PREDICAMENT

Mountains and Monks

Cairo

Cairo International brimmed with people from around the world, a swarming mass of wary tourists, clutching their bags like mothers protecting their young. Security was, as always, on high alert. Adam knew US attacks on terrorists had made it dangerous enough for Americans traveling in Egypt, much less a former CIA operative, especially with the recent riots. He scanned the crowd, wondering which one might follow him to St. Catherine's.

From the seat behind the pilot, he could see everything at take-off. Sand dunes and tarmac turned into bright sky as the craft rose, cruising low above the golden ridges of the Arabian Desert. For centuries people had scratched an existence out of this barren land. Somewhere beyond the Gulf of Suez and the Tih Plateau that stretched across the peninsula, the vast expanse of sand gradually yielded to mountain ranges, at first small and unimposing, then enormous precipices, craggy humps of brown and purple and blue in the distance.

As the small plane climbed, Adam recognized that it was traveling back in time since all about him were archaeological sites over 6,000 years old. Long ago the sand had covered ancient Egyptian turquoise and copper mines as well as Persian, Hellenistic, Nabatean and Roman settlements. Adam knew that St. Catherine's was a newcomer in the region, built by the Byzantine Emperor Justinian in the 6th Century A.D.

"Might as well be landing on the moon," he muttered to himself as he surveyed the peninsula's rugged triangle of granite, limestone and sand.

Suddenly, as the little craft lifted on the wind over one more mountain, the pilot pointed at the horizon. There it was in front of them. Mt. Sinai. *Jebel Musa,* the Arabs called it. The mountain of Moses, the sacred sierra, the *axis mundi*—the geological link between time and eternity. Adam knew that modern archaeologists had questioned its authenticity but he didn't care. The sight of it nearly stopped his breath. Its monolithic size dwarfed the little monastery, which clutched its base like a child holding on to her mother's skirt. Adam had scaled taller peaks, but nothing of this magnitude.

Near the plain of El Raha, Adam and a couple of scholars from England and Germany landed on a narrow airstrip generously called St. Catherine's Airport. The beat-up all-terrain vehicle they'd crawled into bumped along the tarmac, swerving past Bedouin encampments, doing its best to miss camels and mules that acted like they owned the road.

Weather-beaten faces stared at the intruders with suspicion as they passed. Adam wondered who they might be working for, these aged but timeless natives of Sinai, personified by the Bedouins or *ba'adiya,* the Arabic word for desert. Even their women, hiding half their faces behind colorful hijabs, made him wonder which ones were plants.

From the air, the tiny monastery had reminded Adam of an Arab child's dollhouse. But as they pulled up in front of it, the ancient monastic retreat looked more like the embattlement it was. Adam stared at the six-story fortress wall before him.

A bearded monk, dressed in black-on-dusty-black, opened the ancient entrance gate in the western wall, which faced the courtyard, the cemetery, the oasis and garden. To the right hung an even older gate now permanently sealed.

Above it, Adam saw the funnel through which boiling oil had once been poured on attackers in earlier centuries.

Once he walked through the gate with its three iron doors Adam knew there would be no turning back. He knew he was entering another world altogether.

*   *   *

The Sicilian assassin named Marcello huddled at the back of the little clump of scholars as he watched Adam move into the monastery. He studied the corners of the old stone structure measuring their plumb lines for a possible escape.

It was his job to make sure Adam never left.

Careless Curiosity

Maryville

R enie decided to spend the afternoon at home staring at the computer while she sipped a steaming cup of gourmet coffee. A lawyer's work is never done, she thought. After an hour or two, she glanced away from the screen at a disheveled stack of National Geographics on the floor by her bed. Picking one up, she thumbed it. It was on Egypt, a place of myth and mystery she'd always wanted to see. Renie loved faraway places. She looked up at photographs on the wall of herself with her father climbing Mt. Kilimanjaro, or hiking up the Matterhorn in the Alps. She needed to get out of town. She knew it.

The house was much too quiet, so she put on a compact disc of Andrea Bocelli, her favorite tenor. On weekends during law school, she'd slipped away to Manhattan whenever she could to take in an opera at the Met. Eric, her old high school boyfriend, who had moved from Maryville to work on Wall Street, would meet her by the fountains out front each time. Every evening had been magical. When she became a corporate litigator in New York, Eric had bought her season tickets to the Met. Weeks after her daddy's death had brought her back to Maryville, Eric had proposed and agreed to move home and start his own financial planning firm.

Everything had been perfect until....

She looked at a picture of Eric on her desk and wondered why she couldn't cry anymore.

Nessun Dorma from Puccini's *Turandot* resonated through the house.

It was time to warm her coffee. She got up and waltzed her way to the kitchen, serenading the furniture and the numbered Pat Buckley Moss and Catherine Wiley paintings on the walls along the way. She danced, eyes closed, attempting her own private duet with Bocelli.

"O Sole Mio, O Sole Mio..." she murmured to herself a little off tune. Completely entranced in the music, she twirled through the living room like a ballerina on a music box. Her chestnut brown hair floated as she moved in her own dream-like world, absorbed in the rich timbre of Bocelli's grainy voice until—

The ringing doorbell startled her.

She wasn't expecting anyone. Moving to the living room, she looked out the front window, wondering who might have been watching her. She slipped to the front door and peeked through the peephole. A distorted stranger stood before her, checking his watch.

"Whatever it is, I don't want any," she yelled.

"Adam Hunter sent me."

She slid the chain lock in place and opened the door a crack. "Did you say Adam Hunter?"

"He needs your help. May I come in?"

"No." She shut the door in his face.

"He's in trouble."

"Why should I believe you?" she barked back at him.

"Because we're old friends."

"Where is he?"

"In the Middle East."

"I don't believe you."

The stranger paused long enough for Renie to squint into the peephole again to make sure he was still there.

"You'll find an answer to Eric's death."

Renie stopped breathing. She opened the door and stared at him through the crack, her face lit up with anxiety and hope.

"Hope your passport's up-to-date." He handed her a card through the narrow gap in the door. "Call me."

Renie watched him walk to his car. She shut the door and locked the dead bolt, then collapsed in the nearest chair, feeling faint. She wondered if she'd been dreaming.

Shaken, she picked up the phone to call Frank Harkin, the town curmudgeon and publisher/editor of the local paper, *The Daily Times*, hoping he'd be in his office. He was the only man Renie knew who was all bark and no bite, but she loved him anyway. He was like an uncle.

After two rings, he growled, "Harkin, here!"

The young lawyer froze and hung up quietly.

As soon as she had put the receiver down, she wondered if she'd done the right thing. No, she said to herself, I can't tell anybody else about this, not even Frank. I've got to deal with it myself. Her face was flush. She caught a clouded glimpse of her own glow in the reflection in the window.

She held her breath, peeking around every corner as she moved through the house. In her bedroom she crashed on the tangled covers of the un-made queen-size. "I must be crazy!" she thought, lying spread eagle, staring at the ceiling. "Crazy."

Then she stood up and put on the nearest pair of glasses. She began rifling the second drawer of her dresser, pawing through bright pink and chartreuse exercise clothes. When she found her passport with the hurried mug-shot she hated so much, she studied the smudged rubber-stamps from around the world. She wondered where they might take her this time or whether she should go at all.

Then suddenly, with a resolve she could not explain, she began to pack.

She glanced at the name on the card—Conrad Docherty.

No Turning Back

St. Catherine's Monastery

The air was clear and cool the day Adam ducked his head under the ancient stone doorway. He entered the 1400-year-old outpost of Byzantine orthodoxy with a growing sense that something was wrong. For centuries, St. Catherine's, the world's oldest surviving monastery, had been a haven for pilgrims from every nation in search of a site as holy as Mecca or Jerusalem. Adam and his fellow intruders were simply the latest visitors among hundreds of thousands who had gone before them.

A Cambridge professor who had joined the group of scholars in Cairo broke the silence. "First time?"

Adam nodded, taking in the details of the Englishman's dress and manner.

"Allow me to introduce myself. I'm Oliver Stratton from Clare College, Cambridge."

"Adam Hunter." The two shook hands.

"I remember my first," mused Stratton. "1979. Was in graduate school at the time. Marvelous place, don't you think?"

"Yes, remarkable."

The British scholar seized the opportunity to flaunt his knowledge of the monastery. "You know, Mohammed himself once graced this old citadel with his presence. He placed his seal of approval and protection on the place, and the monks have a letter from him to prove it, the authenticity of which no one has ever questioned, at least not to their faces. As a result, St. Catherine's has remained safe from Muslims bent on plunder down through the centuries."

Adam could tell the Cambridge don was just getting warmed up.

"European notables," continued the professor, "like Henry II of Brunswick, Philip of Artois, Duke Albert of Austria, a Florentine named Frescobaldi, various Augustinian monks from Verona, and the Ladies of Castlebrae—manuscript scholars and professors at Cambridge who happened to be sisters, Agnes Smith Lewis and Margaret Dunlop Gibson—all made pilgrimage here, not to mention the French author Alexander Dumas and the German scholar Constantin von Tischendorf."

"How interesting." Adam wished the professor would take a breath.

"Furthermore," continued Stratton, "did you know that in fourteenth century Britain the most widely read book after the Bible was *Travels to Sinai* and that, in the eighteenth century, ships that sailed under the flag of St. Catherine's could travel with safe passage through all sorts of troubled waters?"

"I had no idea."

As they made their way into the heart of the ancient fortress, it seemed smaller to Adam than he had imagined. Buildings were crammed together helter-skelter. The bell tower and the minaret of the mosque for Islamic servants rose well above the other hastily-built structures.

The Cambridge don, the Sicilian, Adam and the other visiting professors were led to their quarters—austere monastic cells in the Hospice, each with nothing more than a bed, a table and a pitcher of water. On the whitewashed walls in his cell, Adam saw the scribbled names of pilgrims from all over the world next to Greek, Russian and Arabic graffiti. A thin layer of dust coated everything in the room. A rancid mildew made him step outside to snatch a fresh breath of air.

Adam withdrew the manuscript page from the briefcase and placed it in a small brown knapsack, which he slung over his shoulder. He was anxious to explore the place. But first he had an audience with Father John who was in charge while the Archbishop was attending ecclesiastical meetings in Cairo.

A Bedouin servant appeared at Adam's door. He was a dark-skinned man of medium height and build with deep lines in his face. He wore ragged, baggy laborer's clothes; a red-and-white keffiyeh covered his head. There was something about him that seemed familiar to Adam. Something about those eyes, Adam thought, but he couldn't remember why. He wondered if he'd seen him before, but couldn't remember where. Without speaking, he led Adam through the labyrinthine warren of dark passageways running in all directions, then up a narrow tunnel of ancient steps onto an uneven rooftop. From there they entered Father John's office, a simple chamber with white walls, rickety chairs and an old wooden desk stacked with papers, a phone, a laptop, a printer and a fax machine.

Father John, like all the other monks, wore a dusty, black gown that covered his body and skirted his ankles just above black, rubber-soled, walking shoes. He sported a ragged, salt-and-pepper beard and a flat-topped, black hat pulled down snug just above the ears. His long hair bunched itself into a bun at the nape of his neck.

Father John peered over the top of ancient, wire-rimmed spectacles with a twinkle in his eye that conjured a Greek Santa Claus.

"*Kalemera, Pater* Adam."

"*Kalemera*," replied Adam, surprised at being called 'Father.'

Father John showed Adam faxes he'd received from the Archbishops of the Greek Orthodox Churches in Cairo and Jerusalem as well as one from the Patriarch of the Greek Orthodox Church in Istanbul, all of which introduced Adam as a Protestant pastor from the United States who should be treated with the respect and honor of a foreign dignitary and should have the run of the place, including the world-famous library. All three faxes were typed in Greek with the appropriate ecclesiastical imprimatur. Adam, surprised to be received with such beneficence, remembered the CIA had connections even in the church.

After an extended exchange of pleasantries complete with the strongest black coffee Adam had ever tasted, a shadow crossed Father John's face.

"Because of the recent robbery and murder, our librarian, Father Euthymios will need to be present when you look at the manuscripts. How long will you be staying with us?"

"As long as my research takes," replied Adam. "Perhaps a few days or a week."

Father John yelled at the door. "Ammon! Take our guest to Father Paul's quarters."

The Bedouin surfaced, nodding and bowing humbly ready to lead Adam to another part of the fortress. He moved like a shadow.

Father John handed him a note scribbled in Greek and added in Arabic, "I'd like for you to give our American friend a proper inspection of the monastery, more than the tourists get."

The Bedouin nodded, almost managing a smile.

Adam understood every word.

"To tell you the truth," grumbled Father John, switching back to English, "I wish we didn't have so many sightseers barging in here, busloads of them from all over the world. If it were up to me, I'd send them all packing, even if they do bring in some extra revenue. The original hermits who founded this monastery would never have allowed all this commotion. We all came here to escape from the world. Now the world comes to us!"

The Bedouin listened patiently to Father John's

litany. When the monk finally bid Adam "good day," the Bedouin began showing Adam the way. A man of few words, the Bedouin appeared to be simple-minded with the kind of uncomplicated life, which appealed to Adam. Bedouins have their own linguistic and nonverbal ways of communicating. When Adam, greeted him with the Arabic, "*Salaam Aleikum,*" the servant mumbled the traditional reply, "*Aleikum Salaam,*" but volunteered nothing more.

From the Cambridge professor's running commentary of Sinai trivia, Adam had learned that the majority of the Sinai peninsula's over 200,000 inhabitants were Bedouins with each tribe following its own particular customs. He also learned that the monastery's Bedouins, called the *Jebaliye* or "mountain people," were descendants of the two hundred Wallachian and Bosnian families the Emperor Justinian had assigned to work for the monks when he originally built the place in 527 CE as a protection from the marauding Saracens.

Father Paul, a ruddy-faced man with a ready smile, met the two of them at the top of the steps that led down to the church. The Bedouin disappeared silently into one of the many tunnels nearby before Adam realized it. Below, Adam saw fanny-packed, camera-laden tourists looking terribly out of place in the old fort. Adam could hear snatches of French, German, Chinese, Arabic and English as the various parties gaped in amazement. Some of them stared at him as he moved away from them on the other side of a rope and sign that read, **NO ADMITTANCE**.

"G' day, m' friend," said Father Paul with a drawling brogue.

"New Zealand?" guessed Adam, testing his ear for accents.

"Excellent, my good man!" exclaimed Father Paul. "Ever been down under?"

"Long time ago."

"Don't see a lot of Yanks all the way out here. What

brings you to St. Catherine's?"

"Manuscripts."

"Just like the other blokes. I'll warn you, there's a closer watch on all the codices since the murder of Father Nicodemus."

Adam glanced around. "Doesn't look like there's any extra security. Thought I'd see some armed guards," said Adam.

"Not at St. Catherine's, matey. The Archbishop won't stand for it. We're just more careful than before. We've got the most important manuscripts locked up tight in a place so secret that only Father Euthymios knows where it is. The library up there," he said, gesturing to the top floor next to the Icon Gallery and the Archbishop's quarters, "is about to close for the day. I'll show you around the rest of the monastery. You can begin with the manuscripts in the morning."

"Fine," said Adam, looking over his shoulder, sure he'd seen someone in the shadows.

As the Egyptian sun crept closer to the edge of the old mountain it smothered the ancient fortress with an odd mélange of golden browns, old ivory and a muddy burnt orange. Adam followed Father Paul from tunnel to tunnel as they bent low to avoid bumping their heads. The entire convent was an entanglement of galleries, arches, stairways and cloisters. Father Paul could have given the tour blindfolded. He ambled through the old place like a lion in his lair. As they walked along the top of the eastern wall, which afforded them both a clear view of the mountain and the valley that stretched in both directions, Adam imagined how easy it would have been to defend this old fort.

"This is where Father's Nick's murderers went over the wall," Father Paul said, pointing to a spot above the site of the Burning Bush. "We can tell by the tracks their feet made right there." Both of them tottered a little to keep their balance as they peeked over the edge of the massive fortress wall and inspected the dirt at the bottom.

As they approached the church, Adam noticed a man surveying the three-story campanile, a gift from Russia nearly a century earlier. They entered the enormous cedar doors, intricately carved in the eleventh century by Crusaders and divided into four parts with bas-reliefs of birds, animals, leaves and flowers.

When Adam entered the church, the musky odor of incense bowled him over. But not as much as the sight of the narthex that exhibited only some of the cache of over 2,000 priceless icons, "One of the largest such collections in the world," said Father Paul. The glittering glow of ancient faces staring at him gave him the eerie feeling he was surrounded. He listened to the low rhythmic chant of monks warming up for Vespers.

He glanced to the right and peered into the dark corners of the church designed and built by an architect named Stephanos in the 500s, according to Father Paul. As Adam stepped into its cryptic interior, he marveled at the webbed beauty of the old Romanesque church with its granite walls, twelve granite columns and dozens of stunning German chandeliers suspended at various heights from the ceiling. Huge golden candlesticks guarded the enormous seventeenth century iconostasis painted by Cosmos of Crete around 1612. Behind this wall of icons stood the holy altar that hosted the great mosaic of the Transfiguration, which only came into Adam's view as he made his way across the elaborate eighteenth-century marble floor.

Father Paul explained the history and significance of each icon, but Adam seemed overwhelmed by the gilded splendor of it all. Father Paul had seen the glazed-eye look before. Like a recording stuck on *play*, he continued as if Adam were actually listening.

The pungent incense and gold-plated glory of the old church dizzied Adam. He forced a yawn down his throat. Centuries of orthodoxy overlaid more centuries everywhere he looked. Strata of candle smoke caked the walls with the odor of burnt offering. He jumped at the bong of the talanton, the great wooden bell, which announced Vespers.

Father Paul waved him back toward the nave of the basilica.

The service, with its chants and venerations, the kissing of the icons and readings from the large wooden podium, seemed foreign to Adam. The whole thing was so unintelligible that he fell asleep in one of the narrow straight-backed upright benches that lined the length of the worship space.

Tischendorf Returns

The monk said, "Father Adam? Vespers have ended."

Adam sat up and gawked at a young man's face. Rubbing his eyes, he quickly surveyed the room as light from the outside cascaded off the chandeliers in ever-changing hues of blues and slate grays that enhanced the mystical look of the place.

"Jet lag?"

Adam nodded.

"Happens all the time."

Adam winced a little as he rose. He had snoozed in the same position for too long and had a crick in his neck.

Then he reached for the knapsack. Where was it? It wasn't on his shoulder. It wasn't in his chair either. He patted his body frantically and became short of breath.

"Lose something? Is this what you're looking for? I believe you dropped it when you dozed off." The sentence came from the single pew next to his. Adam noticed the question had been posed in perfect English sprinkled with a dash of Mediterranean seasoning. Tuscan? No, it was more southern than that. Naples perhaps. The hand that accompanied the voice offered the knapsack to him, but Adam still could not see who held it.

"Yes, thank you," replied Adam.

"My name is Marcello Zanetti," the man said as he shook Adam's hand in a single graceful motion. "And you would be Adam Hunter. I'm delighted to make your acquaintance."

"How did you know my name?"

"Father John told me."

"Oh, yes, of course. And where are you from?"

"I teach ancient literature at the University of Rome. I'm here to review some of the old manuscripts. You?"

"The same." Adam homed in on the Sicilian's face. He had been trained by the CIA to spot the most skillful liars. The eyes always tell the story, he'd learned. This one had told him the truth.

Or he was a master liar.

Adam thanked Father Paul for the personal guided tour, bid the Roman professor adieu and announced he would be turning in. He decided to go outside for a little fresh air. Ducking through a small door for tourists in the northern wall he noticed the old basket, the original visitors' entrance to the monastery. The six to nine-feet thick walls appeared even more imposing from the northern side. An old dromedary gawked at Adam with a blank stare and ground his mouth from side to side in a slow, rhythmic chewing motion.

Adam climbed up the side of the mountain directly in front of St. Catherine's. While surveying the fortress and Jebel Musa that soared high above it, he studied the scruffy looking northern expanse of the structure that had been damaged many times. According to the Cambridge don, its most recent repair had been engineered by Napoleon on his 1801 foray into Egypt. The descending sun sent glints and sprays of saffron rays across the valley then abruptly disappeared.

Feeling a sudden chill Adam scrambled down to the flatland in front of the monastery, slipping a little on loose rocks as he went. On the way to his cell, Adam noticed a light in Father Paul's room. He saw Father Paul at prayer with the shadows of smoldering embers flickering across his face.

"Would you like some coffee?" said Father Paul without looking up.

"Thank you, yes," said Adam, wondering how the monk knew he was there.

Father Paul handed him a small mug of his best brew. Adam sipped another cup of coffee so strong you could stand your spoon up in it, he thought. He pretended to drink it and set it down on a crude little end table.

"This is the room, you know," Father Paul said. "The one where Tischendorf discovered the original codex."

"Here?"

Father Paul nodded. "They used it as fuel for the fire, you know."

"The *Codex*?"

"That's right, mate. Edges of it were singed by burning coals."

"Hard to believe."

"Very appropriate since Tischendorf's people were charcoal burners," Father Paul said. "Think of the similarity to Petrarch."

"Petrarch?"

"His father burned some of the books he'd hidden in his room when he was a boy, but saved Cicero's *Rhetoric* and a copy of Virgil after Petrarch pled with him to spare them."

Adam said nothing, thinking it an odd comparison.

"This is also the room where Father Nicodemus was murdered." A deep note of sadness rang in his voice.

They both stared at the dying fire. A coal fell and shattered across what was left of the last log then sprayed sparks into the room. Father Paul didn't move. The tiny glows eventually went out one by one.

Silence filled the room. The fading cinders did all the talking.

"Think I'll call it a night," said Adam, finally breaking the spell.

"Suit yourself, mate. Tomorrow, the library."

"I'm ready. *Kalespera*."

"Good night to you, too."

*   *   *

Adam opened the unlocked door to his room and saw a note on the floor with his name on it. The room was a mess. His backpack had been upended and its contents strewn everywhere.

He looked down the hallway both directions and back over his shoulder.

He entered cautiously, but could see the intruder was long gone. One by one, he picked up the pieces, observing that nothing was missing.

He opened the note and translated the Greek sentences. It read: "Tischendorf returns. But Tischendorf will pay for the error of his ways!"

Meeting One's Shadow

Father Euthymios eyed Adam carefully as he and Father Paul entered the monastery library. Adam was surprised to see how contemporary it looked compared to the rest of the ancient fortress. He expected to see something dark and musty. Instead, the walls were bright, the books neatly shelved between startling, white pillars. Not a speck of dust on the floors.

Adam could tell Father Euthymios was one of those fastidious librarians who'd rather not have anyone peruse any of his precious volumes, much less check one out. The old monk glared at Adam, then went back to his work.

"Don't worry about Father Euthymios," whispered Father Paul. "He's never had the gift of hospitality. He'd rather keep the place locked up, especially after the murder. Father Nicodemus was an old friend. They worked together on manuscripts. Now Euthymios is the only one left."

Adam marveled at the rows of darkly bound books of all shapes and sizes, trying to remember who'd said, "A library is but the soul's burial ground."

"Second in importance to the Vatican Library in quantity and quality, you know," Father Paul said as they made their way slowly up and down the aisles of old codices. "We've got over 3,000 of them—mostly Greek, while the rest are in Arabic, Syriac, Georgian, Armenian, Coptic, Ethiopian and Slavonic."

Father Paul showed him *Codex Syriacus,* dating back to the 5th century. The longer Father Paul and Adam stayed, the more agitated Father Euthymios became. He kept throwing dark stares Adam's direction. Finally, he got up and walked to a door at the end of the library, which he unlocked and entered quietly.

Father Paul watched Adam closely as he turned the old vellum pages. Father Paul was not a scholar like Father Euthymios, so he didn't really know how to read any of the books. But he was still proud of them.

A large crash coming from across the monastery startled them both.

"Mother of God!" said Father Paul bolting out to check on the sound.

As soon as Father Paul was out the door, Adam knew he had only a few minutes to find the missing page. He moved quickly from shelf to shelf, pulling different volumes off. He thumbed them then replaced them. He knew any moment Father Euthymios would return.

Making his way around to Father Euthymios' desk, Adam looked at the old manuscript spread open on top. Sweat moistened his palms. The knob on the door at the end of the room clicked, but no one came through it. Adam turned the vellum leaves of the Coptic text one by one as he held his breath.

The knob turned again.

Then he saw it.

A note scrawled in Arabic tucked between two pages. It read, "Meet me at the charnel house at midnight, next to the mound of skulls and bones. I will show you the leaf you seek."

No names.

Adam slipped out the front door of the library as Father Euthymios returned.

*　　*　　*

At dusk, Adam crossed the large sandy courtyard in front of the monastery. He passed the meager garden and the cemetery and arrived at the old charnel house. There was no one else around. He entered the ossuary slowly. Like an ancient monastic scarecrow, the skeleton of the 6th century monk known as Stephanos hung lifeless before him, stopping his breath.

Then he saw mounds of skulls. Hollow eyes deep-set in hundreds of toothless cranial faces that all seemed to stare directly at him. Shadow faces upon shadow faces, mouths all agape. Thousands of them piled together. Each one had been placed one on top of the other with great care.

"Father Adam," said a voice in a whisper.

Adam could see nothing but hundreds of empty eyes staring at him.

"Father Adam? Can you hear me?"

Adam stood motionless.

From behind the great heap of heads stepped the Bedouin.

"You?"

"Are you surprised?" the man answered in English.

"You are not like the others."

"There is much about me you do not know."

"Why here?"

"The monastery walls have ears. Here it is safer. The dead repeat nothing."

"What is this place?"

"There is only so much room in the cemetery. It has been so for centuries. First, they bury their dead. When all the flesh has fallen off, they dig up the bones and bring them here to spend eternity in peace with their comrades. Desert monasteries always display the skeletal remains of their ancestors as a reminder to the monks of their mortality."

"Very effective." Hundreds of hollow eyes and faces sent a chill up Adam's spine.

"You have come for the other page of the manuscript," the man said.

He unfolded an old vellum page written in Greek

uncials. Adam removed the page he had from his satchel and held it next to the one the servant had displayed. He studied it for a few moments.

"You have been chosen to deliver this manuscript."

"Where?"

"To the head of the Catholic Church in Rome. That's all you need to know for now."

"Why can't you tell me more?"

"An assassin has been sent here to kill you for this manuscript. He will certainly move to eliminate you now that you have both pages."

"What assassin?"

"Do not return to your room tonight. He will be waiting for you. Sleep outside. Tomorrow morning early, around 3:00 a.m., there will be tourists coming to climb Jebel Musa. Meet me at the Central Tower. We will blend in with the tour group and climb Mt. Sinai with them. There will be hundreds of them from all over the world as there are every day."

"And then?"

"Patience, Father Adam. You will see."

The Bedouin blew out the lantern and disappeared behind the bones.

Adam stood still for a moment. He poked his head out the front door and moved under the moonlight to the far side of the monastery. He passed the sleeping dromedaries and worked his way up the hill opposite the monastery. Wedging himself between some rocks on a bed of gravel, he hoped to catch a couple of hours of sleep. The old mountain loomed above him in the twilight.

Making Up Excuses

Maryville

Evelyn Hastings had not heard from Adam for days. Not even a message on her answering machine. She was beginning to worry. The calls to the office from people wondering where he might be annoyed her. She'd finally decided to tell them that his aunt had taken a turn for the worse and that Adam didn't want to leave her side, an approach that worked pretty well for a while. But when Renie disappeared too, the whole town was abuzz. Gossips worked over time inventing creative scenarios not even Evelyn had imagined.

The whole thing had gotten out of hand.

Evelyn thought about the two of them together somewhere alone, looking into each other's eyes, making love passionately in some exotic place. It nearly drove her crazy imagining it. Renie hadn't cared much about anybody after her fiancé's death years ago until Adam came along.

The phone rang.

"Hope Church, may I help you?"

"Hey, Evelyn," growled Frank Harkin.

"Oh, Hi, Frank."

"You heard anything from either one of them?"

"Not a word."

"I can't figure it. First him, now her."

"I wish I knew," said Evelyn.

"It's not like her to leave without calling me and letting me know where she's going. I'm afraid something's

116

happened to her. God, I hope we don't find her in a ditch somewhere up on Andrew's Bald or something."

A chill went up Evelyn's spine. She hated the mountains and anything to do with being in the woods.

"Surely not that, Frank. We need to hope for the best. Does the Sheriff have any news?"

"Nothing. No sign of her anywhere. You don't suppose they're together, do you?"

"Why would she be going to visit his aunt?"

"Come on, Evelyn. You don't still believe that cockamamie story, do you?"

"I'm only going by what he told me."

"I've wondered about that guy since he came to town. There's lots more to him than meets the eye. I'm sure of it."

Evelyn remembered that the publisher had been the only one in town who'd questioned Adam's story. He had been suspicious from the beginning. No proof, just a bad gut feeling.

"You hear anything, please call me. Okay?" barked Harkin.

"You will be the first to know, Frank."

*   *   *

St. Catherine's Monastery

Adam turned on his side and heard the gravel he'd kicked ripple down the hill. For an hour or so, he'd slept soundly, but his internal alarm finally went off. His mind awakened as his body unfolded and stretched like a plant in search of the morning sun. He glanced at his watch in the dark. He could barely make out the time by the moonlight. 2:47 am. He re-oriented, grabbing a secure rock so as not to slip down the hill then gathered his things. When he tucked his hand inside the briefcase, his fingers groped the old vellum pages.

He had wanted to begin reading the second page as soon as he'd gotten it, but knew any kind of light on the side of the mountain would have alerted his assailant.

He could hear noises and voices below. People had already begun to gather in front of the monastery for the hike up the old mountain. Flickers of flashlights crisscrossed the ground and pierced the night sky. Dromedaries yawned and honked a symphony of deep nasal grunts. Arab drivers and shop salesmen up and down the mountain readied themselves for another morning of business.

As Adam neared the bottom, he saw more people arriving. Groups from around the world. Tourists, believers. Curiosity seekers, most of them. He looked for the Bedouin servant, but he was nowhere in sight.

He glanced at his watch. 3:00 am. Still no Bedouin.

A small group of French women, all in their twenties, appeared. They snickered and teased their Egyptian guide.

Adam looked every direction, but no sign of the Bedouin.

The guide told the young French women to use their "torches," as they called their flashlights, to stay together and especially avoid the camel drivers.

Other groups began to materialize.

Adam's instincts told him to blend in, so he moved toward the women from Paris and Lyon. A keffiyeh surfaced, then vanished around the corner of the monastery. It wasn't the Bedouin.

More groups appeared. The crowds in front of the old fortress shushed each other so as not to awaken the monks. Flashes from the torches angled and splintered the darkness.

The French women bundled up to leave.

Suddenly, a tap on his shoulder made Adam jump. He turned to attack, but instinct stopped him.

"*Salaam*, my friend," said the Bedouin. "Are you ready to go up the mountain?"

"I was about to join this group."

"Good idea. It will give you better cover."

"You sure someone is after me?'

"Trust me, my friend. I know everything that goes on here. I can spot an assassin a mile away," said the Bedouin as he stared directly into Adam's eyes. Adam wondered what he saw there.

"Yalla! Let's go!" yelled one of the Arab guides. The groups began to inch at a caterpillar's pace up the old peak.

*   *   *

From the backside of St. Catherine's, the Sicilian watched the great mass of people begin its assault on Sinai. He flipped open his cell phone. "Yes, he has the page now." Marcello felt like an ant next to Mt. Sinai. He adjusted his hiking boots then skittered across loose rocks down the side of the fortress wall and caught up with the convoy.

*   *   *

Washington, DC

"Drew, I want some answers!" President Sanchez said on the phone.

"We're doing all we can," said Farley.

"That's not good enough! Can't you people work some magic with all those computers and all that money we keep sending you?"

Farley simply listened. He'd learned to let the President rant until she finished. He put the call on speakerphone and, without making a sound, checked his latest emails.

"I don't trust anyone over there anymore. With the spies we've caught lately selling us out to the other side, God only knows how many there are still over there, poisoning our jambalaya."

Farley muttered, "Yes, Madame President..." continuing to check his email.

"...and why we don't have any more control over our own people, I can't figure out for the life of me. Bunch of Benedict Arnolds if you ask me..."

Farley clicked his mouse across the computer screen before him.

"Whoever did this to Stump is going to pay..." droned the President.

The last email made Farley stop cold. He stared at the screen in disbelief.

"If you learn anything, I want to be the first to know."

"I will, Madame President," Farley said, then hung up.

He clicked "Reply" and began typing. Suddenly, he stopped and highlighted his entire response.

He thought for a moment then hit "Delete."

Tapping his fingers on the desk, he looked at the clock then picked up the phone and punched in a number. "We have to meet. Tonight."

He punched up the file on Adam Hunter. For the next twenty minutes, he read the file thoroughly.

Then he noticed something he hadn't seen before.

Not What It Seems

Mount Sinai

The trek up the craggy crevices of Mt. Sinai reminded Adam of other excursions he'd made in the Alps and the Himalayas. This one was much easier although he wasn't accustomed to hiking in the dark. His mind was a newsreel of forced marches around the globe as the swollen line of pilgrims, like a huge python, twisted and turned its way up old Sinai.

Along the rocky trail, merchants in little shops offered cigarettes, strong coffee, tea and rich chocolates. There were camel rides for those who'd had enough walking. Daylight was still a couple of hours away. Adam watched his back.

As they neared the top, he saw more climbers who apparently had left earlier. Some of them had camped out overnight. Though it was still dark, a hint of early light began to surface on the horizon. The black humps of the mountains spread before him. The accents from different world languages came at Adam in sighs and murmurs from all sides. Tourists stood three or four deep at the wall, readying themselves for the spectacular sunrise that would soon appear. They pulled breakfast from their backpacks and bought coffee at the little shop on top.

Both Adam and the Bedouin were surveying the crowd's faces when a shot rang out.

An old man next to Adam took a bullet in the shoulder. People screamed and scattered as Adam hit the

121

ground and yelled "Get down!" to those around him.

No one paid attention and began trampling others.

Adam knew he was the one drawing fire, so he bolted for higher ground on the other side of the little coffee stop. He ran as fast as he could in the dark, tripping and scraping his hands on the rocks. He knew turning on his "torch," would make him more of a target. Shots ricocheted off rocks and echoed all about him, but he never looked back.

The Bedouin servant was right behind him with someone in hot pursuit.

"Father Adam, wait for me," called the Bedouin as a bullet grazed his side.

Adam's initial thought was to keep going so he could find a place from which to mount a counter-attack. Instead, he stopped and turned right into the fire, bobbing and weaving his way back to the Bedouin. As Adam dodged through the flashes of gunfire, he recalled the night in Prague when he'd charged back into the heat of the fight for his best friend who'd been downed by KGB fire. That night he hadn't made it in time. This time he would.

"You came back for me?" said the Bedouin, holding his side.

Before Adam could respond, a bullet caught him in the left thigh and another in the shoulder, which sent him reeling back to the ledge. Teetering at the precipice, he did his best to right himself, but still tripped and stumbled over the edge to another cliff. He sprained his ankle, breaking the fall. Between that and the leg wound, he could not move.

In less than a minute the Sicilian Adam had met in the chapel stood over him, a silencer in his face.

"Give me the briefcase. Then I will put you out of your misery," said Marcello.

Adam held it over the ledge of a cliff. "Go ahead. You'll have a hard time finding it down there."

"Yes, but I will find it. They said you were one of the best. Too bad you came back for the servant. Touching, but unwise for someone in our profession."

The Sicilian was right. He should not have gone back. His shoulder was numb and the pain from his ankle and thigh streaked up and down his leg.

"*Arrivederci, mi amico,*" said Marcello as he aimed the silencer at Adam.

Before he could take the shot a bright light splashed their faces, a spot so radiant neither one of them could see. A roar filled the air, halting the pandemonium atop Mt. Sinai. Awed and mute, the pilgrims turned to the light.

Marcello was blinded by the light and staggered under the force of the wind. Stumbling on the rocks, he tripped and hurtled over the cliff's edge.

A voice boomed, "GRAB THE LADDER."

Adam realized what hovered above him was a helicopter. A rope ladder drifted in and out of the beam of light. He caught the pendulum's rhythm, grabbing the third rung. Pulling himself up clumsily, he secured one foot on the bottom rung while his injured leg hung free in space. The shoulder wound had soaked his shirt in blood and sapped his energy. By sheer force of will he maintained consciousness as he clenched the briefcase handle.

Slowly, the helicopter lifted. The whir of rotors and engine reverberated across the old mountain and through desert ridges below. The bright light rose. Adam hung precariously as the copter gained altitude then banked and angled into the approaching sunrise.

Faint yellows and oranges spread across the edge of the morning sky, gradually penetrating pewter-gray clouds as Adam floated in what seemed like suspended animation. His body twisted in slow motion. His hand ached as it clung to the tethered twine. His leg and shoulder throbbed. Ancient boulders below beckoned him, offering to end it all if he'd only let go. The handle of the briefcase nearly slipped from his left hand as the sun peeked over the mountaintops.

As the helicopter passed over St. Catherine's and

neared the desert, Adam realized that the rope ladder was being hauled up. When they pulled him in, one of them stuck a needle in his arm and he was gone before he could even get a good look at any of them.

Gone...a million miles away.

* * *

Vatican City

Don Mazzini stepped from the black limousine.

The Swiss Guards stood their ground until they saw who it was. He'd paid them handsomely for years, so they let him and his associates pass through the Bronze Doors as pre-dawn glimmer bathed the buildings of the Apostolic Palace.

Flanked by his bodyguards, he made his way across the Court of St. *Damasus* and up to Lorenzo's apartment a floor below the papal chambers. It was early. Five in the morning. The Cardinal had not risen from his bed.

The Don wanted to surprise him.

He did.

The knock on the huge door jolted the Cardinal.

"Whatever it is, come back later," whined the Cardinal.

No one spoke. The knock came again.

Exasperated, the cleric worked hard to untangle himself from the covers. Leaving them in a heap on the bed he threw on his black silk gown and gathered himself as he moved to the door, still half-asleep.

As he cracked it open, Don Mazzini greeted him with, "Lorenzo! How kind of you to get up!"

"Vicenzu!" sputtered the Cardinal.

"Well..." said Mazzini, "are you going to invite me in?"

"Oh, yes...of course," replied the Cardinal, rubbing

the sleep from his eyes.

"Do you have any coffee around this place?" said Mazzini as he entered.

"I'll have some brought immediately," gulped Lorenzo.

Mazzini gave Lorenzo a fat envelope. "Something for the Vatican Bank."

"*Grazie.*" Lorenzo felt the weight of it in his hand. "Every little bit helps."

Mazzini strode slowly around the apartment taking it all in. "Very nice, Lorenzo. It's *molto bene.* Looks like religion pays."

The coffee appeared.

When the attendant had gone, Lorenzo asked, "Why are you here?"

"I like the neighborhood!"

"But your coming here could ruin my chances of ever being elected pontiff. Then, where would you be? Who would give you absolution then? The present Pope will never do it."

"I know. That's why he has to go. He's way too pure for a bribe."

Mazzini paused and changed countenance. "The manuscript we're chasing has slipped out of our hands. Marcello has dropped out of sight."

"My God, this is awful. Is he dead?"

"I don't think so. The professor is very resourceful."

"But the American got away?"

"Apparently so, and with the manuscript...."

Mazzini looked out the window with his back to Lorenzo, noting that it was almost the same view of St. Peter's Square as the Pope enjoyed...almost.

"This Adam Hunter is CIA, posing as a Protestant clergyman," said Lorenzo. "But what does the CIA care about an old manuscript?"

"I'm not sure. All I know is there are a lot of people

interested in it and even willing to die for it."

"Whatever we do, we've got to keep it away from the pontiff. There is no telling what he will do with it."

"His day will come."

Moshe's Method

Adam lifted his head and peered at the inside of a large sandy-colored tent planted in the middle of the desert. He could tell it was daylight, perhaps afternoon. The signals to his brain said "pain" the moment he moved.

"Don't try to get up just yet," said a trim, sun-tanned, middle-aged man.

Adam squinted, trying his best to take in a face he'd never seen before. The man spoke perfect English, but the accent was Mediterranean with Hebraic flavoring.

"I'm Adam Hunter."

"Yes, we know. We've been tracking you for a while now. Here, drink this," said the man handing him a cup.

Adam winced as he leaned forward and took a few sips. Throbs of pain coursed through his body. "I thought I'd bought the farm."

"You Americans have a funny way of putting things," replied the man laughing. "Our medic treated your shoulder and your leg and wrapped your ankle. You'll be up in a few days once you've begun to heal."

"My briefcase!" said Adam in a sudden panic.

The man smiled, pointing to the corner of the tent. "It's right there. Besides, no one here can read what's in it. We've already tried."

"Who are you?" Adam asked.

"My name is Moshe." The man seemed very calm.

"Israeli?"

127

"Good guess."

"Aren't you a little out of your territory?"

"Our territory is the world, just like yours."

"Mossad?" said Adam.

"And you are CIA."

"Ex."

"Apparently you've been called back into service."

"Apparently," replied Adam, cautiously. "What Mossad unit?"

"*Kidon,*" said the man.

"Assassins," noted Adam.

Moshe nodded. "Like you."

"Not anymore."

"Right," said the man with a knowing smile. "I also serve in the Matkal."

"Rapid Deployment, like our Seals," said Adam probing.

"Something like that," said the man.

Adam heard voices outside speaking a mixture of Hebrew and Arabic. Suddenly, he felt terribly drowsy. His view of everything dizzied.

Now the man had a twin. The sentences came at him with an echo. He stared at the cup. "What did you give me to drink."

The man smiled. "Something that will help you sleep and the medic gave you an-n-n-other sedat-t-tive. You need to r-r-rest. We will talk more l-l-later," reverberated the voices in Adam's head. "You need to give yourself t-t-time to g-g-gain your strength before you do anything el---"

The whole tent began to swim...then came the blackness....

*　　*　　*

Washington, DC

Drew Farley never drove anywhere without protection. But, after being dropped off at his colonial redbrick estate in Alexandria, he waited until the limo had slipped away before entering his garage and sliding into his silver Jaguar.

It was exactly 11:15 p.m. when he pulled into a parking garage at Reagan National. Resisting the temptation to do his Grand Prix imitation all the way to Level 3 he angled carefully into his usual space. He checked his watch. He was on time. He heard a plane land in the distance. "757," he said to himself. He could tell by the sound.

He glanced at his doughy face in the rearview mirror. He turned on his CD player and cranked up an old Hal Ketcham song. None of his wives ever liked Country/Western, but he lived by it. When his stomach growled, he rifled the glove compartment and found a package of M&M's.

A little after midnight the American Airlines flight from Dallas, a Super 80, made its landing. "Quiet enough for National's ten o'clock curfew," he muttered to himself. Built-in hush-kits were wonderful additions to those planes, he thought, wishing he could put them on some of the leaks at Langley. He tapped the steering wheel and glanced at his side view mirrors. "Where the hell is he?" he fumed.

A forest green Explorer pulled in beside him. The driver got out and hopped into Farley's Jag.

Farley glared at him. "You're late."

"Someone followed me. Took longer than I thought to shake him."

"Excuses, excuses. So…what have you got?"

The man stared straight ahead. "It's higher than you think."

"The White House?"

"She knows more than she's telling you."

Farley thought for a moment as he stared directly at the concrete wall in front of him. He furrowed his brow. "You think Hunter's working for the President?"

"It's possible. You think he did Stump?"

"No way. He worshiped the guy," Farley said. "Where is he now?"

"Somewhere in the middle of the Sinai desert. When we can get a bead on him, we should be able to track him via satellite."

"Let me know the minute you locate him."

Desert Surprises

The Sinai Desert

A dam tried to turn on his side, but couldn't.
"Don't move, Adam."

It was a woman's voice…Adam was certain of it.

When he opened his eyes, he thought he was dreaming. Renie Ellis sat next to him and patted his forehead softly with a damp washcloth.

This was a trick, he thought. A cruel trick.

Then the mirage continued and the half-delirium. Was it his wife's face in front of him or was it Renie's? Images swirled about him.

He collapsed again on the cot.

*   *   *

Hours later, Adam awakened. He ached all over. He wondered how long he'd been there. Days, perhaps weeks. Desert sand peppered the side of the tent as the wind whipped up in fits and spurts. Moshe pulled the flap back and entered. His strong frame bent from the waist like a drawn bow. "The patient has awakened. How do you feel?"

Adam offered a raspy, "I've felt better."

The Israeli knelt beside Adam's cot and pressed a cup of water to Adam's lips. "Not too much at first. Easy. There's someone who's here keeping an eye on you. Come on in," said Moshe to the shadow dancing on the canvas wall.

Renie ducked her head through the tent flap and the rest of her followed. Adam blinked and rubbed his eyes to make sure he wasn't seeing things.

"Renie, is that really you?"

She stood before him in a blue denim shirt, unbuttoned at the top, collar up in back, sleeves rolled up, khaki shorts and hiking boots. Her hair was pulled back in a ponytail. She flashed a smile.

"How long have you been here?" said Adam.

"Since just before you made your grand entrance. But you have been out most of the time."

"What are you doing here?"

"Your friend from the CIA was very convincing."

Adam thought, "I don't have any friends there. He must have brought her here to get at me, to make sure I do whatever he wants."

"Where is he now?"

"I'm not sure. We flew to Cairo together. An Egyptian guide he hired drove me out here in a Land Rover. He said he would meet me here later. That was it."

Adam shook his head. "Do you realize how dangerous this is?"

"Looking at you gives me an idea."

"I think I'll leave you two alone for now," said Moshe suddenly. He slipped out quietly as Renie moved toward Adam and sat down beside him.

Neither of them spoke for a while. They listened to the sounds of the desert, the wind flapping the tent wall.

Finally, she broke the silence. "Are you in much pain?"

"I've had worse."

"Some wounds go so deep that the healing hurts more than the injury."

Adam nodded, surprised at the depth of wisdom her comment betrayed.

The stillness between them returned as the wind

whipped up again. The tent billowed and shrank as the heat shimmered on the desert.

"What's all this about anyway?" asked Renie.

Adam nodded in the direction of the briefcase. "Give that to me and I'll show you."

Renie handed him the attaché. Adam reached inside and pulled out the two pages.

"What does it say?" she asked.

"I don't know yet. I can only pick out a few words and a phrase here and there."

"How can you tell what the words are? Everything seems crammed together like one long word?"

"That's how manuscripts from this period are written."

"And what period would that be?" said Renie.

"Fourth century AD."

"These are that old?" she said, her eyebrows arched.

"Maybe."

"What are you supposed to do with them?"

"Deliver them to the Pope."

"The Pope? Why you?"

"I wish I knew. Where did Moshe go? Maybe he has some answers."

"I'll get him."

She disappeared through the front tent flap.

Adam heard her talking to one of the Kidon unit then their voices were muted.

In a moment, she re-appeared.

"He drove over with some of his men to a ridge further south to check on something."

"How many did he leave behind in camp?"

"Only a handful."

"I wish you weren't here."

"I can take care of myself," said Renie. "You're the one who needs taking care of."

"Anything to eat around this place?"

"I'll see what I can scrape up," she said as she patted his hand and moved gracefully through the front flap.

Maneuvering painfully, Adam looked at the two pages of palimpsest once more, trying his best to decipher some of the words on the second page. He could make out one or two of them, but not in sequence, so they never seemed to make any sense. Unable to reach the briefcase, he tucked the manuscript pages under his cot and dozed off again.

Angry voices awakened him suddenly as shadows silhouetted the canvas above him. Gunfire crackled in all directions. A couple of bullets whizzed through his tent just missing his head. He heard screams then silence. Adam hated the helplessness. It was torture to move and nothing seemed to work as if his whole body had atrophied.

The attack flared up again then stopped.

Adam could hear intermittent bursts of gunfire throughout the camp, then voices approaching his tent.

Bishop's Move

Vatican City

The Pope had just finished meetings with papal nuncios from South and Central America, and was going over unsigned documents with his priest secretary when the Cardinal appeared at his door unannounced.

"Lorenzo! What brings you here this afternoon?"

"*Santissimo Padre.*" Lorenzo, dipped his head to kiss the Pope's ring. "I have a matter of utmost importance that I want to discuss if you have a moment. I know your calendar is tight today, but this won't take long."

The Pope looked at the papers stacked before him and said to his assistant, "We both need a break anyway. Go. Return in half an hour. My next appointment isn't until 2:30."

The young man leapt at the opportunity.

The Pope peered into Lorenzo's face. "Something is troubling you, my friend. Tell me."

"Someone tried to kill the man with the manuscript, but he escaped."

"God means for him to live," the Pope said.

"Perhaps so. But is it good to have an old manuscript like that floating around?"

"Old manuscripts have been floating around for centuries. Why should we worry about this one?"

"Because the word is the man is bringing it to the Vatican."

"What's wrong with that?"

"It may be part of *Codex Sinaiticus* and there's no telling what it says."

"Scholars would have to verify its authenticity."

"But, can we afford to take that risk? We might find something that would change the Church."

"Well, that's not a problem. The Church needs change. As long as I am Pope..."

That is exactly the problem thought Lorenzo.

"You trouble yourself too much about this, Renzo. You should turn it over to God."

"God helps those who help themselves."

"You do know that's not in the Bible," said the Pope drifting into one of his monastic moments of meditation.

Yes, thought Lorenzo, but most of the world lives by it. He excused himself without speaking since the pontiff was already off in another world. He will drive me crazy, Lorenzo groused silently as he slipped through the door and started for his office across the Courtyard of *Damasus*.

Road Kill

The Sinai Desert

Adam reached for anything he could use for a weapon. But there was nothing close by. He heard Renie scream, "No!" throwing herself in front of Adam's tent.

Renie came tumbling in to Adam's side.

The Bedouin servant from St. Catherine's followed.

"You've led me right to him, woman."

"You?" said Adam.

The Bedouin smiled.

"Leave her alone!"

"Give me what I want," replied the Bedouin

"What could I have that you would want?"

"That briefcase."

"You want the page back?"

The Bedouin picked up the briefcase, poked his hand into the bottom. Pulling the leather bottom back, he pulled out a small strip of microfilm. "No, I want this."

"And now the card," said the Bedouin looking at Renie.

"What card?"

"Conrad's."

"You mean this one?" she said removing it from her purse. He grabbed it from her hand.

"What is it?" queried Adam.

"The knock list of CIA operatives around the world. With the code on the back of the card your woman brought you just signed their death warrants."

"I wondered what that number was. Adam, I thought Conrad Docherty was your friend."

"He isn't," replied Adam now pulling himself up and staggering like a drunk toward the Bedouin.

The Bedouin pushed Adam over easily, opening both wounds.

Enraged, Renie kicked the Bedouin hard, but he slapped her across the face and sent her tumbling over on top of Adam. "Two lovers finally together," said the Bedouin.

Renie ran at the Bedouin again, but he grabbed her and held her tight against his body.

She screamed as she tried to elbow him in the side.

"Go ahead," laughed the Bedouin. "Scream all you want, woman. No one will hear you out here."

He wrenched her arm as he dragged her from the tent.

Adam struggled to get up again, but could not. He had used all his energy to make his first attack.

He heard Renie scream once more, then silence.

Anger Can Be Blinding

Washington, DC

The reception in the East room of the White House began promptly at 7:00 pm. The guests stood in line on the oak floor of Fontainebleau parquetry to greet the President and the First Gentleman. With their drinks and hors' d'oeuvres, they milled about the 1938 Steinway under Martha Washington's ever-present gaze. A string quartet filled the air with Pachelbel's Canon. It was strictly a white tie and gown affair.

Assistant Chief of Protocol, William P. Briner, flanked by the President and her husband, nodded and smiled cordially as he introduced generals, admirals, heads of state, members of the Cabinet, the Supreme Court, and leaders from the Congress, their spouses and friends. Briner's memory for names and their correct pronunciation was unequaled in D.C.

"Madame President . . . Andrew Farley, Director of Central Intelligence, and his friend, Miss Lilly Bridges of New Orleans."

"Madame President," drawled Farley.

"Drew, glad you came. And Miss Bridges, I am delighted to meet you."

"It's an honor, Madame President!" Lilly extended her hand, attempting a curtsey.

The First Gentleman's response was not nearly as warm. The President felt the chill. He'd never trusted Farley.

The line of guests moved through quickly since there

139

were less than a hundred of them. It was to be a special evening as they celebrated new European countries' alliances.

A staffer began motioning everyone to dinner which was to begin promptly at 8:00 pm in the State Dining Room.

"Hope this doesn't go too long," Farley said to his date. "The speeches at these things are always dreadful."

"I'm just excited to be here!" gushed Lilly. Farley just smiled and shook his head.

At the end of the dinner, the President offered several toasts to a couple of Heads of State. Champagne goblets clinked around the room. Finally, the sounds of a band the President liked warmed the East Room, summoning them all back to the dance floor where the evening had begun.

Farley hated to dance. He was always two left feet. So, he took a couple of spins with Lilly, pawned her off to the nearest three-star and headed for the spiked punch bowl where his Deputy Director found him.

"We have to talk. Perhaps, we should go out into the hallway, Sir."

That line got Farley's attention. His Deputy Director hardly ever called him 'Sir.'"

Dodging twirling gowns and tuxedos, the two of them zig-zagged their way across the East Room to the hall outside.

"What's going on?" Farley asked.

"There have been some hits on some of our people."

"Hits?"

"That's correct, Sir."

"Who? Where? How many?"

The Deputy Director gulped before speaking. "Practically all of our Middle Eastern people. Tunis, Tripoli, Cairo, Khartoum, Beirut, Damascus, Amman, Tehran and Baghdad."

"What?" Farley fell backwards into the antique Queen Anne chair next to him. The hulk of his frame nearly broke it.

"The estimate is between 35 or 40 operatives. It happened sometime this afternoon."

"Mary, mother of Jesus!"

"No one is claiming responsibility."

"And you have no idea?" said Farley, his head in his hands.

"None at all."

"Well, someone's going to pay for this!" said the CIA chief, suddenly on his feet. He charged back to the East Room like a raging bull.

Dancers scattered as he stormed across the floor. Farley passed off his startled date to the general who would take her home. Turning for a moment, he glared at the President, then disappeared through the door.

* * *

The Sinai Desert

When Adam woke up, he saw the Bedouin sitting across the tent from him eating what appeared to be lunch. The Bedouin handed him a water bottle and a plate of thick stew. Adam knew better than to ask what was in it. The gruel tasted like cooked cardboard, but he surprised himself at how much he ate. When he said he needed to relieve himself, the Bedouin motioned to one of the guards to go with him.

The afternoon sun blinded him. As his eyes began to adjust, he surveyed the whole camp. Only eight tents. Bedouins scattered here and there. Looked like twenty or thirty of them. All with weapons.

Adam explored possible escape routes but there were none. The problem was there was no place to hide. It was open desert in all directions. The tiny oasis was the only reason the camp could survive at all.

Back in the tent, he said, "Where is Renie?"

"Safe," the Bedouin smiled. "Yours?"

"Just a friend."

"You know the sand is a beautiful thing," said the Bedouin.

"Hadn't thought about it much," said Adam.

"It's like the human race. Like all creation. We shift from here to there, blown about by the wind. Each of us is nothing more than a grain of sand," he observed. He shoveled a handful of it up and let it pour from his palm like water onto the ground.

"And your point would be?" chided Adam.

"Just reflecting on the transience of things. Like those CIA operatives who are gone now." The Bedouin gathered another fistful. As the grains cascaded to the ground he said, "Gone with the wind."

The Bedouin smiled, got up and left Adam completely alone.

Adam reached for the two pages of manuscript and began studying them again. Surely the answer was in there somewhere.

Eye in the Sky

Langley, Virginia

Drew Farley summoned those he could trust into the satellite reconnaissance room.

"It's coming into focus now, Sir," said the technician.

"Good." They all moved to the flashing screen. "What are we looking at?"

"A Bedouin encampment somewhere in the Sinai desert."

As the satellite passed nearer the target, the image sharpened.

"Can you draw us in closer?"

"Yes Sir," said the technician. He enlarged the picture, bracketing the surrounding territory. They could see figures moving around. Some were cooking, others loading equipment.

"What makes you think this is where our man is?"

"Mossad gave us the location, Sir," said another operative in the room.

"What do the Israelis know about all this?"

"They were working a project in deep cover there when our guy stumbled across the one they've had their eye on."

"And who might that be?"

"A Bedouin terrorist who has been hiding out at some monastery in Egypt."

"What's the story on him?" Farley looked at the

143

screen more intently.

"We're working on that."

"What the hell is our guy doing out there in the middle of all this?" said Farley.

"He's not our guy anymore."

"I know that. But what's he doing there now?"

"Seems to be caught in the middle of a very odd game. Something to do with a manuscript."

"What manuscript?"

"Something very old that a lot of people seem to want. It has to do with this ancient monastery somehow." He flashed a picture of St. Catherine's on another screen. "Here are all the reports we have on this situation." He handed him a thin file.

Farley turned, his back to the large computer screen as he rapidly scanned the sketchy report. He stood with a couple of the others looking at the file.

Then the technician said, "Sir? Sir? You might want to look at this."

By now everyone in the room was back in front of the screen watching what looked like an attack in the making.

"Enlarge the view, son, so we can take it all in... There...that's good...hold it there."

"We only have a couple of more minutes until we lose the satellite picture," the technician said, wiping his brow.

"That's all right, son. Just hold that sucker as long as you can."

On the screen they saw soldiers approaching the camp from the west.

"Who's that?" asked Farley.

"Maybe Mossad? Our intel informed us they are out there somewhere."

"Wait a minute!" said Farley, "Is that a woman?"

"Where?" said one of the others.

"Over there," said Farley, pointing. "Being held by that one. See her now? Where'd she come from?"

Just as one of the Israeli commandos raised his gun to fire the first shot, the screen went blank.

Peeling the Onion

A dam was up now on the edge of his cot. Gunfire crackled all around. He could hear soldiers yelling. He could hear them dying. A spray of bullets shredded the tarpaulin and whistled through the encampment. One of the Bedouins fell in front of his tent, shot between the eyes.

Renie's scream brought Adam to his feet and out into the open. Amidst smoke and sand, he saw Israeli commandos moving through the camp, slitting throats and firing point blank at their targets. It appeared that the Bedouin's men were getting the worst of it. It was a fierce battle, up close and personal. He saw the Bedouin slip away out into the desert leaving his men to die.

Adam could only watch with his bum leg and weakened condition. He heard Renie scream again and saw two Bedouins yank her behind a tent. Clumsily, he hobbled his way through the melee. Bullets whizzed past his head as he rounded one of the tents and came face to face with the three of them. Renie's shirt was ripped open, her face bruised. Adam could tell they'd been having their way with her when the attack had begun. One of them tossed her aside and turned to Adam. Instinctively, Adam swept him with his bad leg, using his good one for traction. The man went down hard, cracking his head on a metal tent stake, killing him instantly.

"Adam, watch out!" screamed Renie as the other one charged with a huge knife. Adam kicked the knife from the man's hand, took his arm and flipped him on his back. The man rebounded immediately, grabbed his friend's automatic, and aimed it at Renie, but a shot from behind split his spine. He fell forward on top of Renie as Moshe appeared from behind the tent with a little Beretta M21 in his hand, a favorite of Mossad.

"Get this creature off of me!" she wailed, then snapped. "Where have you been?"

"*Thank you* would suffice," said the Israeli.

Adam noticed the gunfire had died out. "Is that all of them?" he asked, grimacing. His whole body ached.

"Yes, we've sent them packing," said Moshe, "as you Americans put it. Two of them took off to the north, but my men will get them."

Two more shots reverberated in the distance.

"What took you so long?" Renie asked.

"We had to wait for the right moment to move in. And this was it. The leader got away."

"Yes, I saw him run off just before you got here."

"And left the rest of them here to die?" Renie asked.

"They would willingly lay down their lives for him."

"Looks like they did," said Adam, gazing at the bodies around the camp. "What kind of man does this to his own men?"

"A very special one."

"You mean there's more to our lowly Bedouin than meets the eye?" said Adam.

"Much more. But let's get you and this camp cleaned up. My men will pull a meal together and I will tell you what I know about him. Then in the morning we must leave this place. Your time here is over."

"That's fine with me," said Renie. "I'm ready for a bath."

"We're lucky to be alive," said Adam to Moshe, "thanks to you. Guess I owe you, twice."

"Just doing my job. Besides, I prefer fighting to

making peace. It's a lost cause."

Renie helped Adam back to his tent. The place was a mess. He looked for his things, which fortunately were all there covered with great piles of golden sand. He dug under the cot and found the two ancient pages partially buried, but still in good shape. He rolled them up and tucked them into his briefcase.

After they'd packed everything up, both Renie and Adam moved to a campfire. They overheard Moshe mutter something to one of his men in Hebrew as the night wind blew the flames.

Moshe stopped talking as they approached.

Adam scrutinized the Israeli. There was something about what he'd just said that didn't sound right. Something didn't fit. But he couldn't figure out what. He quickly forgot it as he turned his gaze on a sunburned Renie. Her skin was a golden brown. Her eyes seemed to sparkle in the dancing light of the fire. He watched her pull a sweater over her head to ward off the oncoming chill of the desert night.

"Let's eat," said Moshe. The meal around the campfire was simple Bedouin fare: goat milk, lamb on a bed of rice and dates for dessert.

By the flicker of the firelight, Adam removed the parchments of old vellum from his knapsack and tried again to decipher some of the words on the second page. He wondered how old they must be and why he, of all people, had been chosen to deliver them.

"Any luck?" said Renie.

"No. I'm going to need some help," he said as he tucked them away again. He looked at Moshe. "Tell us about the Bedouin."

"We think he was the real mastermind behind 9/11. Bin Laden was just a pawn or at best a front."

Adam braced himself against the brisk, night wind.

"His Egyptian name is Ammon which means 'the hidden one.' But he goes by Hakim, 'the intelligent one,' which, in his mind is also short for Al-Hakim. Ever heard of him?"

"Wasn't he a leader or founder of the Druze religion?" said Renie.

Adam sat up and stared at her.

"Don't look so surprised," she said. "I studied world religions at Harvard."

"She's right," said Moshe. "Fatimid caliph Al-Hakim was an Ismaili who, in 1017, was declared to be the first incarnation of God. But when he disappeared four years later, his followers announced that he would return bringing Judgment in about a thousand years."

"Which would be right about now," speculated Renie.

"Give or take."

"Don't tell me, our Bedouin friend thinks he's the return of Al-Hakim!" Adam said.

"Close. He's mixed it with Islam and his own terrorist brew. Remember, the origin of assassins came from an offshoot of the Ismailis who settled in what we now call Iran. You know the story of the old man who lured young boys into the Castle of Alamut, drugged them with hashish, showed them paradise and got them to go out and kill people for him, hence hashishim, the Arabic origin of the word assassin. The Crusaders had all kinds of stories about this guy."

"Right," said Adam. "But what does this have to do with our man?"

"Well, he sees himself as a mythical figure, a metaphor for a whole millennium. He gets young Arabs, Bedouins especially, as his assassins. They're willing to die for his cause, which is pretty much whatever he tells them. He only uses Islam for his own purposes."

"I thought Bedouins were mostly peace-loving people," said Adam.

"Most of them are until pushed to the limit or

wronged in some way. Then they muster the most creative forms of vengeance and they are very patient about getting even. They never quit until they have gotten their revenge. Remember, Muammar Qaddafi started out as a Bedouin."

"And?" queried Renie impatiently.

"And," continued Moshe gazing at Renie, "Hakim has become one of the most feared, respected leaders in this part of the world. Much more than Saddam Hussein, Qaddafi, or Osama bin Laden ever thought about being. He's been one of the main leaders of ISIS."

"Why have we never heard of him?" asked Adam.

"Because he has so many disguises and has remained hidden for so long."

"Where did he come from?" asked Renie.

"He grew up at St. Catherine's Monastery, one of the children of the Bedouin servants there. But he was always more rebellious and brighter than the others. As a teenager, he grew restless and thumbed his way to Cairo. He studied at both Cairo University and al-Azhar University, the center of Islamic studies. He took courses in law and Islamic revolution, a card-carrying member of the Muslim Brotherhood, the Islamic Group, and read everything Sayyid Qutb ever wrote."

"The one martyred in 1966?" asked Renie.

"Correct," replied Moshe as Adam stared at Renie, amazed she knew so much. "Trained by your CIA and fought in Afghanistan, and like so many others, he came home to Egypt to overthrow a secular government by participating in the assassination of Sadat."

Adam could hardly believe what he was hearing. This was the same shy, retiring servant who had taken him to Father Paul at St. Catherine's! The simple man he'd met by the skulls and bones in the charnel house. The man who led him up the mountain.

"How has he avoided being caught?"

"He's brilliant. Except for a failed attack in New

York a few years ago, he's been in hiding at St. Catherine's since September 11. Perfect cover, wouldn't you say?"

"Incredible," Renie whispered. She gazed at the bright stars exploding above them.

"But now, he's come out of hiding," Adam said as his own, botched New York bomb flashed in his mind.

"That's right. He was hidden until you came along. You both must figure in his plans somehow or he would've killed you. He could have at any time."

Moshe threw a few more small logs on the dying fire. Sparks peppered the sand at their feet as the flame licked the night sky, brightening their sun burnt faces.

"I thought your rescue seemed a little too easy," Adam said. "Why don't you arrest him?"

"Not our territory."

"And you don't want to kill him because…"

"Because we want to find out what his full plan is. He's the only one who knows all of it. And torture won't work since he was weaned on it in Egyptian prisons, which is why he's a hero with HAMAS and other terrorist groups. His stoicism in prison is legendary."

"Surely there's some way to find out what he's up to," Adam said.

"Not until someone translates those manuscript pages."

Adam unrolled the pages once again, examining them closely by the light of the fire. He thought about how Tischendorf had done the same over a century and a half before. As the blaze turned to smoldering cinders, he wondered what secret was hidden there.

Gray ashes flickered upward, merging with sand and night sky.

PART FOUR: PRETENDERS

Evelyn and Al-Hakim

Maryville

Evelyn Hastings hadn't talked to her friend Ruth Gibbons for years. Ruth, who had been at the CIA for a decade worked for Drew Farley.

"Evelyn, it's Ruth."

"Hey Ruth. Long time, no talk. You still at Langley?"

"Where else?"

"What's up?"

"We know about your boss who's disappeared. And the young woman. We think they're together."

"Where?" said Evelyn.

"Somewhere in the Middle East."

Evelyn's heart leapt. "Are they alright?"

"Don't know. We've lost them."

"But you didn't call just to tell me that, did you?"

"No, I wanted to let you know that someone will be coming down to talk with you. It may not be safe for you."

"What's this all about?"

"I don't know, but your boss is in some kind of trouble."

"I was afraid of that."

"Watch for our guy. And call me if you need any help."

"I will."

"*Ciao.*"

Ruth was gone before Evelyn could reply. She sat at her desk imagining the two of them together, in each other's arms. She'd lost him. It was her last chance to find a decent man.

It was getting late. She'd worked well past 7:00 pm again since there wasn't anyone to go home to. The setting sun filtered soft light through the branches of the tree outside her window. The only real shadows were on her face.

Then came the sound from around the corner. It startled her. She knew the janitor had already gone for the day. Normally he locked up when he left. There were no meetings at the church that night. She wasn't expecting anyone.

She heard it again. Creaky noises in the old church echoed everywhere.

She decided to call Frank Harkin or 911. Fumbling the phone, she wished she'd not made so much noise. Then she heard the sound again. It was getting closer.

"Come on, answer!" she said in a tense whisper. The phone at the publisher's house rang until his voicemail kicked in. Her heart raced as she hung up. "Okay," she said to herself, "911."

She was so nervous, she missed and hit the 8 instead of the 9. She tried again. But this time, somewhere between the 9 and the 1, the phone went dead.

A man's thumb held the cradle button down.

*   *   *

Cairo

On the broad square of Al-Hakim Mosque next to the Northern wall of Islamic Fatimid Cairo, between Bab al-Futuh (Gate of Conquest) and Bab al-Nasr (Gate of Victory), hundreds of people milled about awaiting Hakim's arrival. They spilled in and out of the surrounding shops and bazaars. Muezzins wailed "Allahu Akbar! God is Greatest!" Beggars offered outstretched hands. "Baksheesh! Baksheesh!" The day teemed with chaotic energy, strong aromas and sounds that had echoed across the centuries.

"Mother of the World, my ass!" said Conrad Docherty to his Egyptian escort as they stood at the edge of the square. "Cairo is nothing but a squalid, parasitic cesspool of half-forgotten dynasties. What's the fascination?"

"I do not know."

A sea of beggars battered them from all sides. Conrad resisted the urge to slap away a couple of them. He had more pressing business and wanted neither a skirmish with a mob nor a tangle with the police.

"Your boss fancies himself as the new Al-Hakim," Conrad said.

The Egyptian nodded.

"Do you believe it?"

"Hakim is a great leader."

"But Al-Hakim was an eccentric murderer."

The man said nothing.

"Where is he? Isn't he supposed to speak?"

"He will be here soon. Just watch."

"What's that roar?" Conrad asked, gesturing in the direction of the rumble.

Then they saw it. A large mass of people, pouring into the square like lava, pushing everyone aside. Conrad and the Egyptian got up on their toes to glimpse the Bedouin leading the mob. The massive throng sent chills up and down the American's spine.

Bandy-legged men portered a large pulpit on their shoulders. Conrad could see it was inlaid with variegated marble and wood.

"Must be heavy!" Conrad yelled, barely hearing himself.

"They would carry it to the sea for him," shouted the Egyptian.

A chant began all around them and built quickly.

"Hakim! Hakim! Long live the great Hakim!"

"Do they believe he is the return of Al-Hakim?"

"Some of them do," replied the Egyptian. "He has not publicly identified himself as such. But that is only a matter of time."

The roar was so deafening that Conrad had to cover his ears. "Ha-kim! Ha-kim! Ha-kim! Ha-kim! Ha-kim!" The litany crescendoed.

Government police at the edges of the square lifted their rifles to the ready position.

The Bedouin raised both hands and the silence was instant. His ability to mute the mob stunned Conrad. Slowly, the Bedouin lowered his hands and stared at the crowd. The whole scene reminded Conrad of film clips he'd seen of Hitler at the Nuremberg Rally. The masses were ready to march into battle for him, and he hadn't spoken a single word. Conrad glanced over his shoulder and noticed that hundreds more had arrived. A full-blown riot was imminent.

Then the Bedouin spoke. *"Salaam Aleikum!"* he yelled to the crowd.

"Aleikum Salaam!" they replied as one.

He repeated his greeting, and they parroted the refrain once more, their collective voice filling the bright sky.

When he said, *"Allahu Akbar!"* they went mad.

The police tried to hold their ground, as the hordes got bolder. People were pushing and shoving each other. The Bedouin could have led a full-scale revolt at that moment.

"Remarkable!" Conrad said.

Then the Bedouin raised both hands, and again the noise stopped as if he had turned off a switch. He stood there and stared at them.

No one moved.

Then he began. "Do you know that this was once a prison where we put Crusaders who tried to take our families and our land! Perhaps it should be re-opened for the infidels!"

The crowd went wild. Conrad felt their hot breath on his neck. He wondered if the Bedouin could contain them. Sticks and clubs were hoisted into the air as the people shouted, "Death to the infidels! Death to the infidels!"

The Bedouin raised his hands again.

Silence.

"Once this place was a stable for Salah al-Din's horses...." He paused for effect. "But a warehouse for Napoleon? Never again!"

Pandemonium broke out. Conrad suddenly felt completely out of place. It seemed like everyone was staring at his white face. Not even donning his Arab disguise helped. A few of them began taunting him and poking him in the side with sticks. His Egyptian escort yelled something in Arabic and they all backed off.

Again, the Bedouin raised his hands and stilled the cacophony once more.

Then, after a few moments when no one seemed to breathe, he continued.

"The Palestinian poet writes: *I am an Arab and my palm is solid as rock, scratching whoever touches it. You usurped my grandfather's vineyards and left us nothing but these rocks. I do not hate people. I steal from no one. However, if I am hungry, I will eat the flesh of my usurper. Beware of my hunger and my anger!*"

With this line, the speech was over. Not even the Bedouin could quiet the crowd now.

Conrad looked for a way out, but there was none. He knew from experience that once they started on him, they would not stop, and he'd much prefer being hanged or shot than to being clubbed to death, which was his worst recurring nightmare. Glancing up to where the Bedouin had been speaking, Conrad noticed he had disappeared. The police wanted to arrest him. The crowds wanted to worship him. The Bedouin was like a rock star about to be trampled.

Suddenly, Conrad's Egyptian escort began running,

so Conrad rushed down the street trying to keep up with him.

The Government police who had just arrived were clearly outnumbered and were fighting for their lives as the people beat their shields with sticks and clubs. Sirens whined all around them. Conrad saw military troops putting a dent in the crowd, but even they were no match for the fuming multitude. No one had control over the mob any more. It was like a blind, wounded animal ready to thrash whatever got in its way.

One of them tripped Conrad and yelled in Arabic, "American! Death to the Infidel!" Before he could get off the ground, they began kicking him in the belly and the back. The Egyptian tried to stop them, so they turned their fury on him, knocking him over and flailing him with bats and clubs.

"Idiots!" yelled Conrad. "He's on your side!"

Unable because of the din to hear what Conrad was saying, they kept pummeling the Egyptian who was now unconscious on the ground. Conrad knew he had only a second to escape, so he began backing away, leaving his escort behind to save his own life, but it was too late. A dozen of them rushed at him.

Suddenly, a van squealed around the corner and screeched to a halt between him and the crowd. The mob slammed into the van.

Quickly, two men jumped out, pushing and beating people back. They gathered the Egyptian, bleeding and dying, and pitched him in the side of the van. Another one grabbed Conrad's arm and yanked him in as the angry attackers tried to beat his back. The door slammed shut with clubs and rocks pounding its side.

"Who are you?" Conrad yelled. He tried to get his bearing in the back of the dark van, but his eyes refused to focus. No one said a thing. They laid out the crumpled body of the man who had just saved his life.

"What's going on here?! Who are you?" barked Conrad.

No one even looked his direction.

The van, rocking back and forth under the force of the runaway rabble, honked and forced its way through the mob.

Finally, someone in the passenger's seat turned and stared at Conrad. The man's face was covered with the edge of his keffiyeh, but Conrad would have recognized those eyes anywhere.

"How did you like my speech?"

"Not sure I can survive another one," Conrad said, still a little shaken.

The Bedouin moved to the back and knelt over his nearly dead servant. A mess of blood and ooze looked up into his eyes. "I have given my life for you, Master."

"Your place is made for you in heaven, my son. Enter the joy that is before you."

The man breathed his last in the Bedouin's arms.

"Why didn't we meet in a more secret place?" Conrad asked.

"I wanted you to see the larger picture."

"Well, I certainly did! I have fulfilled my end of the bargain. I want what's coming to me."

"Not until the manuscript is translated. When will you Americans learn patience? We know how to wait. A hundred years, a thousand. It's nothing. All you deserve will come to you soon enough. Just pray this Adam Hunter delivers the manuscript before the Sicilian gets to him."

Churches As Dangerous Places

Vatican City

Standing in the cavernous nave of St. Peter's Basilica, Don Mazzini admired the Baldachin that rose far above him. He glanced over his shoulder and noticed Marcello approaching from behind with a slight limp. Without turning to greet him the Don spoke, still gazing up. "Did you know, Marcello, when Bernini built this place, he wanted to create a sense of awe and intimacy all at the same time?"

"I believe I read that somewhere."

"You know what it means? It means that things are not always as they seem. You think you know a person. Then you find out there is so much you don't know. Are you getting my point?" said the Don still not looking at his once-favorite assassin.

"Sounds like a parable."

"You know, the Baldachin was built with bronze looted from the Pantheon," Mazzini said, "which means that even the church steals. Makes me feel right at home." A smile inched across his face.

Marcello didn't say anything. His boss could turn philosophical like this when he was very angry. But it was always with other hit men, never with him.

"There's something else here, Marcello. When Bernini started this job, he saw it through to the end."

"Let me tell you what happened."

Mazzini held his palm up. "When Bernini built St. Peter's, there were no excuses. Only results. Capisce?" The old man turned now and unnerved Marcello with a deadly stare, one he'd never seen before.

"Capisce," said Marcello, his head down in disgrace.

"Look at me!" barked Mazzini.

Marcello raised his face.

Mazzini slapped it hard. "Do not fail me this time, my son."

A deadly mix of shame and anger bubbled up inside his young assassin. Marcello glared at the old man, but kept his weapon holstered.

Mazzini walked on a few steps, continuing to gaze at the great dome.

"How beautiful it is. It's *molto bene!*"

* * *

Maryville

"You don't need to call anybody," said the man, causing Evelyn's heart to skip a beat.

"Who are you?" she said, her voice quavering.

"I'm here to help." The man smiled broadly.

"Could I see some identification?"

Pulling out his billfold, he flipped open his ID card. She took a good look at it. Central Intelligence Agency. He was for real. Ruth had worked fast!

Evelyn relaxed, collapsing back in her chair. Suddenly she was a flood of conversation.

"You got here quicker than I thought. You don't know what it's been like. Worrying, wondering. Then when Renie disappeared...."

All the sudden, she stopped. "So, how can I help you?"

"I need to take you to a safe place."

"Why me?"

"We have intel that they might try to do something to you to get to him."

"Who? Why? What's going on?"

"I can tell you once you're safe. We need to leave now. I'll follow you to your house so you can pack a bag."

Evelyn suddenly felt like the world was closing in on her. Catching her breath, she said, "This is all happening so fast. Where are we going?"

"To a safe house up toward the mountains."

"This is crazy. Are you sure we have to go?"

"I'm sure."

"Let me turn off the computer."

"Hurry," he said, glancing at his watch.

Improvising

The Sinai Desert

Adam readied the Range Rover for the trip to the border as Moshe's men loaded supplies in the back. "Are you staying?" he asked.

"No. We'll probably head northwest across the Negev then go up along the Gaza Strip. We need to check on a Palestinian disturbance up there."

The morning sun beat down as hot wind sandblasted the sides of their tents. Adam could see Renie had not slept well. He guessed dreams of the previous day's battle were making her toss and turn. He knew she was ready for a nap when they crawled into the Rover.

"Your passports are in order," said Moshe. "Remember, go cross-country to the highway from Nuweiba, which will take you to Taba where you will cross the border into Eilat. You'll see the Gulf of Aqaba on your right. In Eilat you'll catch an Arkia flight to Tel Aviv. From there you can fly to Rome."

"Thanks for all your help. Perhaps we'll meet again someday."

"Perhaps."

Renie fell asleep with her head against the window during the drive across the desert. Adam glanced at her wishing she weren't there, but glad at the same time. He wondered if she would ever find out the real truth about what he had done in Manhattan that had changed both his and her life forever.

*   *   *

Renie awakened just in time to cross the border a couple of hours later. Egyptian customs officers surveyed them both smiling and whispering to each other in Arabic. After successfully passing through Israeli customs in Eilat, again getting the third degree, Renie asked, "What were they saying back there? I thought they weren't going to let us through."

Adam laughed. "They were commenting on the contours of your figure in very creative ways."

"Men! You're all alike."

"Hey, I didn't say anything. I was just translating. Besides, it was all positive."

The Israeli security officers at the airport were much more persistent than the ones at the border.

"Just answer honestly," Adam said to Renie. "They're the best in the world at spotting liars."

Attractive young men and women, all of them Sabras, or native Israelis, asked them questions separately. Despite all his coaching, Adam could see by the nervous look on her face that Renie was having a hard time answering the repetitive questions.

Suddenly she got up and ran toward Adam.

The interviewer yelled, "Halt!" Officers with weapons immediately boxed her in. Tourists looked up from their iPhones and iPads to see who had been caught.

One of the uniformed men said to Adam and Renie, "Please come with me." To the others, he said, "Check their bags for a bomb."

Adam and Renie followed the officer into a detainment area where he asked them to stay.

"We'll miss our plane!" Renie said. "We have to get to Rome."

"I have to. You're going home. I work better alone."

"I don't care anymore," replied Renie, crossing her arms and turning her back to him.

At that moment, a man walked through the door, introducing himself as Saul Rosenberg.

"My apologies, friends," he said, "There has been a mistake. I am with Mossad here in Eilat, and we just received word to pass you on through. There will be no more problem here or in Tel Aviv. Your ticket to Rome has been upgraded to first class, courtesy of the Israeli government."

Adam and Renie looked at each other.

"Come now," said Rosenberg. "You must not miss your plane."

As they moved rapidly through the little airport under the glare of the customs officers who had stopped them, Renie waved and smiled at a couple of them and at the startled crowd of tourists in line wondering who they were, then disappeared through the door onto the tarmac.

Over the whir of the jets warming up, she yelled, "You're not going to keep me from flying first class to Rome, are you? Something I've always wanted to do for free. This is the most exciting thing that's ever happened in my life. And you want to send me back to my boring little practice in Maryville. The day Eric was killed, something inside me died. Now, for the first time in my life I feel alive again."

"It's too dangerous," said Adam. "I don't know what's going on here. But whatever it is, I'm used to it. I thought I'd left it behind when I came to Tennessee. But, now…the last thing I want to do is to drag you into it with me."

"Why not let me be the judge of that?"

"Look, you're not going with me and that's final. Thanks for helping nurse me back to health. I will always owe you for that."

"Owe me? You don't owe me a thing. I don't want to talk to you anymore." She turned her head to the window as they passed over the Wilderness of Zin and the Negev. Soon the Mediterranean came into sight on their left.

*   *   *

The layover in Tel Aviv found them both buried in silence.

She shopped the Duty Frees while he bought her a one-way ticket to JFK and Knoxville. Then he sat by himself, studying the manuscript.

As the time for her departure approached, Adam looked around to tell her good-bye, but did not see her. He went to her gate and asked the ticket agent if she'd already boarded. No, she had not. The time for her flight came and went.

Renie was nowhere in sight.

Going All the Way

The voice boomed over the loudspeakers. "Will Adam Hunter please go to the El AL customer service desk?" Adam found it quickly. "I'm Adam Hunter."

"Yes sir, someone left this mobile phone for you," said the agent handing him a smartphone.

As soon as it was in his hand, it rang. Adam heard Conrad say, "Your girlfriend is in need of your assistance. The deal is you keep her with you and complete the job or she dies."

"Bastard! Where is she?"

"In the third stall in the women's restroom down the hall to your right. I'd hurry if I were you. The antidote is in her purse."

Adam charged into the restroom with women screaming and threw himself against the locked third stall door, almost landing on Renie. She was limp as a dishrag. He felt her wrist. Only a hint of a pulse. Fumbling in her purse, he located the syringe. In a few seconds, there was a stir. Then she lurched backward, hitting her head on the wall.

"Ow! What the...! Adam? What happened? My head feels like a melon. One minute I came in here. The next...I don't remember the next."

"Listen, I've changed my mind. I want you to come to Rome with me."

"Don't try to make up now."

"I'm not. I'm hiring you for legal advice."

167

"You can't afford me."

"Come on. We've got a plane to catch."

*   *   *

Russia

The Gulfstream G800 cruised toward Moscow with only a couple of bumpy intervals over the fiords of Norway and the Baltic shores of Estonia. The Paleologos company jet was fully equipped with bedroom, kitchen, cabin steward, three world-class pilots, seating for a dozen and the most powerful computers and technological equipment money could buy. Anastasia had brought her own SWAT team along for protection. Half a dozen mercenaries handpicked by Ian McPherson, all of them experts in hand-to-hand and small arms combat. "Probably more than we need," Ian said. "But it's better to be on the safe side."

Anastasia Paleologos never left anything to chance. Her short four-year marriage to Dimitrios was a happy one, most of it spent traveling the world on islands like Mykonos and Santorini whose stark volcanic cliffs she loved the most. On those trips she began to acquire a taste for highly expensive artifacts. But her fascination with the *Codex Sinaiticus* went beyond mere art collection. It had become an obsession. On one of her many trips to St. Catherine's Monastery in Sinai, she'd heard the story of Tischendorf's robbery of the Codex. She'd already fallen in love with the ancient monastic fortress, its history, its tradition, its monks, its icons and its famous manuscripts. She'd even contributed large sums of money to the foundation established for the monastery by the Prince of Wales. She'd made many trips to Room 30 in the British Museum just to see the old codex before it had been moved to the British Library. Her burning passion was to hold it in her hands someday, then return it to its original home.

When Dimitrios finally died, she put the obsession on hold and grieved his passing for a couple of months. Recovering quickly, to everyone's surprise, she took over all the businesses and soon forgot about the manuscript.

Everything came to a halt with the onset of cancer. Up to then, she'd been running things at a manic pace. All the doctors told her she'd have to slow down. She told them she'd outlive them all, but weeks in the hospital, flat on her back, and several rounds of chemotherapy made her think about religion and her own mortality.

Then came the letter from Father Nicodemus, which reminded her of the old codex.

They circled Sheremetyevo International in a long slow loop. As the G800 banked for its final approach, she gazed out the window. It was a dreary day outside. Moscow gray. But the pall of poverty that hung over the whole country was not evident at the airport. Too many black Mercedes AMGs and top of the line Beemers. Not the dour place Anastasia had heard described. I guess these are the ones with the money, she mused.

The row of bodyguards marched in staggered formation around her. They created a comical scene, but she didn't mind the stares. She enjoyed the attention. She always had because everything she did was in grand style, including this last great act of her life.

Two stretch limos waited for them at the curb. For once, she would hold the renowned *Codex Sinaiticus* in her own hands. The cost was high. But to her, it was worth it. Nothing was going to stop her now.

Leverage

Evelyn Hastings set the alarm at the front door of her house and made her way, suitcase in hand to the man's car.

"Where is this safe house?" she asked.

"In a place called Mountain Homes."

"Oh, I've heard of it, but never been there."

"The owner of the cabin we'll be in is retired CIA. He lets us use it from time to time."

Evelyn was a chatterbox as they headed out of town, but he said nothing. The moon was high as they passed Walland and the entrance to the Foothills Parkway, then turned off Lamar Alexander Parkway onto West Millers' Cove Road. After passing Blackberry Farm on the left, they rounded the corner and headed down the dark hill to the farmer's house at the bottom.

The man punched in the passcode and watched the iron gate swing open slowly. A couple of cows at the edge of the woods on the other side of the cove stirred and mooed at the disturbance. The man stopped and turned to see if he had awakened anyone in the farmer's house, but no light flicked on.

He glanced at the moon then started down the long, narrow road that cuts the large pasture of Mountain Homes in half. Without any headlights, his eyes adjusted quickly to the moonlit stretch of asphalt that lay before him. When he passed the tennis court and the pool, he turned left and disappeared into the forest. He maneuvered the tight tunnel of trees and found the cabin they would be using.

"I'll get our bags from the trunk. Can you grab the groceries I put in the backseat?"

"Sure," Evelyn said nervously.

As they got out of the car, they could hear the muted chatter of Hesse Creek tumbling by the long screened-in porch.

When she leaned in to retrieve a couple of food bags, she felt him hold her shoulder from behind and cover her face with a dampened cloth.

*   *   *

Langley

The next morning Ruth Gibbons turned on the speakerphone and listened to the messages on her voicemail as she poured herself a cup of Starbucks. It was the usual stuff—calls from ambassadors around the world. One from the *Post* wanting an interview with her boss for the Sunday edition. Another one from the *New York Times*. There were also messages from State Department officials wanting a moment of Drew Farley's time. Could she just work them into his schedule? It was very important.

"Yes, it always is," she mumbled to herself. "Blah, blah, blah."

But one voicemail caused her to sit up straight. She set her coffee down, punched the button on her phone and listened to it again.

"Ruth, it's Evelyn. I'm calling from home instead of the office this time. Wow! Your people work fast. One moment I'm on the phone with you, the next he's standing there in front of me!"

Ruth put both hands in front of her mouth in a motion that stopped her breath suddenly.

"Anyway," the message continued, "I've just come home to pack. He's waiting out in the car."

Ruth called her boss on the intercom. "Mr. Farley? Forgive me for interrupting your meeting, but may I speak to you?" She began to cry.

On the speakerphone, Ruth heard Farley say, "Gentlemen, excuse me for a moment. There seems to be a problem. Look over these plans. I'll be right back."

Farley found Ruth agitated when he entered her office. "What's wrong?"

"I think I may have done something terrible. You know that administrative assistant I told you about down in Maryville, Tennessee?"

"The Hastings woman?"

"Yes, that one. I'm so sorry for interrupting your meeting," said Ruth, close to a panic, "but, didn't you say you were sending someone down there to make sure she was alright?"

"Yes. Why?"

"When is he supposed to arrive?"

"Tomorrow. He's in my office right now, getting prepped."

"Oh God," whispered Ruth.

Resilience

The EL AL ticket agent asked, "Does she need a wheelchair?"

"No," said Adam, propping her up. "She needs to be on her feet for now. She can sleep on the plane."

Renie draped her arms around Adam all the way through the tunnel into the First-Class section. By the time they took off, Renie appeared to be in another world.

He watched her for a few moments. A couple of pillows engulfed her face and her firm body slouched slightly to the side. He'd put a blanket over her after take-off, but it had slipped part-way off. Carefully, he pulled it back across her bare shoulders and tucked it in.

She stirred a little, snuggling up next to him. "Hmmm…" she said, smacking her lips. A tiny line of saliva ran down her cheek. He wiped it off with the softest of touches that caused an involuntary stretch. She turned and buried the side of her face even deeper in the pillows on his shoulder, but did not wake up.

As Adam looked at her, he wondered if he could ever fall in love again. After his wife's death, he hadn't looked at another woman.

But this woman. There was something about her.

He felt connected to her somehow. But she only complicated things.

As he drifted off, the scene that swirled into his mind's eye was one of sand in the desert blowing up in his

173

face. Waves of golden granules smothered him. Then the Bedouin, dark and somber. Laughing, mocking. A gritty countenance loomed before him. That face...that mask... suffocating ...strangling him!

"Mr. Hunter? Mr. Hunter?" said the flight attendant. Adam awakened suddenly, lurching forward.

"You alright?" she said.

"Oh, sorry," said Adam. "Guess I was dreaming."

"Must have been a bad one," she smiled as she handed him a thick, manila envelope, sealed and addressed to him. "One of the EL AL officers told me to give it to you after take-off."

"Thank you."

He opened the envelope and removed the file. A memo was clipped to the front.

TO: MR. ADAM HUNTER
FROM: MOSHE
HERE IS MORE DETAIL ABOUT THE BEDOUIN.
Ammon, who is known now as Hakim, is one of the most dangerous men in the Middle East. After growing up at St. Catherine's, he moved to Cairo where he was involved in riots then spent time in the dreaded Tura prison and its torture chambers. By the age of 20, he was a hardened man. He studied law and politics at Cairo University. His training and fighting in Afghanistan prepared him for leadership in the terrorist world. He is much more powerful than Osama bin Laden ever was. We know he is planning something, but we don't know what it is. If we kill him now, we will never know the full plan and it will unfold on its own. Somehow, you and the young woman are involved. The whole thing

*hinges on the two pages of manuscript, which
remain a mystery to us. Good luck.*

Adam stared at the photographs of the Bedouin at St.
Catherine's, in Afghanistan, in Cairo, in Tripoli, in New
York City and in Washington, DC. Then, he scanned a more
detailed résumé provided by the Israelis, which offered a
clearer picture.

Still, he longed for answers. What did the manuscript
say? Why was he the one who had been chosen to interpret
it?

The plane banked for its final approach to Leonardo
da Vinci Airport as Rome spread out before him. He saw the
Dome of St. Peter's in the distance and hoped the Vatican
would provide the answers he sought.

* * *

Rome

Conrad Docherty looked out his window at the Dome of St.
Peter's. He wasn't one for religion. Never had been. Money
was his religion and the power it gave him. The Bedouin had
promised him more than he could ever imagine, which was
quite a bit since he could imagine a lot.

He remembered the first time he'd met the Bedouin
on the training grounds in Afghanistan. Conrad had taught
him and bin Laden everything the CIA had to teach. He'd
shown them how to use the enemy's own resources against
him. The Bedouin had also learned well from Conrad how to
forge strange alliances, stranger than anyone had ever
thought of before. Conrad knew he was a traitor, but he
didn't care. The money he was going to make on this one
would help him disappear and be set for the rest of his life.

He glanced at this watch. He was in Rome to check
on his investment. The key to his payday was the successful

translation of that manuscript and nothing was going to keep that from happening. Nothing.

The phone rang. Conrad answered it.

"I've got her."

"Where are you?"

"At a cabin in a place called Miller's Cove."

"Any problems?"

"None," said the man on the phone. "Piece of cake."

"How's the cabin?"

"Works. The guy who's letting me use it won't be around for quite a while. Neighbors are also traveling. The place is pretty quiet."

"The FBI may come nosing around. If you stay put, they won't find you."

"I'm not going anywhere. There are enough supplies to last for a while."

"Where is she?"

"In the bedroom, out cold."

"Remember, don't kill her. I need her alive...for now."

*   *   *

West Miller's Cove, East Tennessee

The man in the cabin went into the bedroom to check on Evelyn Hastings. She seemed so peaceful under all those covers. Too peaceful, in fact. Then he remembered he hadn't left her that way! He'd laid her on the bed, thinking the drug would keep her under for another hour or two. When he ripped back the blanket, all he saw were pillows puffed up to look like a body.

"Shit!" She couldn't have gotten far. But which direction did she go?

He ran to the long, narrow, screened-in porch and looked up and down Hesse Creek, then plowed through the back door and began wading waist-deep to other side.

Glittering trout scattered as he splashed through the water.

At the creek's edge he charged up the muddy side and ran as fast as he could straight ahead. Through a clump of trees, he looked across a shimmering meadow, wondering where she could have gone. Perhaps to the right, he thought, to stay close to the other cabins and call for help if anyone could hear her.

He charged into the meadow, breathing hard. Conrad was not one to listen to excuses. He knew he'd better find her fast.

*　　*　　*

At the top of the meadow, Evelyn crouched like an animal on the edge of the woods, watching her kidnapper move in her direction. Her dress was drenched, her body soaked, her wrists reddened from the ropes she'd worked loose when she escaped. Wheezing like her old coffee pot, she wondered if she would ever catch her breath. When she saw him move to her left away from her, she collapsed on crunched bark next to a tall poplar. Scraping grime from her bottom with her bare hands, she glanced up the incline into a matted tangle of undergrowth.

There was no trail. It was one of the denser sections of virgin forest, straight-trunked grandeur everywhere. She couldn't retreat across the meadow. This was her only way out. Her goal was to get to a road—any road that could take her back to Maryville. She looped back in the direction she thought was toward home, making a wide arc through the forest. She studied her feet, wondering how long her pumps would last, then began clawing her way up the brow of the hill. "I hate the woods," she muttered to herself.

She heard a sound and looked back. He had turned and started her direction again, moving like an animal on a hunt. He was the hunter and she the prey. He was only fifty yards away and closing fast!

Papal Splendor

R enie shifted from one foot to the other. "What do I say? How do I act? I've never even seen a Bishop or an Archbishop, much less a Cardinal or a Pope! No offense, but you're the highest level of clergy I've ever talked to."

She could tell Adam's mind seemed to be somewhere else, perhaps on the manuscript.

"Adam, are you listening to me?"

He'd stopped and made several copies of the document in case something happened to the original, his first chance to do so since obtaining it.

"Adam, have you thought what's going to happen when the Pope thinks we're just stirring up trouble, thanks us, sends us packing and then destroys it?"

"We still have the copies."

"What good is that if you don't have the original?"

"Look, if we can't trust the Pope, who can we trust?"

Renie de-coded and changed the subject, perusing the opulent papal quarters. "Imagine the overhead to keep this place going." She drummed her fingers. "My administrative assistant probably thinks I've really lost it, telling the judge to ask for all those delays and continuances. The very idea that I would just up and..."

The Pope's priest-secretary interrupted, "The Holy Father will see you now."

Renie took a deep breath.

As they walked through the massive doors into the

audience library, she was struck by the size of the room. Three large windows to the left opened onto St. Peter's Square. Friezes and bas-reliefs rose high on the walls. A Barcelona chair accompanied a massive sixteenth century desk on the right. Pearl-like marble floors with large brown squares, spaced in geometric formation, spread out before them. Fifteenth century paintings adorned creamy velour walls. At one end of the room, large bookshelves filled with white volumes surrounded elegant, ivory-tinted chairs with upholstered arms and cabriole legs, strategically placed on an enormous Persian rug. A plushy silence pervaded the room.

Renie whispered in Adam's ear, "Am I supposed to curtsey or something?"

"Be yourself. He'll like you just the way you are." His tone had softened, as if to say he did. She wondered if she would ever figure him out. Eric had been the strong, silent type too, but Adam was different somehow, more mysterious and certainly more dangerous. He seemed to smother a deep hurt beneath all that silence. She wondered if he would ever tell her what it was, or if she really wanted to know. Some things are better left unsaid.

When she turned, there he stood in all his glory, white cassock and sash, and her with nothing but a skirt and blouse. She'd wanted to go shopping, but Adam had said not to worry about it—clothes wouldn't matter to the Pope. But now, standing before the head of global Catholicism without a jacket was like visiting God in your underwear, she thought. She felt naked.

"Miss Ellis, Mr. Hunter," he said in a manner that put everyone at ease. His voice was strong and tender. "What an honor it is for me to meet you both." He took Renie's hand first, enveloping it in his.

Renie froze. She tried to say something but nothing came.

The Pope merely smiled then tried to remove his

hand from hers. Realizing she had not let go only added to her embarrassment. But something about him made her want to hold on.

"The honor is ours, Your Holiness," Adam said, extending his own hand.

"Come, let us have a seat. Would you care for refreshment?"

"No thanks, we're fine." Adam guided a dazed Renie behind the Pope. Barely touching the small of her back, he positioned a chair behind her.

"A glass of water would be nice," she interjected, taking her seat.

"Of course," said the Pope without summoning anyone. Renie had the sense that the order would be carried out, as if the walls had ears. "They tell me you are from a town called Maryville, is that how you say it?"

"That's close enough," said Adam.

"MA-RY-VILLE." The Pope, sounded it out slowly. "Imagine that. A whole town named after the Virgin. What a grand idea!"

"I'd never really thought of it that way." Renie felt the tension go out of her shoulders and her face.

"Not sure anybody there ever has," Adam said.

"Perhaps they can now." The Pope, warmed the room with his gentle smile.

Renie nodded, amazed at how he had put her at ease.

The assistant appeared with a tray and poured glasses of water for all three from a Waterford crystal decanter.

"Your name is Irene."

"Yes."

"We have a Saint Irene from the fourth century. Even before that, Irene was one of the most beautiful names in the Roman Empire."

"I told you I would like coming to this place," Renie said to Adam.

"So, you are an attorney? Harvard-trained, I'm told."

"That's correct...Your Holiness," she replied, pleased she remembered the right title.

"Fine school. And you are here representing Mr. Hunter?"

"Oh..." The question startled her. She peeked at Adam who gave her a tiny nod. "Well, yes, you could put it that way. I'm his attorney in this matter."

"That's wise." He turned to Adam. "It appears that you have hired the best."

"The very best," replied Adam, throwing a glance Renie's direction. She was surprised by Adam's sudden warmth.

"And you are a Protestant pastor."

"Yes, Your Holiness."

"But you have not always done this. Mid-life crisis? Is that how you say it in your country?"

"You might put it that way."

"I believe Saint Paul had one of those."

Renie watched Adam recoil at the comparison to the first century murderer-turned-clergy.

"And what did you do before you found your true calling?"

"I worked for the government."

Renie saw Adam shift in his chair.

The Pope seemed omniscient, knowing everything about them. Almost everything. He was far from the old fool Renie had imagined him to be. "But you are here to show me a manuscript you have found."

"Well, I didn't exactly find it."

"Oh?" said the Pope.

"It was given to me, at least the first page was."

"There are more pages?"

"Yes, Your Holiness, there are two."

"How did you acquire the second one?"

"I had to go to a monastery in Sinai to find it."

"Ah, like Tischendorf!"

Adam raised his eyebrows.

"My degree was in New Testament here at the Gregorian."

"Then you are familiar with St. Catherine's?"

"I went there twice when I was a priest, even climbed the old mountain. Beautiful, isn't it?"

"Breathtaking."

The Pope smiled, staring off into space as if in another world for a couple of moments. "But that was a long time ago," he said, snapping back to reality. "Why didn't you take this manuscript to the Patriarch in Istanbul? A little more his jurisdiction, wouldn't you agree?"

"I am supposed to bring it you, Holy Father, and to you only. You know, I tried to get one of these pages to you before."

The Pope's brow wrinkled. "Giovanni was your contact?"

"I'm afraid so. Someone doesn't want you to see these pages."

The Pope nodded slowly. "Do you have them with you now?"

Adam opened his knapsack and removed the two pages, looking a little crumpled after all they had been through. He paused before handing them to the Pope. "You are not afraid of what the manuscript might say?"

"Why should I be? If the message is authentic, I need to listen to it. If it isn't, then we have nothing to worry about, right? Besides, I have been looking for a sign in the new Millennium."

Adam handed him the pages.

The Holy Father slid a pair of golden reading glasses halfway down his nose and peered over the top as he probed the first page.

Adam and Renie fell silent. Not a breath between them. Only the rustle of crisp vellum crackled softly as the Pope drew the page close to his eyes.

For a long time, he said nothing. Finally, he spoke. "Greek uncials?"

"Yes, Your Holiness," replied Adam.

"Like *Sinaiticus*?"

"The same."

"It's more difficult to translate with no break between the letters, isn't it?"

Adam nodded in agreement.

"Why do you suppose they did it that way?" Renie asked.

"Perhaps to conserve space," said the Pope. "These vellum pages were precious in their day. Animal skins to be exact, and they didn't want to waste even a millimeter of them." He removed his half-moon spectacles slowly. "Have you translated any of it, yet?"

"Only pieces here and there," Adam said.

"Any idea what it is says?"

"Something about leaders coming together."

The Pope's eyes sparkled like diamonds. "I like the sound of that. Show me what you've discovered so far."

Adam moved around to the Pope's chair. "Well, I'm not an expert, but I think if you look there you will catch the word *kingdom*. There. ΒΑCΙΛΕΙΑ *Basileia*. Do you see it?"

The Pope returned his glasses to the bridge of his nose and peered closely. "Yes, I do." He sounded it out slowly, syllable by syllable, "BA-SI-LEI-A. Yes, I see it!" The Pope was pleased with himself. "Show me another one, *per favore!*"

Before Adam could speak, the Pope interrupted, "Wait, I think I see one!"

"May I look, too?" Renie asked.

"Of course!" the Pope said like a child with a new toy. "Come, stand next to me."

Renie moved to his side and watched him point a bony index finger at the beginning of a line. "See, there?"

"You mean, the one that starts with a K?" Renie asked.

"Yes, that's the one. Do you see it, Mr. Hunter?"

"I do now."

"Do you know the word?"

"I believe so," Adam said.

"Let me take a guess," Renie said.

Both of them looked at her, surprised.

"Be my guest, Miss Ellis!" said the Pope.

"Well, I'm not sure, but I studied some Russian in college, and I know there's a connection between Greek and Russian with the Cyrillic alphabet. If I remember correctly, what looks like a P there is probably an R. In Greek I believe you call it a *rho*. And I'm certain that the 'I' there is just an I in Greek. From sorority days I remember we called it an *iota*. Then you've got a couple of C's there. Let's see, those are probably *sigmas,* which means an S. I don't know if the word goes on further or not since there's no break, but my guess is it's the word *crisis*."

"Marvelous scholarship, young woman!"

Renie saw amazement cross Adam's face.

"And," she continued, "if memory serves me correctly, one of the little-known synonyms for crisis is *judgment*."

"*Si! Si!*" the Pope said. "*Krisis* means judgment." He looked at Adam and added, "Mr. Hunter, you have hired an extremely intelligent attorney. Splendid, Miss Ellis! Do you think you could pick out another?"

"If I had a little time..."

"Actually, I think we've probably been here long enough, Your Holiness," Adam said. "Perhaps we could come back after you have considered the possibility of putting some of your best scholars to work translating it."

"Yes. I have another engagement in a few minutes. Let's meet at 1:00 tomorrow afternoon."

"Should we leave the manuscript with you?" Adam

asked.

"Well, I could consign it to the Prefect of the Vatican Library, Giuseppe Giacomo, or perhaps Cardinal Angelo Biondi in charge of the Sacred Congregation for the Doctrine of the Faith. I could give it to Cardinal Carbonari. He's the one I trust the most." He thought for a moment or two. "No, I think, in this case, I should keep it myself. You do have copies, don't you?"

"Yes, of course." Adam handed the crinkled pages to the Pope.

"*Grazie*, Holy Father. Thank you for the time you have spent with us," Renie said.

"*Prego,* my friends. The pleasure has been mine."

The Pope turned to Renie and took her hands, "Miss Ellis, I look forward to seeing you again. Be careful out there. Rome is not altogether holy. The Lord be with you."

"And also with you," they replied, as though from the liturgy.

The Pope smiled and nodded as they departed.

Hazardous To Your Health

In the middle of the massive Piazza San Pietro, Adam scanned the crowd before proceeding. "Well, what did you think?"

"Remarkable! He's so kind," Renie replied. "I had a great time."

"Oh really? I couldn't tell."

Adam smiled at her then suddenly looked away. "Come on, let's walk to the hotel." He started across the square.

"You think it's safe?"

"We've gotten this far, haven't we?"

"Barely," she replied.

*   *   *

From high above St. Peter's at the top of Michelangelo's dome, Marcello had them both in his sights. First, he aimed at Renie, then at Adam. Switching back and forth, he focused the crosshairs of his Steyr-Mannlicher SSG P-IV rifle, a 308-caliber two-piece with a telephoto lens and a silencer. The red laser dot appeared at the base of Renie's bobbing skull.

*   *   *

Adam saw a red dot bouncing on the back of Renie's neck and ducked instinctively, yanking her to the ground. The Sicilian's shot missed by inches as it glanced off the pavement, chips of stone flying from the sparks.

A handful of people around them scattered, some screaming as they ran.

Pigeons flew in all directions.

Tourists took cover, scampering in ever-widening circles as if a pebble had been tossed in a lake.

Adam grabbed Renie's hand. "Let's go!" He jerked her toward the enormous Egyptian obelisk in the center of the square, one of the remains of Caligula's Circus.

Another silent shot ricocheted near Renie's foot as they dove behind the column.

"Who's doing that?" Renie cried in a fetal position against the pillar.

"Probably the one who was after me at Sinai." Adam strained to see where the bullets had come from. Glancing up at the dome, he caught the reflection from the rifle.

The next shot hit the huge fountain to Adam's left.

He squinted into the light to catch a glimpse of what was happening on top of the dome.

Then he saw the struggle between two men. His assailant hung off the edge of the wall. His rifle dropped and clanked down the outside of the great dome. The man almost went with it, but Adam saw him push his opponent back and crawl over the wall to safety. A fight ensued. Fists. Feet.

"What's happening up there?" Renie yelled.

"Looks like we have a guardian angel," Adam said, straining to see. He heard tourists screaming. From what Adam could see, the assassin seemed to be taking a beating.

*   *   *

"Are you hurt, Signor?" said one of the gendarmes to Marcello as he helped him up.

"No," said Marcello. "That man was firing at someone down below. I tried to stop him." He glared at the bystanders, daring them to contradict him. But no one spoke.

"What did the American mean, when he said, 'Leave

my investment alone'?" asked one of the gendarmes.

"How should I know? I was just trying to prevent a murder. He was shooting at someone down there," said Marcello.

"Who?"

"I have no idea. May I go now?"

"Yes, of course, Signor. We may need a statement from you later."

"Fine, here's my card," said the Sicilian. "I am a professor at the university." With that he headed down the stairs.

*   *   *

Berlin

Wolf Schiller, a tall, blond German, watched the shiny, black Mercedes pull up in front of him not far from the Brandenburg Gate. The dark, wet night reminded Schiller of his native Schwartzwald, the mystical Black Forest. Two guards stepped from the limo, surveyed the street then motioned to the man inside. The CEO, Helmut Oberfeld, a portly, bald gentleman, elegantly dressed in cashmere black, emerged from the car with furtive glances.

Schiller, hands in the pockets of a black trench coat, moved slowly but deliberately toward the Mercedes.

"Herr Oberfeld, may I have a word with you?"

The guards stiffened as Oberfeld turned to face Schiller.

The soft puffs of his weapons dropped each guard one by one. None of them had a chance.

Oberfeld stood alone, terror crossing his face with bodies piled around him. "I'll double whatever they are paying you!"

Schiller took two steps closer, dropped one hand then leveled the automatic in the other at Oberfeld's forehead.

One shot between the eyes finished him.

No one else was on the dark street.

Schiller holstered both weapons and retrieved his cell phone. He punched in the numbers and waited. One of the guards moaned. Schiller leaned forward, placed cold steel against the man's temple and fired.

"It's done," he said. "*Ja,* all of the them. I told you I always finish what I start."

The Hunter is Hunted

The White House

The President fidgeted.

Drew Farley sat across the desk from her.

"Drew, what have you got on Stump's death? The FBI's come up empty."

"We're working on it, Madame President, day and night. But there's nothing. It's a black hole."

The President got up from her chair, walked to the side of her desk, arms folded, staring at Farley. Farley averted her gaze. He hated it when the President looked at him like that. The tension between them had been building over the years. He knew the President had been forced to appoint him since her first two tries had miscarried in Senate confirmation hearings. He knew he was a third-choice compromise. It always smarted a little to realize he'd never be in the President's inner circle. But who was these days?

"Well, there is something more," Farley said. He shifted his massive bulk slightly in the chair. "It's about the former CIA op who's tangled with a terrorist in the Middle East."

The President hesitated then spoke. "Did we re-hire him or something?"

"No, Madame President. He's out there on his own. But there may be somebody inside pulling his strings."

"Someone in our government?"

"Looks that way."

The President didn't say anything. Farley had

forgotten how quiet it could get in the Oval Office. His armpits moistened. She turned her back and faced the curtains.

The President finally spoke. "Any ideas on how high this might go?"

"Nothing yet. Should we do something to stop him?"

"Is he a threat to our country?"

"Not that we can tell."

"Then leave him alone. Just keep an eye on him. Is that all you have, Drew?"

"Yes, Madame President."

"Have a good day," said the President, turning and offering her right hand.

Drew Farley returned a vice grip as their gazes locked. "Thank you. The same to you." He left by the door through Esther Adrian's office.

*   *   *

After Farley was gone, the President pulled the secure phone from her desk and punched in some numbers.

"Where have you been?"

"In Rome checking on our boy. Had a close call yesterday. The story of his life."

"What's he up to?"

"Working with the Pope to get that manuscript translated. It's the key to the whole plan."

"Farley was just here. He's rooting around like a backyard dog. It worries me," said the President. "If he digs too far, this whole thing could blow up in our faces."

"You want to call a halt to it?"

"Too late for that."

"What about Hunter?"

"Keep him alive, whatever you do," the President said, "at least until this is over."

The President hung up the phone and turned on the

TV. A CNN reporter was standing in the streets of Cairo. "No one has claimed responsibility for the assassinations of numerous CIA operatives throughout the Middle East. So far, the White House has not commented, but some experts believe it may be the work of an unnamed Egyptian terrorist who was connected with Osama bin Laden and is now one of the key leaders of ISIS. The President is still trying to decide whether or not to attend the upcoming peace summit in Jerusalem. Many in her Administration and Cabinet are advising against it, but Speaker of the House, Joseph Wellington, favors the President's participation. And now back to Atlanta..."

The President winced at the sound of Wellington's name. There'd never been much love lost between them since he was the leader of the opposing party in the House, a self-made man who worshiped his maker. She hit the mute button. There was no turning back now.

*   *   *

Rome

Cardinal Carbonari called Don Mazzini in the Don's suite at The Excelsior. Mazzini had just sat down to dinner for one. There were few things he loved more than eating, even sex. He swirled his linguini with his fork. He spooned a small mound of it then jammed it whole into his mouth. A few flecks of red sauce sprayed across the starched white napkin he'd tucked under his triple chin.

A servant brought him a phone.

"*Buona sera, Eminenza!*" said Mazzini with his mouth full. "What's the matter? You're all excited."

Mazzini listened carefully. "Marcello missed him again?" he said, fisting his fork, prongs upraised, slamming it on the edge of the table.

"Someone bumped him when he fired," Lorenzo

193

said. "His shot went awry."

"Did the intruder kill Marcello?"

"No. The gendarmes appeared just in time."

"Now Marcello must face me. He knows how much I hate failure...what about the other one?"

"Disappeared into the crowd on top of the dome."

"Who is he? Why would he want to save this Adam Hunter's life?"

"I don't know."

"What nationality?"

"The gendarmes tell me he's *Americano*."

"How are the Americans involved in this?"

"I have no idea. But I do know the Pope is meeting with this Adam Hunter and the young woman tomorrow to discuss the translation of the manuscript. There is nothing we can do to stop it now."

"Not to worry, *mi amico*. I have a plan that will take care of Mr. Hunter and the Pope."

"I don't even want to hear what you are thinking," Lorenzo said.

"But first, we must get Marcello's attention. Perhaps, some healthy competition will bring out the best in him."

"I told you," Lorenzo replied. "I don't want to know."

When Mazzini hung up, he called to his servant.

"*Si, Don Mazzini.*"

"Get Wolf Schiller for me, *per favore.*"

Hating the Woods

The Foothills of the Smoky Mountains

Evelyn Hastings was a sopping mess. She'd never felt so grimy in all her life. She'd spent the night in the forest and was tired, hungry, and cold. She'd slept on the ground for the first time in her life. At least, she'd tried to sleep. She'd hated camping, even dropped out of Girl Scouts because of it. Her mother had made her do Tremont for a week. She cried the first half and begged to be sent home the second.

The sounds of the timberland kept her awake half the night. She could see where wild pigs had been rooting around searching for food. She thought about bears that had become so bold they'd even been sighted in town near the college. She remembered wolves had been introduced in the park to decrease the number of coyotes she'd heard howling and yipping the night before. And snakes! Someone had just died of snakebite two nights before. God knows what else! "Varmints," folks in the cove called them. The mere sound of the word made her cringe.

Her feet ached. She was soaked to the bone, and scared.

The sun tried to force its way through the thicket but, like a solar eclipse, the forest blocked its rays. Evelyn estimated it must be midday, but couldn't tell because she'd lost all sense of time. She'd found water when she crossed Hesse Creek again but felt herself weakening rapidly and had no idea how far she'd walked.

She began to wonder if she'd been going in circles. "Didn't I pass that hemlock tree a few hours ago?" she asked herself—the one with the broken limb that hung limp like a dead man's arm. She kept looking over her shoulder to see if he had followed, but there was no sign of him, thank God. Who was he and why had he taken her? How did all this relate to Adam and Renie?

She got her hopes up when she stumbled across an old logging road, but it dead-ended into Flat Creek. Now she knew for sure she was lost. The more she walked, the weaker she got. One of her heels had come off but she didn't know where. She tripped over hidden roots and snarls of undergrowth. She learned the hard way not to step on wet logs or the grayish-green lichen that grew on them. Heavy spring rains and floods had downed many trees. Tulip poplars and pines looked like tall, wiry men dancing in the breeze—thousands of them, moving in rhythm. They reached out for her. Branches grabbed at her as she tried to rush through them. They slapped her face, her arms, her breasts, her legs. They would not let her go. The faster she walked the more they spanked her. Her body was a battlefield of tiny abrasions.

An omnipresent numbness set in.

She plopped down in a patch of shiny galax leaves to catch her breath, then lay still and listened. Flat Creek murmured the sounds of the ages. She thought there might even be a waterfall nearby. Polished granite rocks, worn smooth by centuries of sand and water, glistened in the shallow stream. She inhaled the damp sweetness of decayed vegetation. It was moldy and musty like the old mountains themselves. Out of old death came new life, she thought. She hated admitting it, but the woods she detested provided the camouflage she needed to stay alive. Fiddleheads would eventually unfurl into ferns and Solomon's seal would again hide its beauty. Just the thought of it gave her hope.

She got up and began running through the trees.

Some old roads and trails would appear and then vanish. She plowed up a draw that she hoped would be a way to get to the top of the adjacent ridge. She didn't care how much the trees and the rhododendron and saw briers cut her. She didn't even feel the pain anymore. She just wanted to get out of those woods, to the top of that ridge. Back to civilization, to her home, her life, no matter how meager it was. It was her life, by God! She sprinted now with every ounce of energy left in her body...and floated as if in an awful dream. Maybe she was losing her mind she thought and laughed out loud. She slowed as the incline increased.

Then it started to rain.

First a drop, then a pitter, then a patter. A mist. A drizzle. The soft soaker turned to a steady shower. Then came the cloudburst. The downpour. She remembered how in Texas they'd call it a gully washer. "Great!" she laughed. "This is my life, from bad to worse!" She shook a defiant fist at the torrent that pounded down upon her. A million drops pelted her face and filled her mouth. She drank greedily as she wiped the back of her hand across her face.

She turned to catch a glimpse of a marvelous sight...at first, only a glimmer, then a tiny shaft of light, barely visible amidst the driving rain. She didn't care about the thundershower any more. She focused every ounce of energy on getting to the hint of incandescence that grew before her. She wanted to merge with it, bury herself in it. She wanted to disappear into it.

There, in the middle of a storm, the gentle glow spilled upon her as if heaven itself had opened to accompany everything it had just dumped on the land. Then she began running again, picking up the pace now, her enthusiasm catapulting her up the side of the hill.

The mass of light spread as she scraped and crawled like a wild pig through the brush. At the top, she burst through the last bramble branches like a football team through a paper banner at the beginning of a Friday night game at Maryville High. She almost flew out onto the highway.

"Yes!" she cheered as she smeared the spit and dirt across her face. She got her bearings, looking both directions. "Wait a minute, I know this road," she announced to the air. "It's the Foothills Parkway." Now I can hitch a ride back into town, she said to herself, ambling along the asphalt somewhere between a limp and a hobble.

There weren't many cars but every single one slowed as they approached her, then accelerated and whizzed on by no matter how much she thumbed or waved. Some of them swerved to miss her. Others held their ground and forced her off the road. Most of them honked, streaking the silence with a long-drawn-out whine.

I must look a fright, she realized as she wiped grit and smudge from her body and pushed a hand across her mop of hair. As she got bolder, she tried to stand in front of them to wave them down. Still, they didn't stop.

When she grew tired of walking, she plopped down in a tangled heap by the side of the road, exhausted. I can't go another step, she said to herself.

More cars passed by.

"Why won't someone stop?!" she said punch-drunk, and started to sob.

Then, to her surprise, one of the cars pulled over onto the dead grass right in front of her. She tried to get up, but couldn't budge.

"Don't move, ma'am," said the man, coming around from the driver's side. "I'll help you up."

"Are you an angel?" she whimpered.

"Hardly!" said the man, laughing. "What happened to you?"

"It's a long story. I just need to get home."

"What's your name?"

"Evelyn Hastings."

He paused for a beat. "Oh…really?"

"Do I know you?"

"No. I just thought...what a nice name."

"Well, thank you," said Evelyn, relieved that someone had finally stopped to pick her up. He was so strong that he lifted her with no trouble despite the extra pounds she'd put on recently.

"I'll make a mess of your car," she said.

"Don't worry. I've got a big plastic tarp in the trunk. You can sit on that."

"You've thought of everything," she said with the hint of a smile.

"Here, let me help," said the man, taking her arm.

Evelyn stepped carefully into the large Buick and let him strap her in. Wonder where he's from, she thought, pulling her fingers over her matted hair to push it to one side, knowing she must look a fright.

"Where do you live, Ms. Hastings?"

"In Maryville. Just follow this road down to the bottom of the hill, angle right and turn left at the stop sign. That will take you right into town," she said. "You from around here?"

"No, from up north, in the D.C. area."

"Oh."

She sighed as he pulled back onto the road.

"You must have been through something awful," said the man. "Hungry?"

"I could eat a horse."

"No need for that," he chuckled. "I think there's a little convenience store up here around the corner. Surely, they'll have something."

"Yes, that sounds great." Her head fell back on the headrest.

When he came to Lamar Alexander Parkway, he turned right instead of left.

Evelyn leaned forward. "Oh, did I say right? I meant left. This isn't the way to Maryville. It's the way to

Townsend."

"I know," said the man. His nice smile had disappeared. "We're going for a hike."

More Than Life Itself

In the country outside Moscow

The dinner that night was a grand affair. Sasha, Vladimir and Boris were on their best behavior as they entertained the wealthiest woman they had ever met.

Anastasia Paleologos fell in love with Boris Gromilov's dacha by the Moskva River. It was even more elegant than her Rosedale mansion in Toronto. The rich architectural detail, the intricately carved wood, the tromp l'oeil in the ceilings and the gilded beauty of the place made her want to buy it on the spot.

"A lovely home, Mr. Gromilov," she said, sipping the vodka a servant had brought her. Ian McPherson and two of his mercenaries never drank on the job. Nothing but *kompot,* the Russian fruit drink, for them.

"That was a marvelous meal. But you didn't have to serve me dinner. I would have bought the manuscript anyway," said Anastasia.

"I thought it only the civil thing to do," Boris said. "To capitalism, profit and good fortune!" he said, raising his glass. Everyone joined him.

Anastasia lifted her goblet for the next toast. "To tradition, heritage and sound investments!" Glasses clinked all around the room.

"Let us retire to the veranda."

"Excellent idea," Vladimir said, lighting a cigar.

All were offered a cup of tea.

"Now to business," said Sasha with a flourish. "I

believe we have something you want."

"And I have something you want," Anastasia said.

"Bring it in." Sasha motioned to one of Boris' assistants.

Anastasia thought about all the times she'd seen *Codex Sinaiticus* in the British Museum and later in the British Library. All the times she had dreamed of holding it in her own hands.

When an assistant laid it before her, at first, she sat and stared at it.

"Go ahead," Sasha said, "touch it; it won't incinerate you."

"This is a moment to savor," Anastasia replied.

"We're not talking sex—this is only an old book, for God's sake," said Sasha with an edge in her voice.

"Aleksandra," Boris said. "Let the woman enjoy herself. She's paying a lot for this glimpse of eternity."

"Such passion, Borya," Sasha said.

Anastasia leaned forward, lifted the massive volume slowly, and pressed it to her breast, then sighed.

"Is she going to buy it or make love to it?" whispered Sasha to Vladimir.

Hardly anyone breathed as she opened the book and stared at the first page of the Gospel of John. She seemed to be in another world.

Sasha crossed her leg, her foot swaying back and forth.

Finally, Anastasia spoke. "This is the most beautiful thing I have ever seen." She motioned to Ian McPherson, who left the room.

"Where's he going?" Sasha asked.

"To get the manuscript expert we brought along. You didn't think I'd buy it without verifying it, do you?"

"Of course, not," Boris said.

Ian McPherson entered with Oliver Stratton, the stiff looking professor from Clare College, Cambridge

University whom Adam had met at St. Catherine's. He appeared to everyone out of place, but not out of his league when it came to old manuscripts.

"Professor Stratton, meet Aleksandra Beserdechnaya, Boris Gromilov and General Vladimir Kulikov."

"Delighted," he said nervously, shaking their hands.

"Here is the manuscript," Anastasia said. "Would you examine it, please?"

The professor took one look and gasped. "Madam, you did not tell me. How did you get it?"

"It wasn't stolen from the Library on St. Pancras, but from the British Museum when it was on loan for a few weeks recently."

The Cambridge don looked puzzled. "But no one has reported a robbery."

"That's because they don't know it's gone. Remember, your fee will provide for all your research and a more comfortable life. Just identify this manuscript then remain silent when you return to England," Anastasia said firmly.

"But if the authorities find out...I mean it will be hard to keep this a secret. I'm amazed they haven't reported it yet."

"A facsimile was put in its place," said Vladimir.

"It would have to be a very good one."

"It is," said Boris.

"It will be hard for me to keep quiet about this."

"Let me tell you how you can," Sasha said with a cold-blooded stare. "Listen carefully. If you talk about this to anyone, I will personally have you killed, then your children and all your grandchildren. Is that clear enough?"

Stratton's knees buckled, and the color drained from his face. "Who are these people, Mrs. Paleologos?"

"You can see for yourself," Anastasia said without flinching. "Now, will you please identify this manuscript?"

Stratton glanced around the room and saw everyone looking directly at him. His hand shook as he removed the magnifying glass from his vest pocket and bent over the old book. He stared at it for a few moments then turned the pages. He picked it up and examined the rough cover.

Finally, he announced, "This is the original *Codex Sinaiticus*. 4th century CE."

"That's what I wanted to hear," Anastasia said. "Thank you, Professor. That will be all. You may go home now and enjoy your research and all the money you have made. You are now a very wealthy man."

"And," Sasha added, "may your children and your grandchildren live long and happy lives."

The professor dabbed his brow with a handkerchief and left the room with the help of Ian McPherson.

Not one to mince words, Anastasia announced, "The agreement has been made. We will take it with us now. When our plane lands safely in Tel Aviv, your money will be wired to your account. One billion dollars, American."

"How do we know you won't double-cross us?" Sasha asked.

"Because I know you will find me and kill me if I do."

Boris smiled. "I like the way you do business, Madame Paleologos. No lawyers. No written contracts. Not even a handshake. We take you at your word."

"Thank you for a most wonderful evening," Anastasia said, smiling. With that, she led her troupe out the front door with Ian McPherson carrying the *Codex Sinaiticus* under his arm.

When they had left, Sasha said, "Can you believe she paid that much for a devilish old book?"

"You'll never understand a woman like that," Boris said, wistfully.

The Bigger They Come

The Vatican

Cardinal Carbonari, vested in buttoned-black soutane with scarlet skullcap and crimson sash, dipped his head as Adam and Renie entered the papal library.

"Mr. Hunter? Miss Ellis? How good to meet you. I'm sorry, but the Pope has been delayed momentarily," said Lorenzo. "Would you like some refreshment?"

"No thank you, Eminence," Adam said. There was something he didn't like about the Cardinal. Perhaps it was the saccharine tone in his voice. Renie's face gave the same response. Adam had learned to read her body language and could tell she did not warm to the old cleric.

Lorenzo waved them to a group of large Florentine chairs.

"So," said Lorenzo, "you have discovered a manuscript."

"Well, I didn't find it, exactly," countered Adam.

"I see," Lorenzo said. He steepled his fingers in a pretense of prayer. "Then how did you come by it?"

"It was given to me."

"May I ask by whom?"

"A Bedouin peasant in an Egyptian monastery."

"How mysterious." Lorenzo's black eyes narrowed to slits. "Why have you brought it to the Holy See?"

"I don't know," Adam said.

A tiny smirk appeared on Lorenzo's face. "You were told to bring it here, but you have no idea why?"

205

"Am I hearing an echo?"

"Sounds more like you are hearing voices, Mr. Hunter," Lorenzo said.

"All I know is I'm supposed to bring this manuscript to the Pope."

Lorenzo changed his tack. "You are a Protestant, are you not?"

Adam hesitated, wondering what direction this line of questioning would take them. He looked at the door, wishing the Pope would arrive. "Yes."

"Do you believe in visions?"

"Visions?"

"I'm wondering if you have seen a vision of some kind. Not something Protestants do very often."

Adam stiffened. "All I know is I have this manuscript. And I've risked my life getting it here. And I want the Pope's help finding out what it says."

"How do you think the Pope can help you?"

"By gathering scholars who can translate this thing."

"What makes you think he will?"

"I can only hope."

Adam felt the heat of the Cardinal's penetrating gaze. "Could I see the document?"

"I only have copies. The Pope has the original." The moment he said it, Adam wished he hadn't. Never tell more than you have to—the CIA had taught him that long ago. But the seminary had taught him the opposite. He felt his worlds colliding.

Reluctantly, Adam offered one of his copies to Lorenzo.

The Cardinal held it at arm's length. "Interesting."

"That's upside-down," Renie said. It broke the ice a little as she smothered a laugh, and Adam finally smiled.

"Yes, of course," said the Cardinal, a dash of red brushing his sunken cheeks. Seething, he turned it over and held it to the light, doing his best to recover his composure.

"Renzo, you have met my friends," the Pope said, suddenly striding through the door.

"Yes, Holy Father." They all stood.

"What a pleasant young couple they are." The Pope moved toward them at a good clip.

"*Si*, Your Holiness," said Lorenzo, grinding his teeth through a grin.

"Everyone, sit, please," said the Pope. "I see you have a copy of the manuscript? Amazing, isn't it?"

"*Si*, Holy Father. We were just discussing the merits of reading it. I was about to tell them that you would not approve of scholars translating these two little pages because the Vatican would not be interested. Isn't that right, Holy Father?"

Adam and Renie held their breath as the Pope pondered a question that seemed to hang in the air forever.

Finally, he spoke, "Yes..."

The Cardinal's cracked face broke into the beginnings of a smile.

"Yes, Lorenzo...ordinarily. But in this case, I do want to know what the manuscript says. I want scholars to translate and exegete it. And I want you to be in charge."

The Cardinal sputtered, "But, Your Holiness, there is so much on my schedule now. The Austrian delegation next week, the..."

The Pope raised his hand in interruption.

"I have already put Cardinal Pirandello in charge of that. You must clear your calendar. I want you to focus all your efforts on this project. I want Cardinal Biondi to help you. There is a gathering of text scholars from around the world at the Gregorian right now. Here is a list of their names." He handed it to Lorenzo, then another copy to Adam and Renie who quickly scanned down the page. Adam recognized the names.

"Put them on it right away. It should not take them long to translate it."

Adam could hear the resolution in the Holy Father's voice.

The Cardinal's face crinkled like a medieval parchment. "But, Holy Father, I have no skill as a scholar. I am not the right one for this high and holy assignment. I can't read a word of it!"

"Ah yes, but I don't want you to read it. I only want you to administer its translation. Your gifts are in plotting and planning. Besides, who can I trust more than you, old friend?" said the Pope. "You are now in charge of gathering the team of scholars for the translation of this manuscript."

Adam thought the Cardinal needed resuscitation. His face had lost what little color it had left. All he could muster was, "I am honored, Holy Father...that you would entrust to me such a sacred task. Shall I keep the manuscript until the scholars arrive?"

The Pope thought for a moment, glancing at Adam and Renie. "No, Renzo. I have secured it in a safe place. The scholars can work from the copy. Have duplicates made for them."

Turning to Adam and Renie, the Pope said, "I want to thank you for bringing the manuscript to me. I know it has not been easy for you."

"I had no other choice," Adam said.

"It has been our honor, Your Holiness," Renie added. Adam smiled at her as a thank-you for rescuing his blunt retort.

"Perhaps when the scholars begin translating, we will understand why," said the Pope. "Day after tomorrow, would you return again a little before noon? I would like for you to be my guests when I deliver the Angelus and bless the people from the window."

"We'd love to," Renie said.

"Where are you staying?" asked the Pope.

Renie answered, "A little place called Albergo del Sole."

Adam frowned wishing she hadn't told them.

"Oh," said the Pope, "Not very far from here."

"Yes, I know exactly where it is," said the Cardinal with a nod and a smile.

Dropping the Mask

The Cardinal had never seen *il Papa* look so radiant, so alive. He wondered what the manuscript had to do with it. He wondered what it said as he glanced at the Greek uncials while crossing the *Cortile San Damaso*.

He entered his palatial office suite and called Don Mazzini.

"So, you have a copy, the Pope has the original, and they have the only other copies?" Mazzini said.

"Si."

"When Schiller takes them out, he can get their copies. Destroy yours. With Hunter dead and no one to corroborate the Pope's story, he will look like a fool. You will have nothing to worry about."

"I'm afraid that would be too obvious. I will have to make copies for the scholars or the Pope will get suspicious. He's invited the two Americans to come for his noonday blessing day after tomorrow. I'm worried about what he's going to do."

"The Pope will speak from his window at noon, two days from now?"

"Si. Why do you ask?"

"I would like to come and hear him."

"You don't want to be up here with us, do you?" asked the Cardinal nervously.

"Of course not. I will be on the piazza with the faithful," Mazzini said. "Where will you be standing when he speaks?"

"In the background, as always," the Cardinal said.

"How far back?"

"Out of sight. Why?"

"Oh, no reason, just curious," said the Don. "So, he wants you to assemble the scholars?"

"*Si*. He has already chosen them. They are here for a conference. I worry about what they will discover."

"Leave everything to me," said the Don.

* * *

Don Mazzini said to his servant, "I want to see him now." The servant nodded and left the room.

Wolf Schiller, former GSG9, one of the toughest anti-terrorist teams in the world, strutted into Mazzini's palatial suite. The tall, blond, broad-shouldered German, looking like chiseled marble, stood at attention, still as a statue.

Vicenzu Mazzini paced around him in a measured gait. "Ordinarily, I don't go outside the family, but they tell me you are the best."

"I always finish what I start."

"You have three assignments. The first two are lethal, highly trained. The third one is a puppy but more closely guarded than the President of the United States."

Schiller looked straight ahead. "When do I begin?"

"Tonight."

* * *

Renie knocked on the door to Adam's room. It was slightly ajar.

"It's open."

She entered slowly.

He lay face down on the bed, shirtless. His shoulder wound had nearly healed.

"You're dead tired, aren't you?"

211

"I've felt better," Adam mumbled. He didn't move a muscle.

She took in his room in a single glance. Bed. Chair. Sink. Wardrobe. Bathroom down the hall. Exactly like hers.

"Mind if I sit down?" she asked.

"Be my guest."

She sat on a chair next to the bed.

"Why this place?"

"Didn't want to attract attention."

"Something you learned in your other life?"

Adam said nothing.

"Tell me about your other life." She leaned forward, staring at his strong back.

"It's not worth telling."

"Ever kill anyone?"

Adam paused before he spoke. "Can I take the Fifth on that one, counselor?"

"You don't have to answer. You already have."

Adam didn't reply.

"What does it feel like?" she said, her heart pounding.

"Why is it so important to you?"

"Because someone killed my fiancé."

She watched Adam go up on one elbow, cradling his head in his hand. She saw both sadness and tragedy in his empty gaze.

"All I want to know is what would make a person do something like that?" Tears swam in her eyes. She felt him peeking deep into her soul.

"You really want to know?"

She nodded, wiping her eyes with the back of her hand. Her body slumped in his direction. She focused on his face, his mouth.

"At first," he started in slow, measured phrases, "it's terrifying. You think you can't do it. Then you do it because you have to, because you're ordered to do it. It's him or

212

you…the first time's the hardest."

He glanced away suddenly. She wondered why he couldn't look at her.

"Then the second, the third. Pretty soon you lose count and stop thinking about it. Sometimes you get a rush from it. Then…you feel nothing."

Renie wondered if this was the same man she'd heard preach from the pulpit in Maryville. She shuddered at how cold he seemed. Like ice.

"That's the way it was in Somalia," he said. A deep sadness filled his voice. "You tell yourself you're doing it for your country. You don't think about them as real people with girl-friends or families. They're animals, numbers, things." His calmness unnerved her. "They are the enemy."

Renie crossed her legs and turned away from him, mesmerized and terrified. She marveled at his tranquil demeanor. She wanted him to stop. Yet she wanted him to go on. Why had she followed him? Why did she want him now more than ever?

"Pretty soon," continued Adam, "that feeling comes over you …"

She waited.

"…like you're God, determining life and death. One moment the person is there, the next…all because of you. You change history with one squeeze of a trigger." He pantomimed it as he pointed at her.

Trembling, she gazed into his black eyes. How empty, she thought. How sad. Too much hurt for my words to heal. When am I ever going to know the real you, Adam Hunter?

"It's the most incredible feeling," he concluded, looking right through her.

They fell silent again.

"Why did you stop?" she asked. He looked away. "Something happened, didn't it? Something awful. Whatever it was, you can tell me."

His eyes moistened, bringing a sudden tenderness to them.

"Move over," she said. She lay beside him as he turned and rolled on his back, staring at the ceiling. She put her head on his shoulder and draped her arm across his chest softly. "It's alright now," she said, gently running her hand across his heart.

For a minute or two there were no words between them.

He stroked her hair. "Why are you here?"

"I don't know." Her face pressed against his chest, her lips barely grazing his skin. "I had to come."

She lifted her head and looked at him then rubbed a finger just beneath his lower lip. He smiled at her in a way he had never done before and gently laid her head on his shoulder again.

They held each other for a few precious moments making her wonder if they would make love.

Then a footstep outside their door broke the spell.

Renie thought it was just someone going down the hallway, but Adam leapt from the bed, dumping her on the floor with a thump.

"I heard something," he whispered. He pulled her to her feet. "We have to go, now, come on!"

"What's going on?"

He wedged a chair under the door then grabbed the knapsack and a shirt. He yanked her to the window then jumped alone into the central atrium.

He stood ready to catch her with outstretched hands.

"I can't!" she yelled. But the sound of bullets piercing the door behind her launched her into his arms and sent the two of them tumbling across the atrium floor.

They saw the blond giant firing at them as they ran for the lobby with Adam pulling Renie behind him. Adam charged out the front door of the pensione and looked both ways. They knew they only had seconds. To the left, they could see the edge of the Campo di Fiori.

"Look out!" Renie yelled as a motor-ped ripped toward them.

Adam swept the rider off with one hand and grabbed the handle of the motor-ped with the other, pulling it to a halt. The teenaged rider skidded across the pavement and bounced off the wall on the other side, bruised and bleeding.

Adam righted the bike and hopped on as he said, "Sorry, kid!"

Renie hiked her skirt up and jumped on behind him. Adam gunned it lurching forward, scattering the crowds in the little piazza.

They could hear Wolf Schiller's shots nick the building next to them as they disappeared around the corner of Teatro di Pompeo.

Speeding up Via dei Guibonnari to freedom, Renie held on for dear life, clinging to Adam's chest. They rode through the Piazza Venezia up Via del Corso, turned right, and stopped for a moment at the Spanish Steps.

He squinted, looking up the hill. Revving the engine, Adam took off again, rounding the southern tip of the Borghese Gardens and racing up the Via Vicenzu Veneto.

He pulled in front of The Excelsior and stopped.

The wide-eyed doorman greeted them. "*Como aiutare?*"

"*Si, Grazie,*" replied Adam, handing him a wad of euros. "We're staying here. Park it somewhere, *per favore.*"

"*Si Signor!*" said the young man, staring at the huge tip.

When they walked into the lobby Renie noticed its opulent beauty—the marble floors, the Corinthian columns, the gilded look of it all.

Adam asked for and got one of their most expensive suites.

"Keep things simple, huh?" she teased.

"It's the last place they'd look for us."

*   *   *

Wolf Schiller entered Don Mazzini's palatial suite.

Mazzini peeped over the top of his newspaper. The German was a bust of himself. Mazzini spoke in a cold, dispassionate tone, but a volcanic anger bubbled just beneath his words.

"I can see it on your face," the Don said. "First Marcello. Now you. Is he really that good?"

"I will get him."

"You have two more days."

Academia At Work

A dam watched Lorenzo closely as the scholars entered the Reading Room in the Secret Archives of the Vatican Library. He had heard of most of them, read their works. It was still hard for him to believe his goatskin manuscript was to be the center of their attention that day.

The bust of Pius XI watched over the whole proceeding from the end of the room. The salon's white walls lifted to a high rounded-arch ceiling. Chalk-faced statues of saints stood guard from large niches in the wall on each side. The musty parchment smell of the old scriptorium reminded Adam of the library at St. Catherine's. A long narrow carpet divided the room into rows of ten wooden table-desks on each side.

The professors already knew each other from decades of international conferences. Most of them were editors of distinguished journals and authors of widely recognized books, monographs, articles, and reviews. There was lots of nodding and posturing as they sized each other up the way academics are wont to do.

"Thank you for coming. Please, take your seats," Lorenzo said. His greeting sounded sincere, but Adam could see his heart wasn't in it.

Everyone stood as the Pope entered the room.

"Please, be seated, my friends. I am so glad you are all here," the Pope said. "I have invited you here to translate a very important document presented to the Holy See by this gentleman, the Reverend Adam Hunter, and his friend, that is, his associate, Miss Irene Ellis. Mr. Hunter, Miss Ellis would you please stand?"

The two of them rose, dipped their heads slightly then sat down.

"*Grazie,*" continued the Pope. "None of us would be here had it not have been for the courage and persistence of these two Americans."

Adam could see the Cardinal glowering behind the Holy Father. Why the permanent scowl? Adam wondered.

"We do not yet know how old this manuscript is," said the Pope with a more serious tone, "but we believe that it was written by a monk at St. Catherine's Monastery at the foot of Mt. Sinai. People have already died because of its existence, so it is crucial for you to determine what it says. You must work quickly. Time is of the essence. My closest confidant and associate, Cardinal Carbonari, will make sure you have whatever you need. Please notice before you sealed folders with your names on them. Inside them you will find copies of the codex, which will be the object of your efforts while you are here. If there are no questions, you may begin."

After the Pope left the room, the Cardinal turned a stern stare on the group like a professor monitoring a final exam. Pens and pads of paper were stacked at each place. Spectacles and magnifying glasses appeared. All of them produced either laptops or iPads. Heads bent over the copies as a studious quiet filled the room.

Three hours passed, then four.

Hardly anyone had moved.

They had to separate the words in the manuscript since there was no break between them. Kale Debtere, the Ethiopian, was the first to smile and begin translating. Others noticed his response. Then a Czech professor jumped in with a look of delight, scratching and scribbling across the page.

"Definitely *Sinaiticus!*" muttered the Brazilian under

his breath.

The Russian woman agreed. "But how old, do you think, Alberto?" asked Yelena in Portuguese.

"Not sure," replied Santos. "Fourth, maybe fifth century. Can't tell until I review the original."

Renie tapped Adam on the arm.

"What?" Adam said, still looking at the scholars.

"What's going to happen after this?"

"Depends on what they find out."

"No, I mean what's going to happen to you and...me?"

"I don't know," stammered Adam, "guess we go back to life as usual."

"You really believe that? You think you can pick up where you left off?"

"I haven't thought that far ahead."

"Do you ever? Seriously, what are we going to do?"

"Well, we've done all we can here. I was just supposed to deliver this thing, no more."

"It's become an obsession with you, hasn't it, this manuscript?" she prodded, peering deep into his eyes. Adam didn't deny it. "More important to you than anything else."

Before he could answer, he heard the French Dominican yell something. Others joined arguing over a word or a phrase.

Lorenzo moved to the middle of the room, his hands in the air, trying unsuccessfully to bring peace.

They were on their feet, waving fists of paper in each other's faces. Fingers stabbed the air as they made their points.

Adam and Renie heard them talking about leaders of great religions coming together in Jerusalem but no one could figure out why. They were saying the syntax was simple, the vocabulary almost crude. They wondered if it had a deeper meaning.

One of them asked, "Why all this talk about hearing

a word from Sinai?"

"Because," said another, "Mohammed visited St. Catherine's and put his seal on the place. You know that. There's a mosque there to prove it."

"But who could have written it and why?" said the Czech.

"That's not our job, mates!" drawled the Australian scholar.

"Then what exactly is our job?" said the Dominican.

"It's to translate the bloody thing, no more. Leave the 'why' to the philosophers," the Aussie replied.

"I agree with Todd," said Yelena. "We can't be expected to determine its deeper meaning, that is, if it has one."

"Oh, it has one," the Ethiopian scholar said with a confident smile. "I'm sure of it."

Everyone stopped and stared at the African.

"In the meantime, the Pope has asked us for a translation. And it appears you have one. At least we have a start on one," Lorenzo said. He motioned to an aide to find the Pope.

"While we're waiting," Adam said to the scholars, "I have something to show you."

To everyone's surprise, he held up the two original pages of vellum. Lorenzo's face tightened.

Adam stood on the other side of the first table-desk and laid it out before them as they bumped and jostled to see it up close. A hush fell over the room as trained eyes skimmed the justified lines of old uncial letters on the two sepia-toned skins.

ΙΔΟΥΠΑΝΤΕCΟΙΑΝΑΓ
ΙΝωCΚΟΥCΙΤΟΥΤΟΝΗ
ΒΑCΙΛΕΙΑΤΟΥΘΕΟΥΕ
ΡΞΕΤΑΙΦΕΡωΝΕΛΠΙC
ΤωΚΟCΜωΑΛΛΑΠΡωΤ
ΟCΔΕΙΑΝΘΡωΠΟΥCΑΚ
ΟΥΕΙΝΤΗΝΑΛΗΘΕΙΑΝ
ΚΑΙΖωΕΙΝΑΥΤΗΝΟΤΕ
ΕΙCΑΝΘΡΟΠΟCΠΑCΞ
ΕΙΟΟΛΟCΚΟCΜΟCΠΑ
CΞΕΙΟΤΕΕΙCΑΝΘΡωΠ
ΟCΑΠΟΘΝΗCΚΕΙΟΟΛ
ΟCΚΟCΜΟCΛΥΠΕΙΔΕ
ΙΤΟΝΛΑΟΝΤΟΥΒΙΒΛΙΟ
ΥΜΑΝΘΑΝΕΙΝΖωΕΙΝΕ
ΝΕΙΡΗΝΗΝΗΕCΤΑΙΤΕ
ΛΕΥΤΑΙΟCΚΡΙCΙCΕΝΙ
ΕΡΟΥCΑΛΗΜωCΑΜω
CΕΙΠΕΕΝΑΥωΝΤΗΝΕ
ΘΗΝΤΟΥΗΓΕΜΟΝΟ
CΚΑΙωCΟΘΕΟCΕΙΠΕ
ΕΕΝΤωΑΙΝΙΓΜΑΤΙΤΟ
ΥΖΕΚΙΕΛΔΕΙΗΓΕΜΟΝ
ΟΥCΤΟΥΛΛΟΥΤΟΥΒΙΒ
ΛΙΟΥΕΙCΑΠΟΛΝΑΠΠΙC

ΤΕωCΚΑΙΟΙΑΡΞΟΝΤΕC
ΤωΝΕΘΝωΝCΥΝΑΓΕΙΝ
ΕΝΙΕΡΟΥCΟΛΥΜΚΑΙΑ
ΚΟΥΟΥCΙΛΟΥΟCΑΠΟ
CΙΝΑΗΜΕΓΑΛΗΟΡΟCΟ
ΠΟΥΜωΥCΗCΕΥΡΗΚΕ
ΝΤΤΟΝΘΕΟΝΟΤΕΟΚΑΙ
ΡΟCΗΛΘΕΑΚΟΥCΕΤΕ
ΛΛΛΗΛΟΥCΕΝΕΙΡΗΝΗ
ΗΞΡΟΝΙΚΟCΓΕΝΗCΕΤ
ΑΙΔΕΥΤΕΡΟCΞΡΟΝΟC
ΑΚΟΥCΕΤΕΤΗΝΦωΝΗ
ΝΤΟΥΘΕΟΥΕΝΤωΠΝΕ
ΥΜΑΤΙΑΚΟΥCΕΤΕΤΟ
ΝΛΟΓΟΝΟΝΟΘΕΟCΕΞ
ΕΙΠΑΝΤΙΤωΛΑωΤΟΥΒ
ΙΒΛΙΟΥΚΑΙΟΥΤωCΠΑ
ΝΤΙΕΘΝΕΙΚΑΙΤωΟΛω
ΟΙΚΟΥΜΕΝΗΤΟΤΕCΥ
ΝΑΧΕΕCΘΕΕΝΤΗΠΟΛ
ΕΙΤΗΑΓΙΗΙΕΡΟΥCΟΛΥ
ΜΕΠΙΤΟΥΑΥΤΟΥΞΡΟ
ΝΟΥΟΤΕΟΘΕΟCΟΙCΕ
ΙΔΙΚΑΙΑΝΚΑΙΜΕΝωΝ
ΕΙΡΗΝΗΝΕΠΙΤΗΝΓΗΝ

When the Pope walked in, they barely noticed him.

The Cardinal snapped them to attention by simply clearing his throat.

"I understand you have something for me," said the pontiff with a feathery trace of a smile. "I can hardly wait." An aide slid a chair under him.

The scholars stood in a semi-circle near the front of the room.

One at a time, they began to translate until the last sentence had been read.

Behold all who read this! The kingdom of God is coming, bearing hope to the world,

221

but first it is necessary for people to hear the truth and live it. When one man suffers, the whole world suffers. When one man dies, the whole world grieves. The People of the Book must learn to live in peace or there will be a final judgment in Jerusalem as Amos said while wearing the clothing of a leader and God announced in Ezekiel's dark saying. It is necessary for the leaders of the people of the Book, one from each faith, and the rulers of the nations to gather in Jerusalem and hear a word from Sinai, the great mountain where Moses found God. When the appointed time has come, you shall listen to each other in peace or history will happen a second time. You shall hear God's voice in the wind. You shall hear the message God has for all of the People of the Book and thus for all nations and the whole inhabited world. Then you shall gather in the Holy City of Jerusalem at the same time when God will bring a just and lasting peace upon the earth.

No one questioned anyone else's translation, which Adam thought remarkable. When the last scholar finished reading, they all looked to the Pope for some response.

He paused in thought for a moment. "It is not by accident that this manuscript has survived and been brought here for this moment. I declare that we have been assigned to fulfill the mission outlined here. Tomorrow I shall make an announcement to the faithful."

"But, Your Holiness," one scholar said, "what if there is more to this manuscript than we can see on the surface? Like a deeper meaning."

"Translate, parse, exegete all you want. If you find something more, inform me immediately. But I feel compelled now to let the world know about the manuscript and begin fulfilling what it says. Ladies, Gentlemen—Thank you again for a job well done."

The Pope took the original and left the room.

Lorenzo said, "Please return all copies of the codex and your translations of it to me. The Holy Father does not want anyone to leave the room with any record of the document. You will see it again tomorrow."

The scholars complied, grudgingly. Some of them headed for the door while others lingered to continue discussing the deeper meaning of the old text.

Adam looked around for Renie. He had completely forgotten about her in the excitement. He walked up and down the hallway searching everywhere for her, but she was gone!

PART FIVE: PREMONITION

Never Give Up

Anastasia's G800 took off from the airport in Moscow with only one new passenger. A quiet fella she noticed as she boarded the plane. She decided to ask Ian about him later. If Ian brought him on board, he must be a new member of his team.

She couldn't believe she had the *Codex* in her possession, a dream come true. She spread the volume before her, a thin membrane of cellophane protecting its old pages. Ancient Greek uncial script stared back at her.

She thought about the many monks who'd given their lives copying it, the years it had remained hidden, safe from marauding archaeologists like Tischendorf whose only real goal was fame and money.

She had no appetite. Her head ached and she felt faint. She'd only picked at her food in her private suite. Out of the ordinary for her since it was her favorite—haricots verts, Supreme de volaille with jelly and truffles, poached in butter. A French baguette. Boutari white wine from Santorini. Fresh figs for dessert.

"Ian?"

In an instant, McPherson stood by her side. "Yes, Mrs. P.?"

"Tell Andre to take it away."

"But, you've hardly touched it."

"I don't feel well. The pain in my lower back has returned."

"I thought it was in remission."

"They never promised it would last forever."

225

"Don't talk like that. You're going to see a hundred."

"What's longevity when you get stashed in a home and end up staring out a window or at the idiot box all day?"

Ian said nothing.

She grimaced as she inched toward the bed.

"Let me help you."

"Stay where you are, young man!" She held up her hand as she limped in a half-crouch to the edge of the mattress. "I hate the pain." Shaking a fist at heaven, she muttered, "If it's going to hurt like hell, I hope you take me quickly!"

Ian moved toward her.

"Another step and I'll have you thrown off this plane. I know you're good, but without a parachute?"

"I want to help you, Anastasia," he said softly. "At least, let me turn back the covers for you."

"I can do it myself, thank you."

She retreated painfully across the quilt then pulled at the covers, sorting and maneuvering them. Finally, she was under them. "There will come a day when I can't do it myself. When that day arrives, I will expect to see you and all the others waiting on me hand and foot. And I will enjoy it. Until then, leave me alone."

Ian smiled. "Let me tell the pilots to head for Toronto."

"You will do no such thing. We stay on course for Tel Aviv. You don't understand what I'm doing here, do you? I don't care if I never get back to Toronto. I don't care if I never make another dollar. None of it means anything anymore. I have found my Holy Grail, won the World Cup and the Stanley Cup all in one." She pointed at the old *Codex* on the table. "There is nothing better than this. Haven't you ever had a goal in life, Ian, one that is worth more than life itself? Well, this is that one thing for me. I'm almost there. I have two more destinations—Jerusalem to find the man who has Father Nick's manuscript, then Sinai to return this precious codex to its true home."

"You're sure?"

On her look, Ian got the message.

She fell back on her pillow. "Tell me about the new man. I haven't seen him before."

"I had him meet us in Russia. Used to work with him. He's one of the best."

"Can you trust him?"

"Yes. You want to meet him?"

"No," she sighed. "If you say he's all right, that's good enough for me. But with something this precious along, I don't want to take any chances. I like predictability, something I loved about Dimitrios, God rest his soul." She wheezed. "Now, where is that medic? I want something for the pain. Let him start earning his keep."

Ian summoned the doctor who gave her an injection. She drifted off in a matter of seconds.

*　　*　　*

After the medic had left, Ian moved into the larger cabin up front where some were playing cards and the man who'd boarded in Moscow was reading a paperback.

When Ian went into the cockpit to check on the pilots, the new recruit set his fat novel down. "I'm going to the head," he said to the other two sitting there.

They grunted a reply without looking up.

He moved to the back, hesitated at the restroom then slipped on past the kitchen into the inner sanctum.

There she lay before him like a corpse in a coffin.

He scanned the room and saw it on the table.

*　　*　　*

Rome

Adam pushed through the door of his hotel suite. It was already open. The Swiss Guards were right on his heels.

He glanced into Renie's room and stopped.

She stood at the window, her back to him. "So," she said without turning around, "did you find what you were looking for?"

"Not yet," Adam replied, waving the Guards away.

When he heard the door shut behind him, he moved to the window and stood beside her.

"What makes you think you would find it here?" said Renie.

No Justice, No Peace

Camp David

President Sanchez squinted at the dreary Maryland sky. She'd been at Camp David for the weekend with her Chief of Staff, Pete Ashton, and her National Security Advisor, Anson Avery. Flying in with the Israeli head of state and his guards that afternoon on Marine One was Drew Farley.

The gathering was to be a summit of sorts to continue deliberation on the Palestinian problem. They all wanted to have a private crack at the new Israeli Prime Minister before the rest of the government got their licks in. Security had been beefed up. Mossad had negotiated with the Secret Service to ensure sufficient precaution. One of the Secret Service men had said to Pete Ashton, "Those Israelis are uptight. You'd think HAMAS was going to storm the place or something."

The President sat down for a drink with her Chief of Staff.

"Did you have a good walk?" Ashton asked her.

"Excellent, Pete. Bring me up to date on the Israeli boss. Executive summary, please," the President said, glancing at her watch.

"Okay. David Ben-Shalom. A Sabra. Fought in the Sinai campaign when he was a teenager. Studied at Technion in Haifa, Israel and the seminary at Yeshiva here in New York."

"This guy's a rabbi?"

"Started out that way. Quite a scholar in his youth. Began publishing in his early twenties, first on the Torah, then Judaism in general, then he shifted in theo-political directions. He taught at that seminary for a while then moved back to Israel to lecture and work for peace. His mentors were Rabin and Perez. He was with Rabin the night he was shot."

"Lucky to be alive. You say he's written some books?" the President asked, nursing her drink.

"Twenty-four to be exact."

The President nearly spewed her martini across the room. "And he's not even fifty yet?"

"Most of them aren't more than a hundred pages. But he does have a couple of tomes."

"Any Pulitzers?"

"One," replied Ashton. "*The Earth Is the Lord's.*"

"Oh, yeah. I remember that one. Isn't it still on the *Times* Bestseller list?"

Ashton nodded.

"I knew I should have read it. But, how was I supposed to know the guy was going to get elected Prime Minister?"

"That was even a surprise to him. He was a huge long shot. The groundswell fooled all the pundits. I think it was the book, his lectures and the fact the people really are getting tired of all the fighting."

"What's his thesis?" queried the President.

"A tour de force that suggests we don't own the land anyway, so we ought to share."

"Sounds kind of commie."

"Not really. Capitalism still works with his approach. What's unique is his call for a new way of looking at one's neighbor. A way to reach out without losing dignity."

"It'll never work in that part of the world. He'd better not give up his guns or spies."

"He won't. He's more of a 'wise as a serpent' than a

'harmless as a dove' kind of guy."

"Smart. I'm looking forward to meeting him."

"You're going to get your chance. Here comes Marine One," said the Chief of Staff, looking out the window. The deafening whir of the copter announced his arrival.

The chopper pilot circled Catoctin Mountain and brought the Sikorsky VH-60N Blackhawk down on the helipad not far from Mt. Weather. From the helicopter emerged Farley and the new Israeli Prime Minister and his entourage. They all ducked under the rotors and headed for Aspen Lodge under heavy escort.

President Sanchez met them out on the lawn. She waved at Farley who nodded in reply then offered an outstretched hand to the Israeli staff members as the blades whipped the air.

Behind them walked a man of modest height and frame, with wise eyes set in a face that beamed. He did not bob and weave under the gust of the copter's props as the others had done. He stepped with a regal air, his two bodyguards three paces behind him.

"Madame President!" said the Israeli. "What an honor to meet you!"

"The honor is mine, Mr. Prime Minister. Will you join us inside?"

By the time they had all gathered, the President asked him, "How do you like my little hideaway?"

"I love it. Especially the name!"

Laughter rippled around the room. Political laughter. Nervous laughter.

"Pete Ashton, my Chief of Staff, has lodge and room assignments," the President said. "Dinner will be at 2100. Breakfast tomorrow morning at 0800. Tonight, will be refreshment and relaxation. Tomorrow, we go to work. Any questions?"

No response.

"Pete, they're all yours!" The President turned and headed for her room.

Night fell like a shroud over the camp, making flashlights necessary. As the little group gathered for dinner, they were all in a good mood. The charisma of the new Israeli leader was contagious. The President watched him with a careful eye, wondering what motivated him. She marveled at Ben-Shalom's ability to tell stories that night.

"Remarkable man," said the President to Farley on the porch later that evening after everyone else had gone to bed. Farley puffed on an expensive Cuban cigar.

"Yes, he is," said Farley.

They stood together looking out into the blackness, only slightly illuminated by the flickering embers of Farley's cigar. The sweet aroma of rich tobacco enveloped them. It was a typical February evening in Maryland. Overcast. Not a star in sight. There was a chill in the air, but not as great as the one between them.

"May I ask you a question?" Farley said.

"Of course, Drew."

"What's really going on with our former operative on the loose, this Hunter fella?"

The President stiffened. "You tell me. He's your guy."

"Not any more. There's a lot going on around here that I don't know about," said Farley with enough intensity for the President to feel the heat.

"Perhaps you'll find some answers this weekend." said the President.

"I wonder who will provide them," Farley replied, blowing thick smoke into the night sky.

The President was unnerved by the look in Farley's eyes.

*   *   *

Ian McPherson opened the cockpit door and entered the cabin. He saw the cheap thriller open-face on the seat. He looked at the men buried in their card game. The others napped.

As he stepped into the medial area of the jet, he approached the curtain that led to Anastasia's suite.

With a swift whoosh, he pulled back the drape and saw the old woman flat on her back, completely still.

His heart stopped.

When he saw her chest rise and fall and heard the guttural wheeze of her labored breathing, he finally took a breath himself.

The door behind him opened and the new man stepped from the restroom. Ian could hear the tail end of the flush.

The man offered something between a wave and a salute. "Everything all right, Sir?"

Ian nodded as he watched the man return to the front of the plane. He glanced at Anastasia again, then entered her chamber and stared at the *Codex*. Everything seemed to be in order. Maybe I'm getting rusty in my old age, he thought.

He checked his watch. Only five hours to Tel Aviv.

* * *

Rome

The crowds were already building on Piazza San Pietro by the time the Don's limousine arrived. "I have a room on the third floor," he said to Wolf Schiller, pointing to a building just outside St. Peter's Square on Borgo Santo Spirito. "From there I can see everything. You realize you are altering history today."

"For me, it is just another job," Schiller said.

He stepped from the car with a long black case and slipped into the crowd like a man entering a cornfield six feet high.

Don Mazzini watched his blond hair bob above the congregants until it blended in then disappeared completely. The limo pulled away.

No Greater Target

A t the upper end of the curved Colonnade, Adam and Renie mounted a few steps, checked in at the security desk, and passed by the Swiss Guards, sentried in erect silence with halberds and mace. In an era of high-tech weaponry, Renie marveled at the heavy weight of tradition that dictated the fifteenth century spear-shaped battle-ax and the even older medieval war club, topped with a spiked, metal head. Ancient anachronisms that seemed odd in a church, much less the epicenter of Christendom.

A priest led the way through the Bronze Doors, along Constantine's Portico, up the Bernini Staircase, *Scala Regia,* under Vasari's apocalyptic murals, *Sala Ducale,* then across the Court of St. *Damasus* into Gregory XIII's wing of the papal residence. Renie detected a faint whiff of incense wafting in the air, ecclesiastical aroma designed to portend the halls of heaven.

Moving between the Apostolic Palace and the Bramante and Raphael loggias, they entered the façade and mounted the Papal Staircase, which brought them to *Sala Clementina,* bedecked with dizzying frescoes. Renie wanted to linger for a moment admiring them until Adam tugged at her arm. "I'm coming," she said, thinking this the most amazing museum she'd ever visited.

They rode the lift to the fourth floor.

As they stepped from the elevator, Renie glanced at her shrouded reflection in the polished sheen of Siena marble. It reminded her of the surprise she'd felt looking in the mirror that morning. Sinai sun had darkened her skin to a deep golden tan and put a blonde tint in her hair, which brushed her shoulders lightly. She barely recognized herself, wondering how much the odd journey with Adam had changed her.

When they entered the Pope's antechamber, Cardinal Carbonari was there to greet them with thinly disguised disappointment. Renie could tell Adam was still suspicious of him.

"Eminence," said Adam.

The Cardinal nodded with a tilt of the head.

Renie glanced at Perugino and Pinturicchio paintings that seemed out of place amidst the Spartan simplicity of the papal apartment. She felt the same way.

"I trust your stay in Rome is all you imagined," said the Cardinal.

"Oh, that and more," said Adam.

"Is your pensione meeting your needs? L'Abergo del Sole?"

"Oh, we've..." Renie stopped mid-sentence when she caught the sideways glance Adam threw her direction.

"We've been most pleased with it," Adam said.

Carbonari eyed them both.

"Where is the Holy Father?" Renie asked.

"Preparing his message."

They could hear the growing din of the rabble outside.

"Sounds like Vols' fans just before kickoff at Neyland Stadium," said Renie.

"And where is that?" said the Cardinal, nettled at having to make small talk.

"In Knoxville..."

He shrugged.

"...Tennessee. It's where UT plays. Big Orange."

"You are referring to American football?"

"Yes, Eminence."

"Very odd game," Lorenzo said. "Violent and fast, but too many committee meetings."

"Oh, you mean the huddles," laughed Renie, catching a glimpse of Adam's smile out of the corner of her eye.

"Is this where your athletes plot strategies against their enemies?" said the Cardinal.

Before Renie could respond, the Pope entered the room at an easy pace, welcoming his two American guests warmly. Over his white cassock and narrow-sleeved rochet, he wore a large mozetta trimmed with ermine, the kind of short cape with small hood pontiffs wear, draped with a gold and silver brocade stole. Renie was amazed at how unpretentious and humble he appeared, bedecked in all his liturgical finery.

"Today you will be surprised." The Pope's ancient face glowed brighter than any of his vestments.

"We can hardly wait, Your Holiness," Adam said.

"Come," the Pope said. "I am about to speak."

The Cardinal's countenance reddened.

The numbers below topped 500,000 and continued to grow down Via della Conciliazone. The noise level surpassed anything Renie or Adam had ever heard at Neyland Stadium. The public had been told that the Pope had an important announcement to make at his noonday blessing, so the great square was packed.

*   *   *

Wolf Schiller entered the back of an Italian television van parked near the Egyptian obelisk in the center of St. Peter's Piazza.

A startled cameraman asked, "Who the hell are you?"

Schiller twisted his head to the side breaking his

neck. None of the rest of the crew was armed, so he made short work of them with a few soft puffs of his silenced automatic. His deadly work took only a few seconds, muffled by the hum of the growing multitude outside.

Schiller then cracked the back door and adjusted the telephoto sight on his Hechler and Koch rifle. He aimed it directly at the Pope's famous perch.

Homily On the Edge

The long red-velvet cloth etched with gold had been unfurled and neatly draped over the window ledge. The large, heavy, bulletproof glass lectern had been clipped into place; the microphone was positioned at just the right height. Great white shutters book-ended the window.

When the Pope appeared, the crowd went wild. *"Viva il Papa! Viva il Papa!"* He waved a small wiping motion with a tiny flick of the wrist that only increased the decibel level. The love-fest continued for two or three minutes.

He quieted them. Then he greeted them, reciting the Angelus in Latin, and blessed them. Then he paused.

A half a million congregants held their breath as they waited.

When he began his speech, he spoke in Italian in slow, measured sentences, using simple words and phrases so everyone could understand. He talked about a new day and a new time, "…when we need to pay attention to what God is saying to us. As we move deeper into the 21st century, we need to know where we should go as people of faith."

All eyes were on him now. Not a single person moved, except for the Cardinal, who kept shifting his weight from one foot to the other like a man who had been sentenced to a lifetime of standing on hot coals.

The Pope continued. "I have an announcement to make. A man has appeared here at the Vatican with an important document, a manuscript that comes from the Sinai in Egypt."

A hush shimmered across the spellbound throng.

Then the murmur began again until the Pope raised his hand, stilling the crowd gently like a master conductor softening his orchestra with a delicate decrescendo.

"I have assembled a group of scholars who have translated this document, which calls for me to gather world leaders in Jerusalem for a summit on world peace. Since politicians have already been planning such a conference, this manuscript confirms its importance for people of all faiths as well. Today, with this announcement, I am inviting leaders to join me at the Dome of the Rock as a sign of a new era of peace for the world. A full text of the translation of the manuscript is now being given to the international media."

At first the people were stunned, unsure what to think. Then the applause began. Slow. A clap here, another there. Hardly an ovation.

"This isn't going very well," Adam whispered to Renie.

"I disagree. He knows exactly what he's doing. Watch. They're sorting it out. I've seen the same looks on juries' faces."

Renie noticed the Cardinal's face tied in a knot, telegraphing what his vote would be. But she didn't care. She had been mesmerized by the pontiff's gentle smile.

"This team of scholars was organized and directed by one of the great leaders of our church," continued the Pope, "Cardinal Carbonari, the Vatican's Secretary of State!"

The announcement hit the Cardinal from out of the blue, turning his legs to jelly. Renie saw the frightened look in his eyes. Somehow, he made it to the window on his own strength where the crowds cheered him, but not as enthusiastically as they had greeted the Pope. The applause was merely polite and cordial, but he was still overcome by the moment, grinning and waving awkwardly, fanning the embers of his own insecurity.

After giving his subordinate a brief moment of glory,

the Pope continued, "It is also my privilege to introduce to you the man who has brought this manuscript to us. An American. A Protestant pastor from the United States, the Reverend Adam Hunter!"

The crowd's response surprised both Renie and Adam.

Renie could see Adam wasn't one for the limelight. He'd never stood before a congregation any bigger than the 150, which had gathered weekly in his little Maryville church.

Renie smiled, nudging him forward.

Adam shuddered as he stepped alongside the Pope and scanned the sea of faces. The sustained acclamation that grew gradually rendered him speechless. Renie could tell he was much more comfortable working behind the scenes, camouflaged in an assassin's lair.

The Pope stood between them, the Cardinal on his left, Adam on his right, and took their hands in his, raising them together. The city of Rome shook with the thunderous applause. There was so much noise no one could have heard a cannon fire.

Much less a silencer.

Renie watched the color drain from the Cardinal's face as he began inching back from the window. She saw Adam looking at something in the center of the piazza. Edging forward, she caught a glimpse of it. A tiny reflection from the back of a television van.

Suddenly, Adam pulled the two clerics to the floor with a thud. Surgically aimed shots pierced the wall just behind them. Swiss Guards charged into the tangle of cassocks and instinctively offered their own bodies as shields.

There were no more shots, but the crowd below exploded.

Adam leaped to the window and peeked over the ledge, looking for that reflection or anything else out of the ordinary. Nothing. He scanned the crowd in search of the assailant, but people were running in all directions, bumping into each other, trampling the weak and older ones.

Swiss Guards helped the Pope and the Cardinal crouch across the floor to safety then pulled Adam back and shepherded him to the corner of the room to which Renie had retreated.

Lorenzo, more startled than any of them, could hardly speak. Breathlessly, he managed, "My God, we were nearly killed! Your Holiness, are you alright?"

The Pope smoothed the front of his cassock. "I'm fine, thanks to our new friend." Turning to Adam he said, "Renzo, do you realize this American just saved our lives?"

One of the guards slid the nearest chair under the Cardinal before he hit the floor. He was visibly shaken, his red biretta askew on his head.

Everyone could hear the sounds of people stampeding below. Screams filled the air.

"Holy Father," Adam said, "it appears that someone doesn't like your idea very much."

The Pope nodded. "I've never gotten such a quick, negative response to any speech in my whole life."

"Perhaps, we should forget the whole thing," Adam said.

"*Sì*," the Cardinal whimpered. "He's right, Your Holiness."

"No. Everything will proceed as planned. We will just increase security, which is your responsibility, Renzo. And you are still in charge of this summit. I want you to invite the world leaders, both political and religious."

"But Holy Father, our lives are in danger. And think of the recent violence in Israel."

"Renzo, where is your spine? We're not going to let a couple of assassin's bullets keep us from unveiling the most important discovery of the new millennium. And Israelis and Palestinians have been fighting for decades, which is the very reason we need to go. Nothing has changed. If we give up now, they will have won, whoever *they* are. Then we will never have peace. I will not allow that to happen."

The Cardinal glowered.

"Begin inviting the leaders immediately."

Change of Plan

Across the piazza, Vicenzu Mazzini had watched his plan disintegrate. He never expected the Cardinal to be standing there. He guessed the German had hesitated for a split second when he saw Lorenzo. Schiller had missed his chance to get both Hunter and the Pope.

The reaction of the crowd had unnerved Don Mazzini. He'd never seen the great square empty so quickly. With his binoculars, he strained to see if Wolf Schiller had escaped. Scanning the piazza, he focused in on the $10,000 Heckler and Koch PSG-1 he'd bought for him, angled out of the van, its silencer pointing directly at him. Cold, black steel glimmered in the light.

But the German was nowhere in sight. Carabinieri swarmed the piazza.

Don Mazzini smiled. The master of disguises had disappeared.

But he had missed his mark!

*   *   *

Camp David

"Madame, President, I hate to awaken you, but I think you might want to see this," Pete Ashton said. The sunrise had just begun to warm the compound.

The President, blinded by the light of the TV, recoiled at first, then adjusted her focus. She maneuvered her backside against the headboard.

CNN's account was the same all over the world.

"How the hell do they get this stuff before we do?"

"They were there covering the Pope's announcement when it happened. Our people in Rome just called it in and told us to watch it since it's the most up-to-date report."

"Turn it up, Pete. I can't hear it." Ashton pressed the volume button then handed the remote to the President.

"Little is known about Adam Hunter," the newsman said, "the American Protestant clergyman who saved the Pope's life. He comes from an East Tennessee town called Maryville and apparently worked for the government before that. He is certainly a hero now, not only in the Vatican, but throughout the entire Roman Catholic world. We have tried to get an interview with him but so far have been unsuccessful."

The President hit the mute button and looked at her Chief of Staff. "Better get the others up, Pete. I need to make a call. I'll be out for breakfast in a little bit."

"Yes, Madame President," Ashton said as he slipped through the door.

The President reached into her bedside table and removed the phone in the second drawer. She fingered some numbers and waited.

"I was expecting your call," a man's voice said.

"You see it?"

"I was there when the shots were fired."

"What the hell is going on?"

"If our guy hadn't been there, the College of Cardinals would be stoking the smoke for a new papal election."

"Is Hunter going to live through this thing?"

"I don't know," said the man on the phone. "Funny thing though—he's so popular now, he could run for President over here and get elected. All Italy adores him."

"Should we offer him some protection?"

"No. We don't want anyone thinking you're

involved in any way with what is about to happen. I'm afraid he's on his own. You think Farley suspects anything?" said the man on the phone.

"He's been nosing around some, but keeps running into dead ends," the President said.

"Watch him. He can rise up and snap you when you least expect it."

"I'm not worried about Drew," said the President.

"One in your inner circle is your enemy, Madame President, but which one?"

"I don't know."

Headlines

Maryville

Frank Harkin was on the phone to the sheriff by 8:00 am. "You see it?"

"Yeah, Frank. Who'd have believed it? You see Renie?" the sheriff asked.

"Yeah! Caught her on all the stations. Wish her daddy could see her now..."

"What the hell is going on over there?"

"Don't know. Somethin' about some manuscript."

"'Least we know where they are now."

"Which is more than we can say for Evelyn Hastings," Harkin said. "Any leads?"

"Nothin' so far. I've had my men combing the whole area all the way to Newfound Gap and Clingmans Dome. Thought we had somethin' over between Sugarlands and Gatlinburg, but turned out to be a dead end."

"You think her abduction has anything to do with Renie, that preacher and his manuscript?" Harkin asked.

"Don't know."

"I knew there was more to Hunter than met the eye. Looks like I was right all along. Gotta work on a new headline for tomorrow's paper. Special edition this time. Biggest thing that's happened to Maryville since Ruby Tuesdays moved their headquarters here. We've had Sam Houston. We've had a home-town boy become Governor and US Senator. But we've never had anyone who saved a Pope's life!"

*   *   *

Rome

Adam lay on the bed in his room watching the Italian accounts of the story. He could hardly believe what had happened. Swiss Guards stood outside his door, personally assigned by the Pope. He and Renie had left the Vatican from an inconspicuous exit to avoid the press. His escort had dropped him and the plainclothes' guards at a servant's entrance to the Excelsior.

The phone rang, but he ignored it.

The phone continued to ring. Finally, he rolled over and picked it up.

"*Pronto*," he said.

"He speaks Italian!" Conrad Docherty said. "You always were better than me with the languages."

"Better than I," said Adam.

"See what I mean? Thought I'd forgotten about you, didn't you?"

Adam said nothing.

"Congratulations. You're famous now. Been watching you on TV all morning. Nice move. Just think—if I hadn't sent you on this mission, you would never have gotten your moment in the sun. You should thank me. You're a hero!"

"What's really in the manuscript?" Adam asked.

"Everything will be revealed in time. Don't get ahead of yourself."

"Whatever you do, leave the woman out of it. She doesn't know about our world. Why did you bring her here?"

"I needed a hook to keep you honest. You showed her too much attention. I could tell you'd want to protect her."

"Who do you report to?" Adam asked. "Who's your

boss?"

There was silence on the phone.

"I knew it," Adam said. "Listen, you tell your boss, no matter how high up he is, I will smoke him out before all this is over and he'll wish he'd never started any of it!"

"Pretty tough talk from someone who isn't holding any cards. Oh, by the way. I now have one more insurance policy. Your administrative assistant."

"Evelyn? What have you done to her?"

"Nothing. She's safe and sound up in the mountains."

"If you lay a hand on her, I swear to God..."

"I text my man every day at the same time. Not a minute before or a minute after. We've synchronized our watches. If I miss my text, he has instructions to put a bullet in Miss Hastings' head. And the only reason I wouldn't text is if I'm dead. So, you ought to be praying for my good safety."

The phone went dead.

Poker Face

Rome

Renie walked into the room with a full-length terry cloth robe wrapped loosely around her taut body. She stood by the window fluffing her hair, which shimmered in the Roman sunlight.

"Feel better now?" Adam asked.

She turned and nodded, her supple frame silhouetted against the window.

"Nothing like a good, hot shower to wash away your worries."

"Wish it would." She searched his eyes for answers—answers she could see he wasn't ready to give, perhaps because he didn't know himself.

"You might want to see this," he said. He played a recording of the afternoon's events. She glanced at the TV as he ran it slow motion right up to the moment when he ducked. "Look," he said, pointing at a glimpse of her face. "Right there." He freeze-framed it on her. "You look pretty good."

"Is this Italian TV?" she asked, stepping closer to the monitor and the clear picture of herself.

"No, it's CNN."

"You know what that means?" Renie was adding it all up.

"It means the whole world has seen you."

"Including Frank and Evelyn and everybody in Maryville."

"Likely." She wondered why his gaze telegraphed a stab in his stomach at the mere mention of Evelyn's name. "I need to call Frank and let him know I'm okay! He's going to want something to print."

"Don't tell him anything."

"He's not going to like that."

"He's never liked me anyway."

She could see Adam was dead tired. When he drifted off, Renie went into another room and called Frank Harkin anyway. She wanted to hear his voice, but knew she couldn't tell him anything. It really made him mad. He wanted a big headline. Once he gave up getting a breaking story out of Renie, Frank told her about Evelyn's abduction. Renie was shocked.

She hung up and sat for a few moments thinking how tired she was and how good it was to talk to someone back home. She hated to awaken Adam, but she had to tell him about Evelyn. She knew he'd want to know.

"Adam," she said softly as she sat beside him on the bed. "Adam."

"What?" he replied, rubbing his eyes.

"That was Frank on the phone. I promise I didn't tell him anything, which pissed him off. He still has delusions of snagging the Pulitzer."

Adam smiled and stretched.

To Renie he looked completely beat. Vulnerable. She wanted to touch him, to hold him, to give herself to him. She leaned over and kissed him lightly on the mouth. He returned the kiss. But something kept her from going further. She still wasn't sure what. "There's some bad news."

Adam furrowed his brow.

"They got Evelyn. Took her up in the mountains."

"She hates it up there," he replied.

"You already knew, didn't you?" His silence said 'yes.' "Listen, we can't have any more secrets. You've got to start leveling with me or I'm out of here."

"I will, when the time is right." He smiled at her then closed his eyes.

She leaned over to kiss him again, but he was already asleep.

She looked around the room then decided she needed some air. A walk would do her good. She got up, and slipped out the door.

Dashed Hopes

Camp David

As David Ben-Shalom entered the conference room everyone stood out of respect. "Your Adam Hunter is famous today. Quite the hero, this one," he continued. "The kind of man we could use in Mossad."

"I'm sure he would fit right in," the President said as she waved them to their seats. "Prime Minister, thank you for coming. We want to hear what you have in mind for Israel. After all, if we're going to keep sending money, weapons and supplies, it's only proper to hear what we're getting for it."

"You're absolutely right. You have a right to know that we have not done what we should have done for the Palestinians or any other Arabs living within our borders."

Everyone in the room glanced at each other in surprise.

"I see by your response that you are not used to hearing someone from the Middle East admit doing anything wrong. It's true—for Arabs and Jews, saving face is more important than anything else. Repentance does not come easily in our part of the world. But this will have to change if we're going to have peace. It will be the hardest sell of all with my own people because we have lived with fear and reprisal, attack and counterattack, for so long we don't know anything else. This approach will be no easier in the Arab world because of the pain and frustration caused by 'infidels' which is what Arabs call your people and mine. We

253

represent for them an extension of the Crusaders who raped and pillaged their ancestors."

With this line, he had everyone's attention.

"The Arab community will need a strong, persuasive leader who can command respect across all borders and speaks in a way that both Sunni and Shi'ite Muslims will listen. Someone who has what they call *baraka*—great power and authority—someone who has been blessed by Allah as a true messenger of the faith. Until we find such a person who actually believes in peace for all and the authentic co-existence of different peoples within the same borders, there will be no peace. It won't make any difference how many Camp David Accords, Oslo Agreements, Wye River Memorandums or Sharm El Sheik signings we have. They won't be worth the paper they're printed on."

No one in the room had moved, even to pour a glass of water. "Furthermore," continued Ben-Shalom, "It will take money used wisely to put muscle behind our words. We need to show Palestinians we mean what we say about helping with their self-development. Instead of building settlements on Palestinian property, we should be helping them build schools and clinics. How do you say it in America? The dog rarely bites the hand that feeds it? Helping Palestinians will be the greatest act of security for Israel."

By the tone of his voice, they could tell the Prime Minister was wrapping up.

"Israel, like America, is a very fragile experiment in self-governance. It's a miracle that either one of our countries ever came into existence. The difference is that we live on a tiny slip of land and are under a constant state of alert. Our own internal security and the safety of our borders is the first thing on our minds. I will not change that. Contrary to what some of my opponents in the Knesset think, I am not a naive, idealistic fool ready to sell our country down the Jordan River. In fact, my argument is this—peace for all will make for a stronger and safer Israel."

He paused for a moment then sat down.

At first no one said anything. Like Lincoln's Gettysburg, it was a speech few had heard and they were the privileged few. One of them began to clap. Then another. When the President put her hands together and got on her feet, everyone else joined her in a standing ovation.

David Ben-Shalom waved them down and smiled as the accolade continued.

Then one of his guards appeared and whispered something in his ear. His face blanched.

The clapping stopped.

He pushed away from the table. "My friends, I must go."

"What happened?" said the President.

"A great tragedy. A suicide bomber, cloaked as a rabbi, has just killed himself and seventy-three of my people who were praying at the Western Wall. Reprisals have already begun in the settlements. Forgive me, but I must leave immediately. My only hope is that when we meet again it will be in an Israel that is at one with itself and the rest of the world."

Marine One was ready to take off within minutes. The entire Camp David contingent watched in silence as David Ben-Shalom flew away.

The meeting took on a different tone after he left. The Prime Minister had given the President and the others a glimmer of hope, all dashed by the attack at the Wailing Wall. The Secret Service increased security precautions around the compound at the President's request.

*　　*　　*

Rome

The Swiss Guards insisted they accompany Adam to the

lobby of the Excelsior.

He peered out the front door of the hotel then stepped to the sidewalk with the sentries right behind him. The Regina Carlton loomed before them. Doney's sunny street cafe was next door—Hemingway's old haunt.

No Renie. How had she slipped by the guards, and why? Where could she have gone? People on the street began to notice him. Some stared. Others pointed.

He re-entered the hotel.

The concierge was startled to see Rome's newest hero walking right up to his desk. Yes, he did remember seeing a woman of Renie's description, but he wasn't sure where she had gone.

"Perhaps, this has something to do with it," he said, handing a sealed envelope to Adam.

Adam opened it quickly and read the note. *Looking for your girlfriend? Why don't you join us? Come alone. Conrad.* The directions to Conrad's flat were scribbled at the bottom.

"Is that helpful?" the concierge asked.

"What? Oh, yes. *Grazie.*"

His heart pounded. He didn't want to lose someone else. He'd promised himself he wouldn't fall in love again. Wouldn't care that much about anyone again, but he did.

He wondered how he would ditch the Swiss Guards.

But he knew he had to.

No End in Sight

The Sinai Desert

The Bedouin sat with his men around a crackling blaze. Desert dark had settled in as a harsh night wind whipped their tents. The dancing glow of the fire moved flickering shadows across their sun-drenched faces. The burning odor of hot embers and smoldering wood filled the air with the scent of the hunt triggering an ancient blood lust that yearned to be fulfilled.

No one said anything.

Finally, one of them broke the silence. "Tell us a story, Oh Great One."

For what seemed a long time, the Bedouin only stared at the sparkling flame before him. Then he spoke. "Tonight, I tell you a new one."

"Allah, be praised! A new tale told by Hakim, defender of the faith, servant of God!" They burrowed into the sand, pulling their abas around them to ward off the nightly chill and ready themselves for the adventure.

The Bedouin drew a long breath and began. "There was once a young warrior who grew tired of rushing into camps in the dark, pilfering whatever he could in secret. He longed to lead a raid against the sheikh who had killed his family when he was only a boy. So, he found an old Bedouin who knew more about raiding than anyone in the desert. He implored the old man to teach him everything he knew. The young warrior learned to ride like the wind, to shoot a fly from forty meters, to attack without mercy."

"Like you, Hakim," said one of his men, blind admiration twinkling in his eyes.

"Do not interrupt me."

"Forgive me, Great One," the man said, bowing his head in fear and shame.

The Bedouin glared at the rest of his men. No one dared utter a word after that.

He turned to the inferno again, glassy-eyed. "Then came the day he set out for the sheikh's camp. He and his brothers rode in so furiously that no one had a prayer, but they killed only the sheikh and his men. His brothers wanted to rape the women, but the young man stopped them. He set the women and children free, offering them enough provisions to last for weeks. He told them they could travel under his protection if they joined him.

"The women hated him for killing their men, but were thankful he had spared their lives and saved them from his brothers' sexual desires. Some stayed behind, taking their chances. Others joined his roving troop in silent desperation. Among these, there was one girl who fancied the young warrior. Her eyes danced when she looked at him while her veil concealed her growing smile. Little by little, he began to notice her. Soon they became lovers. She traveled with him and his brothers when they went on their raids, cooking for them and doing their chores. She became his woman.

"One day, while they waited to attack another camp whose sheikh had robbed and beaten some poor Bedouins, they were themselves assaulted. Out of nowhere came a barbarian so ruthless that he and his comrades killed everyone but the young warrior who scrambled to safety, wounded and bleeding. He could hardly believe his ill fortune. His woman had been viciously hacked to death. The barbarian had attacked so swiftly that the young warrior barely saw him. But he vowed he would find that assassin no matter how much time it took. How long do you think he planned to search for him?"

"How long, Oh Leader?"

"For the rest of his life."

"Tell us the end of the story, Great One." They were up on their knees, imploring him to finish. "We must know what happened. Did he ever find the assailant?"

"Yes."

"What did the warrior do? Draw and quarter the barbarian? Pin him spread eagle on the sand to die in the sun? Or did the warrior release tarantulas to crawl over the body of the Hated One?"

"No," replied the Bedouin.

"What then?"

"He waited."

"Why, Oh Great One?"

"Because he knew the most important weapon in a Bedouin's arsenal. Patience."

The Bedouin gazed at the dying cinders.

*   *   *

Jerusalem - The Next Day

David Ben-Shalom stood silently for a long time, staring at blood-splattered rocks on the Wailing Wall, Jerusalem's mute reminder that sadness is the Jewish identification card. The raw egg odor of dead flesh caused temporary nausea, gagging him. He coughed, wishing he could puke the stench of war from his beleaguered land.

The whole area had been cordoned off, even to believers. Hundreds of eyes watched him from behind police barricades. He knew cameras from around the world were catching his every move. Wearing a prayer shawl and yarmulke he shuffled toward thousands of scarlet-stained notes crammed into the wall's ancient crevices.

When he had wedged his own wadded and scribbled supplication between two bloody blocks of stone, he tapped his head against them softly, then turned and waded through the bank of cameras.

*   *   *

From her suite in the King David Hotel, Anastasia Paleologos and Ian McPherson watched Ben-Shalom on TV, then listened to the reports of reprisals in Hebron and Gaza. The body count grew with each passing hour. It looked like there would be no end to it.

Ian saw the pain etched in Anastasia's face.

"Have you contacted Adam Hunter?" she asked.

"He's not in Jerusalem yet."

"Once he breaks the code, we're taking the Codex to St. Catherine's where it belongs."

"What do you mean 'we'?"

"I refuse to die until I have completed my mission." She lurched forward in pain.

Ian reached out to catch her, cradling her in his arms as if she were his own child. Her body seemed lighter than balsa wood and just as fragile. With one hand, he pulled the covers back then gently laid her across the satin sheets.

"Morphine," she mumbled in a husky whisper.

"Let me take you to the hospital."

"That's where people go to die. It's not my time yet."

Love Your Enemy

Rome

Adam took extra precautions not to be followed as he made his way to the rendezvous point in a small pensione not far from the Pantheon. He tapped on the door of the suite.

"It's open," Conrad said.

Adam entered slowly. Before he could speak, he heard a muffled whimper. Turning to his right he saw Renie's hands tied above her head to a large hook in the ceiling, gray duct tape across her mouth. Her face was bruised. She twisted and squirmed, producing little more than stifled yelps.

"Your woman's a pretty good fighter," Conrad said, rubbing the scratch marks on his left cheek.

Adam's eyes were on fire.

"Easy, Cowboy." Conrad pointed his Glock 23 at Renie.

Adam froze. He knew Conrad meant it.

"Sit."

Adam lowered his body into the nearest chair without breaking eye contact. "She has nothing to do with this."

"But she's part of the story, thanks to you."

Renie's eyes widened as she jerked at her bonds.

"Talk, Conrad."

"Patience, parson." Conrad leveled the automatic at Adam's chest.

"You won't shoot. Killing me will ruin your plan."

Conrad turned and aimed at Renie who could only muster a stifled yelp. "Yes, but she's another story."

"No!"

Adam leaped at Conrad but midair he heard a shot from behind him. He saw the pistol fly out of Conrad's hand as his whole body plowed into Conrad.

Renie fainted, her body hanging limp.

Adam glanced back at the door. Marcello stood silhouetted against the hallway light.

"He's my mark, not yours," the Sicilian said, stepping into the room. He pointed his silencer at Conrad's head.

"No," said Adam partly shielding Conrad's body with his. "He has to stay alive!"

"I don't care about that. Move!"

Marcello leveled his Sig Sauer, but before he could fire, shots came blasting into the room from behind him.

Wolf Schiller stood in the doorway with what looked like a cannon, surprising everyone. He hit Conrad in the chest with a blast, then began firing at Adam and Marcello.

Marcello rolled to the corner of the room with a wound to the shoulder.

Adam, grazed in the arm, somersaulted the other direction and grabbed Conrad's Glock. He and the Sicilian fought Schiller back.

Bullets peppered the room from both sides causing the German to duck behind the door. As Adam and Marcello sprayed the door, Schiller took flight down the hall.

Adam scrambled to his feet and ran to the door, but the German had vanished.

Adam re-entered the room slowly, his weapon raised.

Marcello pointed his Sig at Adam.

The two of them froze.

Renie, now awake again, still tied to the ceiling, struggled and moaned a muffled scream. The two assailants locked gazes and began circling the room. "Lower yours first," Adam said.

"No, you."

They continued to revolve around the center as if caught in some deadly dance.

"Drop it or I kill the woman," said Marcello.

Adam saw in a flash all the people who had died because of him, including his wife. He saw all the bodies of his victims, and remembered why he had left it behind. Then he saw something in Marcello's demeanor that made him hesitate but said nothing.

Renie's eyes widened as she kicked and twisted, trying to shout.

Adam and Marcello continued to rim the room, stepping off an ever-tightening perimeter. "When I was in the business and the client sent someone to do my job and me, too, I decided the deal was off," Adam said.

"It doesn't work that way here."

"Then you should change the rules." Adam lowered his weapon then dropped it on the floor. Black metal clattered against a hard wood floor. "Leave her alone. Take me."

The Sicilian smiled, his white teeth gleaming. He pointed the silencer at Renie. Adam did not move.

"It's okay," Adam said.

Marcello fired, severing the rope that held her to the ceiling. She collapsed in a heap on the floor. Adam kept his eyes on the Sicilian until he too lowered his weapon and dropped it.

Breaking eye contact with Marcello, Adam turned to Renie. He couldn't understand her muted whine as he ripped the gray tape off her mouth.

"Ow! I said *slowly*. What were you doing?"

Adam untied her hands and ankles then helped her to her feet. "Trying to rescue you."

"Some rescue!"

"Are you alright?"

"No thanks to you."

"It was okay. I saw it in his eyes."

"Well, what do you see in mine?" she replied, glaring at him.

Before he could answer Marcello called out. "Hey, he's still alive, barely."

Adam was at Conrad's side in an instant. The chest wound was massive and sticky—blood everywhere. The murky smell of the dying man was all too familiar. "Tell me what's happening," Adam said.

Conrad's eyes flickered, rolled to one side then closed.

"Where's Evelyn Hastings?"

Conrad mustered a few hoarse words. "We've known each other a long time, Adam. Too bad it ended this way."

Adam grabbed Conrad's shoulders and shook him. "What's really in the manuscript?" When he said nothing, Adam slapped him across the face, but Conrad seemed beyond pain.

"He's slipping," said the Sicilian.

Conrad mumbled something. Adam leaned closer to hear it. "The Bedouin knows, but he'll never tell," he said, coughing up a handful of blood then drawing his last breath.

Adam pumped hard on Conrad's chest, applying CPR to no avail. Trying to revive him only turned his fists a muddy red.

Marcello pulled Adam back. "It's too late. He probably took the one meant for you."

"Or you."

"Perhaps." Marcello covered Conrad's contorted face with a cloth. "Looks like I have two other targets now."

"I'd disappear if I were you."

"They won't stop until I'm dead," Marcello said. "Why did you want to keep him alive?"

"My administrative assistant's being held prisoner, I think in the Smokies," said Adam, looking at Renie. "If he doesn't check in at regular intervals, she will be killed."

"Do you know how to reach his contact or when to call or text?"

Adam shook his head.

"Maybe he has a mobile." Marcello poked around in Conrad's pockets. "Here." He punched the buttons on the slender phone and smiled. "Looks like two preset numbers."

Adam focused on the display. "The first one's mine. I hope to God the second one's his contact in the mountains."

Marcello handed the phone to Adam who jabbed the send button and took a deep breath, covering the mike with a handkerchief. The call went through, ringing on the other end.

"That you?" said the man who answered.

"Yeah," Adam said with a heavier timbre to his voice.

"The reception's awful here. Speak up!"

"Must be satellite trouble."

"What are you doin' callin' at this hour?"

"Just making sure you aren't sleeping on the job. I'll be calling at noon and midnight your time from now on," said Adam.

"Why the change?"

"Because...wait a minute, I don't have to tell you why! I make the rules. You just follow them. You got a problem with that!"

"No, sir. Sorry, sir."

"How's the woman?"

"Okay for a whiner. She hates the woods."

"What about the authorities?"

"They got squad cars and a couple of choppers swarming the park. But they're a bunch of country bumpkins."

"Be careful. They might get lucky. Where are you now?"

"All I can tell you is we're heading into the French

section."

"The French section?" Adam said. He knew it must be a pre-arranged code.

"When do I get to finish this woman and get paid?"

Adam said, "Not yet, you hear? Or I'll have your ass in a sling."

"I hear you."

"Switching back to texting after this."

"Got it," the man said.

Adam pushed the stop button. His face was covered with sweat.

Marcello was offering water to Renie who was visibly shaken. "What was that about the French section?"

"I don't know," replied Adam, shaking his head. "Got any ideas, Renie?"

"The French section of what?" she asked. She rubbed her reddened wrists that had been tethered to the ceiling.

"The Smokies, I guess."

"Never heard of it and I've been on practically every trail," Renie said.

"Concentrate. It's a matter of life and death."

"Don't rush me." A spark of anger lit in her eyes.

"Help me haul him into the bathroom," Adam said. He and Marcello labored under the dead weight of Conrad's body. In the bathroom, they grabbed at slippery arms and feet, swinging him back and forth, and dumping him in the tub.

"You need a bodyguard," Marcello said. "Looks like I'm suddenly available."

"Might as well put a target on my back."

"You've already got one of those. At least this way, I could see them coming."

"Thanks anyway. But I can take care of myself."

"If you change your mind, here's my number at the university." The Sicilian handed Adam his card. "I'd like to help you in some way. I owe you that much for saving my life."

"I didn't save your life. I just got in the way."

"Whatever, I'm still alive and I owe you."

Suddenly, Renie filled the room with a huge grin.

Adam saw it first. "You figured it out."

"I think so. Has to be either Mt. LeConte or Mt. Guyot."

"I'm not familiar with the area," Marcello said. "Where did you say these mountains are?"

"East Tennessee," Adam said. "I hiked them growing up, but I can't help Evelyn now."

"Maybe I can," said Marcello.

"Guess who knows every inch of the Smokies?" Renie asked.

Adam shrugged.

"Frank."

She dug her phone out of her purse and punched in his number.

Lost and Found

The Smoky Mountains

Frank Harkin knew better than to get separated from the search party as they hiked up Mt. LeConte on the Boulevard Trail, the razor-thin ridge that broke west from the Appalachian Trail. Old timers called it a hogback. Starting at Newfound Gap they'd made the turn after three miles and begun their assault on the ancient peak.

Frank had decided to join the LeConte posse instead of the Mt. Guyot group since he preferred LeConte's winding trails. He liked Boulevard because it started high and retained its heady elevation for the steady climb to the top. With the extra girth Frank had added in recent years he didn't want to have to scale any more than was necessary, but the truth was he'd do whatever it took to find Evelyn.

A diaphanous veil hung low on the hills with a thin, blue haze. A slanted radiance filled the hollows and plunging ravines. Heath balds and fields of goldenrod emerged in the fog, their sweet fragrance wafting Frank's direction. A knot of dead balsam trees stood guard along the trail like great, gray ghosts. He heard the whir of wings as the search party ahead of him scared up a covey of slate-pink juncos. He watched the group of birds bank left, then head south, drumming the air above him.

From childhood Frank had known how important it was to stay within visual contact or earshot of the other hikers. But on this day, he broke his own rule. He had to find Evelyn! He told the guys in front of him he needed to take a leak but he'd catch up eventually. A few paces off the trail he stood spread-legged, facing downhill.

Then he heard it.

Was it the crunch of crushed branches or the crinkle of dry leaves?

When he was by himself in the mountains his mind would often play tricks on him. Sometimes all he heard was the wind moaning in the trees. Sometimes it was the haunting melody of the veery, a small brown and cream-colored thrush whose song descended in a rolling series of flute-like notes dropping down the scale. But this time he was certain he'd heard a noise just the other side of a stand of spruce-firs that lined the pathway. Maybe it was a wild hog, foraging for food. He watched a peregrine falcon fire across the sky and wished he could move half that fast.

He glanced up the knife-edge trail. No sign of the patrolmen who'd preceded him. "Hey fellas, I think I heard somethin' down here!" He waited for their response.

Nothing.

He said it again and heard only the murmur of his own gravelly voice echoing across the mountains until its reverberating resonance faded to nothing.

It had been a long time since he had done any off-trail hiking. Even though he was out of shape, he knew instinctively how to negotiate the labyrinth of undergrowth and clear away brush with his walking stick as he labored through the tightly woven thicket. The whole side of the mountain was a riot of plant life, most of which would explode in a kaleidoscope of color come spring.

Down he went, following the sound he had heard, plunging deep into the dark, primeval timberland. His pulse quickened as he crab-walked along a steep slope through a tangle of doghobble. He stopped for air, leaning against a beech tree like a drunk on a lamppost. He felt like one. Dizzy. Light-headed. Craning his neck, he tried to see how far he'd come off the trail, but the thick foliage had blanketed it. Hoping to catch his breath he tried to focus on the location of the sound that had lured him off the beaten path.

Then he heard it again. A good fifty paces to the left and further down the wooded glen. It was muffled and faint like the purr of a kitten. Subdued sunlight, nearly eclipsed by the woods, peeked in and out of the dusky mists that shrouded the old hills that day.

By the time Frank had reached the spot where he'd heard the sound, it appeared to have moved deeper into the forest. He felt his chest tighten. He knew he should never have left the search party, that he'd better turn back now or he would never find the trail. In a fleeting glimpse of his worst recurring nightmare, he saw himself lost forever in the woods.

His body told him to sit down, or he wouldn't have the strength to get out on his own. His knees cracked and popped as he collapsed on an enormous log wrapped with a thick coat of sphagnum moss that moistened the back of his pants. Clam-like stacks of rubbery-tough fungus that clung to the recently felled tree provided a soft, bumpy couch. Catching a glimpse of a deer disappearing into the underbrush, he leaned forward and spit on the ground between his feet.

He opened his water bottle and sucked his last swig until it was all gone. After a few minutes, he struggled to his feet as the sun filtered shadows across his face. Re-attaching his backpack, he turned to begin his ascent and mopped the sweat that soaked his face.

Then he heard what sounded like the low hum of a dying animal no more than ten feet behind him. "Evelyn? That you?" Adrenalin kicked in as his heart raced. "Evelyn?"

Then he saw her, bundled on the ground under a thatch of witchhobble. Hands and feet bound together tight enough to cut off circulation. Her clothes hung on her in shreds. Her face was smudged and bleeding, her hair a tangled mess. But she was still alive. He was sure he'd seen her move, if only a twitch.

He leaned over her and called her name softly. "Evelyn."

His words startled her. When she awakened, what he saw in her eyes was the look of terror. The frantic gaze she shot him made him recoil, the wild eyes of an animal about to be devoured.

"Evelyn, it's me, Frank." He couldn't understand why she continued to struggle, furrowing her brow and moaning with the deep, guttural honks of a goose, attempting to escape its assailant. He tugged at the knot at the base of her neck, hoping to release the gag stretched taut across her chapped lips.

"There." He tossed the twisted red bandana aside.

She sputtered, gasping for air, trying to speak, but she could only produce a few small, raspy sounds. Finally, she sucked in enough air to blurt out a single sentence. "Get away from here now!"

Leaning over her bruised body, Frank caught the look in her eye aimed somewhere over his left shoulder. But it was too late.

A blunt object landed full force on the back of his head.

*   *   *

Adam texted from his hotel room at the newly appointed time.

"How's it going?"

"I've picked up another one," was the reply. "The woman calls him Frank. He's out like a light with a good knot on the back of his head."

"Got a place you can lay up until you make your move?"

"Yeah. Plenty of rations and warm sleeping bags. Nobody's ever going to find us down here."

"Think of it as survival training then."
"I'll survive. I just don't know about these two."
"Keep them alive whatever it takes."
"Will do my best."

Fools Rush In

Adam saw the grimace on Cardinal Carbonari's face when he walked with Renie into the Hall of Benedictions, just above the portico of St. Peter's. It seemed to Adam that Lorenzo was in a permanent state of irritation. The Holy Father had broken precedent by holding his big announcement to the journalists in something other than the Press Room of the Holy See located just outside Vatican City.

A phalanx of cameras representing media from around the world formed a semi-circular wall in front of the Pope and the twelve scholars. Renie, Adam, and the Cardinal stood in the background with the Noble Guard and the Swiss Guard. Gendarmes stationed themselves around the room. Over a hundred reporters jostled for position. Some were *Vaticanisti,* regulars in the Press Room.

The bank of mikes squeaked as the Pope cleared his throat. "Welcome, friends. I wanted the world to meet the scholars who translated this remarkable manuscript."

Adam shaded his brow with his left hand to blot the bright lights and eyed the crowd as the Pope presented the academics to the assembly. Adam felt his throat tighten as he saw a shock of blond hair move behind the cameras.

The Pope opened the floor for questions. Hands shot up around the room. "Who are the People of the Book described in the manuscript?" asked a Belgian reporter near the front.

"Adherents of Judaism, Christianity and Islam."

"And who will represent Judaism and Islam, presuming you will be there for Christianity?" asked a reporter from China.

"Before mentioning the Jews and the Muslims, I will tell you I have asked the Patriarchs of the Greek and Russian Orthodox Churches to join us, despite tensions between them and us. In addition, I intend to ask the Protestant clergyman, Adam Hunter, to join me."

Renie smiled at Adam as he nodded to the army of reporters.

The Pope continued. "As for Jews and Muslims, I have asked David Ben-Shalom, Prime Minister of Israel, and the Jordanian Prince, Abdul Al-Salaam, to join us in this most holy of pilgrimages of peace for the world. I have also invited the Presidents of the United States and the Prince of Saudi Arabia to accompany us."

"I'm from the *Chicago Tribune*, Your Holiness," a reporter said. "Isn't it a little dangerous to be in Jerusalem with the recent bombings that have occurred there?"

"No more dangerous than the South Side of Chicago."

The swarm of correspondents chuckled and grinned at the Trib writer who waved a "touché" salute in response.

"Besides, if this is a divine document, God will protect us for the cause of peace."

More hands, more questions. The Pope had a field day with them, ever the master at working the crowd.

Adam saw the blond hair again.

"What is it?" Renie asked.

He didn't reply, his eyes focused on a fistful of Asian reporters over to the right. Then he saw him. Adam had learned to spot an assassin by watching his eyes. The blond giant had the same cold stare Adam had seen before. He strained to see if the man had a weapon.

He glanced at the door to see what Swiss Guards

might be close by. When he looked back, the tall blond was nowhere in sight.

"What's wrong?" said Renie.

"Nothing," Adam lied.

*   *   *

The White House

Drew Farley stood with the President in the Oval Office "So, what are you going to do, Madame President? A summit like that will be a terrorist's dream, come true. I don't trust those people."

"You don't trust the Pope?" the President asked.

"You know what I mean. Our operatives are working with Mossad on security issues, especially after the recent homicide bombings."

"What do they think?"

"That we're walking into a snake pit," Farley said.

"Security will be fine, Drew. I have to go or there will be no summit. If I stay home and everybody else goes, it will look like we're not for peace. I'd be seen as a coward. The Majority Leader is not sure but the Speaker of the House is certain this will be good for the country. I have to go. Besides I trust Ben-Shalom. He's a man of honor."

"It's not him I'm worried about."

The look the President gave Farley put a chill on him and ended the conversation abruptly. Farley could tell he'd worn out his welcome.

When Farley had left the Oval Office, the President went to her secure line and punched in a pre-set number. No answer, even after six or seven rings. The President felt short of breath. Her contact knew the agreement. He was to keep the cell phone turned on at all times. No excuses.

She eyed the official invitation that had come from the Vatican. She knew she had to go now. She had no choice, with or without her contact.

She tried the number again with no success then hung up quickly. The only reason he might not answer, he'd told the President, would be if he were dead. Nobody else even knew what was happening. There was no one else the President could call. She would have to go to Jerusalem not knowing whether her contact was dead or alive. Worst of all she might be walking into a trap, one she had set herself.

PART SIX: PREDATOR AND PREY

The Shadow Knows

R eligious people, politicos, courageous curiosity seekers, and the world press made travel plans for Israel to attend the great Peace Summit. Since lodging was nowhere to be found in Jerusalem, both Palestinian and Israeli residents charged astronomical prices to rent their flats to the highest bidders. Adam and Renie were guests of the Pope at the Pontifical Institute Notre Dame of Jerusalem Center. They shared adjoining quarters with a view of the old city. Other leaders had moved into the King David Hotel where Anastasia Paleologos had fought for her life until Ian McPherson finally took her to Hadassah Hospital, a place she'd long admired because of the stunning Marc Chagall windows.

The phone rang in Adam's room. "*Salaam Aleikum,* Mr. Hunter" a voice said when he answered. "How are you today?"

Adam paused, recognizing the inflection. "I knew you'd be here."

"Have you figured it out yet?" asked the Bedouin.

"The manuscript? It's all translated if that's what you're asking."

"Yes, but do you know what it means?"

"We have all the words and sentences. What are you talking about?"

"All those scholars from around the world," laughed the Bedouin. "The best and brightest and not one of them

278

could figure it out."

Adam remained silent. He knew he was being baited.

"Come meet with me and I will give you a hint," said the Bedouin.

"What if I don't want to play your little game?"

"You'll always wonder if you could have stopped it when things start happening."

Adam hesitated. "Where shall we meet?"

"In the Muslim Quarter of the old city. Enter the Damascus Gate. Turn left at Aqabat Rissas then right on Aqabat esh Sheikh Rihan."

"When?"

"This afternoon. Three o'clock. Do not be late. Come alone."

Adam hung up the phone and looked around the room for the silenced pistol he'd picked up when he'd arrived in Jerusalem. It was in his bag on the table. He fingered it then put it back in the bag when Renie walked into the room.

"What are you doing with that?"

Startled, he replied, "Oh...nothing." He was finding it more and more difficult to lie to her. There was a tenderness to her confused look that made him want to hold her and send her home all at the same time, his heart churning with a potpourri of emotions.

"You're going somewhere, aren't you?"

"For a walk," he said.

"Alone?"

He nodded then turned and gazed out the window, looking at nothing in particular. Renie moved to his side. After a few moments, he turned and kissed her softly on the mouth, his lips gently coaxing hers with feather-light kisses. He felt her whole body responding warmly. He wanted to make love to her, sensing she was ready for it, but something held him back, something that had nothing to do with her.

"I gotta go," he said. "I'll be back."

He planted a soft kiss on her forehead, and backed away.

"Be careful," she whispered.

Adam had been through the Damascus Gate many times, but the decibel level in the Old City seemed to be higher than ever. Everyone was excited about the upcoming summit. They were tired of endless war, which had put a dent in the tourist business. Maybe, with peace, Christians and Jews would start trooping to the Holy Land again.

Adam walked up and down Aqabat Esh Sheikh Rihan, humoring the vendors who hawked their wares, amused at how fast the prices dropped as he walked away from their tables. He'd been there for two hours before becoming impatient. But he didn't want to show it. Finally, one of the peddlers surprised him by offering him a beautiful bracelet for his woman at no charge.

"I'm sure she is worth it," the merchant said.

"For free? There must be a catch," said Adam.

"Well, actually, there is," the man said. "Meet with the Great One and you can have it. Follow me."

Adam looked up and down the narrow, winding menagerie of shops. The man had already disappeared behind a dark, silk damask curtain. Adam followed.

The passageway to Hakim's apartment reminded Adam of the twisted tunnels that snaked their way through St. Catherine's Monastery. Bobbing, weaving, and ducking their heads, they climbed ancient stone steps worn smooth by centuries of foot traffic.

Suddenly, Adam entered a plain apartment where two men frisked him the moment he walked through the door. He'd expected it.

"Welcome," the Bedouin said. He sat behind a plain wooden table, surrounded by his soldiers, a broad smile on his face.

Adam surveyed the simple room. "What can I do for you?"

"First things first, Mr. Hunter." The Bedouin turned to his lieutenants. "Tie him up."

Adam recoiled as four of Hakim's men approached him. He sized them up. All four had weapons. Only a fool would try to take them.

After fettering his hands behind his back, they heaved him sideways into the nearest chair. Adam straightened himself and watched the Bedouin pace the perimeter of the room in long, slow circles. Adam started the process of loosening his bonds, an old trick he'd learned during CIA training at Camp Peary. The idea was to keep the body completely still while plying the threads with one's fingers. He focused on the Bedouin as his hands went to work.

"Where do I begin?" Long pause. "Ah yes, it was a few years ago in New York City. Wonderful place, don't you think, Mr. Hunter?"

"If you like burnt chestnuts," Adam said.

"Even without the World Trade Center."

Adam looked surprised.

"Brilliant, wouldn't you say?"

"For a madman."

The Bedouin smiled, not taking the bait. "It was masterful. But not nearly as exquisite as what's coming."

Adam surveyed the room. He counted four large bodyguards and one outside the door. Each had an automatic.

The Bedouin stopped pacing to stare at Adam. Adam quit fiddling with his fingers as the Bedouin leaned close to him, his spicy, shish kebab breath causing Adam's eyes to water.

Finally, the Bedouin broke eye contact and began walking again. "Do you remember where you were when your wife died? I do."

Adam's eyes widened.

"You see that, men? He doesn't know who I am.

Let's make sure he is paying attention."

Three men surrounded Adam. One of the men grabbed his feet. Another held his shoulders. The third one began pummeling him across the face with his fists.

"That's enough. I don't want you to kill him. Not now, anyway."

Adam's face was a mess. The blood from his nose ran down into the side of his mouth; he could feel his right eye beginning to swell, as well as a large bruise on his left cheek.

"Now, do I have your attention, Mr. Hunter?"

"Yes." Adam licked the trickle of blood at the corner of his mouth.

"I was with a woman in New York City, my woman. We were about to release a biological weapon. You had been hired to kill me. Do you remember any of this?"

Adam knew exactly what the Bedouin was describing, but his response came too slow. The Bedouin nodded and one of the men punched him hard in the ribs.

Adam doubled over in pain then coughed violently, trying to catch his breath.

"Do you remember now?"

"Yes!"

"Well, let me refresh your memory. It was the Upper West Side. Three-story brownstone. Black minivan out front. The driver was an old friend of mine. But the woman who got into that van was my woman. She was carrying our child and she didn't want to come to New York, but I insisted. Do you hear me? I insisted!" He composed himself, turning on Adam. "And you planted a bomb meant for me in that van."

Adam stared at him, stunned. So, this was the man.

Adam kept working his fingers. Until now, he hadn't known who the mark had been. The time and location for the hit had come at the last minute. He hadn't even recognized the Bedouin when they'd met at St. Catherine's.

Adam's body remained still as a statue while his hands fingered the ropes. The knot was tighter than any he had ever untied. It matched the one in his gut and the one on the Bedouin's face, twisted with guilt and fury.

"Now you have a question for me, don't you? You want to know why I haven't killed you before." He paused. "First I had to find you. I got some help from an old CIA contact who trained me and Bin Laden in Afghanistan years ago."

That line stopped Adam cold. He hadn't put Conrad and the Bedouin together.

"That's right. Conrad Docherty. He told me how you went to seminary. You, pretending to be a man of God! Killing you would be too easy. Your punishment is the knowledge that what's about to happen here in Jerusalem has been set in motion by your little manuscript. And if you try to stop it, I will make sure your woman never lives to see another day."

"She's not my woman."

The Bedouin bent close, his rancid breath bearing down on Adam. "Of course, there was another woman there that day, wasn't there?"

Adam stared at the floor.

"Your wife. You killed your own wife, didn't you?"

"It was an accident."

"On that day in a single moment, you killed your woman and mine," the Bedouin said, his voice lowering ominously. "And because of it, many more will lose theirs in this holy city."

He nodded to one of his men who tapped a hypodermic then moved toward Adam.

"Don't make me fight you," Adam said. "I don't want to fight anymore."

The Bedouin laughed out loud. "You won't have to. You will soon be asleep." His soldiers chuckled with yellow-toothed grins as the one with the needle swabbed Adam's arm.

Suddenly, Adam stood.

His hands now free, he hit the Bedouin in the stomach with a single front snap kick sending him sprawling across the room. Next, he upended the man with the syringe. When a second one came at him from behind, Adam dodged and flipped him on his back.

He grabbed one of them and swung him around just in time to shield his body from bullets flying from two automatics. When the wounded one dropped to the floor with a thud, Adam picked up his weapon and rolled to the side while shooting the pistols from his attackers' hands, surgically nicking their wrists.

The Bedouin got up, his body coiled like a viper, ready to strike. He began circling the room, startled to see how quickly Adam had dispatched his men.

Adam dropped the automatic on the floor. "Tell me what's going to happen."

"Never."

Adam pointed at the silencer he'd just released. "If killing me will stop what you're planning, then go ahead. Take my life. God knows I've taken enough already. I deserve to die but not thousands of innocents."

"Touching speech, Mr. Hunter. But not very convincing. Only a word from me will stop what's about to happen," said Bedouin, moving in. Adam did not resist. With a single motion the Bedouin brought him down, his hand on Adam's throat.

At the same moment, Moshe burst through the door, taking aim.

"No, don't shoot!" yelled Adam, but it was too late.

The Israeli fired his Beretta M21.

The Bedouin grabbed his chest and collapsed to the floor.

"I told you not to!" said Adam.

"He was going to kill you. Besides, I just grazed him.

284

Why did he grab his chest?" Moshe's Mossad operatives moved in behind him and began arresting the Bedouin's wounded lieutenants.

"How did you know I was here?" Adam asked.

"We've been following you since you got here. Figured he'd make contact and you'd lead us right to him."

"I wish I hadn't."

Adam leaned over the Bedouin's body. "You can't die now!" He felt his neck. "Oh God, no pulse. It's cardiac arrest."

Adam tore open the Bedouin's shirt, straddled his stomach and began administering CPR, depressing and releasing his chest. Then kneeling beside him as if in prayer, he placed his mouth on the Bedouin's and blew hard. Leaping back on his torso, he overlapped his hands and began pushing in a steady, rhythmic motion. Then he was at his side again, bellowing hot breath into the dead man's lungs.

"It's no good. He's gone," said the Israeli. "You've done all you can, just let him go."

"No! We have to find out what's going to happen!"

Adam moved like a madman. Back and forth he jumped, pressing and exhaling until, "Yes!"

He fingered the Bedouin's neck. "I got a pulse! Where's the closest hospital?" Adam bundled the Bedouin into his arms and carried him like a baby, teeter-tottering to the door.

"Why do you care what happens to him?" said Moshe.

"Because, we don't know what the plan is, and he's the only one who does."

Amnesia

Jerusalem

Adam and Moshe burst through the emergency room doors of Hadassah Hospital, the Ein Kerem campus with two of Moshe's men carrying the Bedouin. Moshe's Mossad status got them quick entry and the best doctor on duty. They whisked the Bedouin into an examination room and the physician asked everyone to leave.

After twenty minutes, the doctor appeared in the waiting room.

"One of you must have saved his life. But I'm afraid he's lost his memory."

"Amnesia?"

"Well, sort of. The cardiac arrest did it. Too much blood was cut off from his brain for that brief period before you brought him back."

"Does he even know who he is?" Moshe asked.

"Yes, but that's about all."

"Then, what has he lost?"

The doctor hesitated, looking back and forth between Adam and Moshe. "Well, I'm not exactly sure. But it looks like the last twenty-five years or so."

"How long will he need to stay here?" Adam asked.

"It's hard to tell. I'm having him moved to ICU for observation."

"Can we talk to him?"

"No. He's very confused. He has a weak heart and may not make it."

"Please," Adam said. "I'm the one who gave him CPR. I have to talk to him."

The doctor eyed Adam carefully. "I don't know."

"I'm a minister."

"All right, but only you, and five minutes."

Adam nodded affirmatively.

Adam knew ICUs quite well. He'd spent plenty of time in them. He knew the look, the smell, the routine. He sat next to the Bedouin whose pallid skin made him appear anemic. Ghost-like. The Bedouin seemed to be staring into some awful abyss.

"It's me, Adam. It's very important that you tell me what is going to happen."

"What do you mean?" The Bedouin startled Adam with his words.

"You know. We were just talking about it in your apartment. New York. Your woman, my wife. The manuscript, the plan. It's over. Call it off before more people are killed."

"I have no idea what you are talking about or who you are," the Bedouin said. "I've never been to New York City."

Adam had spent a lifetime reading people's eyes. His truth barometer had never failed. For once he wished he could be wrong. But he knew he wasn't. The man lying on the bed before him was telling the truth.

He rose and started for the door, but a tall, lean man stood before him, blocking his way.

"You looking for someone?"

"You. Are you a clergyman?" said the man with a British accent.

"I am," replied Adam. "Protestant."

"That will do. There's a woman on the floor above who is dying of cancer. I work for her. Could you have a word with her, possibly a prayer?"

Adam glanced at his watch then back at the Brit,

wanting to say "No." But the persistent, look on the Englishman's face turned Adam's "Sorry," into "Take me to her."

No words passed between them on the elevator.

Adam stood beside her bed, holding her hand. "I'm Protestant. Hope that's all right."

"I'm Greek Orthodox. My man here is Church of Scotland. I don't care what flavor you are as long as you believe in God."

"Lately I've begun to wonder."

"Don't most priests, sooner or later? Most honest ones anyway."

"What can I do for you?"

"I have to tell you the truth. I brought you up here on false pretenses."

A question mark creased Adam's face. "You're not the first one."

"My name is Anastasia Paleologos. This is Ian McPherson, and you are Adam Hunter."

"Have we met somewhere?"

"No, but I know all about you. Where you came from and what you really are."

"So, you've done your homework. Fine. I think I'll be going now." Adam turned to leave. The Brit didn't try to stop him, but Anastasia's words did. "I have a manuscript to give you."

"Another manuscript? Why me?"

"Because you seem to be quite skillful at delivering them safely."

"No thanks."

"Don't you even want to see it? It's the original *Codex Sinaiticus.*"

Adam felt his face light up. "You mean the one in the British Library?"

"No, the one that was on loan from the British Library in the British Museum, then stolen before it was returned to the British Library."

Ian McPherson pulled a large canvas bag up on the bed. With great care, he removed the old volume from the bag and opened it. Adam stared at it in astonishment then leafed the delicate parchment pages as if he were handling a small bird.

"What do you plan to do with it?"

"Return it to its rightful home."

"St. Catherine's?"

"Tischendorf should never have stolen it from the monks in the first place."

"How do you propose to get it there?"

"You are going to deliver it."

"Me?"

"That's right. But first you're going to use it to help you crack the code in the manuscript you had the Pope's scholars translate."

"How did you know?"

"Father Nicodemus told me in a letter."

"But the Pope had all the best minds working on it," countered Adam.

"So what? The best minds have been working on the Bible for a couple of millennia and they're still arguing over what it all means."

"Touché."

"A bishop here in Jerusalem can help you if you take this Codex to him now."

Adam felt like he was peeling back layers of an onion, one at a time.

"His name is Father Nikopoulos, the Bishop of Jerusalem. His flat is on the second floor of the Monastery of St. Abraham across the small square from the Church of the Holy Sepulchre in the Old City. He will be expecting you this evening."

Adam gazed at the Codex for a moment then looked up at her. "You have cancer?"

Her eyes, bloodshot and worn, still shone with expectancy.

"Six weeks tops, if that. Doctor says I might get a tiny reprieve before the worst comes. All I want now is to see if the *Codex* can help you crack the code, then assure its safe return to St. Catherine's before I die."

"Perhaps you can deliver it there in person," said Adam.

"That would be heaven," said Anastasia.

"But not likely," interrupted the Brit. "The trip alone would kill her."

"It would be preferable to rotting in this tomb." She coughed violently, hacking green-gray gunk from her lungs and then rasping in a hoarse whisper, "Now go, before it's too late. And good luck. God knows you'll need it."

"Would you like a prayer?" Adam asked.

"I need all the prayers I can get."

Adam wondered if he could remember how after all that happened to him. Holding her fragile, wrinkled hand in his, he mustered a brief intercession then left the room quietly.

*   *   *

Bishop Nikopoulos, a short, bearded fire-plug of a man with legs as thick as tree stumps, sported a large smile as he ushered Adam into his flat, a warren of small, over-furnished rooms near the Church of the Holy Sepulchre. Golden icons glittered on the walls, dressers and tables. The pungent aroma of Orthodox incense permeated the entire suite. His tiny Greek mother nodded, and mumbled, *"Kalespera."*

"Kalespera," Adam said, wishing her a good evening as well.

"She speaks no English," Nikopoulos said. The woman continued bowing and smiling.

They sat in the living room by a window that

overlooked the square. The bishop's mother served them strong black coffee and dark chocolates, dipping her body in a half-curtsey.

"*Efkaristo,*" Adam said, the traditional Greek thank-you.

"*Parakalo.*" She backed into the kitchen, shutting the door behind her.

"She helps me around the apartment. We keep each other company."

Adam thought it odd that the cleric felt obliged to explain why he was living with his mother but saw no reason to pursue it. "Your English is very good."

"Three years at Florida State and a couple at a parish in Manhattan. I miss the hot pastramis."

"Yeah, me too." Adam sized him up quickly and decided he could trust the squat, stout man, so he quickly moved beyond small talk. "I want you to keep the *Codex* until it is returned to St. Catherine's. Anastasia says there's a clue in it to translating this old manuscript." Adam handed him a copy of the two pages the Pope's scholars had labored over. "When you find something to crack the code, don't call me. Email your information to a man named Coleman Ashburn in Maryville, Tennessee. He's a retired classics professor there. You can trust him. His website is ashes.com. You realize this may be dangerous."

The bishop nodded. "I would do anything for Anastasia. I believe in what she is doing. I've led many pilgrimages to Mt. Sinai and agree with the monks. Tischendorf should never have stolen it in the first place. St. Catherine's is its rightful home."

Adam gently removed the ancient manuscript from the old canvas bag.

He could tell by the reverent look that softened the bishop's ruddy countenance that for him, the *Codex* was a sacred object. "Tell me where you are going to hide it in case…"

"…something happens to me? It won't." The bishop continued to gaze at the old book.

The bishop scribbled a few words on a piece of paper and handed it to Adam who furrowed his brow. "It's in Greek." Adam checked a Greek/English lexicon on his iPhone then smiled. "Oh, I see."

Nikopoulos took the note from Adam, struck a match under it, and dropped it into a dish as it crumpled to ashes.

Ignorance is Bliss

The President entered the presidential suite at the King David Hotel near the Jaffa Gate across from the Old City walls. She had just finished a meeting with other dignitaries that had gone very well, but it was late and she was tired.

"Madame President," said an aide. "There is someone to see you."

"At this hour?"

"It's Adam Hunter. I told him it wouldn't be possible, but he insisted."

The President glanced at her watch, wondering why her contact hadn't returned her calls to alert her Hunter was in Jerusalem. "Okay, show him in but tell him five minutes."

Adam walked through the door and shook the President's hand.

"Mr. Hunter, what brings you here this evening?"

"Something I need to tell you, Madame President...alone, if possible," he said eyeing the Secret Service men standing close by.

"Don't worry about them. They're paid to be deaf-mute. Have a seat."

Adam sat on a sofa across from a wingback that placed the President slightly above him.

"You must be very excited, and very proud." Before Adam could respond, the President continued. "What a remarkable turn of events, all because of your discovery. We're on the verge of an era of peace in the Middle East that will change history."

"That's just it, Madame President. I think we should

call the whole thing off."

"What? The Summit is the day after tomorrow."

"I've had a bad feeling about it ever since we arrived in Jerusalem. Now I'm certain something terrible might happen. I just don't know what it is."

The President twisted in her chair, studying Adam closely. "What proof do you have?"

"Just a hunch."

"So, I'm supposed to call off the greatest step toward world peace in history on a hunch?"

"I think there is something hidden in that manuscript that we haven't discovered yet."

"You had the best text scholars in the world analyzing that thing."

"Yes, that's true, but—"

"There are no buts. Until you have quantifiable proof, the Peace Summit is still on. And I would suggest you keep this little conversation between us to yourself. Is that clear?"

"Very clear, Madame President."

"Is that all?" The President stood and extended her hand.

"Yes, Madame President. Thank you for your time."

"My pleasure. I'll see you the day after tomorrow. It will be a great day."

Once Adam left, the President punched numbers on her secure phone. No answer. "Where could he be?"

*   *   *

Renie was bent over her laptop when Adam entered their suite.

"What are you doing?"

"Surfing the Web," she said without looking up. "I figured you needed all the help you could get." Her glasses had slid down to the end of her nose, giving her a young, granny look.

Adam peered over her shoulder. "The papal website?"

"No, it's a chat room some Stanford scholar set up for anyone who wants to take a shot at finding a deeper meaning in the manuscript. It's already received several thousand hits from all over the world. Textual interpretation via social media."

Adam was amazed. "Anybody got anything yet?"

"Nothing so far." She glanced his direction then got up from her chair. Removing her glasses and setting them on the desk, she stepped close to him and ran the back of her soft hand across his right cheekbone. "What happened to your face?"

"I fell down and cut it."

Seeing right through it, she said, "Pretty clumsy for someone so agile." She moved close enough for him to feel her supple but firm body against his. He sensed a small grin tugging at the corners of his mouth as he took her in his arms. His lips found hers. He tasted the sweetness of her smile. Tilting his head back, he framed the outline of her delicate jaw with his left hand and felt the tingle of her hot breath on his neck. He kissed her again, more deeply this time. As she molded herself into the length of him, a wave of heat pulsed between them.

Her whispered words, "I think I can forget about the chat room for now," snapped him back to reality.

He released his grip on her, summoning all his willpower. "Oh, no, we've got to keep trying." He glanced over her shoulder at the computer then back at her. Her eyes told him he was making a mistake. He knew his eyes agreed, but love would have to wait.

"Rain check?"

"It's not raining," she replied flatly. "I'm thirsty. Want a drink?"

"Sure. Whatever." He watched her smile disappear

as she slipped out the door.

Adam's mind was already on the two script pages at the edge of the desk. He took the pages of vellum skin over and sat on the bed. He stared at them wondering how many times he'd studied the document that had sent his life into a tailspin. How many ways he had analyzed its words trying to find a deeper meaning. He knew what every word said. The whole world did by now. But there was something there they hadn't found yet. Something only the Bedouin knew, except now he didn't know anything. Adam tried to focus on the pages but couldn't get the sight and smell of Renie out of his mind.

Just then she appeared at the door, a tumbler in each hand. She stood before him in a sheer nightgown, her bare body silhouetted against the light. She moved toward him with the drinks then set them on the night stand. She took his hands in hers and stood him up facing her then pulled him toward her and held him so close it seemed she would never let him go. Then she surprised him by lifting his shirt over his head and pushing him on the bed.

After a moment, she dropped her nightgown on the floor. A fleeting glimpse of Emma flashed across his mind— then she was gone. Now it was Renie...only Renie. She guided him gently through something he'd almost forgotten how to do, it had been so long. The delight he experienced in that moment was a sensation he thought he'd never feel again.

Afterwards, they lay in a tangle of covers, all arms and legs, not wanting to move. Finally, he lifted his head and smiled at her. No matter how hard he tried, he couldn't help but love her. He knew it now more than ever.

She had turned his world upside down.

Digging Deep

Frank Harkin wiped the grit from his mouth with his tongue and washed it down with his own spittle. He glanced at Evelyn, amazed at how composed she looked after all she'd been through. It seemed to him like she'd marshaled some strength in the time they'd been with "the Animal" as Frank liked to call him but never to his face.

Before, Evelyn had only gaped into the woods with an empty stare. Now, Frank was sure he'd seen a spark, the glimpse of a fire he had no idea was down inside her. He knew she hated the woods. That she'd rather be dead than go through any more of this hell.

Both were tied up, as was the Animal's pattern when he went off to gather food and supplies. Frank had finally figured out he must be stealing them from the Lodge at LeConte. Little bits at a time. Sometimes from the campers who overnighted there. Sometimes from the Lodge's storehouse of provisions. It was a good thing or they would have died. The Animal had confiscated excellent tents and camping equipment. Plenty of warm clothes for all them. He got food that didn't have to be cooked since a fire would have given away their location. Frank was impressed that the Animal even knew how to put Iodine tablets in their water, one per liter, to kill the Giardia, a parasite that caused violent diarrhea. Frank figured the Animal must be some kind of a survivalist. He couldn't believe no one had found them yet. The search party had come near once, and Frank had wanted to yell. But the barrel of the gun in his face and the other one pointed at Evelyn's head had stopped him.

That was two weeks ago. He knew the search parties must have given them up for dead by now. No one imagined they would still be alive. Temperatures had dropped to freezing and below several nights in a row. It had already snowed twice. Frank looked up. Something like great puffs of pipe smoke had settled on top of the mountains. He tried to speak, but his throat was too dry. He could barely manage more than a grunt.

"Evelyn," he croaked in a hoarse whisper.

Nothing.

He tried again. "Evelyn? Can you hear me?"

No response.

"I know you're in there somewhere."

She turned her head toward him, but merely stared.

"Morning," said Frank.

She only mumbled something. But at least it was something. For days she had said nothing. Like the life had gone out of her. Her face was chapped and hard like the jagged gray bark of the red spruce tree against which she leaned. Her hands were as rough as corncobs, her hair a matted bird's nest. She blended right in with the woods. Catatonic camouflage. He could tell she had long since stopped worrying about her appearance. And yet, to Frank she looked more beautiful than ever.

The Animal had given them both warm clothes and fitted Evelyn with a sturdy pair of hiking boots. He'd made them get up and walk, hands bound, a little bit every day so they wouldn't waste away. At first, Frank hated the forced marches but couldn't tell what Evelyn thought because she never said anything. Each day they'd hike a little farther. It had been rough going at times, especially through the thick laurel slicks and rhododendron hells. It seemed to Frank that the Animal was preparing them for something, but what?

He heard the Animal coming from a long way off.

Frank's ears had become attuned to every little sound. If a Blackburnian warbler or a red-breasted nuthatch stepped on a single pine needle in search of food, Frank heard it. He could even distinguish which direction the wind blew by the sound of it whispering through the tallest trees as it blew over the lee side of the mountain. He could tell which varmint was which by the crunch of the forest under its feet. Most of all, he could distinguish their kidnapper's gait from every other creature in the Park.

Frank thought the Animal seemed to be in a hurry this time.

"Morning, children! Another great day at Camp Kidnapped. Looks like things are drawing to a close and we may leave this beautiful mountain resort. Isn't that a pity? 'Course, if my man doesn't check in, then you get to stay here forever. But he will. He always does. And guess what? Someone's going to fly us out of here."

"Fly?" said Frank. "How?"

"Helicopter, what else?"

"From where?"

"LeConte. How do you think they get provisions up to the Lodge?"

Frank remembered that the llamas came up three times a week, but in March the bulk of the supplies for the spring and summer were hauled in by helicopter off of Clingman's Dome. The Animal was right.

"You mean we're going to hike back up to the Lodge from here?" grumbled Frank.

"Well, you can do that or I can shoot you. Take your choice. Personally, I'd much rather shoot you and leave on my own. But those aren't my orders and I always follow orders."

"Or you don't get paid."

"Something like that. Anyway, you don't have a choice. I gotta get you both outta here before you die on me, and I don't know how much longer you're going to last. Me?

I could stay up here a long time, supplies or no supplies. But, you two? Not a chance. So, get ready to move."

Evelyn remained silent. Frank thought she seemed more at peace than he'd ever seen her before. He wondered if it was the calm that comes just before death when the body knows the end is near. He thought he almost caught a hint of a smile on her face. He wondered what she was thinking.

The Animal gathered some of his things into a backpack.

Frank noticed he wasn't dismantling the tents, which meant he intended to assault the mountain in a single day. "We'll never make it by nightfall through all this thicket."

"You're right, newspaper man. That is, if we went cross-country. But we're going to head up this way and catch the Boulevard Trail. Then it will be clear sailing to the Lodge."

Frank glanced at Evelyn who looked a wreck, but seemed remarkably composed.

The Animal untied their hands so they could keep their balance then pointed the way. He'd actually made something of a path on his many trips up and down, but not too much in case a hunting party returned. Steadying himself, Frank began the climb looking at old gnarled trees that clung to the edges of rocky crags. Evelyn stepped up behind him in silence. The Animal took another look at the campsite and brought up the rear.

About a hundred feet from the Boulevard Trail, the Animal, said, "Stop here."

Odd, thought Frank. He'd never given them that kind of reprieve before. He seemed to Frank more agitated than usual.

"Put your stuff down. We'll rest here a minute."

Both Frank and Evelyn threw their packs on the ground.

"Why are you staring at us like that?" said Frank.

"Because this is the end of the line."

"What do you mean?"

"He means," replied Evelyn who hadn't put two words together for weeks, "he's going to kill us."

Frank was astonished both at what she had said and how calmly she said it.

The Animal offered a toothy grin. "She's right."

Evelyn glared at the Animal in a way that must have made him feel more like the hunted than the hunter because Frank could see an odd mix of rage and fear bubbling to the surface of her demeanor.

"No. Please," Frank said. "Why are you doing this? I thought you were taking us to LeConte?"

"She knows why, don't you?" said the Animal to Evelyn.

"It's because his contact hasn't checked in," Evelyn said with no emotion in her voice.

"That's right," said the Animal turning and pointing the gun directly at Frank's head. "You first. Don't want you around while I bed the girl."

Frank cowered with arms upraised, tensing in preparation for the end. "No, no!"

Behind his back, Evelyn picked up a large rock she saw near her foot and hid it behind her back.

"Shut up! Die like a man."

Before shooting Frank, the Animal turned back toward Evelyn, and at the same moment she hurled the large rock at him. It hit him right between the eyes, staggering him. Startled, he regained his balance and tried to re-focus.

Before he could get his bearing, Evelyn stepped forward and kicked him full force in the groin, doubling him over in pain.

Then she picked up a thick, sturdy limb of a fallen Sweet Birch tree. She waited until he lifted his head slightly and let him have it square across the jaw.

The Animal was airborne now. He tumbled through the thicket until his body smacked with a thunderous clap into the trunk of a Carolina Hemlock, then dropped to the ground in a heap.

Frank stood stunned. He couldn't believe Evelyn had clocked their kidnapper with the sweetest swing Frank Harkin had ever seen. He wondered if the Animal had taken the brunt of all of Evelyn's frustration toward all the men in her life. He was glad he had not been on the other end of it. He could see the adrenaline coursing through her body as she turned to him with fire in her eyes.

"Don't hit me! I'm on your side!" Frank yelled. Then he stepped forward and embraced her. She started to sob then caught herself, tension humming through her body.

"We've got to go, Frank. Now! He might still be alive!"

"I can't see how, but I'm with you. Let's get outta here."

As they grabbed their backpacks, the cell phone rang. It had fallen out of the Animal's pocket when Evelyn leveled him. Frank found it on the ground hidden in some pine needles.

"Don't answer it! We don't have time."

Frank hesitated.

The phone continued to ring.

Frank picked up the phone, punched the button, and grunted, "That you?"

"Good! I caught you. You haven't killed them yet, have you?"

"What do you think? What was I supposed to do?" said Frank, trying to imitate the Animal's voice.

"Oh my God, no!" yelled Adam now slipping into his own voice. "You weren't supposed to until I told you!"

"Wait a minute..." said Frank. He covered the mouthpiece and whispered to Evelyn, "I think I know this guy." But he couldn't quite place it.

The phrase, "Wait a minute," must have been enough for Adam.

302

"Frank is that you? Is Evelyn still alive?"

Frank stood speechless for the second time in a single day.

"Adam?"

"Yes, Frank, it's me. And Renie is with me."

"What?!"

"Frank. I can explain."

"Frank, we've got to go!" said Evelyn. "I'm sure there's an explanation. But we've got to get out of here."

"Frank, listen to me," said Adam. "I don't know how you got free. But you're not safe until you get out of the Park. What are you close to?"

"The Boulevard Trail. We're gonna head to LeConte."

"Get moving! You can get some help at the top. Go! Now!"

Frank and Evelyn bundled up and started the climb. Neither one of them spoke, not wanting to waste any breath on words. They hoped they were heading in the right direction. But they were relieved to be free. The going was harder for Frank than for Evelyn. She seemed to have more energy than ever before. She looked like she could have run up Alum Cave Bluff Trail, the steepest one around, without stopping. Frank couldn't understand how she'd rebounded from near death to super human power. She seemed to take to the forest like an experienced mountaineer. He couldn't believe how much she'd changed.

"I found it, Frank!" she said. "Boulevard!"

"Good work!" he heaved as his breath plumed in huge, white puffs above him.

As they worked their way through the last branches of the spruce-fir stand alongside the trail, Frank collapsed on the layered gray shale. They looked up and down the narrow ridge-spine that led to Mt. LeConte. A delicate, hoary lace mantled the trees, not snow or ice so much as a thin dusting of frozen fog.

"Come on, Frank," said the tireless one. "We can't stop now. Just a couple more miles."

Frank pulled his exhausted, worn body to its feet and started up the tunnel trail. Evelyn led the way. Fine with him. All he wanted to do was get to the top. Suddenly he felt light as a feather as he followed Evelyn, marching at a good clip between mountain ash and fire cherry trees on both sides of the trail. They clutched the steel cable rail as they traversed the enormous slide of Hurricane Opal. Sheets of water seeped through layer upon layer of shale in what looked to Frank like great mounds of baklava. God, I'm hungry, he said to himself. And thirsty. "I need some water."

"Okay. Quick stop," Evelyn agreed. When she turned to hand him her water bottle Frank caught a look in her eyes that drained the blood from his face.

"Oh my God!"

Frank took a quick glance back and saw the Animal not more than fifty feet behind them, stumbling toward them like a wild man on a mission in a half-stagger, half-run.

The Second Mile

Jerusalem

Adam bent over the Bedouin in ICU, pleading with him. "Surely you can remember something!"

"It's useless," said the Israeli doctor. "We've talked to him several times now and he knows nothing of the recent years of his life. It's as if they never happened. He recalls only his childhood and his early adult years. Beyond that, a blank."

"How long can this last?" said Adam.

"Weeks, maybe months. Sometimes it never comes back. Sometimes it can come back just like that," said the physician, snapping his fingers.

"We don't have weeks or months. We have to know now." Adam paced the floor. "Isn't there something you can do to bring him around?"

"Nothing. He needs rest. I think you should leave."

"Look," said Adam to the doctor. "He's trying to say something!"

All the Bedouin could muster was, "Doctor, who is this man?"

Adam felt the knot tighten in his stomach.

He took the elevator to the floor above and moved down the hall to the old Greek woman's room. "How is she?" he asked the Brit.

"About the same," said McPherson. "Glad you came. She may be nearing the end. She's asleep now."

305

*   *   *

The Smoky Mountains

Frank couldn't take another step. He'd run all he could around the last few bends at the top of Mt. LeConte. He collapsed on the trail just past the shelter.

There the Animal caught up with him.

Evelyn dropped her backpack and sprinted the last hundred feet up to the Lodge.

The Animal kicked Frank across the mid-section. "You're comin' with me so you can see me kill that bitch. Get movin'! Now!!"

The Animal yanked Frank up the trail the final hundred feet. As they approached the cabins, they saw a bearded young man in front of Evelyn and the other campers. He had a shotgun in his hand pointed directly at Brock.

"Mister. I don't know who you are, but you need to drop your gun."

Before the young man had a moment to think, the Animal had nailed him between the eyes. He toppled back in slow motion like a tall tree that had just been felled. Campers nearby screamed and scattered into the woods, but Evelyn stood her ground.

"Smart, Woman," grumbled the Animal as he wiped dried blood mixed with sweat and spit from his face with the back of his hand. A large blue bump rose like an Easter egg in the middle of his forehead. "You knew I would catch you again, didn't you? You're smarter than I thought, lady."

Frank threw up and collapsed on the ground, awake enough to be living the nightmare.

"What a sorry excuse for a human being," said the Animal, glancing at the newspaperman who lay like a lump of clay in the mud.

"Funny, I was just thinking the same thing about you," said Evelyn.

"Sister, I gotta give it to you. You got balls. Certainly, more than this one. Never got banged by a woman like that before. I'm usually the one who's doin' the bangin'."

Frank lay helpless, trying to swallow the fear that clogged his throat while Evelyn stood defiant, hands on her hips, feet firmly planted.

The Animal held the gun steady as their glances locked.

"We don't have time for that now," interrupted a man who appeared from nowhere.

The Animal moved the gun barrel slightly, pointing it over Evelyn's left shoulder at the man who approached from behind her. "Who are you?"

"I'm your flight out of here."

"Where's Ronny?"

"Sent me instead."

"All right. But you're going to have to help me get this one on. He's pretty far gone."

"What about her?"

"She's comin' too. But keep an eye on her. She's more dangerous than a rattler. Where's the copter?"

"Over there," replied the pilot, pointing at a thick weald of conifers.

The four of them navigated the small, narrow trail to the blowdown where the copter sat ready. Frank and Evelyn tumbled in the aft as the Animal and the pilot strapped in up front.

Trees and bushes bent back from the force of the wind as the chopper rose above Myrtle Point then angled off toward Porters Creek Trail. They lifted above the forest and flew a few minutes before anyone said anything.

The Animal was the first to speak. All he said was, "Here's a good spot. Let's drop 'em here."

The helicopter floated through a thick gray mist that drifted in strands and threads like so much gauze over the dense, shrub understory along Brushy Mountain Trail. A light snow had begun to fall, cloaking the whole area with a hoary ashen frost. The craft tilted one way then the other, causing Frank and Evelyn to topple over each other.

"Hold it still, will you?" yelled the Animal, staggering to the back seats.

"Be careful," said the pilot. "When you pitch them out the loss of weight could throw us off balance."

"Just do your job, and I'll do mine!" The Animal glared at the pilot. "Come on, bitch," he growled, reaching for Evelyn, "it's time to fly!"

"Leave her alone," stammered Frank.

When Frank tried to help, the Animal tossed him aside like a small stuffed toy, knocking him out.

He seized the front of Evelyn's shirt and jerked her to the gaping space on the side, a one-way ticket to the trees below.

The wind gusted and lifted the copter off its trajectory. A downwash caused it to dive. The Animal reeled, trying to fling Evelyn out the door, but something stopped him.

The pilot's foot landed in his stomach, catapulting him to the wind-blasted open door. The pilotless copter began to plummet as the pilot planted a hard fist on the Animal's face.

Evelyn screamed, "We're going down!"

"Who are you?" yelled the Animal, barely hanging on with one hand.

The pilot answered with an elbow to the ribs then one good shove, and the Animal was airborne.

The out-of-control copter spiraled toward the snow-cloaked forest. Quickly, the pilot jumped into his seat and righted the craft. Evelyn watched the Animal plunge to the ground, his fall not cushioned by soft pine needles or newly fallen flurries, but by the trunk of a great White Ash tree, which broke his back and shattered his skull.

"Yes!" yelled Evelyn in a blood-curdling cry. "Get up Frank, he's dead! Thank God, that animal is dead!"

"How did you get him?" said Frank, coming back to consciousness, rubbing the back of his head.

"I didn't," she yelled, pointing to the pilot, "he did."

"Who are you?" Frank said.

As they soared over Cove Mountain, the pilot turned and smiled.

"My name is Marcello."

A Painful Truth

Adam punched in the numbers for Coleman Ashburn's mobile phone.

"Hello," said a voice.

"Coleman, sorry about the hour."

"Adam? That you? Don't worry; I'm up. How's it going with that manuscript?"

"Not very well, I'm afraid. Have you got anything?"

"Maybe there's a piece missing."

"I know just the person who can help you. The Bishop of Jerusalem. I gave him your email address. He'll be in touch."

"I'll watch for it."

"I have a private fax machine in my hotel room. Fax your translation to me here and no one else."

"Got it."

"I'm serious. For my eyes only."

"I understand."

Adam gave him the fax number.

"Time's running out, Coleman."

"Already got the coffee brewing. And Adam…"

"Yeah?"

"Thanks for asking."

"Just get to work." Adam hung up and smiled, thinking of his washed-up, old friend getting a chance to show his stuff.

Renie entered the room with a look that said she had

something on her mind.

"Conrad's cell phone rang while you were on with Coleman," she said.

"Who was it?"

"I don't know, but he hung up when he heard my voice."

"Does that thing have caller ID?"

"I'll check." She punched a couple of buttons and there it was. "Looks like a number in the States."

Adam thought for a moment. "I have a friend at the Bureau who owes me one."

He called the G-man in the middle of a meeting. "Sorry, Sam. It's a matter of national security. I want to know whose number this is, and everything about it. When you get it, fax the information to my room and nowhere else." Adam gave him the number. "Thanks, Sam."

He hung up and looked at Renie. Her face telegraphed a question.

"When am I going to find out who you really are?"

"Not now."

"I want some answers or we have no future together."

Adam stared at her. He didn't have the luxury of thinking about the future anymore. For him life was nothing but a dark and ugly past, a past he'd botched himself. Now he was bringing Renie down with him. Why had he made love to her? It only complicated things.

"I'm damaged goods," Adam said. "Whatever I touch dies."

"I've heard that speech. I want to hear the other one. Don't you see? I know you love me. But you have to give me this before I can really love you."

"I've never told anyone. Not all of it anyway."

"Why not start with me?"

He sat on the bed and stared at a point somewhere between his knees. After a pause, he summoned himself and began telling her about his time in the CIA. His brief

311

marriage to the love of his life. How the job in New York, which was to have been his last, went bad. He told her about the Bedouin, the minivan, and the warning that came too late. The slow recovery in the hospital. The years in seminary, then the parish in Maryville.

He omitted only one detail—the young man who also died that day. He couldn't bring himself to tell her.

He didn't have to.

Suddenly, she sat up straight and said, "Wait a minute. When did you say it happened?" Her face turned white as she added it all up.

She stood and slapped him hard, then turned and walked across the room.

"Why?" she said finally, her back to him.

All he could do was shake his head. "You're the reason I came to Maryville, once I found out who Eric was. I thought I could help you or repay you in some way. I never expected to..." He couldn't finish the sentence.

She got to her feet. "I never want to see you again." She stormed out the door, leaving her suitcase and clothes behind.

A Debt Repaid

The Smoky Mountains

Evelyn yelled over the drone of the rotors, "Thank you, whoever you are!"

"Look, another copter!" barked Harkin.

Marcello peered out the door as they crossed Round Top.

Machine gun fire ricocheted off the landing rails as Marcello banked hard to the port side and made a sharp descent into Tuckaleechee Cove. He sailed over Townsend with the other copter right on his tail. The aerial firefight sent cars on the road below scattering.

Like a large humming bird, Marcello's chopper buzzed up and down as Frank and Evelyn, down on all fours, tried to grab hold of anything bolted down.

A hail of bullets showered them as Marcello did his best to dodge right then left. Some of them sprayed the trees below.

Smoke trailed behind them signaling they'd been hit.

Marcello tried every trick he knew to lose his assailant, but he couldn't shake him. At one point the attacking copter came so close that Marcello got a good look at the pilot. It was the shock of blond hair that tipped him off.

"Why is he shooting at us?" Frank yelled.

"He wants me," Marcello said. Just past the Foothills Parkway, he allowed Schiller to settle in behind him and at the last second before sailing through Walland Gap, he angled sharply to the left and headed back across West Miller's Cove. The stratagem worked since the German had no choice but to fly through the Gap then turn around.

Marcello could not believe how quickly Schiller's copter caught up with him as they raced over Hesse Creek. At Top-of-the-World, he did a sharp U-turn.

Schiller had to lift suddenly to avoid hitting the side of the mountain. His copter floated up with a clear view of Happy Valley.

Marcello dashed back over Hesse Creek. Banking around the Foothills Parkway, he flew through Walland Gap and landed on the left side of the road. His wounded copter was a dying quail. He knew it couldn't go another mile.

"Quick, into that car!" Marcello said.

Frank and Evelyn stumbled toward a Dodge Van and jumped in. The van's owner was bird-watching at the edge of the woods.

"Hey! That's my car," the man said, stumbling out of the forest, fumbling his binoculars.

Marcello peeled out onto Lamar Alexander Parkway, but something caused him to veer off the road.

Schiller's helicopter had landed on the highway in front of them.

Marcello steered the van around the copter as Schiller splattered them with machine gun fire.

Frank and Evelyn ducked as the back window shattered, spraying broken glass all over them.

Schiller jumped from his craft and pointed his weapon at an approaching sedan, which squealed to a stop. Its driver willingly gave up his green Mercedes, and ran off the road to hide.

Marcello could see Schiller in the distance in his rearview mirror.

"Stay down! We haven't lost him yet."

Both cars were doing 80, then 90 heading into Maryville. The Mercedes was gaining on them.

Suddenly Marcello hung a sharp left into the parking lot of the Little River Trading Company.

"Get in that store and lock yourselves inside!" yelled Marcello.

Neither Frank nor Evelyn needed any encouragement, nearly flying through the sliding door of the van and stumbling for the entrance of the hiking gear outlet. Frank knocked a display of fleece shirts over as they charged through the door. Startled clerks and customers backed away from them in waves. From a window in the store Frank and Evelyn could see everything, peeking over the edge of the sill from their crouched positions.

They watched as the Mercedes squealed into the lot.

Schiller jumped from it, an automatic in each hand.

Sirens whined in the distance as Marcello stepped from behind the van. There was nothing between him and the German. He pulled a silencer from a holster below his left shoulder. "Thought you were after the American."

"First things first."

When someone from the bike shop yelled, "Watch out!" Marcello glanced away.

In that split second Schiller hit him twice in the chest.

Frank and Evelyn saw Schiller jump in the car and head into Maryville.

A swarm of police cars appeared as flashing lights filled the parking lot.

Onlookers from the stores watched to see if it was safe to go out now.

Frank and Evelyn burst from the hiking store and ran to Marcello's side. Evelyn sat on the asphalt, cradling the Sicilian's head in her lap as a trickle of blood ran from the edge of his mouth. "Hang on!" she pled. "An ambulance is on the way."

Marcello smiled.

Frank knelt beside him and held his hand.

"Thank you for saving our lives."

He smiled again then died.

Evelyn cupped his head in her hands and held him close to her breast.

The ambulance screeched to a halt and paramedics poured around them. They took his pulse. "This one's gone," one said.

For the first time since all of it had begun, Evelyn began to sob. She couldn't help herself. It was a floodgate.

One of the police officers said, "Excuse me, Ma'am. But did you know this man?"

"Can't you see she's in no shape to answer questions now?" said Frank indignantly, his arm around her shoulder. "Can't we do this later?"

Evelyn stumbled away from the body in a daze, hypnotized by the flashing red lights.

"Ma'am," said one of the paramedics, "We better take you two over to Blount Memorial ER. Looks like you've both been through hell."

"And back," said Frank.

Breathless

R enie opened the door to her room and peeked around the corner, making sure Adam wasn't there. She moved with dispatch, cramming her clothes into a suitcase. She thought about all she'd been through because of him. Then she thought about all they'd been through together.

She glanced into his room one last time and saw one of his shirts on the bed. She picked it up and sniffed it. It smelled of him, a deep, musky odor she'd know anywhere now.

Then looking at the desk she noticed a fax had come in. She glanced over her shoulder, thinking he might return any minute. She moved toward the fax machine and picked up the sheets. One of them slipped from her fingers and cascaded to the floor. Her hand quivered as she retrieved it.

The fax was from Coleman Ashburn. She tried to read it, adjusting her glasses to overcome the blur. Finally, it came into focus. It seemed pretty technical from what she could make out. Lots of Greek words with codes and numbers. There were references to scripture passages. She could tell it had been written hurriedly.

Then she read something that caused her breath to stop. She sat down on the edge of the bed to ponder its meaning.

She jumped at the sound of another page printing on the fax machine and snatched it from the tray. It was from the FBI contact. It had the address, the company and the name of the man who had called the cell phone.

She stood there for a moment. My God, she said to herself. This is the only information anyone has about what's really going to happen! Adam would want this. But where is he?

*   *   *

Once Adam had retrieved the Codex from the bishop's safe-keeping, he began pacing the shadowed tunnels of the old city.

"*La Shukron!* No, thank you!" he said to all the merchants, peddling their wares. The strong aroma of paprika, curry, and cumin filled the air. He held the old canvas bag close to him as the strap pulled hard on his shoulder from its weight. Pilgrims and sightseers choked the narrow alleyways in anticipation of the upcoming peace event.

Israeli soldiers stood sentry at each corner. Adam counted scores of them everywhere, all of them carrying Uzis. Their eyes darted about the crowd in search of terrorists. Adam was surprised at how quiet it had been throughout Jerusalem. Not a single bombing or assassination attempt.

He elbowed his way up the Via Dolorosa by the Austrian Hospice and around the corner by the Alawiya School for girls. As he passed the Alexandrovsky Russian Church, he glanced down the long roadway that extended from the Damascus Gate to the southern end of the Armenian Quarter and thought he saw someone he knew. But it wasn't. His eyes were playing tricks on him.

He slipped inside the vaulted entry to the Lutheran Church of the Redeemer. A couple of pilgrims were scattered here and there in prayer. He felt the chill, could see and hear his breath. His soft steps echoed about the great chamber. He surveyed the lean, elegant lines of the old

318

cathedral. Its high-ceilinged rafters seemed forever out of reach. Soaring pillars, capped with Corinthian columns, arched their way from the back of the nave to the chancel. He moved to the front pew and sat down. Taking a slow, deep breath, he wondered if Renie would ever forgive him. If he could ever forgive himself.

He sat there in prayer for a while, then got up suddenly and turned around, certain he had heard someone. He gazed deep into the nave, but the place was empty now. Everyone had left.

He walked to the large, low pulpit on the right and stood in it, imagining the church, full. He raised his hand in the air to make a silent point.

Then a thought came and he headed out of the church quickly.

*   *   *

Back at the suite Adam had shared with Renie, there was a quiet that unnerved him. He approached his bed and saw his shirt had been moved. He'd been trained to notice details.

"Renie?"

No response.

He moved into her room and realized she had gone. She'd left nothing behind except for a hint of her perfumed fragrance that hung low in the air.

He checked his watch. Why hasn't Coleman faxed his translations? Surely, he's decoded that thing by now.

He glanced at the fax machine. There was nothing in the tray.

Quickly Adam punched in Coleman's number. No response.

He pushed the button that identified incoming faxes. And there it was. Two had come not an hour before. But where were they and who could have taken them?

It had to have been Renie when she came back for

her clothes.

But where was she now?

Presidential Prerogative

Renie crossed the lobby of the King David Hotel and stopped in front of the elevator that led to the Presidential penthouse suite.

"That's far enough," said a Secret Service Agent.

"I have to see the President," she said. "It's a matter of life and death."

The agent smiled. "It always is."

"It's about the summit tomorrow."

"Tell me something new," he replied.

"I'm Adam Hunter's...friend, Renie Ellis."

He looked her over carefully, then put his wrist to his mouth and mumbled something.

Renie waited, her eyes searching his.

The agent's whole demeanor changed. "Someone will be down in a moment," he said in a more official tone.

"Thanks." Renie tried to smile, but her nerves took over as she worked hard to remain calm.

Watching the numbers change on the elevator, she looked at the front door and contemplated running. When she began moving toward the front door of the lobby, the elevator door opened.

Pete Ashton stepped from the elevator, a serious look on his face. The seriousness curved into a smile as he extended his hand.

"Ms. Ellis, I'm Pete Ashton. I work for the President."

Renie shook his hand quickly as she studied his face. Motioning to the elevator, he spoke in a calm, soothing voice. "Let's go upstairs."

Renie smiled nervously at Ashton as she listened to the BING of the floors and watched the numbers count up. They rode to the top in silence. At the penthouse floor, they entered a large hallway filled with people. She counted fifteen or twenty Secret Service officers up and down the hall. The President's people had command of the entire floor. There were lots of nods and whispers.

Ashton touched her arm softly as he led her into one of the rooms, a beautifully appointed suite. He offered her a chair.

"Where's the President?" she asked as she sat down slowly.

"What do you have for her?"

"I really wanted to give it to her myself. Perhaps, I've made a mistake." She started to get up.

Ashton replied, "No. You did the right thing coming here. Let me see it."

She took the fax from her purse.

When he got hold of it, she started to pull it back, initiating a slight tug-of-war. Something's not right about this, she said to herself. I should have waited for Adam. I should have given it to him.

"If you can't trust the President, who can you trust?" Ashton asked, pulling it from her hand.

Ashton studied the fax for a moment then returned it to her.

"Wait here."

She nodded as he left the room.

In a couple of minutes, she saw President Sanchez walk through the door, alone.

"Ms. Ellis, how good to meet you." Renie got up, dropping her purse on the floor, and held her hand out.

"The honor is mine, Madame President."

"My Chief of Staff says you have something for me."

Renie paused then handed it to her, wondering if this

was the mistake of a lifetime.

The President examined it briefly with a furrowed brow. Finally, she nodded slowly and looked at Renie. "I'm glad you brought this to me. Could I ask you a question?"

"Of course."

"Who is this Coleman Ashburn who sent the fax?"

"Coleman? Oh, he's just an old classics professor who used to teach at Maryville College."

"In the town where you and Adam Hunter live?"

"Yes."

"Thank you so much for bringing it. Have you told anyone else about this?"

"Not a soul."

"Good. Thanks again for coming. Pete will show you out."

"Thank you, Madame President."

Ashton appeared at the door to lead her to the elevator.

As she walked down the hallway, she felt like she was going to throw up. "God, I hope I did the right thing!"

Illusive Absolution

Rome

Don Mazzini's face said it all. "Forgive me, Father, for I have sinned."

Lorenzo noticed the curtains had been drawn in the spacious suite. Two of the Don's burly guards bookended the door. The Don sobbed. His eyes reflected a broken spirit.

"What's the matter?"

"I have done something terrible."

The Cardinal laid his hand on the Don's. "Tell old Lorenzo."

"Marcello is dead." Mazzini stared as if into a deep abyss. "My God, what have I done?"

"How?"

"Schiller."

The Don looked like a man in front of a firing squad. The Cardinal knew the Don loved Marcello, had taught him everything about the business and groomed him to take over someday.

"I gave the order myself. But I never imagined that the thickheaded German would catch him. There was no one better than my precious Marcello. It was just a test. The boy had gotten sloppy, so I brought in Schiller to push him a little, just like my father did with me. But I never thought for a moment...he was so much smarter than that stupid kraut."

"*Si*, Don Mazzini."

"It was just a test. Do you understand?"

The Cardinal nodded.

"A kind of final trial before I could hand the reins over to him. I never should have brought that Nazi in. But Marcello should have taken him. Something must have gone wrong."

"God will forgive you."

"He was my son."

The sentence sent a chill up the Cardinal's spine. "Your son?"

"*Si*," said the Don, tears welling up. "A woman...long ago...more beautiful than you have ever seen...we were lovers..." He smiled and paused. "But we couldn't marry. Wrong family. She couldn't keep the child, so she disappeared. The baby went to an orphanage. At first, I didn't know where, but eventually I found out and financed his education anonymously, keeping my distance until he was grown. Our meeting at my niece's wedding was no accident."

"He didn't know?"

The Don shook his head. "I never told him."

The Cardinal studied the Don's face. He saw the resemblance now that he thought about it, the eyes especially.

The Don fell on his knees, collapsing across the Cardinal's lap. "God, forgive me for killing my own son!" The lament sounded like the closing aria of a tragic opera.

Lorenzo could not say the words of absolution.

The Don mopped his tears with the back of his hand and got to his feet. "This manuscript is no threat to the church. You were wrong about that, Lorenzo."

The Cardinal dipped his head in deference, at first biting his tongue.

"Schiller must be stopped," the Don said.

"Will you be able to stop him?"

"If Marcello couldn't, I don't know who can."

Cracking the Code

The Dome of the Rock

A dam thought it a golden day that only an act of terrorism could tarnish, but Moshe was in charge of security, and that gave Adam at least a modicum of solace. The Dome of the Rock's bright orb rivaled the sun that day. Inside the Dome, Adam stood with Moshe near the entrance, watching the Jordanian prince, the Pope, President Sanchez, the Israeli Prime Minister and other world leaders lining up for the procession. Protocol officers had argued all night about who should march out first and who should sit where. American Secret Service, Vatican Swiss Guards and Israeli Shin Bet surrounded the little entourage on its way to the large platform at the north end of Haram Al-Sharif. The political leaders waved and gave thumbs up to the crowd. The Pope and Salaam smiled as they strode forward in solemn procession.

Adam estimated the multitude to be a couple of thousand. God only knew how many choked the narrow streets of the old city. Dozens of soldiers on watch, silhouetted against a bright, blue sky, lined the rooftops. He shaded his eyes from the fierce Israeli sun, straining to catch a glimpse of Renie, but she was nowhere in sight. No sign of Schiller, either. He'd gotten the report from home about Marcello's daring rescue then death.

As they approached the specially built platform, Adam noticed a helicopter to the right, an American-built Sikorsky the Israelis called Yanshuf or Owl. It was ready for

326

a quick escape if necessary. The stage, itself, stood nearly one story off the ground. He'd already been informed that, behind the podium there was a trap door that would open automatically if trouble began. The dignitaries had been instructed to leap into it and slide down the custom-made chute into the secure space below. Under the dais was a whole world of Israeli intelligentsia—firepower, electronic surveillance, and an enormous bunker that had been specifically designed to protect its inhabitants from attack.

Adam slipped to the side of the platform as the leaders mounted the rostrum. The crowd's babble escalated another decibel level until the announcer quieted them enough to say, "Ladies and Gentleman, the President of the United States!"

Adam pressed his hand against his side. There was the knot again. He could feel it in his gut. Something was wrong. He surveyed the masses, but saw nothing.

The President began her speech about peace and good will.

Two minutes into it, the sound of a popgun stopped her mid-sentence.

Everyone looked around to see where it had come from. Then there was another.

Secret Service officers pulled President Sanchez to the floor.

Other security officers shielded their leaders.

"What was that?" said Adam to Moshe as he searched the rooftops.

Moshe was on his cell phone to the Prime Minister. "Fireworks," he said with a smile.

Adam watched Ben-Shalom whisper to the President, who returned to the mike and quieted the crowd. "Sorry about the interruption," said the President. "Everything is fine."

People craned their heads in all directions trying to figure out what had caused the noise.

Adam could feel an odd mix of dread and anticipation in the air.

Moshe pointed at the helicopter. "We can see a lot more from above."

They both climbed onto the Sikorsky as Moshe scrambled into the pilot's seat and started the engine.

Adam heard Renie's voice behind him and turned to see her running his direction. A couple of Israeli soldiers held her back.

"It's okay. Let her through," he yelled over the whine of the copter.

"We need to go!" Moshe said.

Renie sprinted through the secure area. "Wait! Your faxes."

The rotors beat the air, nearly blowing Renie off her feet. "Read this!" she screamed, thrusting the documents into his outstretched hand.

"What is it?"

The helicopter lifted slightly, now hovering five feet off the ground.

"The fax from Coleman and the other one from your friend in Washington."

"Are these the originals?"

"No," she yelled. "I gave them to the President!"

"You made copies?"

"I'm a lawyer. Remember?" she yelled with a smile as they pulled away.

He gave her a little salute as the copter lifted high above the crowd. He watched her shrink then disappear into the swarm below.

Adam quickly lost himself in the fax that Coleman had sent. Excitement welled up inside him. He read quickly as the Israeli copter dipped starboard and rose above the old city.

The peace summit continued below. The Pope had the microphone.

The whole world watched.

Adam dug his cell phone out of his pocket and punched in Coleman's number in Tennessee.

"Coleman!" yelled Adam.

"Adam? You get my fax?"

"Yeah, just now. How'd you figure it all out?"

"It all came together when I remembered that Greek letters are also numbers and the numbers had to refer to scripture verses. You'd better get outta there now."

"Why? These are just verses." Adam read the fax again hurriedly.

"Hardly. Hidden in them is the mode of terrorism and who's behind it all. The Bedouin must have put it in this riddle form to protect himself if one of them turned on him."

"What riddle?"

Adam noticed Moshe had piloted them back over the Western Wall in the Jewish Quarter. He held on as they rose high above the Al-Aqsa Mosque on the other end of the square.

"Well," said Coleman, "the II Chronicles 3 passage is about Mount Moriah, which is the old name for the Temple Mount..."

"Where we are right now!"

"That's right," said Coleman. "The Ezekiel 3:12 passage, 'Then the Spirit lifted me up and as the glory of the Lord rose from its place, I heard the sound of loud rumbling,' refers to the helicopter. But, here's the kicker. Took me the longest to sort it out. Look at the Ezekiel 1:13 passage. I have it printed out there for you. Do you see it?"

Adam skimmed the verse that read, "In the middle of the living creatures there was something that looked like burning coals of fire ..."

"I see it, but what does it mean?"

"Think Greek, Adam, not Hebrew. I didn't get it until the Bishop emailed me the clue."

The helicopter now hovered directly above the dais.

Prime Minister Ben-Shalom was wrapping up his speech.

"What clue?"

"The word for burning coals in Greek."

Adam gulped. The knot in his stomach scorched his insides. "Oh God. Anthrax."

He glanced at the other fax Renie had thrust in his hand, the one from the FBI. The phone number for the man who'd called Conrad's phone was from a biotechnology lab in Boulder, Colorado.

"That's right," said Coleman, "and the names for those involved are all there too and the first one is Moses!"

Adam looked at the pilot next to him.

"I see you have figured it," Moshe said with a broad smile. As the copter banked to the port side then starboard, it began to soar across the great square from north to south. Lifting over the Dome of the Rock, Adam caught a glimpse of the fine spray trailing behind them spewing over the crowd. Around the great mosque, the chopper blanketed them with a silky death mist.

"Stop! Take it down, now!" yelled Adam, but Moshe ignored him.

No bombs. No assassin's bullets. Only a fragile gossamer grave.

Adam grabbed at the controls causing the Sikorsky to lurch.

People below screamed and began stampeding in all directions. The religious and political leaders leapt for the trap door on the stage, but it did not open. Adam could see them pounding on it from above as he and Moshe buzzed the platform.

The guards covered the leaders' bodies, guns raised.

Moshe and Adam wrestled in mid-air as the chopper dipped then righted itself and aimed up again.

Adam fell out the side, hanging onto the rail with one hand.

Like waves of wheat in a fierce wind, the people

rippled this way and that.

Adam pulled himself up and swung at the Israeli, but missed.

"It's too late," yelled Moshe. "I have released it all now. Watch out. I'm going to land."

Adam wondered why Moshe wouldn't fly away to safety and kill him.

The helicopter settled on the ground right in front of the platform.

The dignitaries and the people were quiet. Everyone in Jerusalem knew about biological weapons. But no one was really prepared for it. Especially not a virulent form of anthrax.

"Why?" Adam yelled at Moshe as two Israeli intelligence men restrained him.

Moshe mounted the stage and addressed the leaders with the microphone turned off.

"This madman has brought us here to die," Moshe said pointing at Adam. "He lured us here under the pretense of peace. But it was really so he could kill us all with anthrax."

"I don't think so," said a man who had just walked up on the stage.

Adam couldn't believe his eyes.

Out of the Shadows

It was Stump Stevens in the flesh! The night Adam thought Stump had been blown to bits flashed before him.

"Arrest that man!" Moshe said, pointing at Adam.

"No, arrest Moshe," said Prime Minister Ben-Shalom.

Moshe, startled, began to charge off the stage, but was wrestled to the ground by a squad of Israeli Shin Bet officers.

President Sanchez stepped to the microphone with hands raised as she motioned for Stump and the Israeli Prime Minister to come stand at her side. "First, I must tell you that you're not going to die," she said.

The people in the crowd from around the world turned to each other with looks of relief on their faces. Their many languages filled the square with a cacophony of sound. They could hardly believe what had just happened.

President Sanchez quieted them again then invited Stump to the mike.

"Just this afternoon," Stump said, "we uncovered a plot, thanks to the help of a professor named Coleman Ashburn. He rightly surmised anthrax would be the weapon. Airborne aerosol release was the only way to distribute it, and the only aircraft cleared for flight in a ten-mile radius was this Israeli helicopter. Mr. Ashburn uncovered the name Moshe in the manuscript. So...just before he took off with Mr. Hunter, we switched the canisters. Prime Minister Ben-Shalom approved it. Mr. Hunter did not know when he boarded the helicopter. Do not worry. You are all going to live!"

Moshe struggled to get free, but was restrained by his own men.

"You mean that wasn't anthrax?" called out a reporter nearby.

"No. It was nitrous oxide or laughing gas. But it was so diluted by the time it hit the air, it probably won't have any effect on you at all. We also put water into the canister, which created the fine mist that was just sprayed on you. There is someone high up in our own government who is the mastermind behind this whole sordid plot."

He turned around and stared at the Americans.

President Sanchez looked at the Speaker of the House, Joseph Wellington.

"It's over," said Stump to the Speaker.

Wellington, brandishing an automatic, put the President in a chokehold, holding her at gunpoint from behind.

"There's no way out," President Sanchez said.

"For you, maybe."

Secret Service and Mossad officers moved toward him slowly.

"Stay back or she's dead," Wellington flashed his automatic at Adam. "It was perfect until the Bedouin brought you in."

"It's over, Joe," said Stump. "We know you sent someone to kill the Veep. He's been stopped. You'll never be President now. Give it up."

Adam walked toward Wellington calmly. "Shoot me, instead."

"One at a time." Wellington's eyes glazed like a wild, cornered animal's. He aimed his automatic at Stump Stevens.

The President elbowed the Speaker in the gut, and dropped to the ground.

Stump and Adam charged him at the same moment.

Wellington shot Stump in the arm a split second before Adam knocked the weapon from his hand.

Secret Service officers subdued Wellington and wrestled him to the floor.

The President dusted herself off and turned to Stump. "Are you alright?"

"It's nothing," he replied, rubbing his arm. "Just a flesh wound."

The President pointed to Wellington. "Get him out of my sight."

The Secret Service officers hauled the Speaker off. Shin Bet officers followed with Moshe. The cameras of the world caught it all live as stunned reporters began barking rapid-fire questions in the languages of the world.

President Sanchez moved back to the microphone. She invited the Pope, the Israeli Prime Minister and the Jordanian Prince to join her.

The babble of the crowd drowned out the reporters' questions.

The President shushed all of them by simply raising her hands and tamping them down on the air. "Terrorists tried to block the peace process today, but they were unsuccessful. Everything will continue as planned. Tomorrow evening we will hold a press conference to announce the next steps."

Adam looked around for Renie, but she was nowhere in sight.

*   *   *

Maryville

Coleman Ashburn sat on Frank Harkin's back porch, nursing his second glass of Frank's best single malt Scotch—the good stuff Frank kept for special occasions. They had been watching the whole peace event gone wild on Frank's small flat screen.

"Coleman, you're famous!" Frank said to the professor.

"All I did was translate a little manuscript, something I do every day."

"Perhaps, now you can get one of your books published after all these years."

"That'll be the day."

The phone rang.

Frank answered it. "Yes, he's here." He put his hand over the speaker. "It's President Sanchez wanting to speak to Professor Ashburn. Can't run, can't hide. Not anymore!"

"Wonder how she found me here?"

"Think about it, Coleman. She's the President! She can find anyone anywhere."

Coleman took the phone. "Yes, this is Coleman Ashburn...Thank you, Madame President. Yes, I can come. Right away? Well, er uh...yes, of course. An Air Force plane at Knoxville Airport tomorrow? Thank you, Madame President. I'll be there."

He hung up and stared at Frank, his mouth agape.

"Call from the President? Air Force Plane?" Frank said. "Your life will never be the same after this. Mine won't either. I'm going to have one helluva story to write!"

Coleman was speechless.

"Tell Adam and Renie it's time to come home."

Unpacking the Riddle

Jerusalem

Adam looked at Stump Stevens over a steaming cup of coffee in an outdoor café near the Old City. "I want to know what's going on, and I want to know now!"

"Easy, old friend," said Stump in little more than a whisper. "You ask the questions. I'll answer them if I can. Most of it's classified, and you and Renie are not completely out of danger. We're still not sure who we can trust."

"Don't give me that top secret clearance crap. I want some answers now. Did the President know about all this?"

Stump nodded as he sipped his coffee. "We stumbled across a plot to destabilize the peace process. We knew Conrad Docherty was involved. He was worse than Ames, Nicholson, Groat, or Hanssen, but not smart enough to be the brains. We knew he was connected to the Bedouin, but we never saw the link to Moshe or the Speaker. That's where you came into the picture. I happened onto your part by accident the night you came to my house."

"The night you died," said Adam, "...supposedly. Don't tell me—you had to go underground."

Stump nodded.

"I couldn't trust anyone except the President. And along you came with this manuscript like a puppet on Conrad's string. At the end, I thought her phone was bugged, so I had to stop talking to her until we got to Jerusalem."

"Why didn't you throw me a lifeline?"

"You had to be kept in the dark or they would have

called the whole thing off. Besides, you had insurance. The Bedouin and Conrad had to keep you alive until the plan had been completed. They used your girlfriend for collateral."

"She's not my girlfriend," insisted Adam, wondering why he had protested so much. Maybe he really was in love with her. Why couldn't he admit it?

"Whatever. The problem then was sorting out what was going to happen once Conrad was dead and the Bedouin had lost his memory. Enter Coleman Ashburn."

"It was in the manuscript all along?"

"That's how we finally made Moshe. He was one prize. The Speaker was the other."

"Why did the Speaker do it?"

"He wanted the White House. With the President and the Veep both dead, constitutionally, he was next in line to take over. He got himself vaccinated with Moshe. That's how I picked him out," said Stump. "Everyone else doubled over in terror when they thought anthrax was being released. Even the President did an Academy Award performance to keep up the illusion. The Speaker knew he'd never get to the Oval Office on his own. He wanted more arms for Israel to keep the war fires stoked and he knew the President would never agree."

"What was Conrad Docherty giving the Bedouin besides me on a plate?"

"Several things. The knock list for one. We would have stopped the whole thing if we'd known about that. But once it happened, there was no turning back. Conrad also gave the Bedouin a virulent strain of anthrax, and the vaccine for it."

"The call from the chemist in the bio-technology lab in Boulder," Adam said.

"Yeah, the guy from Boulder flew to Tel Aviv a couple of weeks ago and set up shop. He already had the anthracis. All he had to do was develop the final vaccine in the series. Shin Bet picked him up tonight. The final part of the deal was the robbery of the *Codex Sinaiticus* from the British Museum in London, which the Bedouin promised the monk who created the bogus manuscript for him. There's nothing those monks want more than the return of that old *Codex*, after some German scholar named Tischendorf swindled them out of it. We know it was stolen. Then the Russians got it. We think they sold it to some wealthy, old Greek woman."

Adam played dumb. "What was Moshe's angle in this thing?"

"He hates Ben-Shalom's guts because he can't stand peace initiatives. He thinks he's too soft on the Palestinians, so he figured he'd eliminate all the people for peace in one strike, fan the flames of Middle Eastern war for another century or so and get to lead it all. He needed our money to keep the war going. That's what connected the Speaker, the Bedouin and Moshe. But Moshe had already decided to double-cross the Bedouin in the end, so the real story would never get out. I mean who would ever believe he'd make a deal with an international Islamic terrorist? He almost got away with it."

"What was Conrad supposed to get out of all this?"

"Money. Lots of it, which is the reason he was in such a hurry for you to get the manuscript translated. The code for a large Swiss bank account is supposedly hidden in there."

"You mean there's something we haven't deciphered yet?" Adam asked.

"That's why the President is flying your professor friend over here. It's the only part of the code he didn't crack."

Adam got up to leave. "Do me a favor."

"What?"

"Next time you cook up a little scheme like, leave me out of it."

"Not a chance."

Adam saw Stump glance over his left shoulder.

Suddenly, Renie was standing by their table, having appeared from nowhere. She wasn't happy. In fact, mad was written all over her face.

Stump got up. "I need to let you two lovebirds have some time with each other. I'm sure you have a lot to talk about."

Renie didn't acknowledge Stump as he slipped away, leaving them alone.

Renie just stood there, arms crossed and stared at Adam in disbelief. Adam knew there was no arguing with her. He knew she would never understand his world, his life.

"I'm gone for good, Adam. You're much too dangerous for me," she added, smearing her mascara with the back of her hand. "Good-bye."

Adam tried to say something, but nothing came. He watched her leave and did nothing to stop her.

He knew there was no stopping her now.

The Final Puzzle Piece

Jerusalem

Adam stared at Anastasia. "How is she?"

"Worse, I'm afraid," Ian said. "The doctor doesn't think it will be long, but there's still a possibility for a slight reprieve."

Adam stroked the old woman's hair.

"Got the *Codex?*"

Adam held up the canvas bag.

"God knows that bloody thing has caused lots of trouble."

"Watch your language, Ian! It's a holy book," Anastasia grumbled, her eyes closed.

Adam smiled. "Let me know if she improves enough to move her. I'd like to take her to St. Catherine's myself and watch her deliver that old book in person. It would be an honor."

"The Gulfstream is ready for take-off at any moment. If she has an ounce of strength left, she's going to want to go. But it doesn't look very good right now."

Anastasia turned her head.

Adam was sure he'd seen her toss a little wink at him.

He left the room, walked down the hall to the elevator and rode it to the Bedouin's floor. He pulled up a chair beside the Bedouin's bed.

"You are a nice friend," the Bedouin said with a hint of a smile.

"What makes you say that?"

"You are the only one who visits me."

"We have known each other before."

"I wish I could remember you."

"Perhaps some things are better forgotten," Adam said. "How do you feel?"

"Not good. Tell me, why are Israeli soldiers outside my door? Am I under arrest?"

"Let's just say they're here for protection."

"From whom?"

"You never know in a world like ours."

"I've heard on the news about some manuscript. Do you know anything about it?"

"A little. What about you?"

"When I close my eyes, I see old words."

"What kind of words?"

"I'm not sure. They're not Arabic."

Adam reached in his pocket and pulled out a copy of the two-page manuscript. He opened it in front of the Bedouin. "Is this what you see when you close your eyes?"

The Bedouin stared at it for a moment then nodded. "Yes. That's it." Then he stopped as if he had withdrawn to another life, another time. He closed his eyes. "I see myself as a child at the monastery. The old Greek monks are my friends. They call me Ammon. I remember it now. They talk to me about a book, a very old book. They tell me long stories by the fire, stories of the German scholar who stole it from them."

"Tischendorf?"

"Yes, that's the name. They hope someday to get it back no matter how long it takes. I want to help them, but I don't know how. I am only a young lad."

"Go on."

"That's all I see." The Bedouin opened his eyes.

Into the room walked Coleman Ashburn with one of the President's aides and two Secret Service agents.

"Coleman, how good to see you!" He and Adam

embraced as kindred spirits. Adam motioned for them to go out in the hallway. "How does it feel to be famous?" Adam asked.

"You tell me."

"I wish I could crawl in a hole and disappear. I just want to live a normal life."

"You can forget that. Your life will never be the same. The President has briefed me on the problem—one last piece of the code to be cracked. Any luck with the Bedouin?"

"Nothing. He seems to have lost all his recent memory."

"I spoke with the doctor. He said even in extreme cases like this you never know when little snatches and pieces of information might come back all the sudden."

"The trick is being here when it happens," Adam said.

"I've studied the manuscript from beginning to end," Coleman said. "I know every inch of it, every syllable. All I need is a hint and I can crack it. I'm that close. What we're looking for is a number to a Swiss bank account, right?"

"Apparently," replied Adam.

"We need a word whose letters will spell out the right numbers."

"There's no time to go through all of them."

"I know, so keep him talking. All I need is a whiff of it."

"Okay. But let's give him a moment. He seems to be in some nether land. The doctor says he needs to remain quiet or he could have another cardiac arrest."

"How's Renie?" said Coleman.

Before Adam could answer, the Bedouin spoke. "That's it!"

"What?" said Adam as he and Coleman re-entered the Bedouin's room.

"Renie."

"What about her?" said Adam.

"Not her. The word *renie*. That's the word." The Bedouin's eyes danced with delight.

"What are you talking about?" said Adam.

"He's talking about peace," said Coleman, "the key that opens every door. Renie's name comes from Irene, which is the Greek word for peace. That's it. I'm sure of it, and the Bedouin just confirmed it. If you add up the numbers from the letters in the word for 'peace' in the manuscript, you'll have a numbered account in the Swiss bank."

"You mean it was Renie all along? I could kiss that woman!"

"Why don't you?"

"It's too late for that." Adam looked out the window sadly.

"Why?"

Suddenly, the Bedouin grabbed his chest and went still.

"Quick, Coleman, get someone in here now!"

Adam knew his call for help was only in desperation. Something to do in the presence of death. He'd seen enough of it to know. The Bedouin was gone. Doctors and nurses were at his side in seconds. But it was too late. It was written on their faces. They checked his pulse and covered his face with a sheet.

"Too bad," Coleman said.

"I don't think so," said Adam.

"Come again?"

"He's found some peace in his life."

"Odd way to get it."

"It comes to us in different ways. At least he's found his."

"You okay?" Coleman asked.

"Yeah. I think I'll just stay here with him for a while. Don't feel right leaving him here all alone."

"I'll see you later at the press conference."

Adam stared at the Bedouin's body. "I have one more stop before that."

"Where are you going?"

"To find a priest. I have a lot to confess."

Answered Prayer

The Pope's Suite

The Pope welcomed Adam into his suite and waved his
Swiss Guards away.

"Something troubles you, my son," the Pope said.
"Sit down. Tell me about it."

"Perhaps this is not the best time for you. I can come
back."

"No, my son. I am here for you now. Unburden your
heart. Please. I will listen."

Adam didn't know where to begin. Every time he
took a run at it, he had to stop and start over. He didn't want
to unload his scarred adolescence or introduce the pontiff to
his wounded child. He didn't want another shrink to unpack
his numerous neuroses. He wanted to warn the Pope that his
life was still in danger. But before he could get the words
out, he found himself talking in riddles about Renie. He
couldn't get her out of his mind.

"What do you do when you've hurt someone so
deeply, you know you'll never be forgiven?"

"Never give up hope, my son. Forgiveness may be
long in coming, and even the worst sins can be absolved."

"But only by the one who's been wronged, right?"

"That's certainly the most satisfying route. And
when it comes—"

"You mean, if it comes."

"No. I mean when it comes, then you will know true
peace. Only then."

The pontiff is right, Adam thought. Sounds like doggerel. Simple. But right somehow.

"There's something else I need to tell you," Adam said. "It's about Cardinal Carbonari. I don't know exactly how to put it."

"Put what?"

"Well, it's kind of a delicate matter."

"My ears are not indelicate."

"I think…"

"Holy Father!" said the Cardinal, barging into the room.

"Lorenzo, I am in a meeting. Did my priest secretary not tell you?"

"Yes, he did. But I have the most astonishing news. Of course, I can come back, if you like."

"No. You are here now. Tell me. What is it?"

"They have broken the final code in the manuscript. It's a numbered account for a Swiss bank. Billions of dollars!"

"That's remarkable, Lorenzo. Have they decided what to do with it yet?"

"No. But, the decision will be announced at the press conference this afternoon."

"The young man who brought the news wants to meet you. He has admired you his whole life and would think it the privilege of a lifetime to shake your hand."

The Pope looked at Adam.

"Should I step out of the room?" Adam asked.

"No. Stay. You can meet the young man too."

"He is a young German," the Cardinal said. The German walked through the door. "His name is Wolf Schiller."

"Oh, no," said Adam now on his feet. "He's the one who tried to kill you at St. Peter's."

"What?" said the Cardinal, with what appeared to Adam a fake look of surprise.

"Silence!" barked Schiller as he entered the room. The German seemed in no hurry. He pulled a large automatic from a holster and attached a long silencer to the end of it.

"Oh my God!" Lorenzo said.

"I said, 'Silence!'"

Adam thought the Pope seemed amazingly calm. "My son, I think we should pray about this." Then he did.

Adam couldn't believe it. He watched the pontiff descend into one of his reveries.

"What is he doing?" Schiller asked.

"Praying," Adam said. His eyes scanned the room. Not a weapon in sight.

"I can see that, you dummkopf. Why is he praying? Don't answer that. You!"

"Who me?" quaked the Cardinal.

"*Ja du!* Wake him out of that stupor."

"I may not be able to do that."

"Then I'll shoot you instead."

"No. I'm not the mark, you idiot! They are!"

"What did you call me?"

"Uh, Herr Schiller, of course."

"That's what I thought. Now wake him up!"

Adam still had his hands in the air, but no gun. No opportunity to attack or defend.

The Cardinal was doing his best to stir the Pope, but it was not to be.

"I don't care which one I shoot. It's you or him."

Lorenzo grabbed the Pope's shoulders, but the harder Lorenzo shook him, the deeper the pontiff went into his meditations.

Adam could see from Schiller's eyes his patience was razor-thin. He was only moments away from firing.

The Cardinal shook the Pope feverishly.

Adam was ready to give his life for the Holy Father, so he leapt in front of the Pope at the same moment Don Mazzini burst through the door, yelling "No!"

The Don hit Schiller in the left leg with a shotgun blast, which caused Schiller's shot to go awry, hitting the Cardinal just below the heart.

Hobbled by the Don's attack, Schiller turned on him and nailed him in the chest.

As the Don went down, he got off another scattershot that caught Schiller in the gut. The German hit the floor, dead.

It was all over in a matter of seconds.

Adam couldn't believe he and the Pope were still alive.

The Swiss Guard swarmed the place instantly.

The Pope began to stir a little, his eyes still closed. The German was gone. Adam knew Mazzini and the Cardinal wouldn't last long.

Adam rushed to the Don's side.

"You!" sputtered the Don, "You're the reason my precious Marcello is dead. Get me Lorenzo. I'll not have last rites from a Protestant."

"The Cardinal is nearly dead himself. Perhaps you would like the Holy Father instead."

Don Mazzini began to sob, at first low and resonant like an aria of lament, then a wail that crescendoed but finally turned to a whimper.

Adam watched Swiss Guards move with dispatch, making sure the Pope was alright then securing the room. He heard the Pope say, "Soli Deo Gloria, Amen," then open his eyes. "Holy Mother of God, what has happened?"

The Pope eyed the Cardinal on the floor next to him. He knelt beside him then took him in his arms. The Cardinal had lost too much blood and was barely conscious. "Renzo, my friend. You have remembered my admonition to you when you became a Cardinal. You have shed your blood for the faith. My poor Lorenzo. How devoted you were to the end. Look, Adam, he saved my life!" He rocked back and forth with the Cardinal fading in his arms.

Adam thought to correct him, then stopped before he could form the words in his mouth.

The Pope offered his old friend makeshift last rites, then laid his head on the floor. He was dead.

"Holy Father, I think this one needs it, too."

"What is his name?"

"Vicenzu Mazzini. I believe he also...saved your life," Adam said, amazed at the irony of it all.

The Pope knelt beside Don Mazzini, cupped his head in his hands and whispered into his left ear, "*Si capax, ego to absolvo a peccatis tuis, in nomine Patris, et Filii, et Spiritus Sancti. Amen.* If it is possible, I absolve you from your sins, In the name of the Father, the Son and the Holy Spirit." No Extreme Unction. Just a few papal words uttered in haste.

The Don died seconds later with a hint of a smile on his face.

The Pope traced a blessing in the air.

Adam could not believe what had just transpired. "Are you alright?" he asked the Pope.

"*Si*, Prayer is a marvelous thing, my son."

Adam stared at him in amazement as he watched him move to Schiller's side and say a prayer over him, too.

The Pope's white cassock was stained a dark, dull red.

Adam looked about the room and saw bodies everywhere. Their blood soaked the chalk-like carpet.

"I will miss my dear Lorenzo." The Pope stared at the Cardinal who lay crumpled before him. "He's a real martyr, you know, for saving my life."

The Swiss Guard began removing the bodies one by one.

Adam had never seen the Pope's face so downcast.

"Do you feel up to attending the press conference after this?"

The Pope paused before he answered as if he had

been jerked suddenly back to reality.

"*Si*, I think I should go. The death of loved ones and friends should not stop us. It only slows us down. Life must go on."

"I agree," Adam said, thinking about Emma.

A Fragile Alliance

The press conference at the Knesset hosted media from countries Adam had never heard of before. He didn't realize that there were that many cameras in the whole world. He looked for Renie, but she didn't appear.

Adam stood beside President Sanchez who was ready to march out with the other leaders.

"Thought you hated crowds," the President said.

"Do you people know everything about me?"

"Almost."

"This is where I recede into the woodwork," Adam said.

"Thanks for everything. Try to stay out of trouble," she added with a campaign smile.

The press conference proceeded pretty much as Adam had suspected. Lots of posturing by the politicians, especially the President. The Pope seemed subdued. He did mention the heroic and tragic death of his favorite Cardinal and longtime friend, Lorenzo Carbonari. What baffled Adam the most were the leaders of the PLO, HAMAS, the Muslim Brotherhood and dignitaries from all the Arab countries who had come, not to show solidarity with the Israelis, but to begin conversations that "might lead to peace if the conditions were right for all parties"—something he never imagined he would see in his lifetime.

Then the President made the announcement. Standing with the Pope, the Israeli Prime Minister, the Jordanian Prince, and the Prince of Saudi Arabia, she announced that 40 billion dollars, which had come into their hands from a Swiss bank account, would be used for the establishment of an international commission to bring peace in the Middle East. "This commission," said the President, "will include representatives from surrounding Arab nations along with Israel to develop, with the three religious leaders, a program that will lift the economy for everyone and will allow the 'People of the Book' to co-exist along the lines of Shimon Peres' vision for peace and Anwar Sadat's dream before he was assassinated."

A hush fell over the crowd as the Israeli Prime Minister stepped to the microphone and began to speak. "With the money and Israel's willingness to admit wrongs," Ben-Shalom said, "we can create jobs and homes and have real action for both Israelis and Palestinians, not just promises anymore." Then he joined hands with the Jordanian prince who took the Pope's hand. The Pope took the Russian Orthodox Patriarch's hand, who grabbed the hand of the President of the United States. In unison, they lifted their hands together.

Cameras captured the whole scene for posterity. The entire world watched.

At first there was only stunned silence. Then a few began to clap slowly, rhythmically. Then cheers began resounding all over Jerusalem. All over Israel. All over the world.

There was so much celebrating and partying the Israeli Prime Minister and the Jordanian Prince couldn't even continue to present the details of their plan. People would have to read about it on the Internet and in the newspapers. They'd have to hear about it on CNN.

Ben-Shalom said to Prince Salaam, "What's going on here?"

The prince replied, "I don't know. Looks like peace is breaking out all over. I think it's out of our hands now."

The Pope overheard them and added looking to heaven, "Perhaps it always has been."

Adam thought of how the Bedouin's poor excuse for a human document had been turned miraculously into something good.

* * *

The drive to Ben Gurion Airport in Tel Aviv seemed a blur to him. Before taking off, he stopped for a drink at the bar. The celebration continued. Everyone seemed glued to the tube. The place was abuzz with talk of peace.

The man next to Adam said to the bartender, "Amazing, isn't it?"

"Most remarkable thing I've ever seen," replied the barkeep as he twisted a lime into a tumbler.

Adam finished his drink then walked to his gate. He stood at the window, waiting for his plane.

He looked around for Renie.

She was gone.

Epilogue

Maryville

By the time Adam had arrived home, he learned he would have to find a new administrative assistant. Evelyn Hastings had given her notice. She and Frank Harkin had announced their engagement. A short one. They wanted to make up for lost time.

Adam's first official act was to bury the Sicilian named Marcello whom no one in Maryville seemed to know but Frank, Evelyn and Renie. Hardly anyone came, but there was one gray-haired Sicilian woman who showed up for the funeral, dressed in black. Adam thought her strikingly beautiful and regal despite her age. She spoke to no one, just attended Marcello's memorial service and left. Adam wondered who she was, but guessed because he saw the resemblance.

Adam's last official act was Frank and Evelyn's wedding, which brought out half the town. Celebrity pastor and celebrity couple. Celebrity attendants. Coleman was best man, Renie, maid of honor. Adam thought he saw Renie glance at him once as he led Frank and Evelyn through their vows. He was mistaken. Her eyes searched the stained-glass windows above him.

He did services for a few weeks as crowds packed the place. They came from as far away as Chattanooga and Kingsport. Some even drove over from Nashville just to hear him, not for his sermons but for his notoriety. He knew the difference. He hated the crowds.

354

So, like Evelyn, he gave his notice.

*   *   *

The day was East Tennessee ashen gray. A light north wind whispered through ancient oaks. Grandview Cemetery welcomed a new permanent tenant as Adam offered a Benediction at the graveside service. He had ushered another beleaguered soul into the presence of the Almighty, the great honor all clergy have by providing the final transition from this life to the next.

A slight wind flapped the green awning. Adam gave the widow, a shriveled but wiry woman, a small nod but she never saw him for staring at the coffin. He understood. He was still having trouble letting go himself. The soloist's reedy rendition of Amazing Grace echoed in his ears. Diggers prepared to lower the casket and shovel the dirt, slipping another old soul into the ground.

When the service ended, Adam shook the last hand and started for his car but something caught his eye—Renie was a hundred feet up the hill, kneeling in front of a slab of stone. He stood for a moment watching from a distance, then padded toward her on the moist earth. Like a soldier negotiating a minefield, he stepped gingerly to avoid treading on someone's dear departed.

He watched her tidy the area as he approached. She straightened the tired glads like a bird re-arranging her nest. She stroked the engraved name on the marker with the tips of her fingers. All this he observed without her knowledge. She nudged tears with her knuckles, adjusted her glasses and brushed a wisp of chestnut hair off her forehead. Her blue print dress fluttered in the breeze. He'd been looking for a tiny glimmer of redemption by being close to her and helping her in some way, or maybe he wasn't sure what he was looking for anymore. He'd searched for God at the divinity school, but found practically everyone there preferred spending time analyzing and speculating about the Almighty, not becoming acquaintances.

"That you, Adam?" she asked, squinting as his dark shadow spilled across her body, eclipsing the sun. She rubbed her eyes, trying to focus.

"Yeah."

"Had a funeral?"

He nodded.

"Whose was it?"

"I didn't know him. Funeral home asked me to do it."

"Must be hard burying people you don't know."

A newsreel of his former life played in his mind—all the people he'd killed for his country who'd had it coming, but not the Bedouin's girlfriend in the minivan or Renie's fiancé or Emma. They were innocent.

He took her left hand and helped her to her feet. Her firm grip sent a charge through him that reminded him of Emma.

She brushed particles of damp sod from her knees then stood her ground.

"What are you doing out here on a cold day like this?" he asked.

"Same thing as you I suppose." She rubbed her arms to ward off the chill.

"I'm saying good-bye."

"Me too." Renie glanced at Eric's grave. "To him and to you," she said as she looked over his shoulder at nothing in particular.

A junco bounced on the ground nearby, then fluttered to a limb.

"So," she said finally. "I heard you were leaving. What're you gonna do?"

"Go back to work for the government, I guess. Can't keep this up. It's not for me. I'm nothing but a sideshow in a church now."

Her brow furrowed.

Adam shook his head. "No. I could never go back to that. They've asked me to help head the international commission to establish self-development of the peoples in the West Bank. The CIA will be helping Mossad monitor the effort for security. But they need someone to get things stabilized and do some refereeing over there. Could get pretty nasty. Reprisals and counter-reprisals. I know the languages fairly well. Know the area. Small learning curve."

"Thought you'd had enough of Israel."

"Me too." He kicked the dirt. "Guess not."

"I do have one question," she said.

"Yes?" He lifted his face and searched her eyes.

"Where did that Swiss bank account with the billions come from?"

"Oh that. It's money Bin Laden got from a Saudi prince who supported his and the Bedouin's terrorist efforts, but wanted to remain anonymous. The Bedouin had big plans for it after what was supposed to happen in Jerusalem."

"Wow. I guess that's a good example of 'What others meant for evil God meant for good.' Isn't that from somewhere in the Bible?"

"Yeah, it is. You learn that at Harvard?"

"No, in Sunday School at the church you're leaving."

"Oh."

"It's what happened in Jerusalem."

"Yeah, I guess so," he said as he forced a half-smile. "Say," he started then caught himself. "No... it's a bad idea."

"What?"

"I may need a good lawyer over there."

"I told you before. You can't afford me. When do you head for Tel Aviv?"

"In a few days. But I have to make one stop along the way."

"Really? To see anyone I know?"

"Don't think so."

Renie blushed then stiffened. "Oh, well..."

Tears blurred his vision. She seemed to fade into the mist as she backed away from him one step at a time.

"...have a nice life."

Adam didn't know what to say. So, he gave a little wave and felt stupid for it.

*   *   *

St. Catherine's Monastery

Winter wind from old Sinai whistled through St. Catherine's like a blue northern across a Texas prairie. Adam sat by the fire with Anastasia in one of the old monks' cells and listened to her wheeze. A steward had set the blaze so large it sounded like a Fourth of July celebration run amok. It popped and sizzled, playing shadows across Anastasia's face like an old silent movie.

"This is the greatest day of my life," she said.

"Don't try to talk. You need every breath."

The fire weakened.

"It needs more fuel! Pitch another log on. I'm cold." She pulled the wool blanket tighter around her frail body.

"But it's a furnace blast now."

"Do it!"

Adam obeyed.

"Not like that, boy. Put it on cross-wise. Don't you know? A fire has to have air to breathe!"

Sparks spit juices. Gasses hissed and spewed as flames licked around the new log.

"Where is he?"

"I'll check."

"No. Don't leave me. Ian's out there; ask him."

Before he could get up, the Archbishop entered the cell.

"Archbishop," Adam said. "We've been expecting you. *Kalespera.*"

"Kalespera," he replied. "And to you, Anastasia. Sorry you are not well."

"Everything is fine now, Archbishop," said the old woman. "Can we begin?"

Adam could see she was putting the best face on it.

"You understand the arrangement?" Adam asked the Archbishop. "Mrs. Paleologos has left to the Monastery an endowment of one billion dollars. The corpus is not to be touched. Ever. The interest may be used at the rate of five percent per annum for upkeep and expenses. In return for this gift, you will keep it a secret that you have the original *Codex Sinaiticus.* The British Library now knows their copy is a fake. They've begun a world-wide search for the original. No one must know you have it, or someone like Tischendorf will try to steal it again someday. Is all of this clear?"

"I understand, Mr. Hunter."

"There are no papers to sign, just a handshake agreement."

The Archbishop nodded.

"Anastasia? Are you ready?"

"Yes. Set me up straight and give me the *Codex.*"

Adam tried, but her pain was too intense, her hands too weak.

"Help me, Adam."

Adam held the *Codex* in both hands then placed her right one on top.

"Can you feel it?" he asked. The fireplace grew dimmer.

"Yes. I've got it. Get on with it."

"Go ahead. Say it."

"Archbisho–..." her voice broke. "You say it for me."

Adam looked at her then began. "Archbishop, it is my honor and privilege to return this fourth century manuscript, the *Codex Sinaiticus*, to St. Catherine's

Monastery, its true and rightful home. The British Museum was too embarrassed to admit it had been stolen, but the British Library has a remarkable facsimile," said Adam, reading from the prepared script, "such an exact replica that tourists will think it's the real thing. And now…"

Anastasia interrupted, her eyes closed, a hint of a smile on her face. "I can take it from here. And now I can die in peace. I want to be buried here, and my bones and skull put into the charnel house with the rest."

"It will be done, Anastasia," the Archbishop said. "God bless you."

Anastasia smiled and drifted off. Adam could see she was gone.

He stayed with the body long after everyone else had left, except for Ian McPherson who waited outside the door to say his last good-byes. Adam watched the dying embers until they were little more than a flicker. He looked around the room, remembering it was the same chamber where Tischendorf had first discovered the *Codex*. He leaned over and planted a feathery kiss on her cheek. It was still soft and warm.

He left her cell and walked for a while, going up and down through the ancient tunnels. He had no particular destination in mind. He just kept walking until he found himself near the Round Tower of the ancient fortress looking over the wall. He stood there for a long time, surveying Mt. Sinai silhouetted against the night sky.

"Bigger than it looks, isn't it?"

Adam turned, startled, trying to focus on the figure in the twilight. "Renie? That you?"

"Who else would follow you to a God-forsaken place like this?"

He stared at her, trying to make her out in the dark.

"We're even out here, you know?"

"What do you mean?" he asked.

"Both a little blind."

Adam didn't know what to say.

"Don't worry," she said. "I can talk enough for both of us. I liked your touch with the old woman tonight. I watched it from a distance. There's something very real and true about you."

"What's going on?" Adam said. "You've changed."

"Mr. Stevens stopped by the other day. Believe you call him Stump. He told me the story of your life. The parts you left out."

"Sorry you had to hear it."

"I'm not. He told me how many lives you saved in New York the day Eric died."

"That won't bring him back."

"I know, but it brought me back."

"What're you doing here?"

She turned and gazed into the dark blue expanse in the distance.

"Let's just say I've developed a sudden fondness for the desert."

"But, you're a mountain girl," he replied.

"Voila!" She waved her hand in the air at the great mass that loomed above them.

"Why are you here?"

"I decided you were right."

Adam stared at her quizzically.

"You are going to need a good lawyer where you're going."

She moved toward him.

He felt her warm body against his.

"I thought I couldn't afford you," he said, drawing her closer. His lips searched hers in the dark.

"You can't." She kissed him lightly on the mouth then more firmly. "I'm strictly pro bono from here on out."

They embraced the way they did the night they made love.

Adam took a deep breath.

ASSASSIN'S MANUSCRIPT

The mountain air was sweet.
The old knot was gone.

THE END

Author's Note

*Why would I write a novel about an assassin-turned-minister? Here's why. It was another ordinary day except for one thing: Alex Haley, the author of **Roots**, was sitting in my office visiting. He asked me, "Bill, have you written anything?"*

"Yes," I replied, "a few books, all nonfiction."

"Let me see one of them."

I pulled one off the shelf—a set of lectures I'd given at Princeton—and handed it to him. For the next ten minutes, he skimmed and perused, flipping pages here and there. Suddenly he looked up and said something that changed my life, "Bill, you need to write a novel!"

"What makes you say that, Alex?"

"Two things: you know how to write and you know how to tell a story. That's what a novel is."

I was stunned by his second observation since Haley was a world-class story-teller himself, something he had proven at a small dinner party the night before as he regaled me and his fellow diners with some "edge of your chair" tales. One more thing about Alex. He was the consummate cheerleader. "Find the good and praise it" was his mantra. He saw things in people they didn't see in themselves. "Bill, you need to write a novel. Just think about the novels you like reading, then write about something you know."

I loved Clancy, Ludlum, Forsyth, and Daniel Silva, and knew a lot about ancient manuscripts. I was also intrigued by the kinds of books Dan Brown writes. Being a Greek scholar myself, one of the true stories that's always fascinated me is the saga of Constantin von Tischendorf, a mid-1800s German archaeologist who on his third try discovered the oldest, most reliable version of the Bible **(Codex Sinaiticus)** *at St. Catherine's Monastery at the foot of Mt. Sinai in Egypt. I figured "Jason Bourne and Indiana Jones meet* **The Name of the Rose***" or "Dan Brown meets Daniel Silva" would make an interesting story. So off I went to the races, never realizing what an adventure lay before me—a little bit like Alice tumbling into wonderland or Edmund, Peter, Lucy and Susan stepping gingerly into C.S. Lewis' mysterious wardrobe.*

"Bill, you need to write a novel." So, I did, starting with research trips to foreign countries, interviews with former American, Russian, and Israeli assassins and with Buck Revell, whom I mentioned in the Acknowledgements.

What emerged was a mythic story a la Joseph Campbell in his **Hero with a Thousand Faces** *or Christopher Vogler in his* **The Writer's Journey***. The challenge in writing this story was shaping a clergyman (something I know a lot about) with a dark and murderous past (something I know nothing about). Of course, the biblical model was the Apostle Paul. Adam is a mythical character whose name in Hebrew means humankind. He is the quintessential human being with an ineradicable flaw in his character—one he cannot correct on his own. Adam is tortured, flawed and broken because of his own self-inflicted wound. He is desperately in search of peace, like all of us. Unlike other books with international espionage, my novel does not follow the traditional "good guys/bad guys" approach since it demonstrates how flawed we all are, appropriating the idea that there is good in every evil person and evil in every good one.*

Renie, whose real name is Irene, which means "peace" in Greek is clearly what Adam (humanity) needs. She is the only one who can complete his mythic story.

William J. Carl
Maryville, Tennessee

List of Characters

Egypt
The Bedouin
The Bedouin's men

London/UK
Nigel Rupert, Gallery Warder/British Museum
Arthur Bledsoe, Gallery Warder
Conrad Docherty, CIA operative
The Supervisor, Nigel Rupert's boss

Maryville, Tennessee
Adam Hunter, Protestant clergy, former CIA
Irene "Renie" Ellis, attorney
Coleman Ashburn, Classics professor
Frank Harkin, Newspaper publisher
Evelyn Hastings, Administrative assistant
"The Animal"

Washington, DC
President Sanchez and her husband
Stump Stevens, Former CIA Director
Drew Farley, CIA Director
Esther Adrian, President's assistant
Joseph Wellington, Speaker of the House
Ruth Gibbons, Drew Farley's assistant
Pete Ashton, President's Chief of Staff
William P. Briner, Asst. Chief of Protocol
Anson Avery, NSA Advisor

Jerusalem
Moshe, Mossad operative
David Ben-Shalom, Israeli Prime Minister

Merchants in the Old City
Father Nikopoulos, Greek Orthodox Bishop
The bishop's old Greek mother

Sicily and Rome
Don Vicenzu Mazzini, Sicilian Godfather
Marcello Zanetti, Professor and Hit man
The Pope
Giovanni, Adam's CIA contact in Rome
Angelo Biondi, Head of Sacred Congregation
Lorenzo Carbonari, Papal Secretary of State
Giuseppe Giacomo, Prefect of the Vatican Library

St. Catherine's Monastery in Sinai
Father Nicodemus, Greek Orthodox monk
Father John, Greek Orthodox monk
Father Paul, Greek Orthodox monk
Father Euthymios, head of monastery library
Oliver Stratton, Cambridge Don, also Moscow

Moscow
Vladimir Kulikov, Russian army general
Alexandra Beserdechnaya, "Sasha" (FSB)
Boris Gromilov, Russian mafia chief
The Patriarch, Russian Orthodox Church
The Metropolitan, Russian Orthodox Church
Sergei Makarov, Russian cyber-hacker

Toronto
Anastasia Paleologos, Greek Billionaire
Ian McPherson, Anastasia's bodyguard

Berlin
Wolf Schiller, German Assassin
Herr Helmut Oberfeld

Made in the USA
Middletown, DE
21 May 2024

54656271R00227